LIFE

IN

L O N D O N.

𝔄 Romance.

By HERBERT THORNLEY

WITH NUMEROUS ENGRAVINGS ON WOOD.

LONDON:

E . DIPPLE, HOLYWELL STREET, STRAND.

—

MDCCCXLVI.

PROLOGUE.

We are entering upon the nineteenth century.

Yet, in this great Metropolis, gorgeous pomp, and hideous beggary are approximate, separated but by a wall; in one mansion the rich man has not a wish ungratified, his coffers full of coin, his tables groaning under every dainty, every quarter of the globe contributing to his enjoyment, and almost every breeze wafting him over wealth and prosperity. In a cellar hard by, lives the modern Lazarus. What a startling, heartrending contrast! His career of vice, misery, penury, and starvation, all of which may be summed up in that one word, poverty; commences with his first breath, and terminates only with his existence.

In this city are co-existing, riches, virtue, and happiness; poverty, vice and misery.

In it there are holes and corners, through which the pure stream of fresh air never flowed, teeming with noxious vapours, generating disease, and entailing misery on generations yet unborn. In it too there are palaces and mansions, whose profuse splendour, and glittering mirrors, dazzle the eye; in it there are churches and chapels, to which the rich and pious resort; in it there are dens of infamy and shame, gin palaces, boozing kens, hells, and harems. In this land of bibles and missionaries, houseless vagrants everywhere wander through the streets, with scarcely a rag of clothing, exposed to all the bitter inclemency of the weather; the rich monopolise everything, while the poor man is put to his wit's ends, to earn even an honest living.

Hunger is gnawing at the entrails of a mighty population; vice, and with it its twin sister disease, is disseminating far and wide; yet, is there not wherewith to satisfy the cravings of the one, or to check the fatal progress of the other. Assuredly the social condition of this city is a very lamentable one. It is the heart of a great nation, nevertheless, it is

1

going to decay, and gradually becoming corrupt and rotten.

But wherefore have we commenced this undertaking?

It is our object to lead the reader through the gay and attractive avenues of fashion, through the noisome mazes of vice, chicanery, and dissipation; to introduce him to the cellar, as well as to the mansion; to the alley, as well as to the abode of opulence; to lay before him all the frauds, follies, and depravities of the Metropolis; to present him with an ungarnished picture of "London Life;" in short, to produce a complete reflection of the present state of Metropolitan society, in the higher, as well as the lower circles, in various classes, professions, trades, and localities :—may he draw wholesome inferences therefrom.

CHAPTER. I.

THE JEW.

It was a dark stormy night in the autumn of 1843, when a man, muffled up in a cloak, emerged from a dirty looking house, in the low neighbourhood of Shoreditch. His whole appearance, combined with a long flowing beard, betoken advanced age. After casting a furtive glance towards either side of the road, as if to assure himself that nobody was dogging his steps, he proceeded by a circuitous and lengthy route to Smithfield.*

He passed through several dark alleys, and dirty courts, inhabited by the very scum of London. It seemed as if the Metropolis had been one vast cauldron, and having boiled over, had deposited all its refuse in these foul quarters. All the houses bore a dilapidated, miserable appearance, and occasionally were so close to each other, that out of the attic windows the inhabitants could, with the greatest facility, have shaken hands across the footway beneath. In the middle of the pathway of these alleys, there invariably ran a narrow stream of filth and decomposed matter, generally stagnant, but now in a state of turbid commotion, from the falling rain. These receptacles must inevitably have produced *malaria* to a frightful extent, had it not been for the occasional intervention of a friendly shower. In such neighbourhoods as these, nature seldom fails to take upon herself what civilization and refinement omit

Cold, biting cold blew the wind, the storm came on with increased violence, the rain poured in torrents, falling upon the heads of the inmates of the half ruined houses—for few were provided with a covering capable of resisting the wet, on such a night as that on which our narrative opens—till the Israelite was compelled to take shelter under the doorway of a building, the exterior and interior of which alike baffle description.

The wind howled through the apartments of the dreary pile, hurrying to and fro, from one empty room

* Smithfield was originally a spot where jousts took place, but it afterwards became the scene of unparalleled cruelty, and of frequent executions. It is at present used as a cattle market.

to another, whistling through the long narrow passages, getting in and squeezing out, at every chink and cranny, and every now and then moaning as if in remembrance of some sanguinary murder or fiendish plot, which had been enacted or concocted in that ill-looking fabric.

At the first available opportunity, when the storm had somewhat abated, he wrapped his cloak more closely round his shrivelled anatomy, and sallied onwards.

"I hope he will be here to-night," muttered he to himself, his teeth chattering with cold and rain.

He had reached Smithfield, and stood opposite St Bartholemew's Hospital, when a young man, semi-fashionably attired, crossed over the road to meet him. There was an assumed gaiety in his bearing, that but ill contrasted with his haggard countenance, and bloodshot eyes; the fresh tinge of health had for ever fled from his cheeks, and his whole appearance two plainly denoted the effects of by-gone folly and past indiscretion. What a scoundrel may a man become, when he once consents to follow indiscretion as a guide!

"Ah, ah! Frederick, my dear," chuckled the Jew, "you cannot for a moment conceive how glad I am that you've come my dear. It's very cold, isn't it my dear?"

"Rayther so."

"A nasty, rainy, windy night. Are you better off for cash than you were?"

"Devil a bit. The Baronet's involved over head and ears; so he can do nothing, that's plain. If I had some money in hand now, I could quite make a little fortune. It's tantalising, isn't it? By Jove, I must raise the wind somehow."

"Haven't you had any answer from your uncle, the reverend preacher, yet, my dear?"

"Oh yes The old humbug wrote to tell me that as I had thought fit to cut myself *out* of his love, he must as a matter of principle, necessity, decorum, and all the rest of it, cut me *off* from what would have been my share of his fortune."

"Like the man.'

"And, moreover, that he would pray, heartily pray for me, if he didn't think it would be wasting his breath to do it. Ha! ha!"

The Jew gave a hoarse laugh.

"'Tis very cruel for a young fellow like me to be pushed for a guinea or two with an avaricious old devil of a miser like you; got more ready and swag than he knows what to do with; it is infernally cruel; but I suppose it's nothing but what we must all come to one day or another."

"Fortune's wheel, my dear, is always turning," said the Jew.

"And you have one great consolation, that any turn it makes just now must be materially to your advantage."

"Yes; only I should rather like giving it a turn myself."

In short you want to borrow money of me?"

" Now you *are* a jolly old brick, a trump, a perfect prince of money lenders. That's exactly the ticket."

" I am poor, very poor," said the miser, " but on one condition I'll do it."

" Name it."

" You are next heir to Sir Richard Vyvian, when he dies."

" When he kicks the bucket, you mean. He won't be long doing that, his body is so rotten now, it can hardly keep his soul out of hell."

The miser shuddered. Any train of ideas bearing reference to a future state, even if uttered by a dissolute young scamp, were unpalatable to him. Perhaps he thought he should keep the Baronet company hereafter.

" Go on and be alive, the cold has nearly cut me in two."

" When he dies you get his estates, his money, in fact, his everything."

" If the lawyers leave me anything, I suppose I shall."

" His estates are pretty well all mortgaged, and his property will be pounced upon by a set of insatiate duns, whom he has thoroughly diddled. Under these circumstances will you sell your chance? If you will, I'll buy it of you."

" You're confoundedly generous. I dare say you will, old 'un, and sell me in the bargain. You want to make another Esau of me, not but what I should rather like some hot porridge on such a night as this."

" I have made you an offer, and can do no more."

" Well, I'm awfully short, and also have a good opportunity of multiplying what I may get. What will you give me for it ?"

" Sign me a paper, and you shall have a couple of hundred immediately."

" Tush! you must double that at least."

" I can do nothing of the kind."

" Make it three hundred. Meet me half-way."

" If you take my advice, you will accept my offer. Believe me, it is good counsel."

" I suppose I must."

" Call on me in the course of a few days, when I hope to have scraped the money together."

" All right."

" Good night, my dear."

" Good night, Levi," was the reply, and he turned on his heel and was gone.

The Jew for a moment watched the retreating figure, and then hurried off in the direction of Shoreditch.

Here he would meet some miserable attenuated object, the prey of disease and starvation ; there he would pass a band of drunken revellers, going out to their nightly debauch.

As the Jew entered the house in Shoreditch, the distant bell of St. Sepulchre tolled the solemn hour of midnight.

How strange is the construction of the human heart ! how various its windings ! how complicated its mazes ! At one moment success became full upon us, dissipating misery and despair, with its genial rays: at another, and our fond hopes are blasted, and our fair prospects blighted, and we seem beings doomed to drain the bitterest dregs of misfortune's cup. Not so with the Jew. The cares and pleasures which alternately chequer life, were strangers to his breast. Heart he had none. With him, an inordinate thirst after gold was the ruling passion. All the better feelings of his nature had one by one withered away, they had all shrunk and dried up before the blasting influence of avarice ; there was nought left in his breast but a dreary, desolate, inhospitable wilderness. But now a smile played around his withered lips, for he thought that he was inveigling another victim in his snares. The most designing and wary, not unfrequently slip the oftenest. But to return to our narrative.

After his crafty looking eyes had peered into every corner of the room, he threw himself hastily on a tent bedstead, and overcome with fatigue, sank into an uneasy slumber.

The apartment in which Abednego Levi now lay had a low ceiling, ornamented with mouldings and grotesque figures of every description ; the wall was full of odd niches and corners, and of yore the house had probably been the property and residence of some wealthy citizen. At present the furniture in it was very scanty ; there was an old deal table, a ricketty tent bedstead, three or four broken old chairs, a one-legged stool, which the miser had bought about ten years previous at a sale, and a dirty worm-eaten portmanteau, looking for all the world as if it had been saved from the deluge by the venerable patriarch Noah.

To the good and virtuous sleep is indeed a rest from worldly cares, but not so with the miser Abednego. His sleep was made hideous with frightful dreams, peopled with creations of his own fancy ; countless myriads of imps hung in clusters from the ceiling, peeping from behind every nook and corner, and playing at bow-peep with his tortured brain, like wanton youngsters on a summer's holiday. Then came a long—long procession, wearing the sable uniform of the grave, pointing their long bony fingers, as if to denounce vengeance on Abednego's head ; mid this troop of grizzley skeletons, many a long forgotten victim did the miser recognise ; suddenly these phantoms of the grave set up a dismal howl, and Abednego, with a wild cry, awoke and started to his feet.

He pressed his clammy hands on his throbbing temples, and for a moment his reason seemed to be tottering upon that awful verge, which constitutes the sole barrier between man in a rational and an irrational, a responsible and an irresponsible state.

" It was but a dream that discomposed me," he said at length ; but a very—very fearful one."

At this critical juncture, a shrill whistle reaching his ear, apparently proceeding from the street beneath the window, he cautiously crept down the stairs. Free from all further apprehension, on hearing three significant kicks on the panel, he immediately opened the door, when two young boys entered.

"Got any swag?" asked the Jew in a brutal voice.

Both answered in the affirmative.

Here the conversation dropped till the trio had reached the first-floor, the only inhabitable one in the house.

"What have you got, Neddy? always the eldest the first, my dears."

"Wipes."

"You're a clever boy. You'll one day be an ornament to your perfession, you will," continued the Jew, carefully examining the texture of the handkerchiefs produced.

"Well, and what have you brought me, Tibby? something good I hope, ay?"

"A ticker."

"That will do. You'll rise to be a great man, you will."

"I cribbed it from such a jolly green chap."

"All the better. He will learn to be more wide-a-wake another time."

"You're both quite sure you're got nothing else," said the Jew, casting an inquiring, searching glance on both of them."

"Are you?"

"Yes," exclaimed the two boys in one breath.

"Then you had better go to bed my dears. But stay, you can pick these handkerchiefs first. Your suppers are in the next room; there, go along."

They left the room together, taking the handkerchiefs with them, and the miser was once more alone.

He again flung himself on the tent bedstead, anxiously awaiting the hours of morning. He counted all the church clocks, as they struck; clocks whose voices in the day-time were drowned in the noisy tumult of the metropolis. With the first blush of morn—for even in murky smoke dried cities like this, a fine summer's morning is a lovely sight—Abednego Levi was seated at the only table in his room, or rather apology for a table, counting over and over again, and closely scrutinising the booty he had obtained by robbing his fellow-men, and depriving himself of the common necessaries of life. Abednego Levi was at once a receiver of stolen goods, a money lender, a miser, and an outcast. Truly a deplorable combination of characters!

CHAPTER II.

THE HELL.

WHEN Frederick Vyvian left the Jew-miser in Smithfield, he pursued his way at a rapid rate towards the west end. On arriving at the Fishmonger's-hall,* alias the Crack—a hell-mart for gudgeons,

flatfish, and pigeons—he sought admittance by performing a species of tattoo with his knuckles on the door. It was some time before his summons was answered, but at last a bolt was withdrawn; the door partially opened, and a man, with a very repulsive-looking physiognomy, gruffly inquired "who he was, and what he wanted?"

"All right," was the reply.

Upon this the door was closed, the chain withdrawn, and a moment afterwards Vyvian passed through the passage, and entered into a room fitted up in a style remarkable for its costly extravagance.

The apartment was well lit, and everything in it was intended either to dazzle or to muddle. Champagne and other wines, with the choicest liquors and spirits, were gratuitously supplied by the liberal-minded proprietors of the establishment: a servant attended to supply the different gentlemen as often as they required it.

The altar erected by these worshippers of chance was an oblong table, on each side of which was seated a croupier, whose office it was to call the game, rake up the winnings, and perform other mechanical offices. A small tin box, denominated the "bank," was also entrusted to his charge.

The haggard countenances of the players, the sunken eye, the quivering lip, contrasted mournfully with the glittering heaps of gold and the numerous bank-notes. A horrible silence prevailed throughout the apartment, broken only by curses and execrations, not loud, but deep. Some seemed eager, others cautious; some, flushed with momentary success, madly staked their all in the vain hope of regaining what they had already lost. A few were busily engaged in making algebraical computations, expecting to arrive at some certain conclusions known or about to be known only to themselves. Vyvian's entrance excited no attention beyond a nod from one or two of the regular frequenters of the place. After he had played a few stakes for the sake of appearance—for he was in reality in the pay of the proprietors, and belonged to that class of pellites denominated "bonnets,"—he took his stand behind a gamester, young in years as in vice, who was loosing, rapidly loosing; yet still he played on, determined if possible to stem the stream of adversity; but the fickle goddess was in an ungracious mood: the young man, who could before have commanded thousands, now rose from the table a ruined beggar.

"Cleaned out," coolly observed a bystander.

"Poor devil! go and hang yourself!" said another.

Casting a hasty look at his antagonist, as if to brave the eye he dared not meet, he withdrew to another part of the room.

By ones, by twos, by threes, the players gradually departed. The croupiers, bonnets, and others, in the pay of the proprietors, alone remained, and, callous to every feeling, stood watching, with a species of fiendish delight, the intense agony of the young

---

*This hell was formerly kept by a ci-devant fishmonger's man, who nightly realised immense sums by it. It was puffed off as a club-house, and, whenever an action was commenced against the proprietor, he invariably expended a large sum in compromising the matter.

gamester, who still lingered as if unwilling to leave the place of his destruction.

"You had better go now," said a croupier, in an ironical, whining tone of voice."

"There is a time for all things," hinted a flashily-dressed bonnet.

"Go!" mournfully echoed the young man; "where can a wretch involved in debt and penniless find a shelter?" A violent burst of tears, accompanied with convulsive sobs, followed this exclamation.

"Come, come, young gentleman," said one of the employed of the establishment, "don't sit howling there; just follow the example of your betters, and move towards the door: allow me to assist you," continued the ruffian, at the same time grasping him firmly by the arm, he endeavoured to thrust him out. The youth, maddened by his losses, and indignant at the treatment he received, endeavoured to resist; a scuffle ensued; one of them, a powerful man, struck him a tremendous blow on the head: the youth fell covered with blood and bruises. No time was to be lost, for a new-comer might take alarm at a sight of this kind; he was therefore hastily dragged into another room, his face washed, a glass of brandy poured down his throat, and, though he was scarcely able to stand, they led him out into the street and left him on the step of a door, while the policeman, who had discernment enough to perceive that his presence was not wanted, obligingly strolled in an opposite direction. Scenes of this description are unfortunately but too common in these receptacles of vice. The heartless devils who keep them even feel a sort of demoniacal delight in beholding the sufferings of their infatuated victims, till, plunged in a chaos of inextricable wretchedness and ruin, they either put an end to their existence, or become as hardened in villany as their fiendish associates. But let us return to the saloon. A new batch of players had entered; the croupiers had resumed their office. At one of the tables Vyvian had taken his seat; he was playing for two thousand pounds, the best of five games. What with superior skill and a little sleight of hand, about one thousand five hundred pounds had found its way into his pocket.

"I am really ashamed of receiving this large sum," said he, evidently elated at his run of good luck; "but it is your own fault—you were so determined to play."

"Since I have been in the habit of visiting these infernal hells," said his opponent, in a surly tone of voice, "I have lost no less than thirty thousand pounds—rather more than the half of my fortune."

"Ah, Sir Richard!" exclaimed Frederick Vyvian, addressing his brother, a tall, portly-looking gentleman who had just entered the apartment. Sir Richard cast a keen glance at the winnings. "Yonder," said he, looking significantly at a gentlemanly youth, "is a young flat I picked up at Crockford's; I will, if you please, introduce you to him; he has lately come into the possession of a fortune of

thirty thousand pounds, and is as green as a gooseberry."

These words were uttered in an under tone. The baronet advanced towards his young friend, while Vyvian turned to the mantel-piece, upon which he had ostentatiously displayed his winnings.

"Allow me, gentlemen, to introduce you to each other," said the baron, returning with his new acquaintance.

"Mr. Stamer, Mr. Vyvian and I sincerely hope that an intimacy will spring up between you as I think it will be to the advantage of both.

"For my part," replied the youth, I am so entirely ignorant of the manners and customs of this great city, that I cannot but benefit by the acquaintance."

"My friend," responded the baronet, in rather an ironical tone of voice, "is the best man in the world to give advice, for he has profited by experience; but as a friend I give you this hint, that the less you visit houses of this description the better. I am boy enough sometimes to try my luck . I care not if I win, and it cannot hurt me if I loose; but I only dabble as they call it.

Vyvian smiled, and, taking the young man familiarly by the arm, he led him to a long table covered with red and black cloth.

"The celebrated game of *Rouge et Noir*, or Red and Black, is so styled," said he, "not from the cards, but from the table on which it is played. Any number of persons may play at this game, and we will, if you please, try our luck."

"I am not sufficiently acquainted with the game," replied the young man, "but it appears to be conducted with a vast deal of propriety and fairness."

A sarcastic smile again played over the still handsome features of Vyvian.

"The persons who play the game," said he, "are called punters, and may risk their money on which colour they please. The stakes are to be placed within the outside line. Bankers generally furnish punters with slips of card paper, ruled in columns, each marked N or R at the top, on which accounts are kept by pricking a pin."

The young man, who had listened greedily to the lesson he was receiving, seemed half inclined to hazard a game or two, when, suddenly, his attention was diverted by the noisy exclamations of a young officer who, having lost his all, begged to borrow of the managers, but they, knowing his circumstances, refused to lend without security.

"I have nothing to give," exclaimed the youth furiously, "but my ears."

"Well they're long enough, God knows," said a looker-on.

"Take 'em, take 'em," cried several voices

"A bargain," laughed the baronet.

"So let it be," jeeringly replied the banker.

'You're going to break the bank, ain't you, sir," said another.

The officer, rendered frantic by his losses and their

unfeeling taunts, drew a penknife from his pocket, and, cutting off the fleshy part of both his ears, he flung them on the table.*

This desperate act of courage drew applause from all round. Stamer followed by Vyvian and the baronet, who bitterly inveighed against (what he termed) the unlucky adventure, hastily quitted the hell.

CHAPTER III.

THE BOOZING KEN.†

THE scene changes.

In a low public-house in Rosemary-lane, known as the sign of the "Nimble Fingers," the rendezvous of thieves, cracksmen, footpads, prostitutes, duffers, swell mobites, and other rogues on the town, are assembled a motley group of vagabonds.

Some drinking "jiggered gin,"‡ some smoking, others swearing, one or two quarrelling, a few playing at "head and tail," and here and there some one practising a species of step, peculiar to gentry of this description.

On the floor was a coat of thick dirt, trodden down hard by time, and about a dozen wood benches, few (if any) of them complete in all their members, supplied the place of seats. The whole atmosphere of the place was horribly tainted with tobacco smok. and foul bre

The chief attraction appeared to be a beggar, who was busily employed in defining the various names characters, and callings of different members of his profession.

"Why, there's Tom in the Tub makes from thirty to six and thirty bob§ a week."

"Thirty bob! lauk, sure," said an old red-faced washerwoman.

"Better to beg than to work, then," observed a butcher's man.

"Better to prig than do either," added a swell mobite.

"Oh! that ere's no nothings to vot some on us gits: vy, look at Bill Biler, the cove as used to pretend to have a mortified leg. He *vas* a knowing cove. He used to lay flower and ship's blood so artful, that a young genelman passing one day giv "him a tanner,** and svore he'd git 'im into the 'ospital, and no mistake. Vell, next day up comes the young genelman agin, says he, "I'm a surgeon myself, but I couldn't git yer into the 'ospital, howsomdever, I've got yer a room for yer, and here's a man and a wheelbarrow to take yer there." Up jumps Bill Biler; my eyes, didn't he cut up the court! and a parish prig began a prating, and would go on calling it a miracle, although the people told him they'd pump upon him

if he didn't hold his jaw. And then he called 'em vicked wretches to think of such a thing.

This anecdote produced an universal laugh.

"And there was old Mother Muggins, who kept a night school, principally for females, for teaching the art of scolding and begging. She turned a pretty penny."

Here the dialogue was interrupted by the entrance of two men who, seating themselves apart from the rest of the company, called for some hot gin and water. This being supplied, and the money paid for it—for the keepers of these kens never give credit—they conversed in a tone audible only to themselves.

The occupants of the "boozing ken" were now getting uproarious in their mirth.

"A song, a song!" cried one.

"Stay, I've got a toast to give," bawled another—"Here's confusion to all honest men." This was unanimously drank, and vociferously received.

"Have you heard about Ned Darby's being magged?" asked one of the new comers of the other.

"Yes; the traps hunted him down at last, poor fellow."

"Lord, vot a mortal sight of care a beak takes of a cove in trouble. 'Mind you don't commit yerself, whatever yer do,' says he. 'Don't say nothing to hurt yerself.'"

"Fair play's a jewel, I'm blowed if it ain't; ven ve comes to consider who is it as keeps all the judges and counsellors so fat, and sleek, and fine; vy us, to be sure. It's ve that keeps 'em. Ve causes it all. They owes it all to ve. And they ought to be grateful to ve for it.'"

"Very true. I'm a thinking that arter all the criminal code isn't nigh so bad as it's thought to be. Vy, if a genelman cotched us a prigging his wipe or cracking his crib, and thought there was no law to redress him, he'd explode on the spot, and we might git roughly handled."

"A jist observation," observed his companion, puffing out volumes of tobacco smoke.

"But now look what lots of holes there are for a feller to git out at, under the laws. I mean the laws of England. A slip of the pen, a flaw in the indictment, and a dozen other perpitious circumstances."

"If it varn't for the laws, every man, woman, and child 'd turn prigs, and then think vot'd be come of onr perfession." The two men now drew close together, and conversed in a lower tone.

"Have yer heerd anything more about the job somewhere up by Grosvenor Gate?" asked the shortest of the two ruffians.

"Yes," replied the other, whose countenance was hardly so repulsive as that of his companion.

"Who's crib is it?"

"A swell of the name of Vyvian. The old Ikey* set us up to it."

"What, Abednego Levi?"

"The same."

* This occurrence actually took place.
† A low pothouse.
‡ A pernicious liquor frightfully adulterated.
§ Shillings.
** Sixpence.

* A receiver of stolen goods.

"Who's engaged in it?"

"The Duffer, myself, and you, if you like it."

"That's the ticket. Much swag?"

"Lots."

"Many servants?"

"A butler and two women."

"Nothing to fear from them, then."

"All we want is a darkey."

"The Duffer's got a good 'un. That ere vun he used up Hammersmith way."

Here they were interrupted by the arrival of Abednego Levi.

"I want a word with you both, my dears," said the Israelite.

They immediately got up, and followed him out of the "boozing ken."

"What is the best news?" demanded the Jew.

"It is for you to tell *us* that," replied Ben, the shortest of the two cracksmen.

"Why," said Abednego, as they proceeded down Rosemary-lane, "the Duffer's contrived to get over one of the women, by rigging himself out in the cast-off regimentals I had by me."

"There's nothing like flash togs with the gals."

"And he's poisoned the favourite poodle dog," added the Jew.

"Good move that. Those little infernal howling curs, tarriers 'specially, make more noise, and bother us more, than all the big 'uns put together," said Tim Roper, the other cracksman.

"Very true," soliloquised Ben Bendy, as if recalling to mind some past event of his life.

"Have you got a boy?" asked Tim.

"You can get lots of them; there's plenty on 'em hanging about," suggested Ben.

"What does he say?" asked the Jew.

"Pal's a-thinking we arn't got no one to sarve our own parposes; but there he's in the wrong: arn't he, old 'un?"

"To be sure he is."

"You're doing business woundy slow, ain't you?" interposed Ben, rather stung at the last observation. "What's to be the upshot of all this palaver?"

"You and your pal there," croaked the Jew, "must be at the ken in Saffron-lane at eleven o'clock on Thursday night. The Duffer'll meet yer, and bring the necessaries with him; and you can leave one at a time, and nobody will be any the wiser. Ay, my dears?"

"So let it be," said both the cracksmen.

The Jew and his confederates now talked over certain little preparatory arrangements necessary to be completed before the intended pannie* could possibly come off. Ben Bendy was by both admitted to be "one of the concern," yet they rather wished to employ him as a cat's-paw than allow him an equal share of swag with themselves. The miser's reason for leaguing himself with Tim Roper in pre-

* Burglary.

ference to his companion was, that by this means he obtained a champion of gigantic force, and one who, though of inferior stature, was possessed of far greater physical strength than most men. Tim Roper, on the other hand, readily and closely connected himsel with the Jew, because he knew that, by his threats. he could always intimidate him, and thereby claim from him the lion's portion of the swag. Such was the position in which these three men stood with regard to each other.

"I say, Tim, who's that ere cove going along there?" said Ben, addressing his companion.

"He's a green 'un, and no mistake," was the reply.

"He doesn't seem elevated."

The ray of a lamp now shone full upon another figure, which was evidently following in the wake of the first. This was the Duffer.

"I see how it is. Mum's the word." And, so saying, Tim Roper stole over the crossing, and concealed himself in an open doorway.

A shrill whistle was heard.

This was answered by another.

The first proceeded from Tim Roper, the second from the Duffer.

When the stranger, little thinking that he was about to be the subject of a premeditated attack, had reached the doorway in which Tim was concealed, his assailant suddenly rushed upon him, and puffed a volume of tobacco smoke in his eyes. The stranger instinctively raised his hand to preserve them, when he felt a sharp tug behind, for the Duffer had possessed himself of his pocket-book. When he recovered himself both his assailants had disappeared. With a species of demoniacal delight, the eyes of the Jew were glaring full upon him.

"What is the matter?" asked Ben, in an almost motherly tone of kindness.

"Have you seen anybody running away," demanded the stranger, furiously.

"Ah, to be sure I have."

"Which way did he go?"

"Why, straight up the street, and then round the corner. He's a-sitting down on a doorstep."

With many an oath and protestation of future vengeance, the stranger pursued the route pointed out to him: perhaps more in hopes of meeting with a constable than the thief. The Jew and Ben, not liking to remain on the spot—although on any emergency the police are generally invisible—the two worthies separated for the night. The Jew bent his steps to the den in Shoreditch, while those of the other were directed back again to the "boozing ken."

When he entered there was a woman standing at the bar literally dressed in rags, smoking a tobacco-pipe, and drinking gin wholesale.

The woman was the *Barker*.

She belonged to that class of street imposters who pretend to be suddenly seized with a fit, and she was nicknamed the Barker from a habit she had under these circumstances of imitating, as near as possible, the bark of a dog. By this rather novel manœuvre she generally succeeded in exciting the pity and compassion of passers-by, and not unfrequently obtained a tangible proof of the sincerity of both. She also carried on an extensive busines in cats'-skins and dogs'-teeth, which latter she knocked out of the heads of dead dogs in the road, and sold to bookbinders, carvers, and gilders, as burnishing tools. She was now dissipating the few halfpence she possessed in gin.

Her husband was a Mudlark.

At home two children were starving.

CHAPTER IV.

THE DINNER.

WE left the baronet, Frederick, and Stamer, quitting the hell. Sir Vyvian and his brother used every artifice to erase the impression made upon Stamer's mind by the scene he had just witnessed, nor were their efforts altogether unsuccessful.

"You must come and dine with me the day after to-morrow, my dear fellow," said the baronet. "Mind I take no excuse." This was spoken with the air of a man who meant what he said.

"You are really very kind, but——"

"There must be no buts in the matter. Come, come, it's all arranged; I shall expect you."

After some further hesitation Stamer accepted the invitation, and the party separated.

On the day, and at the time appointed, Stamer proceeded to the residence of the baronet in Grosvenor-square. On his arrival he was ushered into an elegant apartment, in which a beautiful girl was indolently lounging upon a sofa. Not deigning to rise from her seat, she continued reading, or rather turning over the pages, of a fashionable novel.

"Mr. Stamer," said Frederick Vyvian, advancing towards the new comer, "permit me to introduce you to my sister, Miss Vyvian."

Miss Amelia Vyvian parted her lips just enough to display two pearly rows of teeth. Stamer smiled and bowed his happiness at the introduction.

"A lovely girl," said Frederick, just loud enough to reach the ears of Miss Amelia, "is she not?"

"Perfection," was the response.

There was a silence of some minutes.

"Amelia, my dear," said the baronet, "I fear you, who so seldom play at cards, will find this evening rather dull."

"Not at all," replied the young lady; "besides, I do sometimes you know."

At this moment a precocious young black, probably about fifteen, whom Amelia very aptly termed a creature, announced the name of Mr. Tift.

"Mr. Adolphus Tift, how do you do?" said the baronet, shaking him rather freely by the hand.

Then, turning to the black, "Here, James, take this parcel immediately: remember, there's no rest for the wicked." This last observation was intended as a hint for him to run all the way.

Mr. Adolphus Tift now turned towards Miss Amelia, who, with more than usual animation, had risen to receive him, being delighted, as she said, to find anybody so innocent and natural in this world of sophistication and art as Mr. Adolphus.

Mr. Lift was more than half a dandy, without possessing the finished appearance of the baronet, or the devil-me-care carriage of his brother Frederick, yet there was a self-confidence, almost a self-sufficiency about him, inseparable from a man of the world. He had been handsome, but excess had brought on disease— that species of disease which disfigures the appearance without, at all events in its first stages, diminishing the powers of the body. He had spent his life almost alternately on the continent and in the Queen's Bench. His intellects were to a certain degree muddled, and his ideas appeared to run one upon another quicker than he could find words to express them. He imagined himself ill-used by the world, and that he had all along been the sport of a malicious fortune, and therefore felt no repugnance at tricking mankind at large. He looked upon every man as an enemy, and upon himself as an enemy to every man.

The commonplace observations of the day having been bandied threadbare, the intervals were only enlivened with a sort of cross-fire of occasional chat of more smartness than humour, and more wit than meaning: indeed, the conversation flagged most terribly.

"The flies still continue to be extremely annoying," said Amelia.

"Dear little depredators," replied Mr. Tift.

"Talking of depredators," said Frederick, addressing the baronet, "have you heard of the trick played last night on our brother?"

"What Francis?" exclaimed the baronet.

"Ay; as he was going up some hole or another he was robbed of his pocket-book in a rather ingenious manner."

Frederick Vyvian briefly related the circumstances already known to the reader.

"Thieves have fine invention; no man is fit for one without it," said the baronet.

"Has he got any clue to the rascal?" asked Stamer.

"Not that I'm aware of. He has offered a reward of five guineas for his apprehension and the restoration of the pocket-book and its contents; but, as the sum he lost considerably exceeds that amount, it is not probable that any of the parties mixed up in the transaction——"

"There I hold a different opinion from yourself," interrupted Sir Richard.

"Nor," continued Frederick, "were the thief taken, could my brother identify him, for he never

caught a glance of the fellow who stole his pocket book, and but very imperfectly recollects the features of the one who puffed in his face."

"That's awkward," said Mr. Tift.

"The lower classes are vilely bad," whined the baronet, stroking his whiskers.

"What a blessing it is that such a yawning gulf separates us from the contaminating creatures!" said Amelia Vyvian, in an affected tone.

"It is, indeed, an inestimable blessing, for which we should at all times be grateful," soliloquised Sir Richard.

Stamer fidgetted uneasily in his chair.

"The feelings of the aristocracy are so refined, compared with those of the class alluded to."

"Thank God, we have something else to distinguish us but our *feelings*," laughed the baronet, chinking his pockets. "But pray have done with sentiment."

"But even in the higher classes," said Stamer,

The baronet, Frederick, and Tift, interchanged "there are many doubtful characters, and some, unfortunately, which admit of no doubt at all." glances.

"But they are even as spots in the sun," suddenly exclaimed Mr. Tift, as if mentally illumined by the glittering chandelier above his head.

"How strange it is that Captain Dashington and Doctor Dunwiddy, and my brother and his wife, have not arrived yet!" cried Sir Richard.

"Very."

Here Captain Dashington and Doctor Dunwiddy were announced, and shortly afterwards Mr. Francis Vyvian, with his wife leaning on his arm, also made his appearance.

The new guests had not seated themselves many minutes, when the party adjourned to dinner.

The supper-table was laid out in a sumptuous manner; the wines were excellent; the dishes supreme; and every dainty of the season figured in abundance.

The sideboard was loaded with family plate—even the baronet's gilt spurs were not omitted.

The covers being removed, the soups appeared; they were three in number :—Turtle, Purie de paix, and Soup à la Julienne : these were by all declared faultless.

After the discussion of the soups, the course of fish was announced : this consisted of—Colvert Salmon, Bouquets à la Cardinale, and Crimped Turbot : this proved a very acceptable course.

After this a quarter of lamb, Bœuf à la Jardinière, Jambon à la Brétonne, and that delicious dish Suprême de Volaille aux truffes, were produced, and pronounced excellent.

The next course was—Dindon Roti, Asperge, Charlotte Rape, à la Shakerley, Homard à l'aspie, Merinques à la crême, Tartettes d'Abricots.

Then came ices in every shape, colour, and flavour, favourite and rare wines, and choice liqueurs.

After dinner was over, and the ladies had retired, cards and billiards were resorted to, as a means of whiling away the time; and although the Scotch doctor produced sundry instances of the ruinous effects resulting therefrom, with all of which the baronet perfectly coincided, all present turned a deaf ear to his warnings.

It now becomes our imperative duty to give some account of the agreeable individuals who form our delightful dinner party.

The reader is already acquainted with Amelia, the baronet, Frederick Vyvian, Tift, and Stamer.

Mrs. Vyvian was at once gay and grave, flighty and sentimental, tender and severe, haughty and humble, selfish and generous, benevolent and satyrical. She was a combination of contrarieties. She was not beautiful, but fascinating. She possessed the art of winning, but not the science of keeping.

Her husband was the youngest and the best of the three Vyvians. He was of a tall stature, a good complexion, and a handsome mould.

Captain Dashington was a thorough-bred man of fashion. He was good-looking, had served in the Canadian campaign, and his age appeared to be about thirty or thirty-five years.

Doctor Dunwiddy might have been fifty or more: He was what in plain phraseology is termed a humbug, and had obtained his degree of doctor by enclosing a five-pound note to the University of Aberdeen.

At billiards Stamer lost a considerable sum. It invariably happened that he won a great deal from the baronet, but always lost a great deal more when he played with Frederick. This strange circumstance raised some fresh doubts in his mind as to the respectability of the firm of Vyvian and Co. How subtle is the voice of flattery! When Mr. Tift, who, like the most of knaves, instilled the destructive venom into Stamer's veins, all his suspicions gradually subsided.

"Was not Lord Oxburn to have been here to-night?" said Frederick, addressing the baronet.

"I believe he was; but he is not a very punctual man."

"Are you acquainted with Lord Oxburn?" asked Captain Dashington of Stamer, with some degree of *hauteur*.

"No, I am not."

"Then I must introduce you to his lordship," said Tift.

Stamer bowed acquiescence.

"Lord Oxburn is a man full of all sorts of fahionable employments, fashionable levities, and immoderate pursuits," remarked Doctor Dunwiddy.

"A coronet and twenty thousand a-year is a rather heavy weight for a young fellow of twenty or thereabouts," said the captain.

"Was he no more than that when his father died?" inquired Francis Vyvian.

"Not a bit," replied the baronet. "I saw him thrown suddenly upon the world, with a handsome fortune, and a heart warm, candid, and innocent. knew that, under those circumstances, he must see every vice in masquerade as it were, and that, if he escaped contamination, he might at least become entangled. Then I said to myself, shall I, who am trotting down the hill of life, fail to open his eyes. And from that moment I was a father to him."

"And you certainly acted in a manner becoming a Christian," said the doctor.

"I flatter myself that I did. I at least acted in accordance with the dictates of my heart; yet he is so basely ungrateful as to blame me as being the sole cause of his present embarrassed circumstances."

"I sympathise with you warmly," said Mr. Tift : "I feel for you, and shall I tell you why?"

"As you please."

"Because I assisted you in what we both deemed a paramount duty."

Mr. Tift rose ten degrees higher in Doctor Dunwiddy's opinion.

Presently the ladies and gentlemen rejoined at supper.

At this meal a cold collation of ham and fowl, and other dishes, were done ample justice to.

After supper there was music, but no dancing.

"Of all follies there is none I dislike so much as affectation," said Mrs. Vyvian, casting an admonitory glance at Amelia, who had just risen from the piano.

"I must say that I am rather surprised to hear you make such a confession," said her husband, laughing.

"I suppose there is nothing reprehensible in speaking one's sentiments."

"I, who am old in years and experience," observed Doctor Dunwiddy, "think that no conclusive arguments have been produced on either side."

"I suppose, my dear," said Mrs. Vyvian, addressing Amelia, "that you prefer the country to London?"

"On the contrary, I have a decided predilection for London."

"Strange that a young lady of your age should prefer the gaieties of fashionable life to the innocent sweets of a pastoral existence. Very odd. Perfectly uanccountable."

"I would rather pass one week in some secluded spot than a whole life in London," cried Miss Amelia, merely wishing to annoy and frustrate the object of Mrs. Vyvian.

"That is more unaccountable still. After having heard so much of your amiable character, I should have thought that the kindness you have received from your brother would have prevented your expressing so strong, and, I may add, unfeeling a preference."

Mrs. Vyvian smiled complacently around, and Dr. Dunwiddy coughed an approval.

The baronet touched his gold repeater as if by accident, and it struck the hour of two.

"Dear me, is it so late as that?" cried Mrs. Vyvian. "We really must take our leave."

"As the weather is so very unfavourable, can you not remain with me to-night?" said the baronet.

"Oh, no; the carriage has been waiting for us these three hours. Poor man!"

After a long lecture from the Scotch doctor on the evil effects of damp on the constitution, and a great shaking of hands, Mrs. Vyvian and her loving spouse drove away from Grosvenor-square.

The rest of the party, being rather elevated, were easily persuaded to pass the night at the baronet's.

Amelia quitted the room.

Her example was soon followed by the remainder of the company.

CHAPTER V.

THE BARKER.

WHEN she left the "Nimble Fingers," in Rosemary-lane, the Barker traced her steps to a house in West-street, which modern improvement has recently swept away.

At the corner of the street two squalid children were waiting for her.

"Have yer got anything to eat, mother?" asked the eldest, in a voice faint with hunger and apprehension."

"Eat! where the h—ll can I get anything to eat?" and she sent the child spinning with a blow from her doubled fist. "To h—ll with yer, and take that to eat."

She now for the first time discovered her husband sitting down on the doorstep.

"What do yer knock the child about like that there for?" asked the Mudlark, for a moment raising his head from his knees; "and, what's more, how long do yer think I'm a-going to be a-waiting out here for you?—all day long I 'spose."

The Barker made no reply, but opened the door with a rusty key, and entered, followed by her

husband and children. What a miserable spectacle did that habitation present!

The broken stairs, the damp walls, the nauseous sickening odour which pervaded the whole atmosphere, all but too plainly indicated the chilling influence of poverty—poverty in its most hideous and appalling form.

In one corner of the room the Mudlark threw himself on a heap of matted straw, and in another were huddled together the two unfortunate children.

The Barker had not yet recovered from the intoxicating effects of the liquor she had imbibed at the "boozing ken." No wonder that she, so deeply sunk in vice and misery, should purchase oblivion at any cost.

The eldest child again craved for bread.

"What did yer go a-getting drunk for, when your babbies were starving?" demanded the Mudlark.

"I only had three ha'porths."

"I knows better than that."

"You knows a precious site better than all the world put together You're often as drunk as a lord yourself," said the woman, with tipsy gravity.

Once more the starving child asked for bread.

"By G—d, I'll do it!" cried tho man, starting up from the straw.

"Do what?"

Without replying to the last question, the Mudlark drew on a high pair of waterproof boots, and, having provided himself with a lantern, walked down the creaking stairs, and left the house.

"Where's father gone to?" inquired the girl.

"To search the sewers, to be sure; and a deal he ever gets by it."

"Will he bring any bread with him when he comes home?"

"Who knows what he'll bring till he comes, yer little fool?"

The child, thus repulsed, was silent.

* * * *

The Mudlark pursued his way, in a dogged mood, till he reached London-bridge: here he entered a long, dark alley, leading from Thames-street to the river. The tide was down, and he descended a flight of slippery wooden steps, and groped along the muddy shore till he came to a small round aperture, just sufficiently large to admit his body, situated under a Roman cement wharf.

With his hands and his knees he climbed into the slimy hole—first casting a glance at the pure heaven above, as if imploring its protection, and then, lighting his lamp, he entered the sewers—that vast subterranean London, more extensive and perilous than even the famous catacombs of Rome. How little do the rich and affluent for one moment imagine that human beings, urged on by despair and starvation, are crawling beneath their stately mansions! How little do the wealthy suspect that *men* penetrate into those filthy quarters supposed to be inhabited only by vermin!

The enormous rats, frightened by the light,

scampered away in all directions, and occasionally some strange insect, unknown but in these damp, unfrequented quarters, with a sting as fatal as an adder's, would threaten and buzz around the adventurer: still the Mudlark scrambled on—now sunk up to his knees, and groping in the fetid stream with a short iron, curved at the end, now passing his fingers through the division of the brickwork, in the hopes of finding some small coin or lost valuable.

He had proceeded a considerable distance:

He had arrived at a narrow turning, branching off from the main sewer.

Here it was altogether impossible for him to maintain the erect posture.

Vexed and jaded with useless toil, he was about to give up further search; but then the recollection of his starving children rushed into his mind. Nearly suffocated by the fumes of the stream in which he trod, the rotten brickwork crumbling over his head, danger and death on every side—still he was loth to return. It was evening when he entered, and for two hours had he been groping in the dark, dank sewers. He heard the carriages and vehicles rumbling over his head; he heard the footsteps passing to and fro, passing and repassing, in all the confusion predominant in the modern Babylon: he heard all, but saw nothing. He was entombed alive, surrounded by vermin and venomous reptiles; and, had many of those who rode and walked over his head seen him in his present plight, they would have looked upon him as hardly less loathsome than the objects with which he was surrounded. How few would have appreciated the motive! yet, what was this man's crime? He was poor! In moral England to be poor is to be criminal! Added to all its other degredations and inconveniences, poverty has an indelible stigma attached to it—a sort of imaginary taint. It is, to a certain degree, associated with guilt.

Misery can only be augmented by reflection; it cannot be alleviated. Such was the argument which the Mudlark's heart suggested to overpower his feelings, and to support him in the execution of the task he had undertaken.

Again he struggled on.

The feeble rays of his lamp fell on some glittering substance in the wall.

Immediately hope animated his breast, so late the abode of despair. He stretched out his hand, and eagerly clutched the promised treasure. Closing his fingers tightly upon it, without a moment's pause, he hurried back by the path he had entered. He listened attentively to hear if any one was coming; for if the sewer-searchers meet in their subterranean excursions, they hesitate not to commit murder, or any other degree of violence, for the sake of obtaining what they may suspect another to have found. Nor is the deed very likely to be brought to light. The carcase is speedily devoured by the rats, so that it becomes impossible to identify the person.

" My starving children shall now have food."

Curiosity prompted him to examine more closely the valuable he had discovered.

It proved to be a ring, apparently gold and studded with diamonds. He conjectured that it was of no trifling value.

To his indescribable horror and dismay, while he was eyeing his treasure with delight, a brawny hand was suddenly laid on his shoulder.

" Vot have yer got there, yer bad lot?" demanded the voice.

Startled beyond measure by so strange and unfortunate an incident, the Mudlark accidentally let fall the ring.

For a time he was speechless with disappointment.

At length he collected his faculties together.

" Biler," cried he, " you've robbed me of the only thing I had on earth—my only chance."

This Biler was Bill Biler, the impostor, mentioned by the beggar at the " Nimble Fingers," the boozing ken in Rosemary-lane.

Biler began groping about in right earnest, thinking, from the last speech of the Mudlark, that he must have dropped something worth having.

" Git off, or I may do you a mischief, p'r'aps."

" Nonsense."

" Git off, I say." And he assumed a threatening gesture.

" Why, d—n it, man, I've as much right here as you, haven't I ?"

Enraged at the taunts of Bill Biler, and the loss of the ring, he closed with him, when both men fell heavily to the ground.

The sensations of suffocation began to creep over the Mudlark.

With an almost superhuman effort he freed himself from the grasp of his antagonist.

Both their lamps were extinguished.

Scarcely had they both regained their feet when the rats rushed upon them from all directions.

" We shall be torn piecemeal and devoured alive," cried the Mudlark, in an agony of fear.

" Have you had enough on it ? or are you grumbling still ?" exclaimed Biler, in a menacing tone. " Don't go a whining there; I'll have a glim in a minute."

Having obtained a light by friction, Biler closed his lamp, lest the gaseous atmosphere of the place should ignite. From the same reasons it would have been highly imprudent to have attempted to light the lamp of the Mudlark.

" If it vasn't for my children," cried he, grinding his teeth with rage and disappointment, " you should pay for this."

" Come, none o' yer gammon; hold yer tongue, and go about your business," ferociously replied the other; " and may be I'll be perlite enough to light yer out."

Although boiling with fury, the Mudlark was forced to submit.

When they had almost reached the entrance, Bill Biler took his leave, and returned to search for the lost treasure.

" You 've got nothing to know the place by agen," roared the Mudlark through the round aperture, when he was once more on *terra firma*. " Ha! ha! ha!" And his laugh rang loud and clear through the vaulted arch.

Bill Biler replied with a tremendous oath.

Even among the dirty denizens of the river shore, whenever the moonlight partially revealed him, his appearance was not unnoticed; but when he reached the streets of London, he became the object of universal ridicule.

" Where did you lay last?" facetiously inquired an overgrown charity boy.

" Vat a lummy plight!" said another urchin.

" Oh, would I be in his shoes!" cried another.

" Drunk!" observed a sallow-looking teatotaller.

" As the son of King Solomon," added a looker-on.

" I bets yer a penny I hits him." And a boy chucked a piece of 'baccopipe with unerring certainty.

This was the signal for a general onslaught.

In no humour to brook such treatment, he endeavoured to escape or give the slip to his assailants. Foreseeing his intention, a butcher ran purposely against him.

Then a police constable came up.

" Here 's the crasher," said a dozen voices.

The Mudlark was instantly given in charge for being drunk.

Without more ado he was walked off to the station-house.

The Mudlark had been three hours absent from the house in West-street.

It was now past eleven o'clock at night.

By this time the Barker was somewhat sobered.

" Will father come soon?" eagerly inquired the eldest girl.

" What do you want to know for?"

" 'Cas I'm hungry."

" Wait a bit, then, and you shall have some'ut to eat."

The Barker quitted the room, and walked down stairs and through a passage into a sort of cellar. When she lifted up the trap-door there came forth an overwhelming stench, but her olfactory nerves were of a decidedly strong order. Having provided herself with a light she descended into the cellar, the filthy state of which fully accounted for the pestiferous odour above mentioned.

In the ground, which was composed of decomposed matter, putrid vegetables, and the intestines of various animals, an immense number of dead cats had been buried head downwards. The Barker always maintained a large supply by stealing stray cats and kittens, and in this posture burying their heads alive. By this precaution they were not only rendered perfectly harmless, and their cries stifled, but they were always ready for use.

She drew a large clasp knife from her bosom, and, slitting the furs round the throats, skinned the poor animals with as much facility, expedition, and address, as the reader may have seen employed by a fishman in performing the same operations upon an eel.

The Barker placed the skins over her left arm, and in her right hand she carried the light and two cats recently skinned. Thus equipped she retraced her steps from the cellar, and carefully closed the trap-door after her.

On reaching the room she put on her bonnet, and, having placed the cats in a large iron pot, and clapped them on a slow charcoal fire, ignited for the purpose, she concealed a green bottle in the flowing drapery of her garments, which she intended filling with the proceeds of her skins.

They soon found a ready market at a marine store dealer of the name of Solomon, where a green and white board stated that " No questions were axed." In that neighbourhood a very necessary announcement to insure custom.

The amount she obtained for them was sixpence.

She spent fourpence of this in gin.

With the other twopence she bought bread.

The two unfortunate children devoured the bread voraciously, and the Barker, having disposed of the contents of the bottle, and left the pot gently stewing on the fire, the miserable trio sank to sleep, in an atmosphere impregnated with charcoal.

For what were the contents of that pot intended?

The fat of the two cats were being melted down, with a view to its being sold to the poor as dripping.

The bones would grind into bread.

The flesh would serve for to-morrow's dinner.

The refuse would be thrown into the street, to assist the offal there collected in creating a pestilence.

CHAPTER VI.

THE BURGLARY.

ACCORDING to the arrangement made in Rosemary-lane, the three cracksmen were wending their way up Oxford-street, accompanied by a boy, towards Sir Richard's residence in Grosvenor-square.

It was a tranquil and moonlight night.

" Have yer got the barkers?"* demanded Ben.

" A brace each," answered the Duffer; " but, mind, they 're only to be used in a case of desperation."

" Vill the cook let us in, or shall we have to operate oursilvs?" asked Tim Roper.

" I couldn't have persuaded her to do that ere bit of kindness, and, vot's more, I daren't tell her half vot ve vere hup to, in case she might nose us."

Here the conversation dropped.

The stars were twinkilng merrily in the heavens,

* Pistols.

and the inmates and guests were in the downy arms of Morpheus, when the burglers climbed over the area pailings of Sir Richard Vyvian's house.

"Now then, light the darkey; let's have a glim," said the Duffer. Ben proceeded to obey.

The Duffer now produced a "centre-bit" from a capacious pocket in his greatcoat, in which he carried all the "necessaries."

He burst open the pantry door with a crowbar.

His object now was to obtain ingress to the kitchen.

The Duffer commenced his operations immediately above the back of the door, so as to prevent the possibility, or at any rate the probability, of the iron work interfering with the progress of the instrument.

He executed his task in a masterly manner, and beyond a little grating not the slightest sound was audible; but when he discovered that the door was coated inside with iron:

"Damnation," growled Tim Roper.

"We must try the winder," said the Duffer.

"That's the sort," cried Ben.

The burglars had broken into the pantry, underneath the doorstep, and thus concealed from observation, had endeavoured to force the kitchen door; but their object was frustrated by the iron lining.

"D—n me, if I don't get a bit of grub," observed the Duffer, inserting a jemmy between the doors of the safe, and forcibly wrenching them asunder.

"Come, pal—don't waste time with guzzling now," exclaimed Tim.

The Duffer was not the man to resign a chance of booty for the certainty of grub, and, moreover, he felt the justice of the observation made by his confederate. He merely replied with a surly "No," and acted on the advice.

The window was protected by several stout iron bars.

The Duffer having again dived into his enormous pocket, produced therefrom a fine hair saw. While his companions remained concealed under the doorstep, he succeeded in severing away a sufficient number of these bars to obtain ample space for the admission of the boy. He then, with great dexterity, cut out several panes of glass with a diamond, and almost noiselessly wrenched the shutters open with his jemmy or iron crowbar. The boy now joined him.

Lifting him up in his arms he placed him through the aperture he had just made into the kitchen, and holding the darkey in such a manner as to afford him light, ordered him to undo the fastenings and open the door.

Having so far succeeded, he crept back to his companions in the pantry.

The door was open and the three ruffians entered.

The Duffer led the way to the plate chest, which was always kept in the library.

Fluttering with hope and expectancy, he tore open the lid, when, instead of discovering a mine of wealth, there was nothing but a few articles, mostly plated, and duplicates of the rest.

"He's popped 'em," solemnly exclaimed Ben.

A muttered execration burst from between the half-closed teeth of the Duffer.

"There's no time to be lost, let's take vot we can git. Vun thing's plain, the plated harticles and them ere tickets are no good votsomedever,"

"Vot *will* be *must* be." said the Duffer with emphasis, and he commenced filling his pockets in right earnest.

The heavier articles were put into a bag provided for the purpose.

"There's not a chance of this 'ere affair being chanted on the leer,"* said Tim Roper; "they won't bother about their gobsticks† and clinkers,‡ 'cos of them 'ere slips of paper."

"Maybe we might as well take a few on 'em with us, so as to hact as a kind of corrective against abuse," observed Ben.

"Agreed," said the Duffer.

They heard footsteps on the stairs.

"Douse the glim and cut your luckey," cried the hoarse voice of the Duffer.

In an instant the light was out.

With wonderful celerity and presence of mind the whole party retreated to the pantry, and thence effected their escape with the booty they had obtained.

The footsteps on the stairs were those of Mr. Tift, whose sleeping room was situated immediately over the library. He had been extremely restless that night, and, hearing a strange noise below, ventured to peep down the staircase, when he saw the reflection of a bull's-eye on the wall.

He re-entered his room, and, without a moment's hesitation, slipped on his trowsers, wrapped a couple of blankets round him, and, having armed himself with a poker, rushed down stairs.

How great his astonishment was at the strange sight that met his eye we will leave the reader to conjecture.

The first person he woke was the housemaid, who, half dressed as she was, rushed up to Amelia's room.

"Missus, missus, mum, the house is broken into, and, please mum, Mr. Tift has gone mad, mum."

"Wake up your master immediately," replied Amelia, whom this complication of disasters completely dumb-foundered; and then, having thrown on her dressing gown and shawl, and slipped on her shoes, she knocked lustily at the door of Doctor Dunwiddy.

"Make haste or there will be something horrid happen; there are strange people in the house."

"I'm not a fighting man mysel'," replied the Doctor, in a voice tremulous with fear. "You have got Captain Dashington there, who was wounded in the back at Canada, and what can ye want with a puir lone body like me?"

"If you do not come *out* they will come *in*," said Amelia, laughing in spite of herself.

"Then I'll just ask them to spare a puir body, who never knowingly hurt a fly."

* Advertised in the newspapers.
† Silver spoons.
‡ Silver milk jugs.

No entreaty on Amelia's part could persuade him to open the door, but he double locked it.

At this moment Mr. Tift appeared on the stairs, accoutred and armed as before described, brandishing the poker, and threatening to " smash" anybody and everybody.

" They are in there," said Amelia, wishing to enjoy a joke at the expense of the Scotch doctor.

" Fire and fury !" cried Mr. Tift. And he commenced desperately fencing at the door.

Here the baronet arrived, carrying in his hand a loaded pistol, while Frederick followed with a light.

Captain Dashington also made his appearance.

" Fire in !" roared Mr. Tift : " the villains are concealed in that room."

" It 's me, it 's me ; it is, indeed," exclaimed Doctor Dunwiddy, in an agony of suspense.

" Oh, it 's him, it 's him ! Doctor Dunwiddy 's a thief ; he says so himself." And then, putting his mouth to the keyhole, he added, " I'm quite ashamed of you, Doctor Dunwiddy."

" What *does* all this mean ?" inquired the baronet.

" Go to the library, but go alone," replied Mr. Tift.

The truth flashed across Sir Richard's mind.

On arriving at the library, the scene of confusion that presented itself fully established his worst fears.

When he quitted the room he fastened the door securely after him, lest the fashionable Captain Dashington or Doctor Dunwiddy—who had the reputation of advertising other people's affairs as effectually as a widely-circulated newspaper—should pry into the disordered sanctum.

" Send for a constable," said Captain Dashington.

" James, fetch one immediately," exclaimed Frederick.

" I do not perceive the necessity of any step of the kind. However, as you please."

" Can I have a word with you, Mr. Tift ?" asked the baronet.

" I am at your disposal."

Sir Richard Vyvian and Mr. Tift retired to an adjoining room.

" I presume, sir, that you will never mention what you have this night seen by accident ?"

" It shall be for ever locked in the profundity of my breast." And Mr. Tift placed his hand feelingly on his heart. " Are you satisfied ?"

" I am."

Now, and not till now, did Doctor Dunwiddy venture out.

" Let us see how the thieves obtained entrance," said Frederick.

The whole party hastened to the pantry.

A constable was sent for to examine the window and door, as well as to keep charge over the house.

" No new hand did that job," said the constable.

" Indeed," cried Sir Richard.

" Have they taken anything ?"

" Nothing of any consequence."

" If you give us a description we 'll frisk a bit."*

" I have no wish whatever to prosecute."

The constable looked up to see whether he was jesting.

" Robberies are now-a-days difficult to be found out without the precurser of a reward," observed Captain Dashington.

" Offer one ; you will at least have the gratification of learning that Jack Such-a-one has the ' thimble,' whether you recover it or not," said Frederick.

A glass of beer was given to the constable, and James, being stationed at the pantry door, provided with an enormous rattle, to give alarm in case of a fresh attempt, the disturbed inmates and guests of Sir Richard's house retired to their respective rooms.

Dr. Dunwiddy slept no more that night.

The baronet, Frederick, and Stamer, congregrated together in the parlour.

CHAPTER VII.

THE STATION-HOUSE.

WHEN we last mentioned the Mudlark, he was on his way to the station-house, in the grasp of a City policeman.

How fluctuating a thing is a mob ! Ten minutes previous he had been the object of its ridicule, its scorn, and its contempt ; but now, that they saw him being dragged off to the station-house on the charge of being disorderly and drunk, when they knew him to be perfectly sober, their hearts revolted at such a piece of injustice : the tiniest urchin added his small voice to the general shout of disapprobation.

The policeman, who was rabid and infuriated at the opposition he met with at every turning, threw the unfortunate Mudlark from one side to the other, and then advised him not to struggle, or perhaps he might get hurt.

" Let the man go, can't yer ? I 'll take him home." said a passer-by.

" I 'll mark you," replied the constable.

The meaning conveyed in these indefinite words half frightened the individual who volunteered his services.

At last the constable slipped, and fell to the ground with the Mudlark.

" Down with the bobby," cried one.

" Liberate him," quoth another.

" Bravo !" shouted numerous voices.

Instantly several brawny hands grasped the limbs of the Mudlark, and the unfortunate man was almost torn asunder between the two conflicting parties.

Here a strange-looking individual assisted the constable.

" What do yer do that for, ay, sawny ?"

" Mind yer own business, can't yer ?"

" Go to the work'us ; you look half starved."

A greengrocer stepped forward, and tucked up his sleeves in an ominous manner.

* Search.

The strange individual, after having made a lame attempt at reconciliation, by speaking of "letting him go by-and-by," took the hint, and obligingly quitted the "scene."

Presently a tall Life-guardsman interposed.

Seizing the policeman by the nape of his neck, with one whirl he sent him sprawling on the ground, and liberated the prisoner.

The Mudlark attempted to escape, but before he had run many yards the constable overtook him, and again grasped his collar.

They were close to a public-house.

Thither the policeman directed his steps, accompanied by the Mudlark.

Before the mob perceived what he intended to do, he jerked the Mudlark in, and, having bolted the door, despatched a messenger to the station-house to obtain assistance.

"I wouldn't be here not if I was you," said a woman, addressing the soldier who had before interfered.

Before much time had been lost, a reinforcement of four constables arrived from the station-house, who took up the Mudlark by his arms and legs—arms and legs that were already nearly dislocated—and carried him off, amid the shouts and screams of the mob, like a bit of dirty lumber.

On arriving at the station-house the charge was entered in a book by the sergeant, and he was pitched head foremost into a cell, tenanted by two drunken men and a couple of other disorderly inmates.

"Ven is a man dead drunk?" asked one of them.

"Sure it's myself that can answer that question," replied a bricklayer's labourer. "He's 'dead drunk' when he can't move, and 'elevated' when he can."

Two gentlemen were now thrust in.

"What will be the penalty of this pastime?" demanded one.

"Oh, five pounds. The beak won't send us to Brixton."

"This is justice," thought the Mudlark.

Profound silence now reigned around, broken only by the occasional chant of an Irish hodsman—

I smokes, I drinks, I eats, I feeds,
A merry, careless life I leads.

But the woman's den, which was near, presented scenes far worse. Blasphemies, mockery, laughter, and fighting—hell in miniature!

Prostitutes, thieves, and honest women, were promiscuously crowded together in one heterogeneous mass.

"What will become of my poor children? they will starve," exclaimed a woman.

"This lady has children," said a prostitute, "give them that."

The present was a blow.

The screams of the woman were smothered by the fiendish laughter of the Cyprians.

At length morning came.

The light dawned through the small hole of the cell, but it brought not gladness with it to the heart of the Mudlark. What had become of his children? What would become of them?

A policeman entered and shook him roughly by the shoulder.

He was taken before the inspector.

After that sage personage had heard the case, with such little appendages as the policeman chose to add, and such tints of colouring as he thought would give it effect, the inspector thought that the Mudlark had never been drunk at all, and the policeman thought so too.

It was unanimously agreed that the soldier was the guilty party.

Two constables were despatched instanter to the barracks.

Of course they came back without him.

They were next ordered to search all the public-houses in the neighbourhood.

This duty they performed by tucking up their sleeves valiantly outside every pothouse, as if they fully expected a mortal struggle, and then returning back to the station-house without him.

After having been torn away from his family on a charge which could not be even established at the station-house, he was liberated.

How generous! How noble! How just!

CHAPTER VIII.

THE JEW AGAIN.

FREDERICK VYVIAN was on his way to the Jew's den, in Shoreditch. It was just such a night as that on which he met Abednego Levi in Smithfield.

He was crossing London-bridge.

The fresh wind blew in his face, and, although the night was indeed a wretched one, he gladly braved the elements, when he thought of the success that had attended his imposition with regard to Abednego Levi. How could he feel remorse at cheating a man who intended to rob him? Moreover, remorse seldom found an entrance to his breast; it was too choked up with vanity and pride.

Before him he saw a young man with his hands clasped together, apparently praying — fervently praying.

One sudden leap, and he stood on the balustrade.

"My God, he means to destroy himself!" cried Frederick.

The figure of the young man shone forth in bold relief from above the dark and lowering clouds beyond. No cry escaped his lip. One convulsive rush, and the jaws of the meandering Thames opened to receive him.

Till now Frederick had been mute and motionless as a statue.

No sooner was the deed done than he collected his scattered faculties together, and gave the alarm.

He perceived a boat and two men push off from the shore.

"Where is he?"

Frederick directed them as well as he was able.

"If we could find his whereabouts, we might pick him up, p'r'aps."

The tide was running strong at the time, and there appeared to be no hope.

Suddenly the men cried out that they had found him.

Frederick Vyvian rushed towards the steps, where a number of persons had already congregated together.

Eagerly he pressed forward to view the features of the young man who had destroyed himself. It was the youth ruined at the "Fishmonger's-hall."

This circumstance tended to considerably lower his spirits.

It caused reflection; reflection brought on indecision; and indecision brought on unhappiness. He saw the effects of that fatal vice—gaming—too plainly demonstrated: he received a sort of prac-

tical lesson—it might have been a warning. Yet gambling was almost his sole source of existence. He had no occupation, nor was he fit for any.

He endeavoured to dispel these gloomy ideas from his mind, and he thought of the sum he was to receive that night from the Jew, but all his efforts fell far short of the mark.*

It was ten o'clock when he stopped at the door of the Jew's house in Shoreditch.

Some time elapsed before he could obtain admission.

"Come, make haste; it is not weather to keep a mangy cur out of doors," said he, addressing the Jew.

"Don't be in such a hurry, my dear. You seem ill-tempered to-night, my dear. What has happened to flurry you?"

* In the second chapter he is stated to have won one thousand five hundred pounds. This amount, as he was in the pay of the proprietor, would have gone to the "concern."

"Nothing."

"So you won't make me your confidant? Never mind."

The Jew, followed by Frederick Vyvian, ascended to the first-floor.

"What's that?" asked Frederick, pointing with his finger to one of the Israelite's youthful pupils, who was sitting athwart the one-legged stool.

"I'm the only friend he's got on earth," said Abednego, evading the question, and patting the boy on the head as he spoke. "Go out of the room, my dear, and amuse yourself; or you may take a walk if you like it." And the Jew gave a significant look.

The boy left the room.

"Now, then, to business," cried the Jew.

Frederick Vyvian perfectly acquiesced.

"You have come to-day to sign me a paper, and to receive two hundred pounds. Is not that the case?"

"It is; but it's a very unfair compact," replied Frederick, laughing.

"If it is not rigorous honesty, you must confess that it suits your purpose as well as mine." And the Jew rubbed his hands together, and chuckled audibly.

He then produced a slip of paper, on which the agreement between himself and Frederick was formally and legally drawn up, and he desired his visitor to sign it.

With this Frederick Vyvian, after having carefully perused the contents, readily complied.

The Jew nervously told out two hundred pounds on the table.

"Guineas," said Frederick.

"I cannot give more," answered the Jew.

"Guineas," reiterated Frederick, striking the table with his knuckles.

"It's of no use, no use whatever," said Abednego, buttoning up the pockets of his trousers as he spoke, and looking towards the ceiling.

"You are a mean old screw," exclaimed Frederick; and he commenced gathering up the money.

"Will you give me a receipt?" asked Abednego Levi, carelessly.

"I have given you one."

"Have you?"

"To be sure I have: that piece of paper is as good as one."

"Well, my dear, you can take the money without a receipt."

"Exactly so. We have had parley enough on that point, and now good by."

"Good by, my dear."

He was conducted by the Jew to the door of the house, which he left with rapid strides.

Each thought that he had duped the other.

Scarcely had Frederick Vyvian taken his departure when a shrill whistle summoned the Jew to the door. He opened it, and there entered Tim Roper, Ben Bandy, and the Duffer.

"How goes it?" asked the Jew.

The Duffer replied by a smile of satisfaction.

Tim Roper, who acted as spokesman of the party, related all the events connected with the burglary in Grosvenor-square.

"Now, then, produce the swag," cried the Duffer, addressing himself to Ben.

Ben opened a large bag he carried under his arm, and laid the booty on the table—not forgetting the duplicates.

"Ha! ha! ha!" And the Jew put his hands on his meagre sides to prevent them cracking—a catastrophe much to be feared. "That *is* good."

"I'm blow'd if it vouldn't have been a precious site better if we could have got the articles themselves. Howsomdever, he's saved us the trouble of popping them, that's all," said Ben.

"He's done it in the name of Walker—William Walker," observed Tim Roper.

"What's yer terms for the silver?" asked the Duffer, addressing himself to the Jew.

"Three-and-sixpence an ounce."

"Four bob, or yer don't have it"

"No quarrelling with your best friends," said the Jew.

"Money perduces even more tragic effects than gin and jealousy put together," cried Ben.

"None of your gammon. Your tollibon* wags a trifle too fast. Remember, there's weighty matters afloat, and, when that ere's the case, there should be no trifling among men of business," said Tim.

"I can get four shillings from Joseph. Yer don't for a moment conceive that we did this ere job for your benefit, when we ran a duced risk of getting 'lagged'† for life," cried the Duffer.

"There are a good many jobs that, if they get wind, or by any chance reach the ears of their worships, would bring certain parties to be 'scragged'‡ for death," said Abednego, fixing his eyes full upon the Duffer.

"And there's more than vun mixed up in those jobs, too; and, vot's more, if I catched any one a-nosing me, I'd rip him up as soon as I would a hog, that I would. But, come, to the point. Will yer give four bob, or not? If yer won't, Joseph has 'em." And the Duffer prepared to depart.

"You jest, my dear."

"Do I?"

"I never lose a customer if I can help it, but I must look after myself a bit; you know, my dear, you would yourself if you were in my position."

"Me in your position! I disdains to do a dirty haction, and never undertakes a job but where there's some credit and character to be got by its achievement."

"And swag," suggested Ben.

The Duffer cast an admonitory glance on the speaker.

* Tongue.
† Transported.
‡ Hung.

"I really don't think I can command the money," said the Jew. "Would you be content to take part for the present?"

"You've no business at all to stick up for a dealer, when you 'haven't got no money to pay honourably for goods when they're brought to yer," exclaimed Tim.

"Josephs carries a thousand in his side pocket,* so we'll wish yer good by if yer please."

"The value of silver has sunk, it has indeed, my dear; it isn't near so saleable a commodity as it was. Now, if you had brought me some shiners,† I could have paid well for them."

"Once more, four bob‖ or nothing." And the Duffer began to collect the spoons and various articles together.

"I don't know how I shall get rid of it," said Abednego; and, what's more, I shan't be able to turn a single penny by its passing through my hands."

"If you can't, why, others can." replied the Duffer. "Nothing's too hot, or too heavy either, for Josephs."

"You'll make a fortune out of me. But we aint a-going to split upon that point." And Abednego Levi commenced the painful operation of counting out the money, after he had ascertained the exact value of the booty. He turned every coin twice over in his hand to see if it was not a double one, while the eyes of the Duffer seemed as if they would pierce him through and through—ay, and th brick wall behind him.

"Now, then, let's snack§ the bit in a reg'lar manner," said Tim Roper.

"Don't be in a hurry," replied the Duffer, as he counted over the sum laid down by Abednego.

The money was equally divided between the three cracksmen, but the Duffer had previously contrived to detain a portion of the booty.

"Will you soon be ready for the other job, my dears?"

"What other?" demanded Ben.

"Pshaw! he knows well enough, my dear."

"We've money about us, just at present, but when we've spent that we shall want some more, and then we'll talk over it," answered the Duffer.

"I don't myself relish more of this sort of work than we can help," said Ben

"Nonsense, you're too chicken-hearted by half," cried the Duffer.

"We lives by levying contributions on the public," exclaimed Tim, with a laugh.

"Oh, yes, only I can't comfortably swallow too much on it; it sticks in my throat."

* Ikey Solomons was in the constant habit of carrying this sum about his person.
† Looking-glasses.
‖ The reason they pay so high for this species of commodity is, that they have a crucible ready, and can sell it immediately after the purchase for its full value, and without fear of detection.
§ Divide the booty.

"And a very comfortable, easy life it is too," added the Jew.

"I axes pardon for having kept yer so long, but now bisiness is done, and we're ready to go," said the Duffer.

"At yer service," replied the Jew, making a formal bow.

The three burglars left the house together and retired to a neighbouring ken, where they spent a great portion of the proceeds of their villainy.

Abednego Levi then re-entered the apartment, and, with all possible expedition, employed his crucible in melting down the plate.

The boy, whom he had sent out during the presence of Frederick Vyvian, now returned.

"What have you brought, Tibby?" asked the Jew, who was in a peculiarly happy humour in consequence of the amount of business he had transacted.

"Bull dogs;* I could'nt git nothing else, it was so plaguey wet that nobody was out."

"Very well, my dear; do better next time. Here, come and help me, after you've emptied your pockets."

The boy did as he was desired, and in a very short time the plate was melted down, when it would have been utterly impossible to detect it. The duplicates the Jew destroyed.

He instructed the boy to remain at home that night, and to tell Neddy to do the same when he returned, as he was himself obliged to go out to transact a little business. Taking a specimen of the metal with him the miser departed.

CHAPTER IX.
THE INTERVIEW WITH THE ATTORNEY.

When Frederick left the Jew he had no distinct idea in his own mind what person or what thing he should next endeavour to do. But, after a little consideration, he determined on returning to Mivart's hotel, where he had taken up his abode. On arriving thither a business-like note was put into his hand, which, conceiving it to be of an unpleasant nature, he deferred opening.

After he had despatched his supper he became anxious to learn the contents, when he read the following aloud:—

"Gray's Inn, Dec. 11th, 1843.
"Sir,

"I must request the pleasure of an interview with you to-morrow morning, as I have some communications to make respecting your pretended claim as heir to the property of Sir Richard Vivyan. I bear not the slightest malice or ill will towards yourself, and am open to enter into a pecuniary arrangement. If you show, or carelessly leave about, this note it will materially injure yourself.
I remain,
Your's, &c.,
PETER PRIGMORE.

* Lumps of sugar stolen from the grocers.

" P.S.—Whatever sum you offer with a view of purchasing my silence must be paid down, as guineas in perspective do not suit my purpose."

" The dirty, sneaking, little scoundrel," exclaimed Frederick. " However, now I have sold my chance, I can snap my fingers at him, but I must not make an enemy of him ; we have done a great deal of business together and I hope may do a great deal more ; besides, if he was to split, Sir Richard would shut his door upon me for ever, and therefore it is to my interest that he does not."

Thinking over the strange events of the day—the suicide he had seen committed—the money he had obtained from the Jew, and the letter he had received from the attorney, Peter Prigmore, all seemed to his confused imagination like the disjointed members of an absurd dream.

Frederick Vyvian retired to rest in no very enviable frame of mind.

At an early hour the following morning he inquired for Mr. Prigmore, at that gentleman's chambers in Gray's Inn.

The man of law was seated at a square mahogany table, surrounded with papers and legal documents, and looking abstractedly over the morning newspaper, which he had taken into his hand on the name of Mr. Vyvian being announced. On the whole, his countenance and manner were infinitely more serene than Frederick had expected to find them.

" Pray be seated, my dear Sir," said Mr. Prigmore, half rising from his own chair.

" I have come to speak concerning a note I received from you yesterday evening, appointing this morning for an interview."

Mr. Prigmore slightly inclined his head.

A pause ensued.

" In short, Sir," said the lawyer, with some asperity, " you have come to make an arrangement, is it not so ?"

" That entirely depends upon circumstances."

" With your permission, may I ask what you intend to imply by the word ' circumstances.'"

" What the devil do you mean ?" half angrily demanded Frederick.

" You are really too hasty, Sir."

Frederick Vyvian involuntarily started. There was something unusually harsh and snappish in the tone of Mr. Prigmore, that grated unpleasantly on his ear.

" It is to be extremely regretted," said Mr. Prigmore, in a sentimental voice, " when friends such as we are, whose interests have on so many occasions been one, it is, I say, to be bitterly regretted that we meet on such terms as we do this morning."

Frederick Vyvian gave an impatient cough, and then said " Certainly."

" You see we have unfortunately run aground on a point of great consequence—a point that involves your position in society and all your future hopes, for if once the truth becomes known that you are not the brother of Sir Richard Vyvian, and consequently not the heir, that in short you are nothing but a low born changeling——"

" And you dare tell me this ?" cried Frederick, rising and approaching the terrified attorney, where is your proof ? where are your witnesses ? you think that anybody would take the single testimony of such a highly respectable gentleman as yourself ? do you?"

" Calm yourself, my dear Sir, and sit down. Pray be composed. If I have said anything offensive, I now retract it."

" You had better," said Frederick, and he again advanced towards Mr. Prigmore.

" No personal violence if you please, or I shall call in my clerk to witness the assault."

Frederick made no reply, but continued smacking his horse-whip, as if he had a real live attorney in his grasp.

" By behaving in this foolish manner you are completely running counter to your own most vital interests," said the lawyer.

" You are very kind I must say ; very obliging, and all that sort of thing."

" That is not the question at issue," replied the attorney.

" Then come to the point at once, and without any more subterfuge."

" You are a changeling, and not the brother of Sir Richard Vyvian. That is the point I wish to come to. Now, nobody but myself is aware of this little circumstance, and therefore, by purchasing my silence, you will inherit a large fortune and a title ; if, on the other hand, I expose you, your infuriated creditors will pounce upon you, which may throw a little business in my way, the baronet will for ever forbid you his house, and you will become a degraded outcast. Honour, affluence, and ease, on the one side ; disgrace, poverty, and misery, on the other. Reflect, young man, reflect."

" In fact, you want me to bribe you to hold your tongue."

" I have spoken plainly."

" You have. Now, if you please, hear me. The available property I have already disposed of. Without that the title would indeed be an empty bauble, and one which I do not at all covet. To be sure it helps one to trick tradesmen. I was well aware that you would take a paltry advantage of what you either *pretend* to be, or *know* to be, the truth ; and I also knew that, if I *did* attempt to purchase your silence, your exorbitant demands would run away with more than half the money. Besides, a little ready cash was what I wanted."

" It's false ; it's nothing but a tissue of lies," exclaimed the lawyer, rising from his seat. " But you shall repent this to the last day of your life."

" Indeed."

" Yes, indeed," replied Mr. Prigmore, becoming

more and more violently agitated. "After what has taken place, everything is at an end between us."

"Very likely."

"But whether what you have stated is true or alse I shall expose you. I shall point you out as a mark of scorn for the world. You were foolish, very foolish; you had bright prospects, but now you have for ever blasted them." And then, in a somewhat softer tone, he inquired, "What did you get for it, ay?"

"I think we may yet make matters meet," replied Frederick. "By your exposing my birth you may, to a certain degree, injure me—that is to say, you might effect my expulsion from the baronet's house. But how would that benefit you? His friendship is worth about fifty pounds to me, and I would rather expend that sum on you than lose the chance of what I may get from him. You have no proof whatever of what you advance, and, as for exciting public opinion against me, for that I do not care one straw."

"Is that all you offer?"

"It is; and, as I am rather in a hurry this morning, if you accept it upon consideration, you can write and tell me so."

"You have defied me, sir, and you shall rue the consequences. I shall be extremely obliged by your immediately quitting my chambers." And Mr. Prigmore pointed energetically with his pen to the door, while Frederick Vyvian snapped his fingers, and abruptly quitted the attorney's domicile.

"I would tell him who his father is, in spite of his menacing and bragging, if it were not for the fortune he would come into. But no, that money must be mine. If I were to prove that he is not the brother of Sir Richard Vyvian, I must of necessity state who his father is, and the money would be lost for ever. Perhaps, on that account, and as he throws a great deal in my way, I had better accept the fifty pounds, and let the matter blow over," soliloquised the man of parchment.

Mr. Peter Prigmore forthwith penned a complacent, forgiving, explanatory, bamboozling, note, and addressed it to, "Frederick Vyvian, Esq., Mivart's Hotel, Brook-street, Bond-street."

CHAPTER X.

MRS. FRANCIS VYVIAN.

On the morning after the party we have recorded in a preceding chapter, Mr. Francis and Mrs. Vyvian were seated at the breakfast table in their own apartments in Belgrave-square. At a little distance sat a young girl working thoughtfully.

"Amelia's affectation is really insupportable," said Mrs. Vyvian, pettishly addressing her husband.

"Amelia was a spoilt child," replied Francis, "and very few spoilt children grow up sensible and

amiable women. But my poor sister," added he, "is not to blame; she was left at a very early age to the care of her brothers, who, too young to forsee the consequences of immoderate indulgence, would, I believe, have made any sacrifice to preserve her bright eyes from shedding tears. But she is a dear, kind-hearted, affectionate girl, and a very—"

"Beautiful one, too, you were going to add," said Mrs. Vyvian sharply. "I really wonder, Francis, that you who are such an admirer of female beauty ever made choice of such a fright as I am, but I have often thought it not improbable that other and more weighty considerations turned the scale of your affections in my favour."

"What do you say, my love?" said Francis listlessly, raising his eyes from the perusal of the *Morning Post*, which he held in his hand; "I really must apologize for my distraction, but my attention was at that moment arrested by a paragraph, and I shall feel obliged by your repeating what you last said."

"It is of no consequence," returned Mrs. Vyvian, rising from her seat and hastily quitting the room. "This is really more than any lady can possibly put up with."

Francis Vyvian, accustomed to these stormy breezes, after poking the fire, again took up the newspaper and commenced reading with the most assiduous diligence.

"You cruel, unfeeling creature," exclaimed Mrs. Vyvian, re-entering the apartment, and sobbing violently as she threw herself into a chair. "I well know that I am become an object of perfect indifference to you, and I am resolved that the base, ungrateful girl who has supplanted me in your affections shall not remain another hour in my house. Miss Agnes Talbot," continued the lady, assuming a constrained and rather haughty manner, "I must request that you will pack up your affairs and seek another asylum."

Agnes turned her eyes imploringly towards her benefactress, who, she was aware, had only uttered this accusation and threat for the purpose of annoying her husband.

Francis Vyvian, disgusted and ashamed at his wife's unfeeling indelicacy, looked unusually displeased.

"However I may feel inclined to overlook your pettish frivolities, I cannot, Madam," said he, "allow the sister of a dear and valued friend to become the object of your unjust and ungenerous remarks."

Mrs. Vyvian was about to reply, when a loud rapping at the hall door announced the arrival of visitors. Agnes immediately witndrew, and Mrs. Vyvian casting a look of anger and scorn at her husband, hastened to prepare for the reception of her company.

"Dear Agnes," said she, running into Miss Talbot's sleeping apartment, "do, pray, go into the drawing room, and say that I am indisposed—not at home, in fact, anything you please rather than let me be subjected at this moment to the impertinent scrutinizing inquiries of that disagreeable creature, Mrs. Peacher.

Without making any reply Agnes prepared to do as she was requested.

"Agnes, dear," said Mrs. Vyvian, following the timid girl to the room door, "you need not mention what occurred at breakfast, you know, love, I only spoke as I did to vex my husband."

With this amiable confession she imprinted a kiss on the young girl's forehead.

"Agnes, Agnes," exclaimed the lady, "stay a moment, I have changed my mind, my eyes are not so red as I thought they were."

Agnes returned and Mrs. Vyvian proceeded to the drawing room.

"How very kind this is of you Mrs. Peacher! How delighted Francis will be to see you! But where is Alice? we expected she would have accompanied us last Tuesday to Lady Stanley's."

"Thank, you my love, but Alice has never been well since we visited the botanical gardens last summer. Dr. Locock, who attends her, is of opinion that she requires a vast deal of attention, at the same time he does not consider that there is any immediate danger."

"Poor Alice! I really think it would break my heart if illness or any other cause compelled me to remain at home against my inclination," sighed Mrs. Vyvian.

"My daughter naturally prefers retirement; she has you know been reared in the country, and after spending a winter in town, always returns to the rectory with unfeigned delight."

"I too have been brought up in the country," said Mrs. Vyvian, "but there is no place I dislike so much, and this is, I believe, the only subject upon which Francis and I cordially agree. But my dear aunt," continued the lady, pressing the hand of her husband's relative with apparent affection, "may I beg your secrecy for what I am going to tell you, and may I also hope that you will not refuse to grant me a favour, for I have no friend in whom I can confide? I am not happy, Mrs. Peacher, indeed I am not happy. Before I was married Francis would have passed whole days and nights in seeing me dance, but now, without assigning any particular reason, he peremptorily forbids me to indulge in this amusement. I am very fond of dancing, and if I could manage to go sometimes to a ball with you and Alice, or any other friends, I think that even the most fastidious could find no fault; and, Francis you know, need never know any thing about it."

"I fear, Mrs Vyvian, that you would find it a difficult matter to deceive your husband, and a still more difficult one, to make your peace with him after having done so," said Mrs. Peacher, gravely;

"but you have spoken thoughtlessly, and I have no doubt on reflection, you will be sensible of the impropriety of your request."

Mrs. Vyvian made no other reply than a violent burst of tears.

"I am shocked, beyond measure, to see you so much affected," said Mrs. Peacher. "Pray compose yourself."

"Indeed ma'am, I am most miserably wretched, and unhappy," responded Mrs. Vyvian, sobbing hysterically; "Francis is so harsh and severe, so regardless of my happiness and comfort, that I shall never cease to lament the day I left my father's home."

If Mrs. Peacher had pleased to do so, she could have reminded her niece, that she was quite as miserable in her father's house, as she had since been in her husband's; but Mrs. Peacher kept these recollections to herself, and contented herself with observing, that, in the marriage state, mutual forbearance was necessary.

"Francis, was always considered good-natured and affectionate," added she, "and I hope, dear Alexandrine, you will take my advice, and not let troubles disturb your domestic harmony; if however," continued the lady, affectionately taking the hand of her niece, "a short absence from home will be agreeable, it will afford us great pleasure to receive you; indeed, the purport of my visit this morning, was to request permission for Miss Talbot to spend a few weeks at the rectory, as her society would enliven, without disturbing, the solitude of my daughter."

"I shall be so delighted, my dear Aunt," said Mrs. Vyvian, smiling through her tears, "and whenever you please, I will pay my visit. As for Agnes, she may remain with you as long as you desire, for I can assure you, she is not a very agreeable addition to my family. Francis appears to think, that because she is the daughter of a gentleman, and the sister of one of his early associates, he can never pay her sufficient attention."

"Well, then, my dear, consult with your husband, and whatever day in the early part of next week suits your convenience, we shall expect you."

"Cannot I prevail with you to stay the day with us," said Mrs. Vyvian, assuming one of her most fascinating smiles, as Mrs. Peacher rose to depart.

"Another day I shall be delighted, but to-day my poor invalid is alone. Peacher dines with the bishops and I have already been absent too long."

No sooner had Mrs. Peacher taken her leave than Mrs. Vyvian, anxious to acquaint her husband with her intended visit, hastened to the library; Vyvian was not there, and his wife, impatient of the slightest disappointment, rang the bell with unusual violence. A servant immediately entered.

"Is your master at home, John?" said the lady in an angry tone of voice.

"In the drawing room, ma'am," replied the servant.

"Impossible," responded the lady, "I have but this moment quitted the drawing room."

The servant retired, and Mrs. Vyvian, extremely ruffled in her temper, re-ascended the staircase.

As she approached the drawing room, the door of which was partially open, the sound of voices attracted her attention. A momentary pause ensued; she approached cautiously, and awaited with breathless anxiety a renewal of the conversation.

"I cannot, indeed I cannot sufficiently thank you for your kind consideration," said Agnes.

"Silence! silence!" replied Vyvian. Alexandrine will hear you. "To-morrow morning, then, about ten o'clock, I shall expect you in the library."

"Without fail," responded Agnes.

Mrs. Vyvian heard no more. Her frame was shaken by a sudden and violent emotion. Should she rush at once into the room and upbraid them for their perfidy, or wait and take a more effectual method of revenging her wrongs. She decided upon the latter, and, stealing softly up stairs, had scarcely reached her apartment when she heard her husband descend into the library. For some moments she remained motionless as a statue, listening as if she expected some new and more convincing proof of her husband's infidelity; but all was silent, and she commenced pacing the room with increasing speed.

"I will this moment," cried she, violently pressing her hands against her forehead—"I will this moment insist upon her leaving my house. Francis will readily beleive that she has gone to his uncle Peacher's, and I shall get rid of her without any difficulty or chance of their ever meeting again."

The immediate expulsion of Agnes was no sooner determined upon than a letter was written and delivered into her hands by a female servant, who had orders to inquire if her assistance was wanted.

Surprised beyond measure, Agnes hastily broke the seal, and was not a little astonished when she read the following lines scrawled almost illegibly upon the back of an old letter:—

"Mrs. Francis Vyvian desires Miss Talbot not to remain in her house one moment longer than is necessary to pack up her clothes. If the assistance of a servant is necessary, Mrs. Vyvian has given orders that one of the housemaids should attend."

When poor Agnes read these unfeeling lines, a sudden sickness came over her; the letter dropped from her hand, and she sat for some moments gazing unconsciously. But she recovered herself, for, though she was profoundly touched by such unmerited cruelty, she still felt grateful for the shelter which had been afforded her, and, determined to obey Mrs. Vyvian's commands to the very letter, she put on her bonnet and shawl, and silently, though sorrowfully, quitted the house.

Mrs. Vyvian, who had placed herself at the drawing room window to witness the departure of Agnes, stood watching the figure of the friendless girl till she was no longer visible.

"Thank God! she is gone,' exclaimed the lady, "I shall now have peace."

CHAPTER XI.

THE SMOKING CRIB.

WE must now return to the Jew.

With feelings of indescribable joy and self-congratulation at the successful bargain he conceived himself to have made with Frederick Vyvian, as well as at the stolen plate he had purchased from the housebreakers, which he was now going to endeavour to sell, he passed among the swarming myriads which, even at that late hour, continued to throng the streets of the metropolis.

He walked rapidly on till he arrived at a low public-house, close to the noses of their worships, situated near Covent-garden. In it there was a vast number of ruffians assembled. A casual passer-by, on looking in and seeing them apparently amusing themselves by playing at cribbage, smoking, and drinking, would have thought them honest, hard-working labourers and journeymen, who had snatched an hour of recreation from their several occupations. But such was not the case—in fact, the "crib" tenanted by this merry, dissolute, careless group, was the *rendezvous* of the very worst characters of the very worst part of London. The landlord had formerly been a' very daring housebreaker, who had afterwards turned fence,* and, having amassed a little money by his nefarious transactions, had become "mine host'· of the "smoking crib." This "crib" was in a very flourishing condition—partly from the reputation of its landlord, and partly from its central position in the most infamous part of the town.

Over the bar was a board, on which was inscribed the following couplet :—

> "The liquor's good, the measure's just,
> But pardon, sir, we do not trust."

The general appearance of the "smoking crib" bore a strong analogy to that of the "boozing ken," in Rosemary-lane. They were both frequented by the same class of characters. In the "boozing ken" cracksmen constituted the majority, while the "smoking crib" was mostly frequented by buzzes.†

Abednego Levi walked straight into the little back parlour, and placing his fingers sagaciously on his nose, as if to indicate that he desired a private interview, seated himself beside a blazing fire. No great interval had elapsed before the landlord appeared, carrying a cannikin of grog in his hand.

"Ah! my dear," said the Jew, "how happy I am

---

* Receiver of stolen goods.
† Pickpockets.

to see you looking so well and comfortable. It does one's heart good, it does. You're tugging away at the old stuff, I see."

" I've lived some few years in the world," said the landlord, "and my hexperience teaches me this ere maxim—'That all but grog is vanity below.' It is better than money, or pleasure, and all that. Money's only worth having for the sake of spending, and what makes one so pleasant as a glass now and then? If hever I leaves a fortune, it shall be on the terms that it arn't to be spent foolishly, but to be got drunk with while it lasts." And the landlord took an enormous pull at the cannikin. " Have a glass of som'ut, won't yer?"

"So I will," replied the Jew, who was feverish and thirsty, for in some instances, success causes as much excitement as disappointment.

The landlord hastened to the bar, and presently returned with a steaming glass of hot brandy and water, flavoured with a slip of lemon. The Jew lifted it eagerly to his lips, and drained it to the last drop.

"Since we're met to-night what luck has attended the job the Duffer had in hand?" asked the landlord.

"That's just what I'm come to talk about. He got a very fair amount of swag, and I bought it of him. And I'd rather lose a little money than run the risk, so I want you to buy it of me," and Abednego produced the piece of metal he had previously deposited in his pocket.

" I suppose you want to "lumber it in another crib.' Are the traps after him."

"Oh no, no. But you know I always like to let it pass through other hands. You understand."

" I twig. What do yer want for it? Now don't be exorbitent."

" Five shillings an ounce: it's well worth another shilling; it is, upon my honour, silver has risen very much you know."

"If it is to you it is'nt to me. Five bob, if yer like it."

After a little hesitation the Jew nodded assent.

"I'll send a cart for it to-morrow; my man's a-going round that way on a little business in the morning, and he can pop it under the greens nicely;* only have it packed up proper, so as it mayn't chink or fall about, or nothing of that kind," and the landlord, after having inquired the exact weight of the metal, paid the sum stipulated to Abednego Levi, with whom he had been in the habit of having frequent transactions, both when he was a "cracksman," and in his present capacity of " fence."

A shrill whistle resounded through the " smoking crib."

At one simultaneous moment the " buzzes" dropt their pipes, and off they scampered to plun-

---
* Booty is frequently conveyed in this manner, the simplicity of the ostensible trade acting as a security against detection.

der the struggling crowd who were endeavouring to get out of Drury Lane Theatre.

While these were actively employed, a constable entered, and walking up to the bar, tossed off a glass of " jackey" to the health and at the expense of the landlord. Having exchanged a few words with some adepts in the art of prigging, this " terror of the robber," turned to retrace his steps to his beat. While this sort of connection is kept up between the officer, the thief, and the receiver, the public duty can never be effectually performed. The flimsy excuse that it is necessary that such a connection should exist, as being the only available means by which stolen property can be recovered, is a mere fabrication; it is indeed the only available means by which perquisites, and a glass of "jackey" on a cold night can be obtained. If justice has its due, all participation must be at an end between the officer and the thief.

As soon as the press was over, the " buzzes" returned to the " smoking crib," and disposed of their plunder to the landlord. They then returned to their seats and quietly resumed their pipes. The landlord generally got back the best part of the sum he paid for the booty in the money they expended on tobacco and drink.

" Ned Darby's examination comes on to-morrow," said a man who had just entered the parlour, addressing himself to the landlord.

" Very well, I'll send a *nose* to watch the case, and try and find out where the swag's lumbered, and git Ned to sell it me before he's lagged."

The reward the man obtained for this information was a glass of grog.

" Now, my dear, I must be thinking of my little family at home; they'll be getting anxious and fidgetty about me. I don't like to keep their young minds in suspense." And Abednego prepared to take his departure.

The weather was more favourable than when he quitted his own den in Shoreditch, and his pockets were considerably heavier, so he walked with a gayer and more elastic step, quite at variance with his generally cautious and steady tread.

CHAPTER XII.

THE ENGAGEMENT AS GOVERNESS.

WHEN Agnes Talbot quitted Belgrave-square, she determined to seek a furnished lodging in one of the most retired and distant suburbs of London. With this intention she directed her steps towards Hyde-park, but she had miscalculated her powers, for she, being unaccustomed to walking, had no sooner traversed the park, and arrived in Oxford-street, than her strength began to fail her. The lamps were already lit, and had begun to cast their shadows upon the pavement, which had become par-

tially wet by the rain and sleet which had fallen at different intervals during the day. Among the busy throng who passed and repassed that crowded thoroughfare, few took notice of the timid, anxious creature who pursued her path with feelings of true wretchedness, meeting with rebuffs at almost every turn she took; still she continued her way.

She passed house after house, stopping at every respectable-looking one, and pondering within herself whether or no her application for a lodging would be successful. Pride—the same sort of pride that renders an Englishman the least communicative of any two-legged animal on the face of the globe—prevented her asking the question: She feared lest the inmates might say or think something unpleasant, and, rather than afford them the opportunity, she continued walking till, overcome with fatigue and terror, she approached the private door of a neat-looking house, and knocked loudly for admission.

"Well, indeed," said a little woman, with a shrill voice, "surely, ma'am, you might give a body time to git up stairs."

"Pray allow me to come in," said Agnes. "I wish to speak to your mistress."

At this moment a matronly, middle-aged-looking woman, popping her head out of the back parlour, exclaimed,—

"Who's there, Molly? Why don't you let the lady in?" Molly closed the door, and Agnes was speedily ushered into a small apartment at the back of a shop.

The room was only tolerably furnished; but the cheerful fire, the merry tea-kettle humming its extravagant melodies, as if in opposition to the subdued, methodical purr of a fine tom-cat, who lay stretched upon the hearth rug; the polished table, on which was placed a black and gold-japanned tea-board, covered with old-fashioned cups and saucers, whose beauty chiefly consisted in their extreme cleanliness. All these auxiliaries, added to the good-natured, smiling, cozy countenance of the matron, gave to the little apartment an air of sunny comfort, which was immediately appreciated by the shivering, weary girl, who readily availed herself of the invitation "to draw near the fire, and warm herself."

A few moments' conversation explained the object of her visit.

" We have certainly got one little room that we could spare," said Mrs. Dobbins, musingly ; " but I am not quite sure that my husband would like to let it. However, if you will give your address, he shall call round upon you in the morning, when you can settle it between you. In the meantime, if you please, I will show it to you."

It had not before this moment occurred to Agnes that it was not probable that any respectable housekeeper would receive her without a reference.

Her heart sank within her at this unexpected difficulty. However, she followed her conductress up the stairs. After trying almost every key in her bunch, she succeeded in hitting upon the right one, when Mrs. Dobbins introduced Miss Agnes Talbot into a small second-floor front room.

" A pleasant situation this, ma'am," said Mrs. Dobbins. And then, walking to the window, she added, " We should have a fine view here of St. Anne's church, if it wasn't for this wall that runs up against the window ; but it's very pleasant, isn't it, ma'am ?"

" Very," answered Agnes.

" We had a gentleman who lodged here, ma'am, that used to say he always fancied himself a hundred miles out of town whenever he was in this room."

" It suits me exactly," said Miss Talbot ; " what are your terms ?"

" Why, ma'am, if you will step down stairs, I dare say we shall very easily come to terms. But it is necessary that we should talk the matter over, for, you see, we have been in the habit of letting to single young men, but now, as our two gals are growing up, we don't think it exactly the thing. They are as innocent as two babbies, they are, ma'am, and what's more, it isn't for the value of a few paltry shillings a week that we would put 'em in the way of becoming otherwise."

This harangue was cut short by the entrance of Mr. Dobbins, a good-tempered, red-faced, little man, who bowed respectfully on observing Agnes.

" Mr. Dobbins, this lady wants to settle about our front room, second floor."

" Has the lady seen it, my dear ?" asked Mr. Dobbins, putting on a pair of green goggle spectacles, and turning with an inquisitive stare towards Miss Talbot.

" Young, my dear, very young to go into furnished apartments alone. From the country, I suppose."

" I have been in London two years," was the reply.

" So much the worse. I'm afraid my apartment won't suit you. I am the father of two innocent girls, and I must look to their morals. I am very sorry to hurt your feelings by declining to receive you into my house."

Miss Agnes Talbot burst into tears.

Mrs. Dobbins appeared to have lost the use of her tongue. Her face became longer and longer, and, she pursed up her mouth till it bore the appearance of an accidental slit, scarcely large enough to admit even a lozenge.

" I dare say you'll find plenty others where they'll be glad enough to receive you," continued Mr. Dobbins.

After the candid manner in which he had spoken his sentiments, his manner, from being cramped and restrained had become free and easy. He appeared to have grown both taller and broader. One moment he poked the fire, and another he would hum the " Pretty Maid of Darby, oh !" Mrs. Dobbins, on the contrary, preserved a most dignified silence, broken only by an occasional " um," intended, no doubt, as a civil warning that the lady's company was no longer agreeable.

The arrival of the two girls put an end to Miss Talbot's embarrassment ; the two young women being in the employ of Mrs. Vyvian's dressmaker, she was immediately recognised by them. In an instant the scene changed. A thousand apologies were offered to, and accepted by, Miss Talbot, and Mr. Dobbins kindly volunteered to obtain the situation of governess for her in the family of a wealthy auctioneer resident in Guilford-street.

This Agnes considered to be a rare and eligible opportunity, and, with this idea uppermost in her mind, she retired to the bed-room provided for her, though not to sleep. She dozed and dreamed throughout the night, and dreamed and dozed again. At an early hour the following morning, scarcely refreshed by her broken slumber, and immediately after breakfast was over, she started for Guilford-street, fluttering with expectancy.

Arrived at a sombre-looking house, the residence of Mrs. Pearson, she gave three timid knocks— knocks that the echoes in the hall thought unworthy to reply to.

A servant, radiant with plush, looked contemptuously at her from the area beneath, and presently opened the door with the manner of one who was performing a menial office utterly derogatory to his dignity.

On meeting Agnes face to face, he immediately ranked her among the class known in his vocabulary as " strange people," and therefore contented himself with showing her into a back room, by metamorphosis termed a library, and leisurely strolling up the stairs to inform Mrs. Pearson that a young person was waiting to see her.

A bell was violently rung, and immediately afterwards the servant came down to the library, and showed Agnes to a room where Mrs. Pearson was waiting to receive her. Mrs. Pearson assumed a rather constrained and haughty manner. She stated that the last young person she had engaged as governess was nothing but a barefaced imposter, who pretended to have learnt the Parisian accent, when she (Mrs. Pearson) had since discovered that she had never been farther than Calais; that she had taught the children nothing, and, besides throwing out shoals of other false insinuations, had declared that it was not her fault, but theirs.

" In consequence of what I have heard from Mr. Dobbins, who was formerly a friend of my husband, I think that I may undertake to say that you may consider yourself engaged."

" Thank you, ma'am," replied Agnes.

" With respect to the salary—considering that you will have very little trouble, good living, a pretty little bed-room at the top of the house, and many other advantages—I think that fifteen pounds a year will be a very handsome remuneration for your services. If that sum suits your views, I will consult with Mr. Pearson on the subject."

" That's rather low, ma'am," said Agnes, with some difficulty, plucking up sufficient courage to throw in the remark.

" Although we live in good style," replied Mrs. Pearson, " our out-door expenses are so enormous, —for we must keep up appearances like other people—that we find it imperatively necessary to be as economical as possible in our domestic arrangements. The way we manage is this:—We send our children to school for one quarter to get confidence and that sort of thing, and then we have a governess for them at home. I am certain that the terms I have mentioned are the very highest to which Mr. Pearson would agree : there are plenty of governesses who would be glad of the offer."

Agnes assented to accept the situation on the terms proffered.

" I could mention several friends of mine whose children receive first-rate education for a more trifling consideration than even that. However, as you have thought fit to accept my terms, to-morrow morning we shall expect you."

Mrs. Pearson rang the bell, and the interview terminated.

Never had the smoky atmosphere of Guilford-street appeared more grateful to the feelings of Agnes than after the twenty minutes she had been in the house of Mrs. Pearson, breathing the air of dependence and servitude.

Mrs. Pearson was looked up to by a great many acquaintances, and looked down upon by a great many others. She had till recently resided at Hampstead, but, on account of her husband's improved circumstances, had purchased the house in Guilford-street. It was the ambition of herself and

husband to form aristocratic connexions, and they aspired, in consequence of the fortune they would give with her, to marrying their daughter to a nobleman—a lord at least. They had taken up their abode in Guilford-street merely as a preliminary step to entering into the aristocratic regions of the West end, as a sort of bridge over the stream which separates the money-making citizen from the money-spending nobleman, and the money-spending nobleman from the money-making citizen. They acted as a great many others do who feel a decided predilection for the fashionable quarter of London, and, being crippled in their means, are content to live on the confines, or in some decayed square, whose grandeur and gaiety passed away long since with their ancestors. Crippled means were not the cause of their acting as they did; but Mr. Pearson was about to throw up the auctioneering business, and did not wish to enter into the world of *ton* till he could do so as a gentleman. Love of money was once the predominant feeling in Mr. Pearson's breast, but since the passion of gain had been thoroughly gratified, ambition had to a certain degree supplied its place. He was very economical, although immensely rich, but would have lavishly spent his money on anybody or anything aristocratic. He had in his possession a watch which formerly belonged to the Duke of Sussex; his coat was of the same piece of cloth as Prince Albert's, and therefore he kept it as a sacred relic. Thus we have endeavoured to acquaint the reader with the chief point of Mr. Pearson's character.

CHAPTER XIII.

LORD OXBURN.

IN a sumptuously-furnished apartment in Hyde-park, the walls hung with portraits of famous pugilists, engravings of successful horses, groups of dogs, hunting whips, and other sporting *et ceteras* was seated Lord Oxburn, whose name we mentioned in a preceding chapter.

" Really, Charles, you are not the man you should be to attend upon me. Poor Willis was a perfect angel! There was so much tact and management about him! I never saw the sight of a creditor all the time he was here."

" I do my best, my lord; how am I to get rid of him ?"

" Ask him if he has got five hundred pounds to cash a cheque, and tell him that, if he has not, he had better call on me the next time he is passing this way. Impress it upon him that he must on no account let it escape his memory."

" Very well, my lord."

Presently the servant returned.

" Is he gone ?"

" Yes, my lord."

"Yah! You will learn to do better by-and-bye. There is another knock."

"Is there, my lord?"

"Stay; you had better say that I have got the scarlet fever, the plague, or any other alarmingly contagious malady: if he is a man with a family, that will take effect. If they continue this game, I really must have a little straw put down before the house."

The servant again answered the door.

"Who is it?"

"Mr. Pearson."

"Ah! indeed, Mr. Pearson. He is a very obliging sort of man; I wish all my creditors were equally so. I have owed him two thousand pounds these three years, and I really believe it would break his heart if I payed him, poor fellow. Show him up immediately."

The servant did as he was ordered, and Mr. Pearson was introduced to the presence of Lord Oxburn.

He remained for some time uneasily fidgetting at the door, as if afraid to trust his plebian self in the aristocratic presence of a lord.

"Come in, my good friend, Pearson," said Lord Oxburn.

Thus encouraged Mr. Pearson ventured in, while Lord Oxburn pretended to be engaged in writing a note. The auctioneer continued standing in an uneasy attitude, evidently not very well knowing what to do with himself.

"Pray be seated Pearson, there's a good fellow," cried his lordship, raising his eyes listlessly from the table, and intentionally letting them fall on the auctioneer.

"You are very good my lord—I am much honoured by your lordship's condescension—I can never sufficiently apologise,—I—I."

"It always gives me the greatest pleasure to receive my friends, but, I had forgotten, have you lunched?"

"I have, my lord."

"Never mind, I dare say your ride has given you an appetite; here, Charles," continued his lordship, ringing the bell vehemently, "bring up some lunch, and uncork a bottle of that superb Madeira. I never open that wine but for my dearest and most intimate friends."

"Your lordship is too good, you are. indeed, you will positively kill me with kindness. I could not eat anything for mines of wealth; but if your lordship commands me ——"

"No, no, my dear fellow, please yourself by all means. How is Mrs. Pearson, and Lucretia, that charming daughter of yours?"

"Both in the best of health, I thank your lordship; and, upon the whole, I think I may consider myself a happy man, blessed with a good fortune, a charming wife, and a pretty daughter."

"Upon my soul, Mr. Pearson," said his lordship, shaking the auctioneer familiarly by the hand, "I quite envy your felicity. Almost time, I should say, to think of providing a husband for the young lady. What do you give with her, eh? Some fifty or sixty thousand pounds, I suppose."

"Why, as for her fortune, my lord," said the auctioneer, feeling considerably more at his ease when money was the subject of conversation, "I should not stand about a hundred thousand or so if I meet with a suitable match."

"That is to say. if you could hit upon a baronet, or some man of title, I suppose?"

"Exactly so, my lord, a man has a right to expect something in return for his money."

"I am quite of your opinion, Mr. Pearson, and have no doubt that you will find many noblemen who would consider themselves but too happy to form an alliance with your amiable family. I have, in fact, serious thoughts of becoming a benedict myself, but where am I to find an object worthy of my affections?"

The auctioneer stared wildly upon vacancy, as if conjuring up in his imagination his daughter Lucretia's nuptials with a nobleman.

"How lonely I am! how solitary and dejected! I am absolutely sinking with *ennui*." And his lordship struck his forehead tragically. "Where are you living, Pearson?"

Mr. Pearson handed him a card, and on it was inscribed his name, place of business, and calling.

"Oh! give me back that one, I have plenty others," said Mr. Pearson, producing a polished one from his case.

"I think I must come and see you and your amiable wife, and your charming daughter."

"Mrs. Pearson and Lucretia would be delighted to receive you—that is, if your lordship could possibly condescend to honour my humble dwelling with your presence."

"I will make a point of calling on you, Pearson; it will give me great pleasure to be able to pay my respects to Miss Lucretia in person. I will put your card next to the Earl of Morton's."

"Thank you, my lord."

"There is a little account, I think; I am indebted to you some trifle."

"Pray don't mention it, my lord. You really quite hurt me by supposing——"

"You mistake my meaning; you do, indeed, Pearson."

"Your lordship will greatly oblige me by dropping the subject; but I am afraid I am trespassing on your lordship's valuable time," continued the auctioneer, rising to depart.

"Oh, indeed! Well, I am rather busy," replied Lord Oxburn, smiling. "A very good morning to you."

"Good morning, my lord."

Lord Oxburn shook Mr. Pearson's hand warmly, and, this formality over, the auctioneer hurried out of the room as if fearful that the last topic should be resumed.

———

CHAPTER XIV.

THE VISIT TO THE ASTROLOGER.

AFTER the departure of Agnes Talbot, Mrs. Vyvian rang the bell for her maid, and commenced the operation of dressing for dinner.

"Tomkins," said the lady, "you have lived many years in our family, and I think you must feel some little interest in my affairs." Mrs. Vyvian paused. "I was going to say something to you, added she, "but perhaps it may be as well not."

"As you please, ma'am," replied the lady's maid, "but I am very sure that if ladies knew their own interests they would oftener condescend to open their hearts to their maids. I don't say all maids are faithful enough to trust, nor valets either, but many are, ma'am, and could often do essential service if they dare only open their mouths."

"As far as you are concerned I believe I might without danger confide in you, but your frequent intercourse with other servants makes it not improbable that you might, without intending it, betray your secret.'

"I am sorry, ma'am," answered the maid, shedding a torrent of tears, "that you should think as vilely of me, though perhaps I deserve it for allowing the name of my mistress to be mentioned without informing her of it."

"My name," said Mrs. Vyvian, whose curiosity was in her turn excited,—"who has presumed to make my name the subject of their conversation?"

"I must not, I dare not tell you," replied the maid, still sobbing violently.

"I insist upon your speaking the truth immediately," exclaimed Mrs. Vyvian.

"Well, then, ma'am if you will insist upon my speaking I must. Captain Dashington's valet only spoke of my master, without mentioning the lady's name. He said that his master was over head and ears in love with a certain lady, ma'am, and that he was sometimes in such a dreadful way, that it was quite shocking to see him, and he was positively afraid to leave him alone."

"And pray what has that to do with me?"

"Nothing, ma'am. Only when I asked him secretly who the lady was, he answered "Who should she be but Mrs. Fran—cis Vy—vi—an.""

"Very impertinent," cried Mrs. Vyvian, adjusting her glossy ringlets in the glass, "I really think Captain Dashington's valet might find better employment than talking about his master's affairs. But to return to my first intention. You know that circumstances have compelled me to send away, without any previous notice, that base, ungrateful person, Miss Talbot. Conscious of her guilt,

she left the house without even making an effort to conciliate me, but no doubt before many days pass she will return and on her knees beg re-admission, but on no account admit her to my presence."

"I am sure, ma'am I have often cried fit to break my heart to see how she took upon herself, and not one lady in a hundred would have been as kind as you have been.'!

"Have you ever had your fortune told?" inquired Mrs. Vyvian.

"What an odd question, ma'am."

"Oh, by no means. It is only a freak of mine."

"If you have any desire to speak with a cunning man, ma'am, I could without difficulty smuggle one into your dressing room."

"Dear, no," cried Mrs. Vyvian, "if I do consult an astrologer it shall be in his own house;—I would on no account let him know either my name or my place of residence. To-morrow morning your master will breakfast early, and after the meal is over I will get ready as soon as possible, and we will set out together. In the meantime you may purchase whatever articles are necessary to disguise me effectually," added the lady, putting a five-pound note into her hand.

The maid dropped a low curtsey, took the money, busied herself a little about the apartment, and then slipped down stairs to the housekeeper's room.

She threw herself into a chair, pursing her mouth and looking as if big with some important secret, which she desired, but had too much discretion to disclose.

"Bless me, Miss Tomkins," said the housekeeper, who was sitting fanning herself furiously by the side of a blazing fire, "how can you burst into a room in that manner; you have put us all of a tremor," added she, glancing with sympathy at a ruby-faced butler sitting opposite to her, whose face was copiously adorned with what the censorious would have been inclined to call "grog blossoms."

At this unexpected reception, Tomkins tossed her head, and sat for some time in silence.

"We were consulting, said the butler with dignified gravity, "on the best manner of putting an end to the imperence of tradesmen, for the grocer has dared to threaten to send in his bill to master himself. What do you think of that Miss Tomkins, eh?"

"Think of it," echoed Miss Tomkins, lifting up her hands as if lost in amazement, "what can any sensible person think of it," but that he is an ungrateful grocer, and a villain unworthy of your patronage? See how I'd serve him!"

"And pray, Miss Tomkins, how would you serve him?" said the butler, with a rather equivocal stare, "for I was not born yesterday, nor christened to-day, these two and twenty years come next March I've been a butler, and never but once or twice been able to match those vagabones when they've a mind to be what they call honest."

"I'm quite ashamed of you, Mr. Harris," replied the lady's maid. I have spirit and sense enough to keep all my people, the dressmakers and miliners, and all that set, in the most perfect subjection."

At this moment footsteps were heard—the wine which had been poured out and remained untouched in the glasses was hastily swallowed—the lady's maid crept into one closet, the butler into another, while the housekeeper, after placing her account-book upon the table, walked placidly towards the door and opened it. "Confound you," said she, on perceiving a large Newfoundland dog; "come out, Mr. Harris, 'tis only Dash."

*   *   *   *

The following morning Mrs. Vyvian, disguised in a common straw bonnet, a thick veil, and a large cotton shawl, proceeded with her maid into the neighbourhood of Oxford-street.

In a sombre apartment hung with black drapery, and lighted only by a dull lamp, sat an astrologer, apparently busily engaged in making calculations, when suddenly his attention was diverted from his pursuit by the violent ringing of the bell belonging to his study, and almost immediately Mrs. Vyvian, followed by her female attendant, without deigning to await the announcement of her name and business, entered the room; but upon being informed that one only was admitted at a time, the lady advanced alone, and seated herself in the chair appropriated to visitors. The astrologer pursued his study for some time, as if unconscious of the presence of a second person, till Mrs. Vyvian, becoming rather alarmed, half rose from her seat.

"Have patience, lady," said the astrologer, gazing with unfeigned reluctance and sorrow upon the youthful countenance of his inquirer. "I have cast thy horoscope—and I behold before me, lady, one who has hitherto basked in the light of fortune's sunniest smiles, but whose future presents—presents——" And the astrologer, bending eagerly over the table, perused the clestial figure before him for some moments in silence.

"Speak, speak!" exclaimed Mrs. Vyvian in a tone of irritable excitement. "The past I care nothing about, it is the future—what say you of the future?"

"That it were better, lady, for thee that the green turf at this moment covered thee, than that thou shouldst live to endure the miseries and the sorrows that await thee. The watery moon hastens from evil to evil till coming in conjunction with Saturn she betokens death and the grave."

Mrs. Vyvian sank back in her chair, watching with increased intensement the countenance of the astrologer, while he, at her request, again consulted the horoscope to see if no friendly sign of mitigation interposed to stay the impending calamities;

but his research was fruitless, and the lady solemnly impressed by his prediction took her leave. Arrived at the outer door, Mrs. Vyvian covered her face with her veil, and taking the arm of her maid familiarly to avoid discovery, proceeded homeward·

"Don't utter a syllable, Tomkins," said the lady "I fear I am recoginsed."

"Recognised, indeed!" re-echoed a voice which Mrs. Vyvian immediately knew to be that of Mr. Adolphus Tift; "I am not at all surprised at your being afraid and ashamed of being discovered. When a young lady, unknown to her parents, condescends to visit impostors and fortune-tellers, I think it the duty of every honest individual to make at least an effort to snatch her out of the fire before she gets burnt; and in this intention I shall make it my business to follow you to your place of residence, where I shall endeavour to obtain an interview with your father, who will, I have no doubt, appreciate my motive."

Mrs. Vyvian gently pressed the arm of her maid, to induce her to reply, which the latter, comprehending,—

"We are two young women orphans sir," said she, "lately come from the country: we lodge at a pastrycook shop in Oxford street, therefore I beg, sir, that, for the sake of our characters, you will go another way."

"I'm ashamed of you, worthless menial," said Mr. Tift, indignantly pointing his finger in the young woman's face. "I'm ashamed of you, but you cannot deceive me though you may succeed in deceiving your silly mistress. I am surprised that, in this age of reason as it is called, young ladies are not more circumspect. However, if my company annoys you, madam," continued he, politely bowing to Mrs. Vyvian, "I will walk on the opposite side, but to follow you I am determined." Mr. Tift crossed to the other side of the way, keeping his eyes fixed on the lady and her maid with the most provoking constancy, and pursuing his path with an air of mystery and ludicrous importance which astonished and amused most of the passers by. Miss Tomkins, exceedingly embarassed, led her mistress up one street and down another, till, arrived in Oxford-street, she, without any ceremony, entered a pastrycook's shop and proceeded straight up stairs, where she explained that a gentleman having followed them, they could find no other way of getting rid of him than by pretending that they were inmates of the house. Notwithstanding her disguise Mrs. Vyvian, who had for years been in the habit of making purchases in the shop, was recognized almost the moment she entered it, and the mistress was quite aware that when ladies take little freaks into their heads, and choose to disguise themselves, they are not at all obliged to those who discover them. The queen of the tarts and jellies behaved therefore as if she knew nothing at all about it, and obligingly offered to let the young women out of the house by a back door, an offer Mrs. Vyvian very thankfully accepted, as she was terrified lest Mr. Adolphus Tift should put his threat into execution and really follow them home, a proceeding which would not only have seriously disturbed her domestic peace, but infallibly have made her the talk of the town.

Mr. Tift, after waiting some time in the pastrycook's shop, turned again into Oxford-street, and, walking leisurely, arrived at the corner of a street just at the same moment with Mrs. Vyvian, who, almost ready to sink with apprehension, earnestly entreated him not to follow them any longer.

"You have discovered yourself, Madam," whispered Mr. Tift, "but depend on my discretion."

Grasping the arm of her attendant, Mrs. Vyvian hurried homeward. On her arrival in Belgrave-square, overpowered by contending emotions, she threw herself into a chair and burst into tears. Ashamed of her visit to the astrologer, of whom, after all, she had not made the inquiries she had intended, impressed with a kind of superstitious dread of the fulfilment of the prediction he had uttered, and, above all, alarmed at her unexpected rencontre with Mr. Tift, she unfeignedly repented of her foolish adventure, and almost determined to tell her husband of it at once, but the thought that he could never have confidence in her again checked the intention.

"It is really a pity, ma'am," said Miss Tomkins, to grieve so sadly about nothing at all. I'm sure, ma'am, if you were to write a few lines to Mr. Tift, and beg of him not to say a word about having seen you, that he would keep the secret.

"That's not a bad thought, Tomkins, but I am ignorant of his address."

"Oh, ma'am, I can very easily learn that; his valet is our under housemaid's brother, and I dare say she'll know where he lives, ma'am.

"Well then," said Mrs. Vyvian, a little cheered by the hope of coaxing Mr. Tift to keep silence, "go down stairs and endeavour, cautiously, to obtain the information desired, but avoid giving the least cause for suspicion, and you may depend on it your services shall not go unrewarded."

"Oh don't mention that, ma'am, I'm sure I'd do anything, ma'am, to save you uneasiness." Tomkins quitted the room, and Mrs. Vyvian seated herself and penned the following lines :—

"Mrs. Francis Vyvian will feel obliged if Mr. Adolphus Tift will favour her with a call as soon as possible after the receipt of this note.

"Belgrave-square."

The letter, sealed, was instantly dispatched by Miss Tomkins, who, in about another hour re-entered her mistress's boudoir with the following answer from Mr. Tift :—

"Mr. Tift exceedingly regrets that a prior engagement prevents his accepting Mrs. Vyvian's invitation, but will not fail to call in Belgrave-square

to-morrow about three o'clock, if that hour is agreeable to Mrs. Vyvian.

"Long's Hotel."

"Here, then, begins the accomplishment of the prediction," sighed Mrs. Vyvian, as she threw the note upon the table, "To-day and to-morrow until three o'clock I must endure the most distressing anxiety. I can scarcely expect that that weakminded creature will have sense and discretion enough to keep my secret, and if he does not I feel that Francis is too severe to pardon my indiscretion.',

"My master desires to speak with you, ma'am," for the third time squeeked a little stylish-looking tiger, who had entered the apartment unperceived by his mistress.

"How long have you been here, impertinent?' asked the lady, whose visionary as well as oral faculties had been entirely absorbed by her meditations. "Another time don't presume to enter my presence unbidden." The tiger bowed and departed, at the same moment as Mr. Francis Vyvian entered, and impressing a kiss upon the forehead of his wife, inquired the cause of her displeasure.

"I have made a purchase this morning that I think will please you, my love ; passing by Regent-street I looked in at Mrs. Day's, and made choice of a turban as nearly as possible like the one you admired the other evening.

"A what!" exclaimed Mrs. Vyvian.

"A turban, my love," placidly returned her husband, at the same time motioning Miss Tomkins to fetch it out of the drawing-room.

"Really Francis," said Mrs. Vyvian, "I never could have believed you could be so perfectly ridiculous as to imagine that when I praised that hideous turban of Mrs. Grimstone's I meant what I said. I can receive your present but as a premeditated insult, and as such will treat it as it deserves," added the lady, snatching the turban out of the hands of Miss Tomkins, and trampling it under her feet. "Another time, Mr. Vyvian, before you take fancies into your head, I hope you will consult my taste, and not go throwing away my poor father's money in this wilful manner

"Mr. Vyvian, half angry, half amused at the result of his endeavour to please his wife, did his best to conciliate her.

"If Miss Talbot," said he, had been faithful to an appointment we made, to meet in the library this morning, I have no doubt that I should, with her assistance, have succeeded better in pleasing you, my dear, but I really thought, from the very extraordinary praise you bestowed upon Mrs. Grimstone's head-dress that I ran no risk whatever in procuring you one similar to it. But what has become of Miss Talbot ; I understand she is not at home ?

"Your aunt Peacher requested me to allow her to spend some time with her daughter," replied Mrs. Vyvian, colouring deeply, " and as I saw no objection————"

"Oh certainly not," returned Francis Vyvian, "that accounts then for her apparent bad faith; but to return to the unfortunate turban; if we cannot turn it to better account, let it remain in your possession, and if an occasional glance at it teaches you to be a little more sincere in the expression of your sentiments, I shall not consider the money it cost wilfully thrown away."

Mr. Vyvian quitted the apartment, and Miss Tomkins, hastily seizing the turban with well-assumed indignation, thrust it into a box, declaring "that it was a shame to treat a poor lady in that manner."

Though accustomed to deviate from truth whenever she considered that circumstances rendered it expedient for her to do so, Mrs. Vyvian was too well instructed not to feel troubled and uneasy. On the present occasion she was more than usually so. She had driven an innocent, inoffensive girl to seek shelter among strangers. Her vague suspicions had been, by her husband's explanation, entirely removed; she felt that it was her duty to seek for and restore the friendless girl to the comforts of a home which her jealousy had so suddenly deprived her of. For a moment Mrs. Vyvian was inclined to follow the direction of her better feelings, but self-love, ever predominant in her breast, stifled in its birth her good intention. She could not disguise from herself that Agnes was prettier, more amiable, more accomplished. These advantages decided her not to subject herself again to humiliating comparisons. To banish reflection she descended into the drawing-room and seated herself at the piano, resolving that if Miss Talbot should return of her own accord, she would certainly receive her.

CHAPTER XV.

THE MEETING OF THE BEGGARS.*

IT was morning. The two children of the Barker were sitting down on the doorstep of the house in West-street.

Presently the figure of the Mudlark appeared, when, accompanied by the two children, he entered, for the door had been left ajar.

"Has yer mother been home yet?" he inquired of the eldest girl.

"No, father, she ain't."

"And we're very hungry," added the other.

As every day came round it brought but the same misery to that poverty-stricken family, the same course of starvation, of wretchedness, intoxication, and degradation.

"She's always gadding about," exclaimed the Mudlark, and, urged on by desperation, he put on his waterproof boots, and once again repaired to the sewers.

* This was formerly called a " Beggars' Carnival."

Scarcely had he quitted the house when the Barker returned in company with a beggar.

"Come, Bill Waters," said the Barker, "make yourself at home. Which of this ere two'll suit yer best?" added she, pointing to her own children.

Bill Waters eyed them with the glance of a connoisseur, and he noted the points of each that would probably make an impression upon the credulity and good nature of John Bull.

"Vy, as to the matter of that, I think the little 'un 'ud do best."

"You needn't pinch her more than you can help," said the Barker.

"Leave that to me: but I must be getting ready."

Bill Waters took his shoes off his feet, scratched his legs about the ankles till they literally bled, and, as a finishing stroke, put on a clean white apron.

"Now, then, my dear, come along with me." And the beggar firmly grasped the hand of the child, and at once took up his station in the middle of the road.

He was still within sight of the Barker's house when he commenced his piteous wailings. A little further on he struck up into a song—for he invariably suited his imposture to the neighbourhood he was traversing—just in the same manner that an itinerant pedlar increases or decreases the price of his wares.

"What a blessing it is when people's children begins to do for themselves!" soliloquised the Barker.

The Barker now went out to impose upon the public in her own line.

Several hours had elapsed before she returned, when she brought home with her some food of the coarsest description, and placed it before the eldest child.

The mudlark and the youngest child were still away.

The Barker seated herself on a heap of straw, and leisurely puffed away at her pipe, awaiting the return of Bill Waters and her youngest child.

She was soon relieved from her vigil by the arrival of the beggar, who paid her two shillings for the loan of her infant, and bargained for it at the same terms next day.

"Now, then, come along," quoth Bill Waters, "or all the fun'll be over afore we can git there."

"There's lots of time," replied the Barker.

The Barker and Bill Waters quitted the house together.

The road of the two imposters lay to St. Gile's, that most delectable of all the regions of the metropolis, well known as the "Holy Land."

Although the distance was considerable, they traversed it in a very short space of time, and arrived at a pot-house denominated the "House of Call for Cadgers."

TENNIS COURT.

In a room in this pot-house ere assembled several beggars, all of them giving way to that mirth and jollity which the discussion of the good things of this world seldom fails to inspire.

In the midst of the noisy group stood the land-lord, alternately wetting his whistle and puffing away at his weed.

In one corner sat a blind man fiddling, in another a black, who was employed in making grimaces, and otherwise contorting his features, for the merriment of those around.

Some of that class who

"Limp all day, but dance all night,"

skipped round and round the room, beating time merrily with their crutches. The Barker and Bill Waters danced a jig. There was an appearance of good feeling and conviviality among these impostors—not one of whom, perhaps, had a shirt on his or her back, as the case might be,—that would have been looked for in vain at many a rout in Grosvenor-square.

One little fellow, on a go-cart, sang uproariously ; and, although in the whole course of his life he had probably never stood upright on his legs, he appeared to be as merry and sociable as any of his more favoured companions.

On a table standing near the door there was heaped together an immense quantity of broken bread which had been given to the beggars to eat ; but, instead of so doing, they were keeping it to sell to the biscuit-bakers, who ground it for the purpose of making tops and bottoms.

At the same table was seated a man who was writing petitions and begging-letters, for which he got from sixpence to ninepence each, according to their length and the talent with which they were compiled.

From a house situated opposite to the "Cadgers' Retreat" rushed two women, with their hair streaming behind, covered with blood, and brandishing knives in their hands. Four constables came up. Two carried one of the wome away on the stretcher to the hospital, and the other two, having first disarmed her, dragged the remaining one off to the station-house.

The landlord of the "Cadgers' Retreat" immediately posted himself at the door.

"That house has five entrances," said he. "Now, I've travellers that have come here these ten years, and had their chop and their bit of mutton, or anything they like, all comfortable. They goes there, and what's the consequences? Vy, they gits their throats cut; and sarve 'em right, too.' Having finished this oration—intended by the speaker more as a puff for his own establishment than for the edification of the million without—the landlord returned to his merry guests—the jovial beggars.

Although for a season given up to mirth, yet they had a sharp eye for business. It was now getting late; so they commenced fixing their different routes for the ensuing day's excursions.

The Barker, being almost tired of it, quitted the "Cadgers' Retreat" to return to her own house in West-street.

CHAPTER XVI.

THE TENNIS COURT.*

In the evening of the same day that witnessed the visit of Mr. Pearson to Lord Oxburn, the baronet and Frederick Vyvian repaired to his lordship's residence.

"I was thinking of you young gentlemen," said his lordship as they entered, raising his eyes from a table covered with bills and memorandums, through which he had apparently been wading.

"Is there anything so very extraordinary in that?" inquired Frederick.

"Perhaps not: but I was thinking how devilish unlike you are to your brother: I should never have imagined that you were related to one another."

"No, indeed!" interrupted the baronet, eyeing Frederick with a scrutinizing glance. "Perhaps there is some truth in what you say. He is certainly very unlike any of our family. I cannot trace a single feature of either my father or my mother in him."

Frederick Vyvian coloured slightly, but he was possessed of too much self-command to betray his emotion.

"You appear to see things through the medium of another man's eyes," at length he exclaimed, with some degree of confusion depicted on his countenance.

* Fives Court was formerly the favourite resort of the "fancy"; but that sport, rendered so classic by the eminent pugilistry, who there displayed their prowess and skill, is now no more. The lovers and professors of boxing have since visited this Tennis Court, which bids fair to rival its illustrious predecessor. It is here that the boxers try their powers previous to more serious combats.

"I have not lost the power of seeing with my own yet," returned the baronet, in a tone which impressed Frederick with the idea that he entertained doubts of the relationship existing between them.

"I should say not," replied Lord Oxburn, who was glad of any opportunity of causing differences between Sir Richard and Frederick, both of whom he hated cordially for having, at his entrance into life, ruined both his fortune and his prospects. "You have caught me with such common every-day affairs, as bills and creditors, and I am by no means in a sublime mood—consequently, I see plain things plainer."

"Looking over bills which you neither can or mean to pay, partakes less of the sublime than the ridiculous," remarked Frederick, in a tone of biting sarcasm.

To this Lord Oxburn volunteered no reply.

"I am sorry to have disturbed your agreeable cogitations," said Sir Richard, making a faint attempt at a smile—an effort that in reality made him look more out of temper than ever.

"Oh, by no means! It is infernally 'slow' sitting here, though. Is there anything going on to night?"

"There is a new piece produced at the Haymarket," responded the baronet.

"But there is no fascinating woman to make it go off with *eclat*," murmured his lordship.

"I have it!" cried Frederick, who was pleased at a chance of escaping from his present state of embarassment. "We cannot do better than go to the Tennis Court."

Lord Oxburn and the baronet looked interrogatively at the speaker.

"Can you doubt my reason for making the proposition?" inquired Frederick Vyvian.

"Oh, I recollect now!" exclaimed the nobleman, smiling at the want of retention evinced by his own memory. "It would have mortified me amazingly if I had not been there to-night. There is to be a 'set-to' between Ben Caunt and Freeman, the American Giant."

"Then I make one of the party," said the baronet.

"And I also," added Frederick.

Lord Oxburn, the baronet, and Frederick Vyvian, were soon on their way to Windmill-street, Haymarket. They were highly delighted with the "setting-to" of the burly champion and Freeman, as well as with the wind-up of Tom Spring and Jack Carter.

A considerable number of amateurs and professors of pugilism had assembled together. The affair had created a great sensation in the fistic world. And in the Tennis-court some of the first noblemen of the realm might be seen huddled together with the vilest scum of society.

Among the crowd, which was exceedingly dense,

Frederick Vyvian had recognised Mr. Tift arm-in-arm with Stamer.

He immediately acquainted the baronet with his discovery, when Sir Richard deemed it advisable to invite Adolphus Tift and his associate to Grosvenor-square, where *Rouge-et-Noir* might be played with both amusement and profit. He had an eye to Stamer's thirty thousand, with which he considered himself to have trifled too much already; but he knew that, with the qualifications for roguery he possessed, there were few persons who could evade his traps, and, when once caught, none were able to extricate themselves from them.

The two parties met. Mr. Stamer and Lord Oxburn were introduced to each other by Mr. Tift, and the invitation to his house was pressed on all by the baronet, so they left the pugilistic arena, and walked towards Grosvenor-square, conversing on pugilistic science and fistic matters generally, in which Lord Oxburn assumed to be especially *au fait*, and calling to memory the efforts and peculiarities of those giants of the ring—Crib, Molineux, Randall, Turner, Belcher, Pearce, and many other scientific and unflinching pugilists.

"I think such combats as those we have just witnessed have a very brutalising effect," said Mr. Tift.

"However much boxing may be railed against by *hypocrites*, it is an art essentially necessary to *men*," replied Lord Oxburn.

"What so effectually screens an Englishman from insult on the continent as the knowledge foreigners have of their deficiency in this respect? When they hear the blessing which an Englishman, in his wrath, pronounces on their eyes, they seldom dare await the result," observed Frederick.

"The common people certainly act a wiser part in arranging their disputes with the fist, than the gentry and nobility, who have recourse to deadlier weapons," ejaculated Stamer.

"Lead is a very injurious thing," said Mr. Tift; "and, when taken inwardly, it frequently operates fatally, and, in my humble opinion, steel is not much better."

This rally produced a laugh, in which Mr. Adolphus Tift heartily joined, without taking the trouble to discover whether it was raised at his joke or him; or whether his friends laughed with or at him.

Thus they whiled away the time till they reached Grosvenor square.

CHAPTER XVII.

MR. DOBBINS'S TEA-PARTY.

When Miss Talbot quitted Mrs. Pearson she returned to her lodging in Oxford-street.

The cloth was laid for dinner, and Mr. and Mrs. Dobbins, dressed unusually smart, were in the very best of temper: something particularly agreeable had evidently occurred during Miss Talbot's short absence.

"Fine day for walking, Miss," said Mr. Dobbins, rubbing his hands. "Hope you succeeded in getting the situation," exclaimed the kind-hearted couple almost in a breath.

"I have engaged to enter Mrs. Pearson's family to-morrow," replied Miss Talbot, smiling faintly, "and return Mr. Dobbins and yourself many thanks for the interest you take in my welfare."

Mr. Dobbins muttered something about being sorry to lose her company, while Mrs. Dobbins good-humouredly intimated that dinner would soon be upon the table—a hint Miss Talbot immediately took, and hurried into her sleeping-room to divest herself of her bonnet and cloak. On her return into the parlour she found the family—consisting of Mr. and Mrs. Dobbins, the two Miss Dobbins, and William, the apprentice, a youth about eighteen—seated round the table, gazing intently upon a beef-steak pudding of unusually large dimensions, the savoury steam of which appeared to have paralysed the senses of the whole party, for Agnes took her seat almost unobservable.

Mrs. Dobbins at last, becoming sensible of her presence, took up her knife, and gave a delicate stab into the right side of the devoted pudding. At the sight of the rich gravy flowing in streams down the sides of the crust, an involuntary burst of approval escaped the lips of Mr. Dobbins. The young ladies exclaimed, "Oh, my!" while the apprentice fidgetted about in his chair as if a needle had inadvertently been stuck into the bottom of it.

"Give me nothing but gristle," muttered Mr. Dobbins, as if half afraid that his wife should hear the observation.

"What did you say, sir?" authoritatively demanded the lady.

"Nothing, my dear, nothing," replied Mr. Dobbins, looking feelingly at his apprentice, whose good-humoured smile had settled into a solemn, sulky scowl.

Mrs. Dobbins had observed her husband's look, and, having nearly finished a very hearty dinner, she became suddenly fastidious.

"Really, William," exclaimed the lady, "you'll make me sick if you keep staring at the dish in that manner."

"I can't eat any more," said Sophia, the youngest daughter, pushing her plate towards William; "if you don't mind my plate, and will take it."

William did not seem to mind anything so as he got enough to eat; but Mrs. Dobbins, who seemed determined that he should not enjoy his additional morsel undisturbed, began railing at him without a moment's intermission.

"Dreadful habit that, William, of eating and drinking at every meal till you can scarcely see out of your eyes! I'm really surprised. Mr. Dobbins, at your patience, sir. How you can sit and see a boy make such a beast of himself! He 's killing himself by inches! I'm no enemy to eating Miss," added the lady, turning to Miss Talbot, "that is to say, when it agrees with the constitution, for my doctor tells me, 'Mrs. Dobbins, eat as much as you can; it's not so good for Mr. Dobbins, and death to your apprentice, who should learn to make as little do as possible if he desires to enjoy good health and long life; but to you, Mrs. Dobbins, I again repeat, your constitution requires support; you must eat or you'll die.'"

Mr. Dobbins coughed two or three times rather equivocally, and, turning to William, he made a signal for glasses, which, with a bottle of home-made wine, spirits, hot water and sugar, were put upon the table before the young man retired into the shop, which he immediately did, not forgetting as he closed the door, to cast a look of gratitude, or perhaps affection, at Miss Sophia, who did not appear at all disinclined to return it if she could have done so unobserved.

"We are now alone," said Mr. Dobbins vainly endeavouring to elongate his round, chubby face, and give an impressive solemnity to his voice. But Mr. Dobbins had swallowed nearly a tumbler of brandy and water, and the brandy and water was determined to have fair play. Mr. Dobbins choaked and coughed, and at last, bursting into an unrestrained fit of laughter, "Dear Lucy," he exclaimed, addressing his eldest daughter, "a certain person of the name of Mr. Thomas Garnet, jeweller, living not a hundred miles away from Oxford-street, has made a formal declaration of his earnest desire to marry, and I, like a blockhead of a father, have consented to give him one of my daughters, that is, provided the young lady herself is agreeable to the match."

"Agreeable to the match! Mr. Thomas Garnet desires to marry! I don't underrtand you, Pa," simpered Miss Dobbins as she pulled out her pocket handkerchief, and either cried or pretended to cry sadly.

"Mr. Dobbins, sir!" fiercely ejaculated his wife, "I'm ashamed of you, sir, mentioning such an indelicate subject before your daughters. Poor Lucy, as innocent as a new-born babe, don't even understand what love and marriage mean, sir."

At the conclusion of this reproof, Miss Lucy sobbed louder than ever, while Mr. Dobbins, struck dumb by his wife's eloquence, and fearing he had greatly erred, remained quietly sipping his brandy and water, till at last, having finished one tumbler and dipped pretty deep into another, he ventured to observe that Miss Lucy must have understood him, as she had for some time clandestinely corresponded with the said Thomas Garnet, and that it was in consequence of one of the letters having miscarried, that he felt, as a man of honour, compelled to come forward, though he had not intended to do so till a

month or two later. Mrs. Dobbins, for some reason best known to herself, was silent, but not till she had made two or three attempts to utter "Mr. Dobbins, sir," but her faithless tongue refused to speak the "once familiar word." She rose from her chair, and, with a semi-theatrical strut, staggered out of the room, followed by Lucy, who still kept applying her handkerchief to her face.

Mr. Dobbins hiccupped two or three times, laid his head upon the table, and in a few moments fell into a good sound sleep, whereupon Miss Sophy, the youngest daughter, slipped out of the parlour into the shop, where she took her seat beside her beloved William, leaving Miss Talbot to amuse herself with the harmonious grunting of the sleeping hosier.

Mr. Dobbins had been engaged in his nap only a few seconds, when an unusual bustle in the shop announced the arrival of either customers or visitors. Agnes was not long in suspense, for the door which separated the parlour from the shop was thrown open, and a natty little man, followed by a tall thin youth, bustled into the room.

Mr. Dobbins was on his feet in an instant. Sophy, running out of the room to call her mother and sister, upset the maid who had that moment reached the top of the kitchen stairs with the tea-things in her hands. The gentlemen, hearing a clatter, rushed out just in time for the tall thin youth to receive the inanimate figure of Miss Sophy, who, alarmed at the accident, had fainted. The young man made an extraordinary effort to carry the lady into the parlour, but would, notwithstanding, have failed in his endeavour, and most probably have discharged his burden unexpectedly upon the carpet had not Sophy, instinctively aware of her danger, in a voice scarcely audible, requested "to be put down;" the youth obeyed, and led her gently towards a seat, but she still continued leaning her head helplessly upon his shoulder.

The apprentice, who had witnessed the fainting, the fair form of his beloved triumphantly borne into the parlour by a rival, could scarcely controul his feelings. He coughed, he gnashed his teeth, gave two or three violent kicks against the counter, and shook his fist at the back parlour, as if he was denouncing vengeance against the whole of the company assembled there.

Mrs. Dobbins, who with the aid of a little soda water, had pretty nearly recovered herself, followed Lucy down stairs just in time to prevent Mr. Dobbins unceremoniously throwing a tumbler of cold water in his daughter's face, the poor man really believing it to be the best restorative.

But Mrs. Dobbins would hear of no such thing: "Leave her alone," said she, "let her come to when she pleases, poor thing; nobody knows what it is to faint but those who are used to it, Mr. Garnet," added the lady, pathetically addressing her intended son-in-law. Mr. Garnet looked wise and intimated that a small scent-bottle would be an agreeable appendage in a house where the ladies were so delicate.

"A very proper remark, sir," replied Mrs. Dobbins, looking angrily at her husband, "and a very beautiful smelling-bottle I had, but one day when we were aboard one of the Margate steamers, Mr. Dobbins comes running to me and asks for the loan of it; I was sick at the time and, innocent like, gave it him, but never, from that day to this have I set eyes upon it, though he has declared over and over again that he'd give it me back. I hope if Lucy gets one given her she'll never let it out of her own possession." Mrs. Dobbins nodded significantly at her daughter, while Mr. Garnet whispered something in her ear which occasioned the young lady to blush deeply, to the great delight of her lover, who from that moment never quitted her side the rest of the evening.

Miss Sophy, whose swan-like neck probably began to ache with holding it so long a time in one position, at length opened her eyes and gently raised her head from the benumbed shoulder of the thin youth, who, alarmed lest another fit should subject him again to the same inconvenience, quitted his seat, and literally insisted upon toasting the muffins and crumpets. The apprentice, who had been called to assist in handing about the tea-cups, took the opportunity of revenging himself upon the prostrate limbs of the thin youth, apologising always for his awkwardness, and treading heavier every time, till, exasperated beyond endurance, the thin youth rose from before the fire, threw down the muffin with the toasting fork, and rushed at his antagonist, who flew out of the parlour into the shop, and turned the key of the door, to the no small amusement of the gentlemen and delight of the ladies, who had begun to entertain fears for the safety of the tea-table and its contents.

The thin youth returned to his chair puffing and blowing with the air of a conqueror. He thought no more of the muffins and crumpets, which were forthwith sent down to Molly to toast at the kitchen fire, and at half-past eleven o'clock, just as the gentlemen were taking their leave, Molly entered the parlour with two large plates full, toasted, buttered, and ready to eat.

———

CHAPTER XVIII.

THE ARREST.

ALTHOUGH, at the commencement of the evening, an ill-feeling had evinced itself between the baronet and Frederick Vyvian, by the time they had reached Grosvenor-square no traces of it were discernable.

Notwithstanding Frederick was frequently rough in his manners, and not altogether delicate in the choice of a topic for conversation, yet—thanks to a

certain polish which he had acquired from the society with which he had mingled, and which served to gloss over his defects—his errors were not glaringly apparent.

The baronet treated his guests with a great show of hospitality, and an unusual quantity of wine was introduced on the table, of which all present freely partook.

The baronet and Frederick continually urged Stamer to drink, while they merely sipped their own glasses, and flung the remainder of the contents beneath the table—a manœuvre not unnoticed by Stamer, for he immediately declined any more wine, and steadily adhered to the determination he had formed in spite of their most persuasive eloquence.

"You are quite a hermit," said Frederick.

"Rather say a Turk," added Mr. Tift.

"Not at all," replied Stamer. "If I must speak the truth, I am very well stocked at present."

"You certainly are exceedingly ascetic," responded Sir Richard Vyvian.

"How long are we to sit looking at one another?" demanded Lord Oxburn.

The hint was immediately taken, and *Rouge-et-Noir* was proposed, which arrangement met with the approbation of all present but Stamer, who appeared to have a decided antipathy to amusements of this description when in company with his present associates.

They had but recently commenced gaming, when a servant intimated to Frederick that his company was required below.

"Tell him I am engaged," replied he, "or ask him to send up his name."

Before this last order had been communicated, a repulsive-looking man, without any previous notice, walked abruptly into the room, and confronted Frederick.

"I believe I am speaking to Mr. Frederick Vyvian?" said the man.

It was a critical juncture. Frederick was disagreeably taken by surprise, and, finding himself so completely hemmed in, he could not quite make up his mind whether to avow or deny himself to be himself.

"What is your business with me?" at length he exclaimed, in a tone strongly savouring with the true feelings with which he regarded his position.

"Oh, I know yer! That ere gammon won't take effect," responded the officer. "I've a right to enforce my question."

"A right!" retorted Frederick. "What the devil do you mean?"

"I'm certain of my name, and, if you are not Vyvian, I'll risk it. Here's an execution out against you for nine hundred and sixty-seven pounds, and, if you can't pay, you had better come along."

"We need not make a noise about it," replied

Frederick. "But—my dear fellow!—you are indeed mistaken."

"Not a bit of it," surlily answered the officer.

"There is an error here," said the baronet; "and, when I give my word, I think my position as will prevent——"

"I understand," interrupted the officer, "and I should be delighted to do anything polite and accommodating always, provided it's possible; but at present it isn't."

"I suppose he can be allowed to sleep in a sponging-house?" resumed Sir Richard, with some haughtiness of tone.

"I am very sorry, sir, to say that he can't: it's more than I dare do, with a heavy sum like that.

"I am convinced that, if you would listen to my explanations," said Mr. Tift, "the result would be found advantageous to both parties."

"Come," impatiently ejaculated the officer, "we must be off. If you don't choose to come quietly, I have the power of forcing you; so submit you must either way."

A second officer now entered the room, tired with waiting in the passage below. Frederick Vyvian again hesitated, and asked them where it was their intention to take him;

"Why, to Whitecross, to be sure," was the answer given him.

"Have you got any money about you?" inquired the baronet, addressing Frederick.

"I'm tolerably off in that respect," replied the young man.

Thus compelled to consent to what was required of him, he left the house in company with the sheriff's officers.

During the performance of this every-day drama, Stamer had not ventured to open his mouth; but, on its coming to a conclusion, in spite of the baronet's endeavours to persuade him to stay, he rather abruptly took his departure.

CHAPTER XIX.

WHITECROSS-STREET PRISON.

FREDERICK Vyvian pursued his way in silence, and indeed, whenever he asked a question no answer was made him.

Rendered miserable by the wretched weather, the thick darkness which reigned around him, and the knowledge of the destination to which he was being conveyed, he imagined that his misery had reached its climax, and heartily cursed the fate that had elevated him from the position in society, which, if Mr. Peter Prigmore's words were true, he ought to have filled. The unfortunate young man would have gladly renounced the name and fortune of the Vyvians, provided he could have found himself once more at liberty. The monotonous sound of the carriage wheels, the clattering of pattens on the pavement, and the deep conviction of his unfortunate position, caused the young man to be sincerely disgusted with belonging to a good family without the necessary appendage of a good fortune.

At length one of the officers informed him that he had arrived at the prison.

It was now nine o'clock.

He was introduced to a small lobby, where a turnkey thrust a loaf of bread into his hand, and another turnkey led him through several alleys to the staircase communicating with the receiving ward.

The turnkey pulled a bell.

"Who rings?" cried a voice from the top of the stairs.

"Sheriff's debtor—Frederick Vyvian—C. M." sang out the turnkey, in reply to the above question.

Frederick ascended the stairs, and at the door of the receiving ward was accosted by the steward, a prisoner who had been appointed to the office on account of his general good behaviour.

"What is your name?"

"Frederick Vyvian."

"Have you got your bread?"

"Yes."

"Then put it in the pigeon-hole. Will you have sheets on your bed to-night?"

"If you please."

"A shilling the first night, and sixpence every night after. As you can afford to pay for sheets you can sleep in the inner room, and sit up till twelve o'clock, those who can't go to bed before ten.'

"I understand."

"If you live at my table, sixpence each for breakfast and tea, a shilling for dinner, and fourpence for supper are my charges."

"I shall certainly avail myself of the opportunity."

"Then write a note to the governor, saying you will be certain to settle your affairs in a week."

"I cannot be certain of that, but I am of the contrary."

"If you don't do it you can't stay here. Here is a sheet of paper; a penny if you please."

Frederick paid for the paper, and taking up a pen, wrote the note to the governor, which the steward immediately took possession of, and carefully deposited in his pocket-book.

Frederick Vyvian now had an opportunity of looking round.

The receiving ward was a long low room, lighted by a single fire, around which the sheriff's Debtors were warming themselves, while the Court-of-Requests men were entirely excluded from this benefit, and sat shivering on the benches at some distance from the grate. The only recommendation of this room was its extreme cleanliness.

The steward intimated to Frederick Vyvian that

he must keep apart from the fellows over there, meaning the Court-of-Requests men, as they had not got a penny in their pockets.

"Who is that?" asked Frederick, addressing himself to the steward, and pointing to a decent-looking man sitting on a bench.

"That is a tailor, who once had a very good business, but he meddled with politics, and ran after every brawler for public liberty till he became a bankrupt."

"Who is that sitting next to him?"

"A bricklayer arrested for eightpence, and the costs are three and sixpence."

"That was abominable," observed Frederick.

"Begging your pardon, we often have worse cases than that," replied the steward.

It was now a quarter to ten, and those who could not pay for sheets were huddled off to bed, and Frederick remained chattering and smoking with the gentlemen of the steward's table.

At twelve o'clock Frederick was introduced to a long room occupied by nine or ten bees.

He awoke early the following morning, and, after performing his toilette in a sort of scullery, where for the use of a towel he paid twopence, for soap, one penny; loan of razor and lather-box, one penny.

The breakfast consisted of dry toast and coffee.

Shortly after this meal was over, the prisoners were removed to the different departments of the the establishment to which they belonged.

As the governor did not comply with Frederick Vyvian's note he was instructed to remove to the Poultry ward, on the London side.

The Poultry ward was a dark room, with several barred windows on each side, a few small tables, and sawdust on the floor. Gamblers, black-legs, sprigs of nobility, fraudulent bankrupts, fortune-hunters, clergymen, quacks, lawyers, thieves, sailors, swindlers, and honest unfortunates were collected together, presenting a confused mass indeed, but yet an animated and true picture of real life.

The turnkey introduced Mr. Vyvian to the steward of the ward.

"If you please, sir," said the steward, addressing Frederick, "being a new member, you must pay an entrance fee of one pound and sixpence; this goes towards paying the officers, adding to the comforts of the place, &c."

Frederick paid the demand.

"If you live at my table the charges will be the same as up stairs in the receiving ward."

"I shall be most happy to do so. Who is that old man, he seems to be a moving mass of filth?"

"He was formerly a scholar and a gentleman, but now he is one of the greatest nuisances in the place; he got out of the Bench a week or two ago, but he has been arrested by some coeditor whom he has offended."

Thus it is that imprisonment for debt exercises its baneful influence in producing self-degradation. Thus it is that the gentleman of former times is converted into an habitual gamester, and the accomplished citizen into a besotted drunkard. While roguery reigns predominant *within* the walls, while to be honest is to be despised, how can we expect a debtor to feel any inclination to pay his creditors *without?* The ability disappears, and, with it, the inclination also.

The steward gave Frederick an account of his *chums*, or fellow-lodgers.

Among the prisoners how much vice predominates. Vice and misery occupies so large a space, that there was not an aperture for virtue to creep in at. On the whole, Frederick began to reconcile himself to his fate. The company was very congenial to his taste, and he found plenty of occupation in gaming by night, and smoking and drinking by day.

CHAPTER XX.

THE SUSPICION.

MRS. VYVIAN'S visit to the astrologer seemed likely to be attended with grave consequences both to herself and Mr. Tift.

Captain Dashington, who was upon chatting terms with one of the young women who served in the confectioner's shop, was informed by her that Mrs. Vyvian, with her maid, had passed through the shop, and been let out by the back door, to avoid the pursuit of Mr. Tift. The Captain, intending to turn the story to account, proceeded immediately to Long's Hotel, and arrived there just at the moment when Mrs. Vyvian's page was delivering to a valet the letter written by his mistress to Mr. Tift.

Dashington mounted the stairs and found Mr. Tift, who exceedingly annoyed at the interruption, behaved so stiff and cool that it was impossible for Captain Dashington to prolong his visit beyond a few minutes. He, however, managed to get out of him that he had an appointment with a lady the following day, that lady, the Captain immediately conjectured to be Mrs. Vyvian.

He left the hotel, and was pondering in his own mind whether or no he should endeavour to ingratiate himself with Francis Vyvian by disclosing to him the intrigues of his wife, when the object of his meditation ran against him in Piccadilly.

A hearty shake of the hand, accompanied with an earnest request that Francis Vyvian would favour him with a few minutes' private conversation, induced that gentleman to turn with him into Hyde Park.

"Mr. Francis Vyvian," said Captain Dashington, seriously, "can I trust you? dare I hope that a secret which will for ever remain entombed in my breast can, without danger, be revealed to its legitimate owner? No! Mr. Vyvian, I cannot, as an honourable man conceal from your knowledge that a lady intimately connected with yourself is guilty of the grossest improprieties. Start not; I cannot expect that you will give immediate credence to so distressing a fact—but convince yourself—to-morrow morning go out early—return home at three o'clock, and you will, if I am not very much deceived, find Mr. Adolphus Tift in company with your wife."

"Impossible!" emphatically exclaimed Vyvian, turning pale with rage and indignation. My wife hold an improper intercourse with that poor wretched creature, Adolphus Tift."

"Incredible, ridiculous as it may appear, it is no less true. The lady has within this hour favoured him with two letters. But your secret is safe with me, and if you take my advice you will, after satisfying yourself of the truth of my assertion, let the matter drop; all married men are liable to some misfortune."

"I am sensible, very sensible of your friendly intentions," said Francis Vyvian, pressing his forehead with his hands, "but really your communication has taken me so much by surprise that I am unable to resolve definitely what course I intend to pursue. The thing appears too ridiculous, and the conduct of my wife is too correct for me to entertain a very serious thought on the subject. I shall, however, inquire about it, and I have little doubt that the result will be satisfactory. If otherwise, I know where to find you, and I flatter myself that you, Captain Dashington, will not refuse, in case of need, to act as my second."

Captain Dashington pressed the hand of his newly acquired friend, and took his departure, while Francis Vyvian pursued his way to the Hummums, where he remained till the following morning.

At three o'clock, in an anxious and troubled state of mind, he hastened to Belgrave-square, and the servant had no sooner opened the door than he rushed up stairs and entered the drawing-room, where, with his own eyes, he beheld Mr. Tift engaged in staying the tears as they fell down Mrs. Vyvian's cheeks. At the sight of him the lady uttered a faint scream, but Mr. Tift, with the most innocent simplicity, explained the nature of his employment.

"Troublesome matter, sir, very troublesome matter indeed to dry up ladies' tears; when once the limpid stream begins to flow it's almost impossible to arrest its progress,"

"Scoundrel!" ejaculated Francis Vyvian, looking scornfully at Mr. Tift, "is it thus you tamper with the peace and honour of your friends? Mrs Vyvian, retire to your apartment."

Mr. Tift turned deadly pale, and, placing himself directly behind Mrs. Vyvian, took tight hold of her gown.

"Pity, very great pity, that Mr. Francis Vyvian should allow his passion to get the better of his reason. Believe my word, sir, passion is not only a magnifier, but a destroyer. By its magical influences, straight appears crooked, and crooked straight—honour assumes the appearance of dishonour."

"Silence, trifler!" furiously exclaimed Francis. "Mrs. Vyvian, will you oblige me by quitting the room?"

"Francis," mournfully exclaimed the lady, "can you—will you forgive me? Indeed—indeed, I will never be so foolish again."

"This is not a time, madam, to talk of forgiveness. The cowardly wretch who shelters himself behind the woman he has irreparably injured is unworthy even my contempt; but——"

"Not another word, sir—not another word, I beg of you; for every injurious expression will by-and-bye occasion you the bitterest regrets. Mrs. Vyvian will, if it pleases her, explain to you the cause and nature of my visit, but if she is unwilling to do so," throwing his card upon the table, "you will find me at home any time this evening after six o'clock."

Mr. Tift quitted the apartment, while Francis Vyvian, with his eyes fixed upon the weeping figure of his wife, his arms folded, waited in silence her explanation.

"Oh, Francis!" sobbed the lady, "only say you will forgive me, and I will tell you everything."

Francis was silent.

"Only say one kind word that I may find courage to confess my folly; for, indeed, as far as Mr. Tift is concerned, you have no cause to be angry with him: he has acted the part of a friend, and I am sure you will say so when you know all."

"If you have committed no impropriety what need have you to fear me?" murmured Francis Vyvian, somewhat relieved by his wife's declaration. "I am not, I think, accustomed to be so very harsh."

Mrs. Vyvian then related her visit to the astrologer's, her meeting with Mr. Tift, and its consequences.

Francis at first looked very grave, though he could scarcely at times repress a smile. However, when his wife had finished her recital, he pressed her affectionately to his bosom, and, after seriously reproving her indiscretion, pointed out the folly of giving credit to the predictions of those ignorant impostors.

"I cannot imagine," said he, "that you seriously believe that those wretched creatures possess the power of revealing the future.. It is well known that they make it their business to learn from servants and neighbours enough to enable them to give a tolerable good guess at many particulars concerning those persons likely to consult them. I

have no doubt that, by indirectly catechising your maid, the man you have visited would, if you had given him another call, have informed you of many past events known only to yourself and those about you."

"That accounts," said Mrs. Vyvian, musingly, "for the very extraordinary family secrets they sometimes disclose."

"Add to that, remember that the man will be sure to boast of your having consulted him, and many poor ignorant creatures may be led by your example to put implicit faith in his falsehoods. But tell me, dearest, on what important subject did you so ardently desire to be enlightened."

Mrs. Vyvian blushed, and, after some hesitation, disclosed the history of her unjust suspicions, and Miss Talbot's departure.

Francis Vyvian was now indeed seriously displeased. He rose from the sofa, and, after pacing about the room for some moments, he decended into the street, intending first to call on Mr. Tift and apologise for his unjust suspicions, and afterwards to use his best endeavours to discover what had become of Miss Talbot.

———

CHAPTER XXI.

THE MUDLARK'S MEETING WITH THE JEW.

PREVIOUS to the Barker's arrival at her own house, the Mudlark had returned to West-street from his visit to the sewers. This time his efforts had been eminently successful.

By some strange coincidence, the ring he had dropped on the occasion of his meeting with Bill Biler had again found its way into his possession.

He was uncertain how to act. He had two loads on his hand—his wife and the ring; and he was aware that it would prove no easy matter to get rid of either of them. His cogitations were disturbed by the arrival of the Barker herself.

During the night several plans for selling the ring suggested themselves to his mind, but they all appeared impracticable on account of the searching inquiry he would have to undergo as to how it came into his possession, till at length he remembered the words " No questions axed," as being inscribed on a board somewhere in the neighbourhood.

Thither he directed his steps the following morning. He passed the shop three or four times, looking furtively in, as if to ascertain who the occupants were, and whether there was any probability of their purchasing the ring.

This shop was a repository of miscellanies strangely collected together, but all of them the proceeds of roguery in some shape or another.

There were old books and clothes, chemical phials and beer bottles, faded finery and cards of invitation, bones and ragged pelisses, and, in short, an assortment of trumpery that seemed hardly worth the room it occupied.

The Mudlark ventured in, when he was accosted by an old hag.

The hag's dull eyes shone brighter when she perceived the diamonds as if illuminated by the transcendent beauty the precious stones possessed. It was but momentary, and its place was immediately usurped by a dull, calculating, greedy stare.

" It ain't of no good to me," said the hag, in a hollow voice. " Will it suit you, Mr. Levi ?"

Previous to this the Mudlark had not discovered the presence of a third person, but now the wasted figure of the Jew emerged from a dark corner.

Abednego Levi and the old hag presented a horrible picture of masculine and feminine depravity.

" That depends upon its quality, my dear," said the Jew.

The hag handed the ring for the inspection of the Jew, while the Mudlark stood by awaiting the result.

The Jew examined it minutely, but he could find no blemish in it : it was perfect.

" What do you want for this ?" demanded Abednego of the Mudlark, in an under tone.

" Ten pounds," was the reply.

The old hag, who till now had leant upon the counter, walked away in the direction of the parlour, as if unwilling to witness any more of the transaction.

" I don't care about having it," replied Abednego, handing the ring back to its owner.

" What will you bid for it ?" asked the Mudlark, without attempting to take it from the Jew.

" Five. A person couldn't well refuse to give six for it, I think : it seems pretty heavy," resumed the Jew, weighing the valuable in his hand. " How did you come by it, ay ?"

" That's no business of yourn," replied the Mudlark, firmly.

" Well, no more it is," responded Abednego. " Will you take five ?"

" That will do," ejaculated the Mudlark.

" You see, these things sometimes lie a long time on our hands," said the Jew, producing the money.

Having obtained the five sovereigns, the Mudlark placed them, for better security, in his waistcoat pocket, and shuffled awkwardly out of the shop. He kept his hand firmly pressed on the exact piece of cloth covering the money, and in a few minutes he had reached his own dwelling. He determined on at once depositing his money in some place of security where it might escape the Barker, who he well knew would dissipate the whole sum in drink.

At the bottom of the stairs there was a crack in the boarding, and, without hesitation, he slipped in his money, sovereign after sovereign, intending to tear up the boards to procure it again. He was not aware of the existence of the Barker's cellar.

Let us now return to the Jew.

Soon after the purchase of the diamond ring Abednego Levi left the old hag's shop, but not without first remunerating her for the part she had taken in the recent transaction with the Mudlark.

Instead of the long cloak he generally wore, a seedy suit of black cloth, trimmed with fur, constituted his morning apparel. There was an appearance of conscious guilt discernable in his bearing, which proved beyond a doubt that he contemplated some illicit proceeding either at the present or some future period.

He soon arrived at his den in Shoreditch.

The two boys had but recently returned from an excursion, and were waiting for breakfast, with which they were never supplied by the Jew until they had earned treble the value of it at least. The booty they had collected was deposited on the table.

Having snatched a hurried meal they were again driven forth into the streets, there to remain till they could obtain a sufficient quantity of plunder to earn their dinner.

They were despatched on the *morning sneak.*

They passed house after house without meeting with an opportunity of exercising their skill, the delay occasioned by the absence of the Jew having caused them to be considerably beyond the hour adapted to this species of depredation.

They resolved on pursuing another course.

Presently they came to a carriage standing at the door of a private house, with an unwieldy coachman sitting on the box, but without any footman behind.

One of the boys passed by the carriage and observed that it was empty, when he returned again to his companion.

" You'd better let me flummux him," said the

* Persons following this species of thieving are termed *area sneaks.* It is their object to enter houses with the doors open, and, while the servant is engaged, to steal anything they can lay their hands upon.

smallest of the two: "I always do your dags that way."

"Go and do it, then," replied the other. "There's no one a-coming, is there?"

"Not a blessed soul."

The youngest boy ran almost under the horse's feet, making a thousand grimaces, and endeavouring by every possible means to terrify the horses. The coachman swore and stamped on his boy till he could tolerate it no longer; but the moment he rose to lash the boy with his whip the other whipped away the great coat upon which he had been sitting, and immediately disappeared up an alley.

The young one ran in the other direction.

By the time the corpulent coachman had descended from his box, it would have been useless to have pursued either.

CHAPTER XXII.

MISS TALBOT ENTERS HER NEW SITUATIO.

THE morning arrived on which Miss Talbot was to quit the house of Mr. Dobbins to repair to the residence of Mrs. Pearson, in Guilford-street.

Mr. and Mrs. Dobbins were loud in their exclamations of regret, especially the lady, who, to increase her regret, had her front room, second-floor, thrown upon her hands. Mr. Dobbins insisted upon seeing Agnes down to the coach, which circumstance tended to excite some degree of jealousy in the breast of his anxious helpmate.

The coach soon arrived in Guilford-street. Agnes was met at the door by the footman, radiant with plush, who carried up her boxes to the front attic, and, having asked whether she required anything more, again descended to the kitchen.

She felt her companionless and unprotected position with arrowy keenness. Unable any longer to control her feelings, she seated herself upon the tent bedstead and wept long and bitterly. Presently the footman knocked at the door.

"If you please, Mrs. Pearson requests your company in the library."

Thither Agnes hastened.

Mrs. Pearson now assumed a more patronising air than she had evinced on the former occasion.

Around the table were seated her future charges.

"Good morning, Miss Talbot," said Mrs. Pearson.

"Good morning, ma'am," she replied, with a curtsey.

"There you will find my regulations and rules written carefully out, and by them you must regulate my children's studies," observed Mrs. Pearson, leading Agnes to a corner of the room, and pointing to a strip of paper pasted against the wall,

"Very well, ma'am."

"Let me see: it is now a quarter to twelve, they ought to be doing arithmetic. However, as it is so near the time for it, let them begin geography. Which maps do you consider the best?"

"I really hardly know, ma'am."

But, after Agnes had made this confession, the lady's countenance assumed such a stern stare, that the young girl glanced timidly at the maps on the table, and replied,—

"I think those you have, ma'am, are as good as any."

"I have many reasons to think so, too," responded Mrs. Pearson; "so now, if you please, we will commence."

"Don't you hate maps, Kate?" asked the boy.

"Hold your tongue, sir, and attend to what Miss Talbot is going to say to you," ejaculated the lady, who had taken a seat by the window.

The three children looked anxious to hear what she *was* going to say to them, while Agnes appeared confused beyond measure.

At last the juvenile trio burst into a hearty laugh.

"I'm afraid you are too young to inspire my children with respect; still I am inclined to give you every trial," observed Mrs. Pearson. "I am now obliged to pay my morning visits. That paper will give you every requisite information; and mind I always have it pasted there for fear it might get lost. There is another in your bed-room—a perfect fac-simile of that; when you awake tomorrow morning read it over, and continue to do so every morning till you know it by heart. You will, if you please, dine in the nursery with the children at one o'clock."

Having delivered these commands, Mrs. Pearson quitted the library.

When one o'clock arrived, Agnes and the children went up stairs to the nursery to dinner, and at the same table was seated the nursery-maid.

"You've been blubbering, haven't you?" said the boy, addressing Agnes.

"Be quiet, Master Richard, do," cried the nursery-maid.

"I shan't for you," was the reply.

"Nor me either," added the youngest girl. "Would you, Kate?"

"I shan't have any more books to-day, I can tell her that," said Kate, pointing with her finger at Agnes.

"Hold your tongue, Miss Kate; for shame!" exclaimed the servant.

The child pouted at the nursery-maid in reply.

The remainder of the day was spent by Agnes much in the same manner, till, at a somewhat early hour, she retired with a heavy heart to sleep.

CHAPTER XXIII.

THE QUEEN MOTHER.

The reader will have already perceived that Mr. Tift was a doubtful character.

It is now our intention to clear up the mist which has hitherto hung over his domestic concerns.

When Mr. Tift left the baronet's residence he proceeded to a house in Euston-square, which he entered in such a familiar manner as to convey the idea that he was no stranger to it.

Having ascended the stairs, and arrived at the front drawing-room, he knocked gently at the door.

"Come in, whoever you may be," said a woman, authoritatively, in a masculine tone of voice.

"I am your Irish Majesty's loyal subject, and your most affectionate and dutiful son," exclaimed Mr. Tift, bowing reverentially as he spoke the words.

Her Irish Majesty took no further notice of her dutiful son than by giving him a terrific nod, probably intended as a signal for silence.

In her years the Queen Mother appeared to have considerably exceeded the meridian of life. She wore on her head a purple turban, and she was seated on an elevated wooden throne. Occasionally a look of idiotic insanity would play across her features. In her diseased imagination she supposed herself to be the next heir to the throne of Ireland, and, although an unfortunate fog hung over the river of linial descent—a lapse of a couple of centuries or so—yet her son, Adolphus Tift—who was hardly less crack-brained than herself—thought fit to coincide with the opinion. During the earlier part of his life-time he had used every effort to persuade people that he was an Irish prince of the blood royal, but, nobody giving credence to his statements but an old, one-eyed domestic, who still resided with her Majesty, he was contented with treating his mother as her rank deserved, and looking upon himself as a man who had been robbed of a kingdom. The father of Mr. Tift had been an Englishman, and, as he himself had never visited Ireland in the whole course of his life-time, there was but little Hibernian matter in his composition.

The income of the Irish Queen being very inadequate to support her dignity, and Mr. Tift being rather a drag upon her than otherwise, she was quite as often an inmate of Whitecross-street as of the palace in Euston-square—in short, she was a notorious swindler, and so was her loyal son, who only lived at Long's hotel till the waiter would wait no longer, and then—unless some providential swindle or lucky gaming transaction should occur - that gentleman would act as he had often done before—by changing his name to *Walker*.

"Adolphus," said the Queen, "provide yourself with pen, ink, and paper."

Adolphus Tift obeyed the royal mandate.

"Now write what I dictate. Are you prepared?"

"I am, my lady mother."

"'*Wanted*, several respectable young women, who may be taught a genteel business, at which they can earn from fifteen to twenty-five shillings per week, and have constant employment.' Insert that in the *Times*, and by that means I hope to settle with one or two creditors, who are insolently pressing."

"But you can hardly do it at your own house, my lady mother," exclaimed Tift.

"Martha, my maid of honour, will personate myself, and I only request that you will do as you are desired."

At this moment an altercation arose in the passage between a desperate creditor and the one-eyed domestic, Martha.

"Her Majesty cannot be seen to-day," said Martha.

"Humbug!" roared the creditor, who was no other than Mr. Dobbins; "do you think you're going to make a fool of me in this manner?"

Mr. Dobbins brushed by the domestic, and fearlessly entered her Majesty's presence.

"Her Majesty cannot be disturbed," said Mr. Tift.

"D—n her Majesty!" replied the now infuriated hosier. "If you don't pay I'll summons you for the money."

"I shall see that my lady mother pays you off, and deals with somebody else," exclaimed Mr. Tift.

"I wish you would," was the reply. "She has owed me ten pounds these two years, and, whenever I come for my money, I get nothing but some cursed nonsense about her being the Queen of Ireland."

Her Hibernian Majesty appeared to be entirely unconscious of the existence of the scene that was passing before her eyes.

"You are nothing but a set of swindlers, the whole of you. But I'll summons you for the money. I'm not going to be done out of it, I can tell you." And, having so far given vent to his feelings, the angry hosier prepared to leave.

His company was not exceedingly agreeable to either the royal mother or the princely son.

"You had better insert that advertisement as speedily as possible," said the lady mother.

"The first thing in the morning," was the answer.

After bowing respectfully Mr. Tift descended the stairs, and directed his steps to Long's hotel.

CHAPTER XXIV.

THE INTERRUPTION.

" WELL, Amelia, you will, I think, be glad to hear that your old admirer, Lord Oxburn, will dine with us to-morrow," said Sir Richard Vyvian, while thoughtfully pacing the room, appearing almost entirely absorbed in studying the pattern of the carpet.

Amelia blushed deeply and bent over her embroidery frame.

" May I hope that my pretty sister will agree with me that, if his lordship should think proper to renew his attentions, a more eligible opportunity of becoming a countess cannot present itself ?"

" If you are really speaking seriously, Richard," replied Amelia, " perhaps it may be as well to remind you that you have more than once lamented his lordship's embarrassed circumstances; and, though I am by no means an advocate for interested marriages, I am not so violently smitten with Lord Oxburn as voluntarily to unite myself to his poverty."

" Ha! ha! ha!" laughed the baronet. " I really congratulate you upon your prudence and foresight —so very, very much unlike your dear little self. But when I tell you, Amelia, that Lord Oxburn is heir to the old Earl of Torrington, I think you will acquit me of any intention to wed you to a beggar."

Amelia at this moment was so busily engaged in disentangling her silk that she did not appear to have heard her brother's observation — at any rate, she made no reply, and the baronet continued,—

" You are aware, Amelia, that, last year, when the old earl, struck with your beauty, endeavoured to interest me in his favour, I openly discountenanced his advances. His age, his infirmities more than counterbalanced the advantages of his rank and fortune : but the nephew, what can you possibly have to urge against Lord Oxburn ?"

" That he accuses my kind, generous-hearted brother of conspiring to effect his ruin," said Amelia, rising from her seat, and affectionately embracing the baronet.

" Well, Milly," returned Sir Richard, " think of what I have said, love. Heaven knows that it will be a sad day for me when deprived of your society I wander solitary about these stately apartments, but circumstances are such that I shall never feel happy till I see you wedded to a husband deserving of you : and I think I can, without fear that you will ever have cause to repent following my advice, recommend Lord Oxburn to you."

" But how do you know, Richard, that Lord Oxburn will take compassion upon your poor sister ?" said Amelia, laughing.

" Leave that to me, Milly : only give me the assurance that you will consent to marry him, and I will take care to bring the match about : only you are sometimes such a whimsical little puss, that I was afraid to take a single step till I knew the state of your feelings towards him ; and now I think there is no occasion for further explanation. Your first blush spoke volumes, and your silence proclaims your consent."

" Gently, gently ; don't, I pray you, draw such hasty conclusions ; but be content that, when I do marry, it shall be with your consent or not at all. At present I can say no more, so let us converse about other things."

" I wish you would agree to accompany Francis on a tour, which he intends to make next summer, to the Highlands. We shall be a delightful party if Mrs. Vyvian—who generally contrives to make everything uncomfortable—will endeavour to control her temper."

" And pray who will the party consist of ?" said the baronet.

" Francis and Alexandrine, the Carringtons, Lady Elizabeth Hamilton, Frederick, and Amelia Stamer (Vyvian I mean)," said the young lady, blushing.

" And Mr. Stamer," added the baronet carelessly. " Well, Milly, we shall have plenty of time to arrange before next summer, and perhaps we may prevail upon Oxburn to accompany us. With regard to Mr. Stamer, I shall confer with Francis upon the propriety of admitting a *parvenu* into the privacy of a family party."

" A *parvenu !*" ejaculated Amelia. " I certainly consider Mr. Stamer as eminently superior to many of the titled butterflies who favour us with their visits."

" Butterfly Oxburn excepted, I suppose, Milly," returned the baronet.

" No, Richard ; I will admit of no exceptions ; and if Mr. Stamer is as you represent him—a *parvenu*—I consider that his superiority more than ever entitles him to our esteem and respect."

" Amelia, I have heard such various reports of his name and origin, that I almost repent having introduced him into our family. However, as it would not be convenient to break with him immediately, I suppose I must tolerate him—at least, for a season ; but, if I am not very much mistaken, long before next summer he will be stripped of his golden plumage, and then we shall see of what material your pretty bird is really made. It is a pity young men will go their own way, and reject friendly advice."

At this moment the door opened wide, and a servant announced " Miss Talbot." The baronet, after changing a few complimentary inquiries, quitted the apartment, while Amelia took the hand of her visiter, and, pressing it affectionately, led her to a couch. Without assigning any cause for having left Mrs. Vyvian, Agnes informed Miss Vyvian of her engagement with Mrs. Pearson.

Amelia, who was too well acquainted with the temper of her sister-in-law not to anticipate that something unpleasant had happened, contented herself with expressing wishes for the happiness of her young friend.

"You are pale, Agnes," said she, in a tone of sympathy that touched the heart of the friendless girl. "Is there anything I can do for you?"

"I have suffered much, very much, since the death of my parent," replied Miss Talbot, and tears filled her eyes at the rememberance of her loss. "They are gone. But the hope of rejoining them in a better world strengthens me to persevere in my endeavours to become worthy of them. Educated and brought up as I have been in the lap of indulgence, it is not surprising that I am painfully sensible of my dependent position."

"Poor Agnes!" sighed Amelia, deeply affected by the similarity of their orphan condition. "How I wish that you had made me acquainted with your intention of leaving Belgrave-square; we should have been so happy to receive you."

"I thank you kindly, Miss Vyvian," said Agnes, rising to take her leave. "I was compelled for a short time to avoid any part of your family till a circumstance, which I knew would soon be cleared up, would enable me to meet Mrs. Vyvian without danger of incurring her further displeasure. I flatter myself that by this time she is fully convinced that her suspicions were without foundation."

"But you are not going to leave us?" replied Amelia. "Surely you can remain the rest of the day."

"It was with great difficulty," returned Agnes, "that I obtained permission to leave home even for an hour. Mrs. Pearson is so anxious for the improvement of her children, that she considers it necessary that I should devote to them every moment of my time."

Miss Vyvian, with tears in her eyes, pressed the hand of Agnes, who, after promising to call as often as she could, hastened down stairs, leaving Amelia painfully impressed with the miseries of dependence.

CHAPTER XXV.

THE HELL IN CASTLE STREET.

In a recent chapter we left Abednego Levi in his own den in Shoreditch.

The evening of the same day that witnessed his transaction with the Mudlark, saw the Jew on his road to Castle-street, Leicester-square.

He was habited in a seedy black coat, trimmed with fur, the same that he had worn when at the marine-store dealer's, and he had evidently been endeavouring to assume as respectable an appearance as his slender wardrobe would permit.

Abednego arrived at a coffee-house in Castle-street, and walked into the back parlour, where there was a trap-door immediately over his head.

He knocked on the trap-door three times with his stick, when it was slowly opened, and a ladder was lowered down, up which he climbed into the room above. No sooner had he entered, than the ladder was drawn up, and the trap-door tightly closed again.

The room into which he stepped was long and dark, very inferior in all its appointments, and tenanted almost entirely by foreigners. There were Frenchmen, Italians, Jews, Germans, and Spaniards, with here or there a Portuguese or an American. The Jew seated himself at a table, when an Italian took up his position opposite to him, and the two commenced playing at *Hazard.*

The Italian was dressed in a double-breasted coat, of blue cloth, and profusely braided on the breast; he wore moustachos, with his hair hanging in ringlets. In this *ci-divant* officer's uniform he was accustomed to parade the Quadrant, the Parks, and other places of fashionable resort; for what purposes the reader will readily conjecture.

The Jew lost sovereign after sovereign without even a prospect of a change of fortune, and the Italian Count pocketed the money, with a smile of satisfaction.

At length Abednego placed his hands upon his knees, and intimated to the Italian Count that he had nothing left to lose.

The Italian looked around to see whether there was an opportunity of exercising his skill, but perceiving none, he entered into familiar conversation with the Jew.

"How goes it vid your business, mine vas nevare more flourishing?" said the Italian.

"Nor mine either," replied the Jew, "but you have made a little hole in my gains to night; it's very seldom, very seldom that I get anything by coming here, yet I'm fool enough to do it."

"You've got a fortune somevere in the country, me feel sure of dat."

"If people will think so, I can't help it, because I don't spend my money as you do, for instance; it's a mistake, quite a mistake."

"It's very unimportant to me whether you have or have not," replied the Italian, carelessly, "but with such smart boys as yours are, and such fly fellows as de Duffare and Tim Roper about you, if you have not made a tidy sum, it's your own fault."

"So it is," said the Jew.

At this moment a Frenchman became extremely noisy.

He had been bilked of a considerable sum, by a Jew sitting opposite to him, and was evidently determined not to quietly submit to his losses.

"*Mon Dieu,*" cried the Frenchman.

"Vat you mean?" asked the Jew.

Another quarrel now occured.

A stranger to the place had won a large sum of money, and was endeavouring to get away with the proceeds of his luck, but this the regular frequenters of the place would on no account permit.

No sooner had he announced it to be his full determination to quit, than a scene of scandalous violence took place.

The lights were blown out; the occupants of the hell struck each other at random, but what appeared to be a sudden affray was, in reality, a preconcerted quarrel, intended as a means of preventing the stranger from leaving the den with a single particle of property about him.

After the Jew had been for some time sheltering himself in a corner, he made a movement towards the trap-door, when his foot came in contact with a soft substance on the ground, which he immediately possessed himself of, and cautiously deposited it in his pocket. He opened the trap-door, put down the ladder, and descended into the room below.

The Italian immediately followed.

Then the ladder was whipped up by somebody above, a fresh altercation arose, and several of the company preferred effecting their exits by tumbling through the trap-door, to remaining in the den above.

Some were stunned, while others escaped uninjured.

A cry having arisen that the Bobbies were coming, the Jew hurried away from the coffee-house, but not till he had ascertained the nature of the article he had posssessed himself of, which proved to be a pocket-book well lined with bank notes.

Abednego Levi returned to his own miserable dwelling.

The Italian directed his steps to Saffron-lane.

CHAPTER XXVI.

INCONSTANCY.

Mrs. Dobbins was sitting at work in her little parlour, when her husband returned home from Euston-square.

"Got the money, dear?" said she, looking inquiringly as he entered the room.

"Money, no; nor never shall," replied Mr. Dobbins; "and, by jingo, we are in a pretty pickle. Scamps and Blubbers have stopped payment, and now how the devil am I to pay my rent?"

"Your rent; didn't you pay it at Christmas, then?"

"Why no," said Mr. Dobbins, looking rather bothered; "I gave a bill for three months, hoping by that time I should make up the money without being compelled to draw upon my banker, but now the game is evidently up with them, and I'm a ruined man. But how confoundedly bad the fire is," and Mr. Dobbins gave two or three desperate pokes. His wife, astounded by the abrupt and sudden disclosure of her husband's difficulties, sat pale, sick, and faint; her spirit seemed entirely to have deserted her, her husband's rose in proportion.

"You certainly told me you had paid the rent," timidly ventured the wife.

"What I told you then was a piece of infernal humbug, what I tell you now is the truth."

Mr. Dobbins might have added that the money he intended for the rent he had foolishly lost in a billiard room, but this he said nothing about, but continued venting his ill humour till Lucy came into the room.

At the sight of his favourite child he extended his arms, and, pressing her to his bosom with tears in his eyes, thanked God that one child at least would be sheltered from the coming storm. Lucy, who was not prepared for this tender reception, burst into tears, and, putting a letter into her father's hand, laid her head upon his shoulder, and sobbed violently.

Mr. Dobbins read the letter; then, dashing it on the table. exclaimed—.

"The pitiful scoundrel! but never mind, Lucy, your father is neither so old nor so crippled, that he cannot pay him off in good style. Dash my buttons if I don't pummel his little marrow bones into a jelly before I've done with him. Gone to be married, eh! The devil choke him. Why did he come here stealing my girl's affections?"

Mrs. Dobbins now took up the letter, which ran as follows :—

"Dear Lucy,—I'm afraid you will not very readily appreciate my motives, because I don't somehow or other think that you are at all up to the right and wrong of things. You know, Lucy, and I dare say will readily own, that though I have talked nonsense to you, as I have indeed many girls before I knew you, I never precisely said that I would marry you, though I should have done so had I found you as I, blinded by your pretty face, at first thought you. But no matter now, your faults or your virtues can be nothing to me, as you will see by the following :— A lady in my first floor, worth some little money, has consented to become my wife. I marry her to-morrow in obedience to the wishes of my parents; and, as I know that a tobacconist in your neighbourhood looks very sweet upon you, take my advice, Lucy, submit to the will of your father and mother, marry the man they so highly approve of; for, take my word, Lucy, that though love is all very well money is a great deal better.

"Now don't take on, and fancy you can't like any body but me, and all that sort of thing; get another sweetheart, and you will soon be as happy as

"Yours truly, Thomas Garnet.

"P.S.—I have sold my business, and shall most probably never again return to London.

"Exeter."

"The villain!" ejaculated Mrs. Dobbins, as she tenderly kissed her daughter.

"Father and I, gal, are talking upon business; go and find Sophy."

"Well now, then, which way are we to turn

curselves?" said Mr. Dobbins, as Lucy closed the door; "troubles seem to beset us on every side."

"And all through your skating on Sundays, instead of going to chapel like an honest man with your wife and family. I am sure of it, sir, and I've told you long enough, that if you didn't reform your manners, your prosperity would soon be at an end. But, oh! I was a fool, knew nothing, no, nothing at all; never set my foot in a decent house till I married you, though you know as well as I do that my poor father kept the sign of the 'Three Tuns,' Fetter-lane, upwards of twenty years, during which time I was never in the bar save twice—once when I was christened, and the nurse, to prevent my catching cold, poured a drop of spirit down my throat; and the other time when you, artful like, came suddenly in, pretending you had the spasms, and I, hearing that a strange gentleman was taken very bad, ran out, and who should I see but you; and didn't you say that you'd soon be well if I'd mix a strong glass of brandy-and-water and bring it you myself? which, fool like, father being out of the way, I did; and that's how you and I first became acquainted, you know."

Mr. Dobbins made no reply, but, deeply engaged in his own meditations, he kept pacing to and fro till suddenly a thought struck him. He took up his hat, and was about to pass into the street, when the entrance of Mr. Pearson induced him to return into the parlour.

"A cold day, sir," said the auctioneer, as he stealthily crept through the shop into the parlour. "Was just passing by, and called in to see how you all get on."

Mrs. Dobbins apologised for the fire, which her husband immediately deluged with coals.

"Smoky chimney," muttered Mr. Pearson, as he retreated from the fire-place, enveloped in a cloud of smoke.

"No, we don't smoke generally, sir," said Mrs. Dobbins: "but I suppose the wind's in the wrong quarter."

Mr. Dobbins now set to work in right earnest in unloading the fire, which soon burnt up briskly, and Mr. Pearson again took his seat by the side of it.

He had evidently something to say, but was at a loss how to deliver himself of his burden.

Mrs. Dobbins, with the delicate discernment of her sex, readily discovered his embarrassment, and, without asking any questions, placed a bottle of brandy, two glasses, some hot water, and sugar upon the table.

Mr. Pearson perceiving the preparations, declared that it was time for him to think of returning home; but Mrs. Dobbins insisted so urgently upon his only tasting the mixture, which she had prepared with her own hands, that he sat down again, and, by the time that the two gentlemen had finished their brandy-and-water, Mr. Pearson and

Dobbins were metamorphosed into the Pearson and Dobbins of former days.

"I say, Dobbins," said Pearson, "I'm going to tell you a capital joke. My old lady's determined Lucretia shall marry a lord. Ha! ha! ha! Only fancy Timothy Pearson's daughter going to court."

Mr. and Mrs. Dobbins joined vociferously in the laugh; the tumblers were replenished, and Mr. Pearson continued,—

"My wife, you know, is determined to go the rig. She bothered me out of my life till I bought the house in Guilford-street, hired servants and governess, and set up for a gentleman. Now you know, Dobbins, I haven't been used to all these figaries, and, upon my honour, I often wish, with all my heart, that I was in our old lodging in St. Martin's-lane. I have never been happy since, Mrs. Dobbins."

"I dare say not, sir," replied the good lady.

"Then there's Lucretia—so proud and saucy; she'll scarce speak to her old father. But she's to marry a lord, and that's the reason, Mr. Dobbins," stammered the auctioneer, with some gravity, "that my wife sent me to tell you that your company won't suit us; it won't do to introduce hosiers to people of quality."

The latter part of Mr. Pearson's speech was lost upon Mr. Dobbins, who had fallen asleep, which Mr. Pearson perceiving had sense enough to rise from his chair, bow stiffly to Mrs. Dobbins, walk through the passage, and call a hackney coach.

"Well, did I ever see such insolence!" exclaimed Mrs. Dobbins, as she vainly endeavoured to rouse her husband. "We are fallen low in the world, indeed. And to think of that nasty, upstart, impudent Lucretia, marrying a Lord. I don't believe it's any thing but a pack of lies." Then a violent burst of tears effected what neither pinching nor speaking had been able to do. Mr. Dobbins awoke, and being able to make neither head nor tail of his wife's story, he took his candle and went to bed.

————

CHAPTER XXVII.

THE ITALIAN BOYS.

THE reader will remember that we left the Italian count on his way to Saffron-lane.

On arriving in that vicinity he walked at a slower pace till he reached a low pot-house, when, although dressed out in his flash clothes, he entered a parlour, in which were assembled nine or ten Italian boys. This was a "Retreat" for foreign "Cadgers."

The toils of the day over, the Italian boys were amusing themselves in an uproarious manner. Some performed feats of strength with their teeth, while others played at games peculiar to themselves.

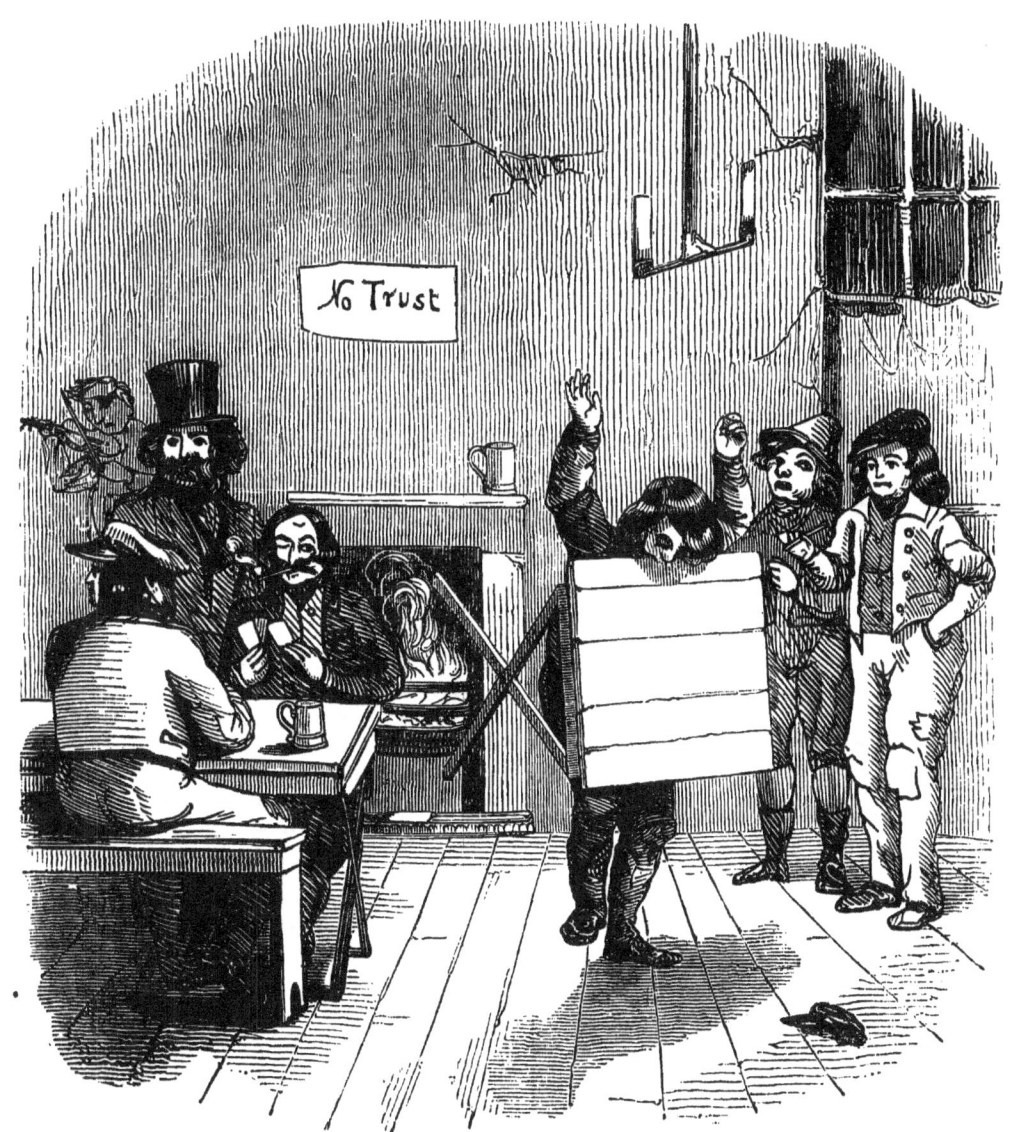

One or two danced round the room, carrying tables with their teeth. Some whiled away the time at a numerical game, and the count seated himself amongst them, leisurely puffing away at a cigar.

The count was the master of these boys, and in the East-end he might be seen dressed as a beggar, but in the West-end he pretended to be a count and an Italian officer. He lived upon what the organ-boys gained, but, besides this, he was a notorious gambler, and a frequenter of all the foreign "hells" in the neighbourhood of Leicester-square. In Saffron-lane he generally wore a patch over one eye, a mangy fur cap, and a ragged coat; but when he paraded the Quadrant, or gambled in a "hell," he was dressed as he was on the present occasion. The Italian now demanded the gains of each.

Eighteenpence was the average amount he received from each boy; only two were minus that sum, and they seemed fully aware of the brutal reception they would meet with from their master. The Italian seized them, one after another, by one leg and the back of their collars, and dashed them savagely against the floor, and, that portion of the punishment over, he pulled their hair and ears with truly demoniacal malice; then he kicked them into a corner of the room, where they continued for the remainder of the evening.

Two other masters entered. One was handsomely dressed, having just returned from a "hell"; the other was clothed in rags. The two gamblers seated themselves together at a table, while the ragged one fell asleep on a bench.

The boys supped off bread and cheese, onions, polonies, apples, and porter: but the two whose individual gains had been minus eighteenpence received no supper at all.

The two gamblers initiated each other into all tricks at cards which they intended practising that evening at one of those "hells" that keep open all night.

"Now, suppose we practise the *bridge*," said one.

"Here goes, den," replied the other.

The *bridge* was a technical term for slightly curving a card, when, shuffle the pack as your opponent will, you cannot fail to be able to cut the bridged one.

"Now I can do dat perfect," said the new comer.

Here a message arrived that the attendance of one of the masters was desired at the bar.

The ragged one immediately obeyed the summons.

After a few minutes' absence he returned and whispered something into the ear of the one who had won from Abednego Levi at the "hell" in Castle-street.

A ferocious frown, pregnant with meaning, was discernible on the ruffian's brow.

"Now, den, boys, get off to de bed," said the sham count. "You can stay," added he, pointing to one of the group, who turned deadly pale at this announcement.

The boys all slept together in one room without bedding or bedsteads, but on the bare ground, while the masters had comfortable, well-furnished sleeping apartments up stairs.

"You *leetle* villain!" said one of the masters, who spoke better English than the other two, addressing himself to the boy who remained; "so you blabbed upon us, did you?"

The olive complexion of the boy assumed a still deadlier hue.

"You shan't have de power to do dat agen," exclaimed the ragged one.

The boy instantly understood his meaning, fell upon his knees, and, in an agony of despair, craved for mercy. The sham count seized him tightly by the throat to prevent his raising an alarm, and, with the assistance of the ragged one, lifted him on to the table. In an instant his arms and legs were pinioned, and a gag was placed over his mouth.

The ragged one then produced from his waistcoat pocket a sharp steel instrument, somewhat resembling a lancet or a penknife, yet materially different to either. Now commenced the horrible operation of cutting out his tongue.

Till the present moment the boy had appeared stunned with terror, but now he evidently writhed in his bonds; the inhuman preparations he witnessed completely roused him from the torpor by which he had been influenced.

All his struggles were ineffectual, but the workings of his mind were fearfully portrayed upon his countenance. His brows were knit, his hands clenched, his pallid lips tightly compressed together, his features were hardly less hideous to behold than those of his cowardly tormentors.

Who can imagine the feelings that were his at that moment! They must have been horrible—very horrible!

The operation terminated in about two minutes; but that space, short as it was, seemed to him whole ages of torment and despair.

The Italian count dangled the dismembered tongue before the eyes of the boy, dancing with savage glee, and gloating over the acute misery of his victim.

How long will such scenes occur in a populous city where a large sum is annually expended on the maintenance and clothing of a body of men who profess to prevent their existence!

"Shall ve hab him fingers too?" inquired the ragged one.

The other master, who as yet had taken no part in the proceedings, interfered in the boy's behalf. Villain as he was, he shuddered at such unparalleled cruelty.

"This will do for de present," said he, in a conciliating tone.

With some reluctance the sham count motioned to the ragged one to carry the boy away. The ragged one obeyed, and, having staunched the blood, and roughly dressed the wound, flung the body into a dark, damp cellar, where, in company with a jug of water and a dozen or two of rats, he might groan and moan to his heart's content.

Before the sham count and his companion were reseated at the table, the ragged one again entered the room, and whispered into the count's ear.

"Him vants some good teeth," said the sham count; "and he shall hab 'em."

"That fellow hab got no tongue; what can he vant with teeth?" exclaimed the other master, in whose breast the hope of gain had stifled all feelings of compunction.

"Very true. Take the dentist with you, and let him extract as many as he likes," cried the count.

The ragged one again obeyed, and presently returned with twelve shillings, the dentist having chosen six teeth, and paid two shillings for each.

"Did he see the tongue cut out?" asked the count.

"No, because I put de gag on his mouth to hinder him calling out," was the reply, coupled with a knowing leer.

"Here's a young gent a-wanting of you," said the landlord, putting his head into the room.

The ragged one followed the landlord out.

"It's a artist that vants a model, so I bid him call agen in the morning," observed the ragged one on entering the room.

"Dat's de way ob doing," responded the count.

Here there were three knocks at the door.

"Come in," cried the sham count.

A short, powerful, repulsive-looking man, with a cadaverous countenance, and a long sack on his back, entered the room. This was a resurrectionist.

" Vell, Tim," exclaimed the count.

" Have yer got the subject?" demanded the man, whom the reader will readily recognise as being Tim Roper.

On a signal being given by the count, the ragged one went to procure the body, with which he presently returned, and deposited his burden on one of the benches.

" It's in deuced bad condition; in my opinion, it's a better subject for sausage meat than for the 'ospitals. Howsomdever, there's your money." And Tim Roper counted over ten sovereigns to the Italian, and, putting the corpse head foremost into his bag, flung it carelessly across his shoulders. " If it vasn't that the law lags a feller for resurrectionising, I wouldn't give that money for it, covered as it is with bruises, and half starved into the bargain," cried he, quitting the room.

The ragged one remained at home to watch the boys, while the sham count and his companion sallied out to one of the " night hells," with the intention of fleecing any greenhorn they might come across. They slept and acted as organ masters all day, but commenced their genteel avocations at night.

CHAPTER XXVIII.

THE ACCIDENT.

FRANCIS VYVIAN returned home after three or four hours of fruitless inquiry.

" I have not heard anything of Miss Talbot," said he, addressing his wife ; " and it is impossible to say what inconvenience and distress your unkindness may occasion her."

" Agnes is quite safe, my dear." replied Mrs. Vyvian, laughing. " The milliner, on whom you called yesterday, has written me a letter, informing me that she has learned from one of her young people that Miss Talbot is in a situation ; so, after all, my unkindness, it seems, has done her an eminent service, for she is exactly made for a governess. So quiet, so demure, so patient, that I often felt inclined to quarrel with her, merely to see if she could possibly fall into a passion ; but I never succeeded: poor Agnes kept her temper, and I my opinion—that she is a poor, inanimate, mean-spirited creature, precisely suited to the occupation she has chosen."

" Whatever Miss Talbot's qualifications may be, I cannot say that I at all agree with you in thinking that poor, inanimate, mean-spirited girls make desirable governesses," responded Francis. " It is, indeed, a painful truth that they require a more than ordinary stock of patience and meekness to enable them to endure, without repining, the affronts, contempts, passions, and sometimes evil words, which assail them ; but surely, Alexandrine, the exercise of these virtues entitles them to respect rather than contempt."

" Pray, Francis, leave off preaching about governesses," said Mrs. Vyvian, " and take the trouble to rise from your seat and look at this beautiful horse kicking and prancing. Oh, Francis! it is Captain Dashington ; he is thrown."

Francis Vyvian rushed from the window down the stairs into the street just in time to assist the captain, who had risen from the pavement, but appeared in danger of falling again. A gentleman, who declared himself a surgeon, very obligingly assisted in leading him into the house, and Francis Vyvian invited the stranger to examine the wounds.

The captain groaned heavily, and appeared unable to utter a syllable.

" I am afraid he is very bad," said Francis, in a low voice.

" It is necessary that the gentleman be kept quiet, but I do not apprehend any immediate danger," returned Mr. Skelton.

" No bones broken or fractured I hope ?" inquired Francis, as he turned into another apartment.

" The external bruises are in appearance trifling, but one of the most important parts of the human frame is injured," replied the surgeon, with rather a ludicrous solemnity. " I allude, sir, to that important member of the body which, by the various actions it enables us to perform, forms one of the principal distinctions between man and the inferior animals. Without the advantage of such an instrument, man, with all his boasted superiority of reason and intellect, could perform but little. The *digiti manus*, situated at the extremity of the metatorpus, are sprained more or less, every one of them."

" If the captain has sustained no other injury than a few bruises and a sprained finger or two, I think we may sincerely congratulate him upon his fortunate escape," said Francis, turning to re-enter the patient's room.

" Gently, sir, gently," whispered the doctor. " I have already expressed my opinion that the patient should not be disturbed, as it is not improbable that hemurrhage may ensue."

The surgeon bowed his leave, and requested that one of the housemaids might be permitted to remain in the patient's room.

For some days the captain was confined to his bed, and not allowed to speak above a whisper.

" 'Pon honour, Skelton, it's too bad of you to keep me stewing here in bed, day after day, upon water-gruel," said Captain Dashington, " I'm so confoundedly hungry that I positively can bear it no longer."

" Patience, patience," cried the doctor gravely,

feeling the captain's pulse. "You are not well enough to go into the drawing-room. The Cutis— an elastic, sensible, porous, and thick membrane— lying between the crete mucasum and the adipose membrane, and covering the whole body, has been partially removed, and——"

"Pray cease your gibberish, Skelton, and take off some of the blankets, or I shall be suffocated," roared the captain, in a voice very unlike that of a sick man.

But Skelton was inexorable, and, instead of complying with the captain's request, when the servant re-entered the room he took her aside and ordered that more blankets should be spread upon the bed, and that the patient should on no account be furnished with any other nourishment than water-gruel.

"Dem'me if I don't pay you off," muttered the captain, casting an infuriated glance at the doctor.

The doctor nodded assent, and desired that, if he made the slightest resistance, force might be used to compel him to submit, as his life depended upon his compliance. "If he 's very unruly," added he, "shave his head and put a blister upon it."

"Larh, poor art, do hark at him, sir," said the nurse, touching her forehead, and looking knowingly at the doctor. "I never eard the like of him."

The captain listened attentively to the directions given by the doctor, and, thinking that he had better submit with a good grace, bore, with exemplary patience, the addition of two blankets, and swallowed basin after basin of water-gruel without even murmuring.

At last he was declared convalescent, and permitted to descend into the drawing-room.

Habited in a very becoming dressing gown—pale, and so weak that he was scarcely able to stand,— Captain Dashington presented himself before Mrs. Vyvian, leaning upon the arm of her husband.

In appearance he was what young ladies call, "interesting." This latest glance in the glass had confirmed him in his opinion, that few hearts could withstand the artillery of his handsome eyes, and he resolved on the present occasion to raise the siege and show no quarter.

But Mrs. Vyvian was in no humour to be courted. Blessed with almost uninterrupted good health, she was exceedingly impatient of the care and trouble incident upon sickness.

She had a decided antipathy to the smell of physic, the sight of water-gruel, and the confined air of a sick room, made her ill. Added to these objections, she experienced a feeling of jealousy that any other than herself should become an object of solicitude and attention.

From her infancy, her parents, her nurse, her governess, her father's servants, had all been perpetually engaged in studying her caprices and anticipating her wishes. What wonder, then, that she was so jealous of attention, so selfish, so un- prepared to fulfil the duties of a daughter, wife, or mother.

Captain Dashington, who had hitherto only seen her in society, had been fascinated by the *piquante naiveté* of her manners, so different from the studied courtesy of the ladies of fashion, in whose society he had been accustomed to mingle, but he was not prepared to find this "child of nature," as he termed her, cold, heartless, and unfeeling.

He had intended to throw himself at her feet, and acknowledge that, made desperate by the difficulty he had found in approaching her, he had purposely arranged the accident. He fondly imagined that his tottering gait, his palid countenance, would have touched her feelings, and have pleaded forgiveness for his temerity more powerfully than even language could have done.

But he had not been more than five minutes in Mrs. Vyvian's company before he discovered his mistake. Extremely annoyed at the fuss he had occasioned, and the interest he had momentarily excited, when he entered the room, she received him very coldly, and was more than usually vexed to find that Francis increased in his attentions towards his guest in proportion as she appeared to neglect him.

If Skelton had not been a party concerned in the scheme, Captain Dashington would undoubtedly have relinquished his attention, but when he reflected that his character as a man of gallantry was at stake, he resolved to turn in his mind the best manner of effecting his purpose. The entrance of Amelia Vyvian put an end to a reverie which he had been permitted to enjoy undisturbed for nearly an hour, an engagement having compelled Francis to absent himself.

Mrs. Vyvian was reading, or rather skimming over the pages of a book of poems. "What a happiness it is you have called this morning," said she, vainly endeavouring to subdue the effusion of scarlet, which, at the sight of her sister-in-law's beauty, covered her face and neck. "Francis has gone out and has left me all alone, that is to say, almost alone, for the company of an invalid is more unpleasant than otherwise. He has been asleep these two hours, snoring, and snuffling, and moaning." The Captain's ears tingled; but he, notwithstanding, still maintained the tranquillity of sleep; conscious, that if Mrs. Vyvian was incapable of appreciating his elegant attitude and appearance, Amelia would not fail to do so.

Miss Vyvian approached him stealthily, and for some moments stood gazing admiringly: flattered beyond measure by this gratification of his vanity the Captain could scarcely contain his ecstacy.

"Pray give me a pencil and a piece of drawing-paper," said Amelia, "that I may scketch this gallant captain, for I have been dying for the figure of a sick linendraper to illustrate a tale which I am writing for the benefit of the distressed needle-women."

If an arrow had suddenly pierced the captain he could not have started from the sofa with greater alacrity. Amelia, who had discovered that he was not really asleep, was delighted at the success of her stratagem, and laughed heartily, but Mrs. Vyvian, believing that he was seized with delirium, pulled the bell, and never ceased ringing till several of the servants made their appearance. The captain explained, the servants were dismissed, and the trio became chatty and pleasant.

Dashington for some time amused the ladies with an account of his travels, then, advancing towards a splendid bouquet, he gracefully presented a flower to each of them, requesting an emblematic response.

"In the bright days of chivalry," said the captain, "love often borrowed the assistance of these pure interpreters of sentiment. Ancient books are full of emblems composed of flowers. Did a disconsolate damsel desire to inform a gallant knight of her captivity or danger, a rose, moistened with her tears, would have divulged her misfortune. But it is in the country," ejaculated the captain, sighing profoundly, "it is in the country, while inhaling a pure atmosphere, and surrounded by beautiful flowers, that lovers know how to appreciate these ornaments of nature. The most timid admirer may find courage to present a flower, though he dare not utter a syllable to express his admiration."

As the captain finished speaking he gazed admiringly at Amelia. Mrs. Vyvian blushed, her jealousy was excited, and she used every possible endeavour to regain her dominion over him, but apparently without avail, for, to the great annoyance of Amelia, he persevered in paying her the most devoted attention till the return of her brother Francis, when his manner gradually subsided into indifference.

"Strange creatures men are," said Mrs. Vyvian, as Amelia was preparing to return home.

"Not more eccentric than many of our own sex," returned Amelia laughing, "but what occasions you to make the observation?"

"I was thinking," said Mrs. Vyvian, "how very suddenly Captain Dashington altered his manner towards you after the return of Francis."

"Very likely, he perceived that his attentions were not agreeable," replied Amelia gravely.

"Why surely you don't mean to say that you do not admire Captain Dashington," responded Mrs. Vyvian, rather pettishly.

"Really Alexandrine, I can't say that I have any very particular predilection in his favour. He is a very agreeable, pleasant companion, but I know very little about him, and have no great desire to become better acquainted."

"The carriage waits," said Francis, popping his head in at the room door, "wrap yourself well up, Amelia, and come down stairs, for it is a very cold night."

Amelia embraced her sister-in-law and took her departure.

CHAPTER XXIX.

THE APARTMENT.

A cold January morning had struggled into existence, when Mr. and Mrs. Dobbins were seated at their own fireside, discussing over their altered position.

"If the rent isn't paid, we can't stay here," said Mr. Dobbins, "the landlord told me so, positively, the last time I saw him."

"Wont Mr. Squezum accommodate the matter by taking a bill, payable in six months?" asked his wife.

"He'll do nothing of the kind," was the reply.

"Then what steps are you going to take, to get out of your embarassments?"

"I owe nobody a penny but the landlord," replied the hosier, "and him I can't pay, that's as plain as a pike-staff."

Mrs. Dobbins rose majestically from her seat, and abruptly quitting the room, ascended the stairs.

Presently she returned, carrying in one hand a small mahogany box, and in the other a hammer. With one blow she split the box in pieces, and fifty sovereigns fell upon the table. An exclamation of surprise and delight escaped from the lips of Mr. Dobbins.

"That money, Mr. Dobbins, sir, I saved from what was left in your pockets of a night, and what was over in the till, and yet it will be the means of saving us from ruin."

Mr. Dobbins volunteered no reply, but inwardly determined to be more cautious for the future, and not leave his money to the tender mercy of his wife.

Mrs. Dobbins defined her husband's thoughts.

"So this is all the gratitude I receive from you, is it sir? you think that I sha'nt have an opportunity of saving you from ruin again, but there you'll find yourself mistaken."

"You're continually nag-nag-nagging at me," replied the hosier.

"And so I shall continue to do, till you reform your habits, and frequent those dens of robbery, the billiard-rooms, less than you do at present."

"Me?"

"You, of course; you never set your foot in such a place I suppose."

"Had'nt we better begin to think of letting our apartments, my dear?" asked Mr. Dobbins.

"Certainly," replied the lady, "and so the best thing you can do, is to write a bill, is it not?"

Mr. Dobbins performed this task almost to the satisfaction of his wife.

The bill ran as follows:—

AN ATTIC TO LET,
To a respectable single man.
Terms moderate, and payment punctual.

"That combines a great deal in a very little, it's a perfect *multum in parvo* lodgin' bill," exclaimed Mr. Dobbins, rubbing his hands in an ecstacy of delight.

The bill was immediately pasted upon the private door, below the knocker, and Mrs. Dobbins prepared herself to see any applicant who might call concerning the lodging.

"Had'nt we better make a little calculation my dear?" said Mr. Dobbins, "to see how we can manage to live respectably on our limited means."

"You can do it if you please; I never expected to come to this."

"Take care of the pence, and the pounds will take care of themselves," replied her husband.

"They'll do nothing of the kind with me, for I shall take care of them myself, without giving them the trouble."

"Pooh, nonsense."

"When you married me, you was going to make a fortin', you was, and now where is it?" Answer me that question if you can?"

"My income is, as near as I can calculate, one hundred and fifty pounds a year; do you think we can manage on that?"

"Manage on it," echoed Mrs. Dobbins, "it's utterly impossible.   There then."

Mrs. Dobbins was one of those people who look upon the mystery of laying out money to advantage, as the great *arcanum* of domestic life; a secret known to them only in the wide universe.

"Mr. Dobbins put on his hat and gloves, and repaired to the office of Mr. Squezum, to pay him the sum due for half a year's rent.

Scarcely had the door closed upon him, when a double knock intimated to Mrs. Dobbins, that some one without was desirous of obtaining admission.

The door was opened, and there entered Mr. Adolphus Tift, but Mrs Dobbins did not recognise him, for the precise reason that, at that period of her existence, she was totally unacquainted with the son of the Queen Mother; nor, although she was considerably indebted to her husband, was the hosier's wife acquainted with the features of that eccentric lady.   Had they once met her glance, she could never have erased the memory of them from her mind; they would have produced such an indelible impression, but they had not.

"What did you please to want sir?" demanded Mrs. Dobbins, eyeing the stranger doubtfully.

"I think you have an attic to let?" replied Mr. Tift, approaching the landlady, and speaking in a tone of confidence.

"What if I have sir? is that any signification to you?"

Now Mr. Tift was not aware of the fact that Mrs. Dobbins was a decided mystifier, that she revelled in mystery of every description, that mystery was her element, and that when she was out of it, she resembled either a fish out of water, or a man in it; that in short, not being always content of mystifying other people, which she generally by some means or other contrived to effect, she frequently mystified herself also.

As we stated before, Mr. Tift was not aware of this circumstance, therefore he thought her question a very odd one, and stood staring at her without making any reply.

"Do you choose to answer that question, sir," resumed Mrs. Dobbins.

"I am in want of one," stammered out Mr. Tift, whom circumstances of a pecuniary nature had compelled to quit Long's hotel.

"Oh, that quite alters the case, sir, will you walk up?"

Mr. Tift, perfectly unconscious of whose house he was in, did walk up, followed closely by Mrs. Dobbins, who introduced him to the apartment formerly tenanted by Agnes Talbot.

"It seems small," said Mr. Tift, purposely raising objections, with a view to lowering the rent.

"It's snug, sir, but not small; the chimbley never smokes, fleas there are none, and our servant, sir, is one of the most attentivest of young women."

"I should occasionally dine at home," observed Tift.

"That maid of mine cooks equal to Crockford's, sir."

"And what are the terms?"

"Let me see—you would sometimes dine at home you say—seven-and-sixpence a week would be the very least I could possibly take."

Mr. Tift immediately agreed to the terms, and laid down half a sovereign as deposit-money, which he had obtained that morning—no matter how.

I cannot afford a higher rent than that as my means are limited, and I always make a point of living within my income," exclaimed Mr. Tift, pompously abstracting the half sovereign from a steel purse, which he kept in a state of turbid agitation, so that the fellow coin to the one he held in his hand might appear multiplied to the eyes of Mrs. Dobbins.

Few people can live *without* their incomes, sir."

"And quite as few know how to live *within* them, ma'am," observed Mr. Tift, who had already impressed Mrs. Dobbins with the idea that he was an 'honourable man,' unfortunately in this sublunary sphere a character very similar in many respects to the 'philosopher's stone,' "but I flatter myself I am not one of those individuals."

Mrs. Dobbins smiled, and, having expressed her conviction of such being the case, proceeded to business.

"When will you come in sir, that we may have all the blankets and sheets aired, and make every thing comfortable to receive you?"

"To-night, at about six o'clock."

"Very well, sir, we shall have time."

"If you require any references as to my respectability I will give you them at once."

"Certainly, I think that ought to be done."

"Oh, oh, very well," said Adolphus Tift, writing the names of the baronet and Lord Oxburn on the back of a card, and handing it to Mrs. Dobbins, "these noblemen will vouch for my character."

Mr. Tift had acquired the appearance of a foreigner from a long residence on the continent, and therefore, on reading the titles inscribed on the card, the hosier's wife conjectured that her lodger was a foreign count in disguise—a count was the precise title, either a duke or a baron would have completely spoilt the whole idea—and a bearer of secret communications or official documents to the government from some foreign court, and very probably a political exile into the bargain.

"Good morning, ma'am; these stairs are extremely awkward."

"You'll find them otherwise when you get used to them, sir. Good morning, sir."

Mr. Tift had not made himself acquainted with the name of his future landlady, although she was cognizant of his; he was therefore unconscious of the fact that he would that night sleep under the roof of one of the Queen Mother's most pressing creditors.

He had perceived the impression Mrs. Dobbins had received of him, and therefore determined to keep up a certain degree of mystery, and if necessary to assume the name of Count Tifteroni, which might have the desirable effect of checking low familiarity on the day when the rent became due.

On his entering the room, after having returned from Mr. Squeezum, Mrs. Dobbins informed her husband that the apartments were let.

"Here is the gentleman's name; he has given two noblemen for his references, and I think he is a foreigner."

"Has he left a deposit?" asked the hosier.

"To be sure he has, and what's more, I saw a thousand pound note in his purse, I'm very sure of that."

"I don't half like foreigners, though," replied Mr. Dobbins.

"Nor I either; and, goodness knows, he looks anything but a saint: but then he is certainly very high and very rich."

"What have you for dinner?"

"Fowls; and beauties they are, too,"

"Fowls; I couldn't touch 'em."

"Oh, they're beautiful! they are, indeed."

"A friend of mine— a poulterer—gave me an account of them this morning: pah! sickening! Says he, 'Fowls are greater travellers than most people imagine; those that are stated to be quite fresh from Dorking, were shipped at least a month ago in the Zuyder-Zee.' What do you think of that?"

"Now, that's an impossibility," said Mrs. Dobbins, "and just a trick of yours to turn me against my dinner. Why, what with sea-sickness and starvation, by the time they had come here, they'd be nothing but skin and bone."

"That's the cream of the thing," replied the hosier. "Their damaged constitutions are gradually repaired on a wholesome diet of gentles, and occasionally a sprinkling of a little damaged barley. But let's look at 'em, and see what country they belong to."

Mrs. Dobbins soon produced the two fowls, when her husband inspected them closely.

"You're thoroughly taken in," cried Mr. Dobbins. "You bought those birds of some man in the street. The fellow has actually had the impudence to sow on a young head and young legs on an old body—a very common trick, as my friend the poulterer told me."

"I'm sure I should never have found out my mistake until I had begun to truss the wretches. However, the man will find himself in the wrong, for I shall insist upon his giving me a goose instead."

"You will gain little by the exchange, for, although Lincolnshire is the reputed birthplace of all the geese in the London market, yet most of them have come up in waggons from Suffolk, where the unfortunate bipeds are suffocated wholesale. You see, I've learned something to-day concerning poultry, and that comes of being a man of observation, for I am one of those people who like to see life in all its varieties."

"I've been infamously used by that monster, but he shall suffer for it, I can tell him that," said Mrs. Dobbins, quitting the room to prepare for the reception of her new lodger.

Mr. Dobbins joined his apprentice in the shop.

CHAPTER XXX.

THE VISIT.

RETURN we now to Agnes Talbot.

She was seated in that formal room—the library —perusing the morning paper, and thinking of happier days. Every now and then a remembrance of what she had been flashed across her mind, and penetrated her heart with a desolate misery.

At this moment Miss Lucretia Pearson entered.

Not only were her features and expression pleasing and her complexion fine, but there was a rich glow of the cheek, and a soft intelligence about the clear blue eye that pointed her out as the possessor of more than ordinary attractions.

Though affected in her manners and conversation, she was more refined in either than her parents.

"How vexed I am!" said Miss Lucretia, taking up a soiled album. "This book was so beautifully bound that it was quite a gratification to look at the outside of it. But, by the time it had travelled round to all my friends for contributions, the morocco and gilding were so wretchedly soiled that I am positively ashamed for any one to see it in such a tarnished state. I never will, on any account, have another one bound till it is filled."

" It was a pity," timidly ventured Agnes.

" A mere trifle unworthy of mention," replied Lucretia, taking up the paper just relinquished by Agnes.

"Dear me, what a heap of governesses are wanted—I mean to say are in want of situations. There must be a great many families in reduced circumstances."

"There must indeed," responded Agnes, almost unconsciously.

"Poor things, they offer to come for the first six months without any salary, and I think none for the next six, for I very much doubt if their faces would ever be seen after the first-named period."

"Whereas Ma gives you ever so many shillings I know," said Miss Kate, who had entered the room unperceived.

Mrs. Pearson followed just in time to hear the last observation.

"Such actions, my dear, are the tenor of my life; when I am charitable I don't do it that it may be known to all the world, but I give alms secretly, to spare the feelings of the receiver, and to render myself happy."

Agnes Talbot blushed deeply, but being seated with her back to the light, fortunately Mrs. Pearson did not observe her confusion.

"But people have no right to put up with the impudent airs of a set of dissatisfied creatures who are for ever talking of the miseries of life—of course their lives must be miserable ; what else can they expect when the fault lies with themselves only," resumed Mrs. Pearson, glancing meaningly at Agnes.

Several loud knocks at the street door terminated the conversation.

Presently the footman, radiant with plush, looked in, and informed Mrs. Pearson of the alarming fact that Lord Oxburn and her husband were seated together in the drawing-room.

Mrs. Pearson hastened to her dressing room.

In an instant Lucretia followed her example.

In the mean time Mr. Pearson called repeatedly for his wife and daughter, in a tone that bespoke furious impatience.

"Really, my lord, I cannot account ——" began the auctioneer for the third time, on entering the room in which was seated Lord Oxburn.

"Nonsense, Pearson, keep quiet, there's a good fellow," exclaimed his lordship.

"How much am I indebted to you for this visit? Mrs. Pearson will be here directly, and I can't think what detains Lucretia so."

"Tell your mother I want her," said Mr. Pearson to a little boy who was building a house with cards upon the table. The child looked up, and, without making any reply, continued his amusement.

Again, and again the command was reiterated, at last the boy moved sulkily off his chair, and quitted the room : presently he re-entered.

"Mother's looking herself in the glass sticking flowers in her cap, and sister's sitting upon the table, kicking up her heels ; Miss Talbot's crying as she always is, and mother says you're a fool and she cant come till she's dressed."

Mr. Pearson's rubicand visage became unusually scarlet as he muttered something about women never being ready, but Lord Oxburn begged that he would not feel annoyed, " there are so many little elegancies scattered about your drawing room," said he " that I could amuse myself here for an hour or two."

" Your lordship is very obliging," returned Mr. Pearson, who prided himself exceedingly upon the profusion of scarce and valuable curiosities which ornamented the apartment. " You see my lord I'm in the way of getting these things without any difficulty, and now I've given up business it's no matter telling how I did it," chuckled the auctioneer. Just in time to prevent a confidential disclosure of the tricks of the trade, Mrs. Pearson with Lucretia, attended by Miss Talbot entered the drawing room.

Lord Oxburn rose and advanced politely towards Mrs. Pearson, conducted her to a seat, then turning towards Agnes, " Miss Pearson I presume."

" Oh dear no !" exclaimed Mrs. Pearson, half choaking with rage, " she is the governess."

Lord Oxburn apologised for his mistake, and advancing towards Lucretia seated himself beside her

Mr. Pearson exchanged glances with his wife, who nodded her approval.

" A beautiful little dog, Miss Pearson," said his lordship, while caressing a French poodle whose innocent gambols made him the pet of his mistress and the family.

" What a profusion of silken curls ! What sparkling eyes !" and his lordship gazed admirably at Agnes.

" Miss Talbot," said Mrs. Pearson snappishly, " your services are required in the nursery."

Agnes blushed, tears trembled upon the lashes of her soft blue eyes, she rose from her seat and bowing gracefully quitted the apartment.

" Your little favourite, Miss Pearson, continued his lordship, reminds me in appearance of a dog purchased by a lady, a friend of mine, from an itinerant dog dealer in Regent-street. For the first eight or ten days the little creature was full of life and vivacity, but he suddenly became dull and stupid, refused his food, and would certainly have given up the ghost had not his mistress sent for a dog doctor who, the instant he set his eyes upon him, revealed the mystery of his ailment. ' Allow me madam,' said the medical attendant, ' to unrip a few stiches and deliver the little animal, which is nothing more than a cur, from the poodle's skin which has become too tight for him ?' the lady consented, and the doctor performed the operation with his penknife ;

in a few seconds the mongrel recovered his liberty, but was banished into the kitchen."

Lord Oxburn had no sooner finished speaking than the ladies began eyeing Mademoiselle Fanchon very inquisitively, but she stood the examination, and was pronounced by his lordship " a rare specimen of the poodle kind."

" Some years ago," said Mrs. Pearson, " I was infamously taken in by a man in Covent-garden, who persuaded me to buy, what appeared to be, a very beautiful green bird; don't you remember, Pearson, how you laughed when I brought it in from outside of the window, where it had been hanging in a shower of rain. All the colour, my lord, had been washed off, and my pretty Poll was nothing but a painted magpie. I paid three guineas for the ugly thing."

Mr. Pearson was about to corroborate his wife's statement, when the door opened, and, to the evident dismay of the whole party, Mr. Francis and Miss Vyvian were announced.

Lord Oxburn, ashamed of being caught on friendly terms with a *cidivant* auctioneer, was exceedingly embarrassed and endeavoured to effect his escape, but both Pearson and his wife were determined not to lose the opportunity of displaying their intimacy with a nobleman. The Vyvians were on the stairs, so that there was but one alternative—either to remain in the room or to bolt down stairs and pass the visitors. Lord Oxburn preferred remaining where he was, and, immediately recovering himself, received the Vyvians with the easy *nonchalance* of a man of fashion.

He took his place by the side of Amelia, who maliciously lamented having disturbed so distinguished an assemblage.

Mr. Pearson, before whom visions of the Vyvian estates, furniture, and plate floated in a sort of demoniacal confusion, was afraid to open his mouth for fear of betraying himself. He felt sure that they had come to speak about some by-gone affair.

Since his retirement from business Mr. Pearson had had time to reflect, and the consequence was that his conscience had become timid and nervous. Some of the elegant furniture in the very room in which he was seated belonged formerly to the Vyvians.

Francis divined the cause of his embarrassment, and, after apologising for the cause of his unexpected intrusion, requested to be allowed the favour of speaking to Miss Talbot.

A heavy load was immediately removed from the breast of the guilty auctioneer, who, glad of an opportunity of slipping out of the room, volunteered to inform Agnes of their visit.

"Mr. Pearson," said his lady, authoritatively, "I do request that you will keep your seat. What is the use of keeping dogs and barking yourself?"

But neither Mrs. Pearson's request nor her witty rejoinder were heard by her spouse, who appeared too glad of the opportunity of escaping out of the room to pay attention to what she said. A few moments after he had quitted it, Miss Talbot again made her appearance.

"Dear Agnes," said Amelia, affectionately, taking her by the hand, "we have come to persuade you to return home again."

Agnes replied but in a low voice—so low that it was not easy to distinguish what she said.

"It is contrary to my custom to allow my governesses to receive their friends in the drawing-room; but, as Mr. Vyvian is an old customer of my husband's, and the servant, I suppose, not knowing who they wanted, shew them in here, makes it that I can't very well object to her meeting them here in the present instance."

"Certainly not," returned Lord Oxburn, to whom these confidential remarks were made in an under tone. "To a young lady possessed of Miss Talbot's beauty and attraction it can little signify where she receives her friends. Adorned by her presence the meanest garret would appear a more enviable habitation than the most costly furnished apartment deprived of her presence." A deep blush suffused the manly countenance of Lord Oxburn.

Mrs. Pearson bit her lips.

"Remember," resumed the lady, in the same tone of voice as she was before speaking, "remember, my lord, that it is not all gold that glitters. Miss Talbot is by some people, it appears, thought tolerably pretty, I can't say that I think her so, but that of course is a matter of opinion, and you will say very unimportant compared with what I am going to tell you. I am sorry to say that she was discharged from her last situation under very disgraceful surmises. When I engaged her I was not aware of the fact, but have since heard the whole history of her and I can assure you, my lord, that it is no very pleasant thing to have people with suspicious characters about one, and, now Mr. Vyvian has taken upon him to call here and visit her, I

think it is high time to have some explanation with her, for I am not to be blinded by his bringing his sister with him."

Francis Vyvian, who, with his sister, had used every possible argument to prevail upon Agnes to return to Belgrave-square, took their departure rather vexed with her resistence to their wishes, for true it is that the rich and powerful almost invariably expect that the poor and friendless will submit to their judgment without presuming to form an opinion of their own.

Mr. Pearson re-entered the drawing-room, and Lord Oxburn, afraid to provoke any further elucidation of Mrs. Pearson's suspicions, advanced to the table and joined the young ladies who were admiring Lucretia's album.

"What a beautiful countenance, and how exquisitely painted!" exclaimed his lordship, examining attentively a highly finished water-coloured drawing. "Really, Miss Pearson, you are quite an artist."

"I draw very little," replied Lucretia, "the portrait you admire was done by my governess."

"Lucretia can draw better than that," observed Mrs. Pearson rather haughtily.

Lord Oxburn endeavoured, but without success, to prevail upon the young lady to exhibit some specimen of her talent.

Miss Talbot remarked that Miss Pearson's time was almost wholly engaged in the practice of music, in which she eminently excelled.

"You must come some evening and hear her play and sing, my lord," said Mrs. Pearson.

His lordship, who was passionately fond of music, eagerly accepted the invitation, and promising to take the first opportunity of doing so, took leave of the company, deeply impressed by the beauty of Agnes, and resolving to seize every occasion of improving his acquaintance with her.

CHAPTER XXXI.

THE QUEEN'S BENCH PRISON.

IT would be superfluous to state that Frederick Vyvian was not altogether reconciled to the incarceration he was suffering, and no wonder, therefore, that he should take steps to obtain his liberation.

He determined on making application to Abednego Levi, and just in the same manner as a drowning man would catch at a straw; he fondly nourished the hope that he might, by threatening to expose his own birth, compel the Jew to advance the necessary amount. But the sum was a heavy one, and he doubted whether Abednego possessed the means of raising even one half of it; and then he felt a secret compunction at paying the debt at all, on account of the shabby manner in which he had been treated.

He also wrote to the baronet, requesting him to

take the necessary steps for obtaining a *habeas corpus* writ, with a view to his being removed to the Bench. With this Sir Richard Vyvian complied.

The morning after these circumstances had occurred, an athletic man, dressed in a velveteen shooting jacket, called at Whitecross-street prison, for the purpose of seeing Frederick. This was Tim Roper.

"Well, my tulip," said Tim, " so it seems you're got into jug* without a chance of getting out of it again."

"I haven't the pleasure of knowing you," said Frederick, who was rather abashed by the insolently familiar manner by which the ruffian spoke, and extremely annoyed at the disdainful glances with which his *chums* regarded him.

"In jug it's all the same whether one's an out-and-outer, downy cove, a lully prig,† a poor *yokel*, or a finished gentleman, but I never was in jug myself but once, and that's vy you cuts me. Howsom'dever, I'm come to do you a good turn!" exclaimed Tim Roper, producing a small bottle of liquor, which he had contrived to smuggle into the prison.

"I knows ven I vos in trouble I drank spirits of wine, vitriol, and every other maddening incentives, as the turnkey called 'em, that I could come across, so I thought you would be in the same predicament," resumed Tim, handing the bottle clandestinely to Frederick.

"From whom are you come, and what is your object in visiting me here ?"

"I'm from an old gen'elman as goes by the name of Levi, and now pra'ps yer can guess what my business is."

"I think I can," answered Frederick, "if you have any communication to make, I shall be obliged by your doing so at once."

Tim Roper handed him a note.

Frederick perused it earnestly, and then cast a glance of mingled rage and disappointment around him ; at last his eyes resting inquiringly on Tim.

"You need'nt try to keep anything dark from me," observed the villian, "I knows all about it already, how I got my information is neither here nor there."

"Then can you assist me ? Can you prevail on that old wretch to advance the money ? Befriend me at this moment, and you may command me for the rest of my life."

"That's an impossibility," replied the ruffian coldly, "so you needn't try to come blarney over me ; you're precious green to think of such a thing, but you must take me to be very raw indeed, and no mistake, if you suppose me capable of such an haction."

"If this was your object in coming to-day, you

* Prison.
† A fellow who steals damp linen off the hedges in the country.

had better have spared yourself the trouble,' sneered Frederick.

"Not at all, because I'd a message to deliver, vich vos to this effect, 'that if you put your threat into execution, we'll have vengeance on yours and yourn;' not that Mr. Levi believes it, or I, or my pals either, but he has promised us our share of the swag, and we don't mean to lose it through a blabbing fool like you."

Frederick Vyvian lost the power of utterance for the moment.

By the time he had partially recovered it, Tim Roper was no longer visible, the ruffian had quitted.

While he was standing irresolute how to act, a letter was placed in his hand by the turnkey ; this proved to be from the baronet. Among other items, it contained the following paragraph :—

"You will be removed to the Bench, or as it is classically termed, to Banco Reginæ, immediately, and as I hope to ease Stamer of his unnecessary *difficulties*, besides wanting your company in several little delicate affairs, not altogether unconnected with the *infernal* regions; I hope to liberate you in a very short time."

"Well," said the young man, "my prospects are brightening a little, I never reckoned upon him to help me out of this disagreeable position."

Frederick Vyvian seated himself upon a bench, and commenced reading an account of the Bench prison, to which he was shortly to be conveyed. It was a parody on Gray's celebrated elegy in a country Church-yard, and was contained in a little volume entitled "Prison Thoughts by a Collegian" :—

The turnkey rings the bell for shutting out,
   The visitor walks slowly to the gate ;
The debtor chum-ward hastes in idle rout,
   And leaves the Bench to darkness, me, and fate.

Now fades the high spiked wall upon the sight
   And all the space a silent air assumes,
Save where some drunkard from the Brace* takes flight.
   And drowsy converse lulls the distant rooms.

Save that from yonder Strong-room,† close confin'd,
   Some noisy wight does to the night complain
Of Mister Jones, the marshall, who, unkind,
   Has, by a week's confinement checked his reign.

Within these strong-built walls, down that parade.
   Where lie the stones all paved in order fair,
Each in his narrow room by bailiffs laid,
   The new made pris'ners o'er their caption swear.

The gentle morning bustle of their trade,
   The 'prentice from the garret over head,
The dapper shopman, or the busy maid
   Will never here arouse them from their bed.

For them no polish'd Rumfords here shall burn,
   Nor wife, uxorious, ply her evening care,
No children run to lisp their dad's return,
   Or climb his knees, the sugar-plums to share.

* A place in the interior of the Bench, in which porter is sold by the authority of the Marshall, to the debtors.
† A solitary place of confinement for such as break the rules of the prison.

Oft did the creditor to their promise yield,
  As often they that solemn promise broke ;
How jocund did they drive the duns a-field !
  Till nick'd at last within the bailiff's yoke !

Let not ambition mock their heedless fate,
  And idly cry, their state might have been better ;
Nor grandeur hear with scorn while I relate
  The short insolvent annals of the debtor.

The boast of heraldry, the pomp of power,
  All wealth procures, its being to entrench,
Await alike the writ's appointed hour ;
  The paths of spendthrifts lead but to the Bench.

Nor you, ye proud, impute to these the fault
  That they are here, and not at large like you,
That they have bills at tailor's, and wine vault—
  Bills that, alas ! have long been over due.

Can story gay, or animated tale,
  Back from this mansion bid us freely run ?
Can honour's voice o'er creditors prevail,
  Or flatt'ry soothe the dull cold ear of Dun ?

Perhaps in this confined retreat is shut
  Some heart, to make a splash, once all on fire ;
Skill that might Hobhouse to the route have put,
  Or loyally play'd Dr. Southey's lyre,

But prudence, to their eyes, her careful page,
  Rich in pounds, shillings, pence, did ne'er unroll ;
Stern creditors repressed their noble rage,
  And froze the genial current of their soul.

Full many a blood, in fashion an adept,
  The dark, lone rooms of spunging-houses bear ;
Full many a fair is born to bloom unkept,
  And waste her sweetness, none know how or where.

Some Cockney Petersham, that, with whiskered
    cheek,
  Once moved in Bond-street, Rotten-row, Pall-mall,
Some humble Mrs. Clark for rest may seek,
  Some Burdett, guiltless quite of speaking well.

The applauses of admiring mobs to gain.
  To be to threats of ruin, prison, lost ;
To see they have not spent their cash in vain,
  And read their triumph in the " Morning Post."

That lot forbade, nor circumscribed alone
  Their growing follies, but themselves confined ;
The bailiff grimly seized them for his own,
  And turnkeys closed the gates on them behind.

The struggling pangs of conscious truth to hide,
  To quench the blushes of ingenuous shame,
The Queen's Bench terribly pulls down our pride—
  For, high or lowly born, 'tis all the same.

Far from the city's mad ignoble strife,
  They still retain an eager wish to stray ;
They hate this cool, sequestered mode of life,
  And wish at liberty to work their way.

And on those walls that still from duns protect,
  Those fire-proof walls, so strongly built and high,
With uncouth rhymes and mis-spelt verses deck'd
  They ask the passing tribute of a sigh.

Their names, their years,—writ by th' unletter'd
    muse,—
  The place of fame, and brass-plate, fill up well.
And many a lawyer's, too, the stranger views
  With pious wishes he may go to hell.

For who, to dumb forgetfulness a prey,
  His pleasing, anxious liberty resigned,
To Banco Regis bent his dreary way,
  Nor cast one longing, lingering look behind.

On some one out the prisoner still relies,
  Some one to yield him comfort he requires ;
E'en from the Bench the voice of Nature cries—
  E'en though imprisoned—glow our wonted fires.

For thee who, mindful of the debtor's doom,
  Dost in these lines their hapless state relate ;
If chance by writ or capias hither come,
  Some kindred spirit may inquire thy fate.

Haply some hoary bailiff here may say,—
  " Oft have we watched him at the peep of dawn,
But—damn him !—still he slipp'd from us away,
  And, when we thought we had him, he was gone.

" Where Drury-lane erects its well-known head,
  And Covent-garden lifts its domes on high,
Morning and noon and night we found him fled,
  Most snugly pouring on us passing by.

" On Sundays, ever smiling as in scorn,
  Passing our houses, he would boldly rove.
We gave his case up as of one forlorn,
  And for his person pined in hopeless love.

" One morn we track'd him, near the accustom'd
    spot,
  Along the Strand, and by his favourite she.
Another came, yet still we caught him not ;
  But, on the third, we nabb'd a youth—'twas he.

" The next, with warrant due, we brought our man
  Snug to the bench, here all the way from town.
Approach and read the warrant (if you can) ;
  You may a copy get for half-a-crown."

THE WARRANT.

Here rests his head, in seventeen and one,
  A youth to fortune and to fame well known ;
But tradesmen trusted and began to dun,
  And Mister Sheriff marked him for his own.

Great were his spendings ; he nought put on shelf ;
  To send a recompense law did not fail.
He gave his creditors all he had—himself ;
  He gain'd from them all he abhorr'd—a gaol.

No further seek his doings to disclose,
  Or draw his follies from this dull abode.
Here he'll at all events three months repose ;
  The Insolvent Act may open then a road.

Having finished the elegy, and after sitting a few
minutes longer on the bench, he entered into conversation with a chum, or fellow lodger.

*   *   *   *

Before two days had passed after the events
above related had taken place, Frederick Vyvian
was escorted to the Queen's Bench.

Being tolerably well supplied with cash, he was
enabled to " pay out " several chums, so that he obtained a separate room for himself.

The morning after his committal he was roused
up by the sonorous voice of the turnkeys, calling—
" Pull up, pull up."

He was then obliged to enter the lobby, through
two lines of curious faces, to have what was technically denominated " his likeness taken."

During this ceremony, or we would rather say ordeal, he was personally and particularly scanned by the whole of the turnkeys; and then he became the subject of the buffoonery of the fellows who were waiting to " quiz" him on his return.

Any introduction to a body of strangers is unpleasant. The new comer is invariably considered a fit object for the gibes and jeers of the multitude; and certainly an introduction to the inmates of the Queen's Bench is not the most agreeable. But Frederick was determined to take all in good part, and, at the expense of a little sacrifice of temper, he achieved his resolution.

Having obtained his *footing*, he made friends as readily at the Queen's Bench as he had previously done at Whitecross-street.

Several of the prisoners confined themselves to their rooms, and adopted the circular hole in the door as a means of carrying on a communication with those persons outside, for fear of becoming contaminated by coming in contact with their fellow prisoners.

Frederick Vyvian took no such precaution, but endeavoured to bury the remembrance of his past follies and his present pain in the company of gay associates.

Thus his condition was little different from when he was an inmate of Whitecross-street.

CHAPTER XXXII.

TATTERSALL'S.

We have already seen that Lord Oxburn visited the residence of Mr. Pearson, and we are also acquainted with the meeting that took place between that nobleman and Mr. Francis Vyvian.

This occurred at about eleven o'clock on Thursday morning.

An hour later his lordship arrived at Tattersall's.

The entrance, which was occupied by several itinerant dog dealers, mostly vendors of hounds and beagles, was through a stable situated in Hyde-park corner, or, as it was technically termed, the " corner," which latter appellation served to designate Tattersall's itself.

After he had been in the place several minutes he perceived Sir Richard Vyvian advancing towards him.

' Well, Vyvian," said his lordship, " how do you intend managing about that brother of yours?"

" Oh, he'll be removed to the Bench for the present, and then I hope to pay the amount shortly, as I have some flats in view whom I have picked up lately."

" I wish you every success," was the reply, " and were you in the same circumstances and I possessed

of the means, you should not find yourself in want of a friend. But that brother of yours—"

Sir Richard Vyvian coloured up, but took no notice of the observation.

" I beg your pardon for touching upon such a sensitive chord," somewhat ironically remarked his lordship, " but I assure you I did so unintentionally."

" Don't mention it, but here is a friend of mine coming up, a well known gammoning cove, he is on the look out for flats, and we are trying to hook one."

At this moment a gentleman of the whip joined the baronet and Lord Oxburn.

" Is that young gentleman one of the fraternity?" asked the knowing one.

" To be sure he is," replied the baronet; " you know Lord Oxburn, don't you?"

" To be sure. That's your sort. He's a bit of a genus in his way; a reg'lar tight one."

" He knows a thing or two," added Sir Richard, carelessly, " but look out there, there's a fellow after my mare Spindleshanks; she's got a wall-eye you know, so keep her against the white wall there, that it may seem to be the reflection, and place her on a rising ground, so that her shoulders may seem square."

" I'm off; you won't match me at that. I'll pigeon him."

" I'm in want of a horse; a good 'un and a cheap 'un," said a cockney, addressing the ostler.

The baronet advanced a few paces, as if he wished to be a spectator of the transaction.

" Here's vone, sir, that will suit you to a hair," observed the ostler, catching hold of a lame, half-starved mare by the bridle.

" I don't think he looks *quite* the thing," ventured the cockney.

" Not the thing! Lor bless yer, sir! I knows vot's o'clock, I do; and, take my word for it, that mare's a good 'un. She's free from vice, sound vind and limb, goes well in harness, von't shy at nothing—in fact, you von't see sich another in a day's ride."

There might have been some truth in both of the last observations.

" She's swapped* under peculiar circumstances," resumed the ostler; " and I'll give you an account of her; and then, if yer like her, you can go and bid up there, where the auctioneer is sitting, in that box at the end."

" You may as well do that," said the cockney.

" She's the property of one of our sporting characters—in fact, one of the first noblemen of the land. She's strong, sturdy, swift, strapping, surefooted, smooth, and showy. Her sire was Memnon, on a sister of Fearless (from the select stud of 'Squire Green), by Victor, a sporting son of Sobersides (by that semnific, superlative stallion

* Sold.

Spanker), who won the gold cup last season at Ascot."

"She seems to be of a good family," quoth the cockney.

"Leave her alone for that 'ere," responded the ostler.

"But she appears rather out of order."

"Vell, sir, there's no harm done if you don't buy. Plenty others will be bidding in a minit.'

"What is the sum bid for that mare?" asked the baronet, stepping up to the ostler.

"We ain't had an offer yet, sir. As soon as I gits back to the end, all them gents as have been admiring the mare's points, will begin a-bidding for her."

The ostler trotted the mare back to the spot where the auctioneer was seated.

The baronet walked up to the cockney.

"The steps of that mare are supereminently stately," said the baronet.

"That may be," cried the cockney; "but somehow or other 1 don't much like her."

"There," cried Sir Richard, taking the cockney by the arm, and pointing to the poor jaded animal, "is the countenance, intrepidity, and fire of a lion."

"There's the eye, joint, and nostril of an ox."

"There's the nose, gentleness, and patience of a lamb."

"There's the strength, constancy, and foot of a mule."

"There's the hair, head, and leg of a deer."

"There's the sight, memory, and turning of a serpent."

"There's the ear, brush, and trot of a fox."

"Those are recommendations," ejaculated the cockney, "and I think I'll go and bid for him."

"I should advise you," carelessly exclaimed the baronet, strolling away.

In an instant the cockney hurried off to the auctioneer.

Presently the ostler came up to Sir Richard.

"Has he bought her, Tom?" demanded the baronet.

"Ay," replied the ostler.

"How much for?"

"Forty pounds."

"Zounds! a dear bargain," observed Lord Oxburn, who was standing by.

"She has been a good mare in her time, though," said the baronet, "but now she has the glanders, and is terribly broken winded."

"And she's a roarer into the bargain," added the ostler, "but the feller that bought her wasn't wide awake enough to try her by hitting her over the back with a stick, and holding her head to his ear."

"Nor did he observe that she had the glanders," cried Sir Richard.

"I trimmed her nostrils well with a pair of scissors, besides which I blew a trifle of pepper and salt up her nose which made her sneeze, and so cleared her head; then I sponged her nostrils, and greased 'em with a tallow candle; this caused the filth to run off the nostril, but he'll find out his mistake in the course of an hour or two."

"So that is your way of *doing* the natives," whispered Lord Oxburn, "but how did you manage about her being broken-winded?"

"I gave her a pound of lard and a quarter of a pound of shot overnight, which will prevent its being discovered for a day or two, or pr'aps more, according to the work the mare does."

"I am only going to the 'Subscription Room,' so you may expect me back again presently," said the baronet, addressing the ostler.

"That's your sort, sir," replied the knowing one.

Lord Oxburn and the baronet took each other's arms and retired to the 'Subscription Room,'

The 'Subscription Room' was an apartment appropriated to the use of subscribers, who paid one guinea per annum each. Here the generality of bets relating to the turf are settled, at whatever place they may have originated; as it is not customary to pay on the spot where the bets have been lost, but at Tattersall's, on the return of the respective parties to town.

"That's a long headed fellow we have just left," said the baronet, referring to the ostler.

"I should think so," replied Lord Oxburn.

"A short time ago he invented a patent fleam for bleeding horses, but it did not answer his expectations, so he had a great many on his hands, and how do you think he managed to get rid of them?"

"I cannot say."

"He went round to half the vendors in London, and ordered a dozen fleams to be sent to Mr. So and So, at this Hotel, and two dozen to Mr. So and So, at that Hotel, when the vendors went to his own house and purchased the fleams from the very man who had ordered them for imaginary people. I need hardly add that my friend Tom got their money and spent it, and they his fleams and kept them."

The baronet laughed at the remembrance of the success that had attended the stratagem.

While he was thus employed Lord Oxburn expressed his intention of leaving Tattersall's.

The two gentlemen wished each other good morning. and separated with professions of mutual regard.

CHAPTER XXXIII.

THE SABBATH.

IT was a Sabbath morning, and a beautiful morning it was, with the bells of the many churches and chapels in the metropolis ringing an inviting peal. "Come, come, come," and the sons and daughters of affluence, habited in every fashionable variety of warm and elegant clothing, stepped lightly, with smiling faces, along the sun-lit pavement. Some were intent upon hearing fascinating, eloquent, preachers, others upon displaying to advantage their beauty or finery. The shabby genteel, painfully sensible that, in this money-making country, to be poor is to be despised, slunk through the back streets into quiet churches, where they took possession of the darkest and remotest corners.

A few, a very few, regardless of their own gratification or the praise or censure of their fellow men, went humbly to worship their creator.

The chapel to which Francis Vyvian conducted his wife and sister was not an exception to the generality of the chapels at the West-end, but was in every respect an assemblage of the votaries of fashion.

A fashionable bishop preached, and a fashionable congregation listened, or rather devoured his discourse. No ill-dressed person ventured within the sacred precincts of this temple of Mammon. It is true that there were, seated on long wooden benches, old men wrapped in brown greatcoats, and wearing grey worsted stockings, aged women and young children dressed in snow white caps and coloured aprons, who were denominated "The Poor." But these were seemingly a set of people made expressly for the purpose of becoming objects of fashionable charity; beings who, in the school of adversity had learned hypocrisy; who, for a scanty portion of coarse food and coarser clothing, had, through necessity, not crime, sold their thoughts, their smiles, their tears, or, in a word, all their better feelings, to become the mere puppets of their wealthy benefactors.

The chapel was crowded to excess.

A charity sermon was to be preached, and the reverend Bishop had chosen for his text the twenty-fifth chapter of Matthew, beginning at the thirty-first verse, " Then shall the king say, &c." After insisting upon the obligations of the rich to bestow relief upon the poor, he enlarged upon the different kinds of charity, and finally wound up his sermon by exhorting them to remember that the charity in question was one of their own creation—that it was a school from which they advantageously procured servants, brought up and trained expressly for the purpose of serving themselves. The concluding remarks had the desired effect; the plates literally groaned under the weight of gold and silver which poured into them as the congregation slowly paraded out of the chapel.

A young girl who had been attracted by the unusual display of gaudy equipages, stood, or rather leaned against one of the pillars of the chapel door. Her teeth chattered, her whole frame convulsively trembled with cold and want of proper nourishment and clothing. One by one the congregation, many of whom had secretly vowed to put in practice the

instruction they had just been receiving; but they were too cold, just coming out of a warm church, perhaps the girl was an impostor, at any rate it was a very bold thing of a poor wretch like that to stand annoying people just coming out of church. So they passed on without even deigning to cast a glance at the sunken eye or pale careworn face of one so miserable.

At length a lady, splendidly attired, moved towards the door, and stood waiting till her carriage drew up.

" For God's sake, lady, bestow a small trifle !" murmured, in a faint and hollow voice, the child of misery.

Frowning severely, and pulling her rich velvet cloak tightly round her, the lady haughtily removed a distance further from the supplicant. But the young girl, emboldened by the opportunity, and rendered desperate by her own and her parent's sufferings, again timidly ventured to urge her necessity.

" What do you want, my good girl ?" said a well-fed, pompous, little clergyman, who had stepped towards the door with a view of inducing the lady to re-enter.

" Really, Mr. Bluster, it is a very disagreeable thing of you to allow the congregation to be molested at the very door of the chapel. Why don't you speak to a policeman ?"

" Oh, sir !" moaned the beggar, " if you only knew how cold, how hungry, how miserable we are !"

The clergyman returned with the lady into the chapel, and the beadle, with the air of a man of business, walked authoritatively in search of a policeman.

Amelia, whose kind and generous nature was ever ready to assist the unfortunate, was engaged in conversation with a party of ladies and gentlemen; but she had noticed the wretched child, had heard her heartrending appeal for assistance, and was only waiting till she could, without exciting attention, relieve her.

On the departure of the beadle she trembled for the fate of the beggar, and could scarcely restrain her impatience. When Mr. Stamer, who had made one of the party with whom she had been conversing, politely stepped aside to make room for some ladies to pass into their carriage, and at the same time took the opportunity to thrust a sovereign into the young girl's hand.

" May God bless your honour," exclaimed the child. And, unable to support the emotion of joy, she staggered and fell to the ground. A slight streak of blood issued from the side of her temple as she lay insensible upon the pavement.

" Come, I say," said a policeman, " how long are you going to lay here ? Come, get up ; I'll teach you to go begging on Sundays."

" The child is faint and exhausted," said Mr

Stamer; "and, I fear, injured by her fall. Cannot you carry her into a chemist's shop, and get her attended to ?"

"Lor bless you, sir! what chemist would pay attention to the like of her? You ain't up to young 'uns of her sort, sir. It's all sham—upon my word and honour it is. These 'ere people are so used to go without, sir, that they care nothing at all about it."

"Habit," returned Mr. Stamer, "can never reconcile human nature to the extremities of either cold, hunger, or thirst."

The child now opened her eyes, and attempted to rise, but seemed unable to do so without assistance.

"Where do you live ?" kindly inquired Mr. Stamer, at the same time motioning a coach. He requested the policeman to lift the girl into it.

A woman in the crowd for a small consideration consented to accompany the child home. The policeman mounted the box, and Mr. Stamer, after explaining to Amelia that the object of her anxiety was recovered from her fit, and on her way home, pursued his way in the direction the girl had given to a small court at the back of Wardour-street.

Having omitted to inquire the number of the house in which she lived, he had some difficulty in discovering it; however, after descending the dirty broken stairs of several wretched habitations he met the object of his compassionate research.

The child smiled gratefully and running forward with the loaf she had been purchasing, she motioned him to follow him down the stairs.

As he descended, a putrid, pestilential smell compelled him to retreat for some moments; the child accustomed to the vile effluvia, and almost unconscious of its existence, was fearful lest the gentleman had changed his intention.

A timid smile replaced the expression of joy which had lighted her countenance ; and, springing forward, she exclaimed to her parents, "The gentleman, the gentleman !"

Mr. Stamer recovered himself and entered the cellar.

Wrapped in a tattered great coat sat a man, whose pale, squalid countenance, and emaciated figure, presented a strong image of disease and famine. He was cowering over a fire which he had just kindled. A child, to whom he had given a piece of bread, was seated on his knee.

On the entrance of Mr. Stamer the man attempted to rise, but being, through extreme debility unable to do so, he sunk into his former posture and burst into tears.

"Come, don't give way but cheer up," said Mr. Stamer, cheerfully, "I have come to see what I can do for you, and have no doubt that in a few days you will be all right again."

The man pointed mournfully to the figure of a female, who was stretched upon some scattered straw, so enfeebled through want and sickness that she was unable to swallow the food put before her. An infant lay moaning piteously by her side.

Mr. Stamer hastened up the stairs, and, calling a boy out of the court, desired him to purchase some brandy as soon as he could, which he administered sparingly to the exhausted sufferers.

When the man was a little recovered, he was desirous of informing his benefactor of the cause of his misery.

"Another day," said Mr. Stamer, "I will readily enter into the detail of your affliction, but at present let us consider the best method of alleviating it."

A ghastly smile for a moment played over the emaciated, sickly countenance of the man, who, unable to utter another syllable, sunk into a kind of languid sensibility.

Mr. Stamer took his leave of the fragile being who had first attracted his attention, and, after engaging the services of a woman in the house to assist in their immediate removal to a more healthy and commodious lodging, he proceeded to the house of a medical man, who, at his request, hastened, without delay, to the succour of the unfortunates.

*　　*　　*　　*

"Half-past six, Mr. Gadabout," said Amelia, as Mr. Stamer entered the drawing-room. "My brother is returned from his drive in the park and we shall dine early to-day as he intends playing a game or two at cards this evening. But what have you done with your protégé ?"

"She is safely deposited in a court at the back of Wardour-street, in the bosom of her own wretched family, but to-morrow they will, if possible, be removed to a more healthy locality."

"I really could not help admiring how cunningly you managed to slip away from us, and place yourself, as you thought unobserved, by the side of the little mendicant. I more readily give you credit for your tactics because it reflects greater honour upon us for having discerned and followed up the manœuvres of a man of your talent and ability. Lady Adela called you a dear, kind-hearted creature ; Alice said——"

"In the name of mercy spare my blushes," interrupted Stamer, "and never mind what either the ladies or the gentlemen said or thought about me, tell me only that I have fulfilled the mission entrusted to me by your own sweet eyes according to your satisfaction, I ask no other reward, I desire no other praise or censure."

"A very gallant declaration," said Amelia, affectionally extending her hand, "and we present our hand in token of our approbation."

Stamer eagerly seized the proffered hand, and was in the act of imprinting a kiss upon it, when the door opened and discovered Sir Richard, followed by Mr. Tift.

"Amelia ! Stamer !" ejaculated the baronet,

"Mr. Stamer, may I request your company in the library," demanded Sir Richard, haughtily.

Mr. Stamer bowed and followed the baronet. Amelia, ready to faint with alarm and confusion, withdrew to her apartment.

CHAPTER XXXIV.

MR. STAMER AND THE BARONET.

WHEN the baronet and Mr. Stamer reached the library they entered, and, after closing the door, Sir Richard sternly demanded of him the meaning of the liberty he had taken with Miss Vyvian.

"My intentions," returned Stamer, "are as pure and honourable as her spotless self, but a promise which I am in duty bound to respect prevents me at present explaining myself more fully."

The baronet for some moments continued pacing the room apparently absorbed in thought; at last, turning towards Stamer, he exclaimed,—

"Young man, it is possible that you may imagine that the fortune of my sister, added to your own, would enable you to maintain her in that style she has always been accustomed to live in; but when I tell you that Amelia Vyvian is portionless, you will no doubt see the folly of indulging hopes which can never be realised. If you really love my sister—for her sake as well as your own—do not endeavour to entice her from the circle of which she is one of the brightest ornaments, but rather strengthen her by your counsel to maintain her position in it, for I tell you candidly that I have promised my interest with her in favour of a man of rank and fortune—one in every respect suitable. You will, therefore, feel that it is impossible that we can avail ourselves of the honour you intend us."

The baronet bowed rather stiffly, and turned towards the door.

"But one moment," exclaimed Mr. Stamer, eagerly, seizing an arm of the baronet. "The peace, the happiness of my life depends upon my union with your sister, who, I have reason to believe, is not indifferent to the respectful tenderness of my affection. I am quite aware that Miss Vyvian is highly connected, but, as soon as circumstances permit me, I shall without difficulty convince you that my family is not inferior to your own, and that my fortune is more than sufficient to maintain a wife and family in affluence. I entreat you, therefore, to tell me frankly whether any other objection has influenced your rejection of me."

The baronet smiled incredulously, but he retraced his steps, and, motioning Mr. Stamer to a chair, seated himself opposite to him.

"Eight or nine years ago," said he, sighing deeply, "I formed an attachment to my own cousin, a lovely creature, the daughter of the Duke of Morton. We were both young, and our affection, which was reciprocal, blinded us to the impossibility of our ever obtaining the consent of our parents. But we loved, and, like other lovers, fondly imagined that our constancy would surmount every obstacle. We vowed eternal fidelity. Six months afterwards, while sitting at breakfast, I read, in one of the morning papers, the following paragraph: — '*Elopement in High Life.*—Yesterday morning the family of a distinguished nobleman was thrown into a state of inexpressible alarm and confusion by the sudden disappearance of the Lady Angelina, second daughter of His Grace the Duke of M——. Upon inquiry it was discovered that the fair fugitive had left —— Park a little after sunrise, and was lifted by a gentleman into a carriage-and-four at the corner of the lane, after which the carriage drove off in the direction of Gretna-green.' I afterwards learned that the object of my cousin's choice was a cornet in the guards, a friend of my own, one whom I had entrusted to convey and receive the letters that passed between us. I mention this by-gone occurrence to show you that, though a bachelor, I am not incapable of judging your case impartially, and rest assured that I wound my own feelings not less than yours when I tell you to review your respective positions; consult your good sense, and you will find my justification and your own peace. I have no desire uselessly to pry into your family connexion or the source from whence you derive your pecuniary assistance. Various reports are afloat, but, as I have no immediate interest at stake, I have not taken the trouble to inquire into their authenticity; but the uncertainty of your position in society is alone sufficient to justify my refusal, and, though probably a spoilt, petted girl may consider that any impediment which interferes with her inclination ought not to be entertained, you, as a man of the world, must be aware that it is impossible, however conscious I may be of your personal and mental superiority, that I can give my consent to the marriage of my sister with the son of, I believe," said the baronet, fixing his eyes intently upon the countenance of Stamer, while he slowly and emphatically pronounced, "a stockbroker."

For a moment a flush of crimson covered the face and ears of the young man, but it subsided, and a smile almost of contempt played over his features as he answered,—

"Not the son, but the grandson, of a stockbroker; a worthy, excellent man, whose fortune has repaired the breach made in our family estate by the profligacy and extravagance of my forefathers. The stockbroker's daughter, my honoured mother, still lives, and it is by her advice that I now travel under an assumed name, as she wished me to see the world without being led into its vices or follies by designing shufflers or gambling knaves."

The baronet in his turn coloured deeply, and, after coughing significantly two or three times, he bowed Mr. Stamer out of the library.

CHAPTER XXXV.

THE BARKER ONCE MORE.

THE day was about to dawn. Dark and ominous clouds hung upon the dreary horizon—clouds that obscured the clear azure of the zenith—and everything foretold the approach of one of those comfortless, chilling, winter days, that so peculiarly appertain to a northern clime—one of those days that are unknown in the fair land of Italy, or in the genial atmosphere of Greece.

The Barker was leaning over a fire she had just ignited, and at a little distance was standing Bill Waters, the impostor, who had accompanied her on the night she visited the "Cadgers' Retreat." The two children were also present.

"Come, Bill, we must be going now," said the Barker.

"Very well; shall we take them brats with us?"

"That, you know, all depends upon what we're going to do: whether I have a fit or hang myself."

"To be sure it does. I think you'd better go and hang yourself first, and then you can come back and get them little 'uns to have a fit with arterwards. They ought to be doing some'nt at their ages, they ought, and, vot's more, if they was mine they should be."

"They shouldn't be idle if it vosn't for my old man, don't you think it."

"Have yer got a bit of rope?"

"Yes."

"All right, then. I've got a knife in my pocket."

And the two impostors sallied out together. Presently they arrived at Cornhill. The Barker walked up to the door of an uninhabited house, where a piece of iron, on which a lamp had formerly rested, protruded over the entrance.

Bill Waters sauntered about on the other side of the way, endeavouring to assume the appearance of a porter out of employ, though in reality he bore a greater similarity to a pickpocket who was pursuing his avocation at his ease.

There appeared the figure of an elderly Quaker advancing towards the spot.

The Barker extracted from her pocket the piece of rope she had previously provided herself with, and in an instant suspended herself from the iron above.

Bill Waters, who was at hand for that purpose, released her from the rope, by cutting her down with a large clasp knife.

For some minutes the Barker lay on the ground, apparently unable to articulate a single sound.

"Poor deluded creature!" exclaimed the Quaker, "What could have driven her to so rash an act?"

Bill Waters, perceiving that the Quaker was in a charitable vein, determined to give that gentleman a full scope for exercising his feelings.

"The times is enough to make any one go to kill themselves; they never were so bad. I'm sure I ain't had a blessed morsel of food these two days," said Bill, as if soliloquising with himself, rather than appealing to charity.

"The times were never better than they are," cried a full-fed looking tradesman.

"I knows I don't find 'em so," replied Bill.

But the attention of the mob, which had gradually collected together, was completely monopolised by the Barker, so that all the efforts of Bill Waters to obtain a share of the notice and charity of the public proved ineffectual.

Presently the Barker opened her eyes slowly, and then moaned audibly.

All were eager to catch the first word she might utter, as that word, skilfully handled, and diplomatically employed, would infallibly prove the key to the whole transaction.

"I could forgive him yet," said the Barker; and then sank back into her former state of stupor.

"She's been betrayed by some wretch of a man," said a dozen female voices at once.

"That never could have been; she's a deal too ugly for that," chimed in a carter's man.

"Hush; she is going to speak," said the Quaker, leaning over the prostrate woman. "What is the matter with you, my good woman?"

"I had one thousand two hundred pounds to live upon till I married an Irish captain, who robbed me of every farthing, and then absconded. This brought on despair and a determination to commit suicide."

After having so far explained the cause that had driven her to make the attempt, the Barker again sank back in a fit of exhaustion.

"Poor critur'!" said Bill Waters, rummaging in his pockets, with pity on his countenance and tears in his eyes.

"My poor children, what shall I do to get you a mouthful of bread?" groaned the Barker.

"God bless me!" cried Bill; "what is the matter with this unfortunate woman? It was a lucky thing I was so near to cut her down."

"It was a perfect piece of providence," said the quaker.

"Here, my good woman, is all I have about me at present," resumed Bill, putting a bad shilling into the Barker's hand; and then, turning to the quaker, he added, "Did you ever see such a scene of misery?"

The quaker's heart melted within him, and his hand approached ten inches nearer his trousers pocket.

"There's half-a-crown for you, my man," quoth the Quaker, placing the coin specified in the hands of Bill Waters. "I'll see to this unfortunate woman."

"Here, my poor soul, take this," cried Bill, giving the half-a-crown to the Barker; "it is the only last penny I have, and that was given me just now; but some of these good gentlemen round will surely give you a trifle."

The feelings of the auditory were now wound up to the highest pitch, and their purse-strings loosened in proportion. Pennies, sixpences, and shillings, flowed into the lap of the Barker, to which the Quaker added half-a-sovereign.

"Bless you, kind people, all," whined the Barker. "My children have had no food for some days. May you never know what want is."

The Barker now appeared convalescent, so Bill Walters assisted her to rise. She limped away from the spot. Bill Walters walked briskly in the contrary direction.

"Three cheers for the jolly old cock!" cried a young scamp with a jaded countenance.

And three cheers were given for the quaker by the mob.

That gentleman had not progressed many yards when he turned after the Barker, and, slipping his card into her hand, instructed her to call upon him whenever she was in want of assistance.

The Barker acquainted him with her own address, when the Quaker took it down in his pocket-book, and agreed to call in West-street the following morning; then the Barker retired to an ale-house, where Bill Waters was expecting her.

CHAPTER XXXVI.

CHARITY.

"Was Mrs. Vyvian in the habit of visiting the poor?" inquired Mrs. Pearson of Agnes, who was repairing the childrens' copy-books.

"Not that I am aware of, ma'am," replied Agnes.

"Well, don't leave off what you are about, because you can talk and work too. But to return to my question: if your mistress had followed the praiseworthy custom of visiting the poor, I should think that you must have been aware of it, as she would scarcely have gone unattended when she kept you on purpose to walk about with her. Pray, what wages did you receive there? you never told me."

Agnes blushed, and, bending her head nearer the table, endeavoured to hide the tears which stole down her cheeks.

"Why, Miss Talbot, your nose is positively touching the table," exclaimed Mrs. Pearson, straightening her back, and drawing in her chin "Really, I cannot allow the children to have a young person about them so full of bad habits."

Agnes brushed away her tears.

"I was going to observe, Miss Talbot," resumed Mrs. Pearson, "that Monday is the day I usually set apart for charitable visits. I send my lady's maid first to open the windows, and let the people know I'm coming but, as Emma is ill in bed, I think of sending you."

Here Mrs. Pearson pulled out of her bag a small pocket-book, in which she inserted the names and addresses of the objects of her charity.

"Number six, seven, or eight, ten, or eleven, I can't tell which, in Little Coram-street, you will find a poor family: go there, and wait till I come. Don't ask any questions, but throw open the windows and doors. Do you hear me?"

"Yes, ma'am," said Agnes, rising from her seat.

"As you pass Mr. Pearson's dressing-room knock at the door and tell him that I wish to speak with him as soon as possible."

Agnes quitted the room as Mr. Pearson entered.

"I was just wishing to speak with you, dear," said Mrs. Pearson, coaxingly.

"Well, be quick, then, for I am going, and have no time to lose."

"Perhaps, then, dear, I'd better wait till you come back again?" ·

"Then you're likely to wait long enough,' returned Pearson, surlily, "for there's been a flare-up in St. James's-street, and I'm in for it nicely, and till I see how matters stand I can't return home again."

"I was only going to speak to you about the policy of getting rid of that Miss Talbot, for I'm quite sure that, as long as she's here, Lucretia will stand no chance with Lord Oxburn."

"If Lord Oxburn backs out of his agreement, d—n me if I don't arrest him directly, for if the game's up in St. James's-street his expectations are all that I shall have to fall back upon."

"Well, then, it's clear we'd better pack off Miss Talbot as soon as possible, and get some plain young woman instead of her."

Mr. Pearson nodded assent, and left the room.

"Miss Talbot! Miss Talbot!" screamed two or three juvenile voices, as Agnes passed the door of the schoolroom, on her way up the stairs, "are you coming to hear us our lessons to-day?"

Agnes explained that she was going out, but would soon be back again.

"Oh, very well, then, we shan't say any lessons to-day; we shall have a holiday."

"You did nothing yesterday," said Agnes, mildly; "therefore make the best of the time while I am absent, and on my return let me find your lessons learnt and your exercises written."

"Let you find indeed!" exclaimed the boy; "we don't learn lessons to please you."

At the conclusion of this speech the little party clapped their hands, and continued doing so till Agnes left the room.

A few minutes sufficed to put on her bonnet and cloak, and she descended the staircase and set out on her mission.

Agnes had proceeded through several streets, when a crowd, principally composed of poor distressed women, vehemently protesting against some apparent injustice, attracted her attention.

The roads being very dirty, though the pavement was dry, she was compelled to wait for some time before she could pass.

"We are not going to be cheated out of our dues," exclaimed several voices. "You don't mean to tell us that there wasn't more money given than what you've divided amongst us."

"What's all this about," inquired one gentleman of another who was standing near him.

"These are the poor women waiting to receive the money given yesterday by the communicants in —— Church, and the women appear to think that the reverend gentleman has appropriated part of the money to his own uses."

"Impossible," returned the inquirer.

"Not imposssible," returned the gentleman, smiling, "but in the present instance highly improbable, because he is a man of high moral character and genuine piety, but the poor creatures, it appears, expected more money. Suffering has made them desperate. They are disappointed, and vent their ill-humour in unjust accusations."

The gentleman passed on, and Agnes took advantage of the opening they forced for themselves through the crowd to continue her walk.

Arrived in Little Coram-street she with some difficulty discovered the objects of Mrs. Pearson's charity, and found that lady, who had proceeded thither in her carriage, standing in a corner of the room, haughtily surveying and approving or disapproving, as she thought fit, the scene which passed before her.

Seated in a wooden chair covered with a faded

chintz, was an aged female, deprived of the use of her right side and unable to articulate.

Hanging over her, in speechless agony, was her grand-daughter, a fair delicate girl who had been blind from her birth.

A man about forty was endeavouring to defend his little property from the landlord.

"It's a hard thing, a cursed hard thing for you to take two pounds worth of goods for a debt of three shillings," said the man, placing himself resolutely before the only bed he possessed. "I don't care for sleeping upon straw myself, but surely you arn't a going to turn the women into the street?"

"What do I care for the women? I want what's due to me," returned the landlord.

"I tell you, by to-morrow night I'll get you the money; you'd a had it this morning if poor Tim Trowel had'nt a died, and you know we've worked a long while together, and I wasn't a going to let him be buried by the parish for the sake of paying you three shillings; was I, do 'ye think?"

"I've nothing to do with Tim Trowel any more than as how he owed me five shillings, and, like a swindler, he died without paying me."

Stung by this aspersion on the character of his departed friend, the man's face was immediately covered with the deepest scarlet; he rushed impetuously at the landlord, and, grasping him tightly by the throat, a violent struggle ensued.

The old woman, conscious of her inability to separate them, shrieked loudly for assistance.

The blind girl covered her face with her two hands, and seemed in an agony of suspense.

Mrs. Pearson, who continued hemmed up in a corner of the room, made several ineffectual efforts to pass.

Agnes, as soon as she comprehended the cause of the disturbance, stepped down stairs and paid the amount due.

"Take care what you're arter; the rent's paid," bawled Mrs. Groggins, in the tone of a Stentor. "Leave their trumpery alone or you'll be liable to a haction."

The landlord immediately desisted and quitted the room as Agnes re-entered it.

"I don't know, Miss, how to thank you," murmured the man as he gratefully approached Agnes.

"Miss Talbot," exclaimed Mrs. Pearson passionately, "I have no further occasion for your services. A person who would have the wickedness to encourage such flagrant dishonesty, I cannot consider worthy of my further countenance. Make no reply, I will receive no excuses," and Mrs. Pearson stalked majestically out of the house.

"Well I never saw the like of such a woman. She little dreams that, thirty years ago, I used to carry her pickaback up and down Lloyd's-court, but we were both chicks in those days, and I should'nt have knowed her now only her mother was so proud when she got a nursemaid's place in

a gentleman's family that she told everybody about it, and when I went to the house with some candles, for I was in a tallow chandler's shop at that time, I see'd her come out with the children, but of course I took no notice, and now she comes here giving herself such airs, and now and then throwing down a shilling, as if we weren't good enough to touch her fingers. But never mind, Miss, there are plenty of sitivations to be got, and I'm a witness that you haven't done nothing to deserve such treatment."

In a state of cruel embarrassment, Agnes took leave of the family, but she no sooner found herself in the street than a full sense of her destitute condition rushed upon her mind.

She felt that to return to Mrs. Pearson was only to subject herself to fresh insult.

She thought of Amelia Vyvian, and her heart beat with a lighter and freer motion as she figured to herself the warm and kindly reception she was sure to receive from that amiable girl. But the baronet, might he not consider her company an intrusion, and decline receiving her? The doubt decided her; she must seek elsewhere. Her whose infancy and youth had been nourished in affluence had now neither home nor friends; she felt like an isolated being, a creature set apart from the rest of mankind, but her spirit was too gentle to repine, she bowed submissively beneath the cloud of misery that seemed ready to burst over her.

Her busy thoughts again and again scanned over her chances for obtaining shelter and protection, but each time the painful conviction was brought home to her heart that she had not in reality a single friend upon the face of the earth.

For an instant she thought of Mrs. Vyvian, but the hope of obtaining any mark of sympathy or kindness from one so utterly heartless she knew would be delusive.

While these thoughts passed in her mind she continued walking rapidly, when suddenly a voice exclaiming "Miss Talbot" arrested her attention. She looked up, and to her infinite delight beheld Mr. Dobbins.

"My dear young lady," said the good-natured hosier, "we were talking about you only this morning; there's been a blow up at one of Pearson's "hells," and I almost suspect that the rascal will be some time before he holds up his head again. He bilked me out of fifty pounds the other week, and would have done it again if I hadn't been too sharp for him. So I very much suspect that we shall have to look out for another situation, Miss Talbot. However, you know where to come when you take leave of your friends in Guildford-street."

Mr. Dobbins touched his hat, and was about to turn away, when Agnes, overpowered by emotion, and unable to articulate, gently laid her hand upon his arm.

"Good heavens! ma'am, are you ill?" exclaimed Mr. Dobbins.

Agnes, somewhat recovering, informed him of her abrupt dismissal.

The worthy hosier made no reply, but, taking the hand of Agnes, he placed it within his arm, and they proceeded in silence towards Oxford-street.

CHAPTER XXXVII.

THE "BOOZING KEN" AGAIN.

Six weeks had elapsed since we first introduced the reader to the "Nimblefingers," the "Boozing-ken," in Rosemary-lane, when the Duffer, Tim Roper, Ben Bendy, and several other members, both male and female, of the profession of roguery, were assembled together.

"Well Tim," said the Duffer, "I've a mind to turn resurrectionist too, but it's a very ugly trade for all that."

"Blow me if it ain't," added Ben.

"There's lots of tick to be got at it," surlily answered Tim Roper.

"I'm agreeable. Come Ben, you must jine us."

"If you both come too, but strike me if I ever go alone. But never mind, on second thoughts, I'd rather decline altogether."

"I always thought you were true as steel," sharply answered Tim Roper.

"I took him to be staunch to the back bone," vociferated the Duffer.

"So I am, but my conscience goes ag'in such a haction as that. If you're thinking of a pannie, or anything of that kind, I'm your man. But I won't wrong the dead."

"Two hands are plenty, so we shan't be put to an inconvenience on that account," observed Tim.

"Pra'ps you'd give me a little insight into the business, as we're going into partnership," said the Duffer, addressing Tim.

Tim Roper glanced uneasily at Ben.

"I never turned nose on a pal yet," cried Ben significantly.

"Well, well; I meant no offence," quoth Tim, extending his hand, which the other readily took. "Come a little closer, both of yer, and then I'll open your hoptics a bit."

The two men drew closer.

"The surgeons pay for every adult corpse, perwided it's neither green nor putrid, two guineas and a crown; and for minors, six bob for the first foot, and a tanner and a-half per inch for all above it."

"Sometimes they pay higher than that, don't they?" demanded the Duffer.

"When subjects are scarce, and there's no felony made use of in getting 'em, that is to say when they're not stolen, they fetch seven or eight times the money. I sold one t'other day, an Italian out of Saffron-lane, for fifteen pound, and paid ten for it; but then, mind yer, the teeth were all complete, and a subject vas vanted on an emergency; besides which, I got it without a chance of getting lagged for it."

"I should like that sort of traffic," chimed in the Duffer.

"Not a doubt of it; but surgeons won't always pay them prices, and perwided they would, subjects arn't always to be got, without going to the churchyard for 'em.

After a pause, the speaker resumed.

"The job we're a goin' about to night is a slap up one, for this reason, that the grave digger lets me take as many as ever I vants, on the condition of my paying him five bob a piece for 'em."

"What use are they to the surgeons after they've dissected 'em?" asked Ben.

"Some on 'em sell 'em ag'in, when the human flesh is frequently converted into a hadipose substance, not unlike spermaceti."

"What then?" inquired Ben Bendy, whose countenance wore an expression of marked disgust at this sickening detail.

"What then—why, this then, the hadipose substance is sometimes burnt as candles, and at others it's used as soap."

A smile played over the cadaverous features of tha resurrection-man.

"An old gent as I knew who styled himself a member of the faculty, used to sell the skulls for nail boxes, soap trays, and handles of knives; and what's more, actually gave an infant's skeleton to his child for a doll, so that the boy might become knowing in the perfession early."

"Resurrectionising's a bad trade," said Ben, "I'd rather beg my bread from door to door, even if I couldn't be a cracksman."

"And vhy should yer mind doing that? begging's a better trade than yer think for, old flick," exclaimed Bill Waters, who had recently seated himself near the two.

"I don't know much about your trade," replied Ben, "but somehow or another I think it's a bad 'un."

"You seem to me to be all alike," added the Duffer.

"Not a bit of it," answered Bill. "First there's the *Rufflers*—fellers as pretends to be wounded soldiers; these, after a year or two's practice, become *Upright men*, still continuing to pretend to have been soldiers, and asking vehemently for work, though they never intend doing it if they get it. They never take nothing but money, and beg all day, but manage to steal grunters (pigs) and poultry from the farmers at night. Then there's the *Hookers* or *Anglers*, who cant (beg) all the daytime, but at night steal linen or anything can catch hold on out of the winders, or else-where, by means of a long pole with a hook at the end."

"You're a nice lot of yer," exclaimed the Duffer.

"Go on," said Ben, who was much interested at the details related by Bill Waters.

"Then comes the *Pallyards*," resumed Bill " coves with rags on, who get votever they can scrape together, and then sells it for ready money ; they put spearwart to raise blisters on their bodies,, or else arsenic or ratsbane to make wounds what can't be cured."

"Are there any more kinds ?" demanded Tim Roper.

"I believe yer," responded the beggar.

"Ain't there fellers vot are called *Abraham men ?*" asked the Duffer.

"To be sure there are, and a deal of money they make, too," replied Bill Waters.

"How do they manage it ?" inquired Ben.

"Vy, they pretends to be lunatics, to be sure, vot 's just come out of Bedlam, where they were well nigh beaten to death. Then they begs money or prowisions at farmers' houses, and at the same time almost frightens them to death by fierce looks and savage sayings."

"They excite both fear and pity ; the surest means in the world of gitting what they want," observed Ben.

"I likes to excite the first-named commodity, but don't at all stomach the second," cried the Duffer, with a ferocious laugh.

"But them as gits more money than all the others put together are the *Dommerars*," continued Bill Waters ; "and, although my friend over there was jist now a sneezing at pity, that 's precisely the way they does it, without there being any fear in the case at all."

"How so ?" asked the Duffer.

"They pertends to be dumb, and keeps their tongues doubled down by main force, then groans for charity, and holds up their hands."

"And what do you call yourself ?" demanded Ben.

"An *Upright Man*," replied Bill Waters. "I was properly installed into the fraternity."

"How was that done ?" said Ben.

"A quantity of liquor was poured on my pate, with these words—'I do stall thee, William Waters, to the rogue, and that from henceforth it shall be lawful for thee to cant for thy living in all places.' All kinds of canters are obedient to the *Upright Men*, and we far surpass the rest in prigging and pilfering."

"You've got a language of yer own, ain't yer ?" cried the Duffer.

"We have. We calls it *Pedlar's French*, or *Canting*," returned Bill.

"It 's time we should be a goin'," said Tim Roper, " for we have some business to night, re-collect." And then, turning towards the Duffer, he added, in a softer tone, " We must be very cautious how we speak on that 'ere subject afore strangers."

"I could have told you *that*," replied the Duffer.

The two villains left the "Nimblefingers" for the purpose of making the necessary arrangements with the grave-digger previous to their commencing their resurrectionising labours that night.

"Which ground is it to be ?" asked the Duffer, as they proceeded down Rosemary-lane.

"Old St. Pancras," was the reply.

Ben remained in conversation with Bill Waters. Presently he got up and quitted the "ken," muttering, as he went, "The sacrilegious villains ! but I'll frustrate their object."

He traced the resurrectionists to Old St. Pancras, when they entered a small house adjoining the burial ground, which proved beyond a doubt to Ben that he saw before him the spot selected by the villains for their midnight practices.

"I cannot turn nose upon a pal," cried Ben ; "but I think my other plan 's a good 'un."

What success attended the housebreaker's efforts another chapter will disclose.

CHAPTER XXXVIII.

THE CATASTROPHE.

IN a preceding chapter we left Agnes and Mr. Dobbins walking towards Oxford-street.

Arrived in his little back parlour, Mr. Dobbins seated his visiter on a chair and motioned his wife to assist in taking off her things, he stepped into the shop.

"Well really, I can't say I expected that my husband would bring you here again so soon, Miss," exclaimed Mrs. Dobbins pettishly.

Agnes explained that she had accidentally met Mr. Dobbins.

"Very lucky indeed, but very strange," murmured Mrs. Dobbins.

"But no more strange than true," said the hosier, who at that moment entered the room, " and I am very sure, Nancy, that when you hear that the poor thing has been suddenly thrown upon the world, you will feel as I do, very thankful that we have a house over our heads in which we can offer her a shelter."

Mrs. Dobbins, though a kind-hearted woman, did not seem quite so well satisfied with their ability to assist Miss Talbot as her husband did, however, she made the best of the matter and expressed herself very glad.

Mr. Dobbins drew his chair towards the fire, took up the paper, and read till dinner. He was in high spirits, and as soon as that important meal was despatched, amused himself and the company by read-ing sundry suppositious paragraphs about Miss Sophy Dobbins and Mr. William Stock, whose nup-tials, it appears, were expected to be solemnized in the course of a few weeks.

Miss Sophy blushed very deeply, and occasionally exclaimed "Don't Pa."

William, who from being a despised drudge, was, by the magical power of a legacy, metamorphosed into Mr. William Stock, rubbed his hands, pushed Sophy with his elbow, and exhibited many silent tokens of ecstacy and delight.

"Don't you tell the 'marrow bones and cleavers,' Molly." whispered Mr. Dobbins, loud enough for every body to hear, "mind you don't."

"La, Sir." responded the maid, "who'd have thought of such a thing?"

Mrs. Dobbins, who seemed amazingly tickled at her husband's wit, laughed immoderately, but being unfortunately minus of two or three of her front teeth, she took especial care to keep her pocket handkerchief before her mouth.

"Do hold your tongue, Dobbins," said the lady, "and don't make such a fool of yourself."

In obedience to his wife's command, Mr. Dobbins made several ludicrous attempts to capture the un-ruly little member, but at last he gave it up as a bad job, declaring that he should never succeed till his wife consented to laugh and talk without apply-ing her handkerchief to her face.

Mrs. Dobbins coloured violently, and, turning to Miss Talbot, informed her that an accident had de-prived her of two of her front teeth.

"But I've no cause to be ashamed of that," ad-ded the lady, looking reproachfully at her husband, "I'll tell you how it happened, Miss, I was stand-ing at the corner of that street which runs across the top of the court, over against a butter shop which nearly faces the street where mother once lived. I was looking up at the old house a wonder-ing who lived there now, when a great big dray horse bounced round the corner and knocked me backwards, flat upon the back of my head. I was picked up by a gentleman who was passing and carried into a doctor's shop where I lay for some time as dead as a rat, but suddenly feeling better I opened my eyes, and the first thing I beheld, Miss, was the handsome face of my preserver hanging over me.'

"Admiring your beauty, I suppose," said Mr. Dobbins, winking at Mr. Stock.

"No sir," exclaimed his wife, "he was examin-ing my teeth. I got up, Miss Talbot, as soon as I was sufficiently recovered and thanking them all round, asked what I had to pay, upon which the handsome gentleman stepped forward, and, putting a card into my hand, gave it a squeeze, and whis-pered 'nothing, my dear.' But I assured him that he quite mistook if he thought my husband was a man to allow me to be knocked down and picked up

and set to rights again all for nothing. 'Then ask your husband, my dear,' said the gentleman, to give you a five pound note, and come to me with it to-morrow morning, for I have been looking into your mouth and I find that several of your teeth are out of order, and others wanting, and I shall have great pleasure, madam, in setting them all to rights, and will attend you two-thirds cheaper than anybody else.' I took my leave, Miss, and made the best of my way home, when, would you believe it, that mean creature my husband refused to give me the money, and has never done so to this day, though he very well knows that I am ashamed to go over the door for fear of meeting the gentleman."

"Well, there's three sovereigns," said Mr. Dob-bins, throwing the money upon the table, "and perhaps you can prevail upon Miss Talbot to go with you, and you must make the best bargain you can."

Agnes assured Mrs. Dobbins that she would be most happy to accompany her, and it was arranged that they should set off the following morning, im-mediately after breakfast.

"I always think it best to go early," observed Mrs. Dobbins," before the instruments have been used, for nobody knows how many dirty mouths they may be put into before the day's over, and I should think that for decency's sake they'd wash 'em at night to be ready for the morning."

Mr. Dobbins who had been nodding and bowing for some minutes, at last indulged in his accustomed nap; Mr. William Stock retired to the shop; and Mrs. Dobbins in a confidential whisper informed Agnes that the latter gentleman was going to marry her youngest daughter, and to pay down two hundred pounds for a share in the business; "besides this,'' continued she, "we have, since you were here last, got a new lodger, I can't find out what he is, but some great man in disguise I've no doubt of. He plays on the guitar, and sings most charming, so loud that he makes the house tremble again, and so hoarse that I can never make out a word he says, but it's very pretty I know that, and so you'll say when you hear him; and then he dances and fences nearly all the night I understand, for Mr. Dobbins and I sleep on the first floor, so we dont know much of it. But the gentleman says he must keep up his practice, and of course if he wasn't used to go to balls and that sort of thing, he wouldn't care about taking all that trouble for nothing, so I say he must be somebody. The first day or two he came here he didn't fancy Molly waiting upon him, he said she looked so uncouth like at him, so he went and brought in a little bit of a crittur not much higher than the table. but I understand she is above four-teen and does his work very well; so if he's pleased, and pays me my rent, it don't matter to me who waits upon him."

Mrs. Dobbins ceased speaking for some moments, then looking affectionately at her eldest daughter, "You know that villian Garnet, Miss Talbot,"

Agnes bowed assent. "Poor Lucy has never held her head up since he left London. Now I say that if she was not a fool, I'm pretty sure she wouldn't stand a bad chance with our lodger. What do you think Miss Talbot?"

"Why really," replied Agnes blushing, "I'm such a novice in love-affairs, that I am quite incapable of giving a satisfactory reply."

"Oh you're a deep un," said Mrs. Dobbins, shaking her head doubtingly, "why long before I was your age I had half a dozen sweethearts. There was Bill Malt the brewer's clerk, Thomas Highlo, the shoemaker, James Roe, the fishmonger's son, and I don't know how many others; but I wouldn't have nothing at all to say to none of them, though they were all dying for me. For a long while nobody knew anything about it, but somehow or other father found it out, and being a funny kind of man, determined to have a joke with 'em, so he asked 'em all to tea on the same evening, without

saying a word to mother or I. They all met about the same time, and father sent for us to come down. The moment I set eyes upon them, I turned back to run out of the room again, but father had locked the door; so up he comes and takes hold of my hand, 'Now gal,' said he, 'which of these ere chaps do you mean to take for a husband.' It was no use mincing the matter, for the night before I'd seen Mr. Dobbins, and my mind was made up, so I up and said, 'neither one nor t'other.' Father set up a hearty laugh, mother said it was too bad of me, and as soon as father unlocked the door, my poor lovers slunk out of the room one after the other like so many sheep without tails, and from that day to this I never saw nor heard any more of 'em, except Bill Malt, so I suppose they must either have hung or drown'd themselves. As for Bill Malt, he went with the rest of them down stairs, but the moment he reached the bar,—for my father was for many years landlord of the Three Tuns, Fetter-lane,

—the moment Bill Malt reached the bar, he called for a glass of brandy, tossed it off, and casting a terrible look at the bar maid, rushed into the street, where he began running and never stopped till he reached the house of his washerwoman. 'Mrs. Soapsuds,' said he, clenching his forehead tightly between his two fists, 'Mrs. Soapsuds, can your daughter be ready to marry me to-morrow morning.' 'Lor no sir,' replied the washerwoman who began to fear that he was mad. Then Bill began to cry, and laugh, and tear his hair, and kick about his hat, so Mrs. Soapsuds promised that her daughter should be ready, and the next morning sure enough they were married, but they never had an hour's happiness, for everything she does is wrong in his eyes; it's always 'Nancy wouldn't have done that, Nancy wouldn't have said this,' she never could please him Miss, up to the day of his death, which took place exactly on the same day fifteen years after I sent him adrift; he died of a broken heart," added the lady in a voice, which emotion, or a conscientious doubt of the veracity of her assertion rendered scarcely audible.

At the conclusion of Mrs. Dobbins's narrative, her husband woke up, and after rubbing his eyes, looked about him, first on one side and then on another.

"Now don't be jealous," said his good lady fixing her eyes smilingly upon him, and shaking her head. "Don't be jealous Peter."

"Lor, bless the woman," said Mr. Dobbins, "what are you talking about?"

Mrs. Dobbins still stared at him till the tears actually started into her eyes.

"Don't cry mother dear," said Lucy, taking her hand and pressing it between her own, "dont cry mother."

"I'm not going to cry gal, though it's enough to break the heart of any one to see how I'm treated by your father there, not one woman in a hundred would have borne what I've borne; they wouldn't indeed, Mr. Dobbins, they wouldn't indeed sir," and Mrs. Dobbins sobbed hysterically.

"Well, if this isn't a rum start, I don't know what is," said Mr. Dobbins who was but half awake. "Lucy dear ar'n't we going to have any tea to night."

Lucy looked very grave and began making preparations for the meal, while Mr. Dobbins amused himself by pulling Sophy's hair, and occasionally, by way of variety, treading upon the cat's tail. Miss Sophy murmured several whining complaints, while the cat expressed his displeasure by what is vulgarly called " swearing."

"Can't you leave the animal alone, you brute," said Mrs. Dobbins angrily.

"The male, or female animal my dear? for I am tormenting two at once." returned her husband.

"You ought to be ashamed of yourself sir, to call your daughter a cat."

"So I am ashamed," replied Mr. Dobbins, pulling out his watch, "for it's past eight o'clock, and I ought to have been out an hour ago."

"That's right," said Mrs. Dobbins. "as soon as ever your mind's at ease, off you go again spending your money like a fool."

Mr. Dobbins made no reply, but buttoned up his coat, put on his hat, and walked straight out, muttering good night to Miss Talbot.

"I would give something too to know where he's gone to," said Mrs. Dobbins looking at the apprentice. "I wish, William, you'd just put on your hat and follow him."

William did as he was desired, but not feeling very much flattered by the commission entrusted to him, he returned almost immediately, declaring "he could not see him any where."

"Just like you," said Mrs. Dobbins, "I never sent you yet, that you didn't come back and say you couldn't find him."

———

CHAPTER XXXIX.

THE RESURRECTIONISTS.

It was half-past one o'clock in the morning when Tim Roper and the Duffer entered Old St. Pancras' burial ground.

" This is the place," said Tim, trying a piece of loose ground with his spade.

While he was thus employed the Duffer appeared to be listening attentively.

" What now ?" exclaimed Tim Roper.

" I thought I heard something," replied the ruffian, trembling with fear.

" No doubt yer did."

" Don't be a fool, Tim; I shall never git on at this sort of job, I can see that with half an eye."

" You can't expect to thrive all at once at a new business," was the brief answer.

At this moment the moon, which had till now been partially concealed, emerged from behind a cloud. The piece of ground on which they operated had been previously loosened by the gravedigger, so that their unhallowed purposes were soon fulfilled.

" This is the stale 'un," cried Tim, " the vun as he vants for the skeleton."

" And a precious stale 'un it is, too," retorted the Duffer; " that is, if we're to judge by our noses."

The resurrection-men now lifted a plain deal coffin out of the hole, when Tim Roper beat in the top of it with his spade, and, having secured the contents, kicked it gently back again into the hole.

The corpse had been so long a time under the influence of decomposition, that it presented a truly revolting spectacle.

"We've come half-an-hour earlier than we agreed to at the ' Nimblefingers'," observed the Duffer, as the church clock struck the hour of two.

"All the better," responded his companion. "What's that a-sticking to the subject?"

"A bit of linen I take it," answered the Duffer.

"Never mind. Pitch it into the bag."

The Duffer obeyed, although his feelings were evidently very repugnant to the filthy task—villain—nay, murderer as he was, he shuddered at participating in the unhallowed proceedings of the resurrection-man.

The moon again retreated behind a cloud, but myriads of stars spangled the zenith.

"I sartinly am gitting a deal bolder," said the Duffer. "All the stiff 'uns in this here churchyard wouldn't make me change colour. By G—d, Tim! what's that?"

"Where?" asked the other ruffian, who was also beginning to be oppressed with a vague fear of he knew not what.

"There," replied the Duffer, pointing as he spoke to a tall white figure evidently advancing towards them.

The two men continued gazing on the object of their terror.

Presently the spectre appeared to sink into the ground—at all events, it vanished from their sight, and they thought they heard a noise resembling the rattling of bones as it did so.

Incredible as it may appear, this apparition so completely paralysed the two ruffians, that they stood fixed to the spot, stupidly gazing upon vacancy.

It is in vain to attempt reasoning upon the springs of human action, but certainly it is that, when the spectre vanished, this circumstance appeared to rouse the Duffer from his strange stupor, for he threw down the bag and its contents, and started off at full speed, as if he every moment expected the dreaded apparition to seize and pull him down.

Tim Roper snatched up the subject, and flew in the same direction as his intimidated comrade, without even venturing to look round, as if fearful of the airy something being close to his heels.

The two men were soon beyond the precincts of the churchyard. Presently a figure rose up from behind a gravestone, in every respect dissimilar to one of the unsubstantial denizens of another sphere, but bearing a strong resemblance to Ben Bendy.

"I've giv' them a sickner," said Ben, liberating himself from a long white sheet, and undoing a pair of stilts he had borrowed for the occasion. "They've got one subject away with 'em, but that wasn't my fault; if I hadn't had that plaguey fall over the gravestone, blow me if I wouldn't have collared that rascal Tim."

Ben Bendy, being unaccustomed to walk upon stilts, had stumbled over a gravestone, which oc-

currence caused the two resurrection-men to suppose, on account of its sudden disappearance, and the strange manner in which it effected its exit, that the apparition was in reality a supernatural visitant.

At length Ben also quitted Old St. Pancras churchyard.

Return we now to the resurrection-men.

They were at a rapid pace threading the intricate streets of Somer's-town, ever and anon casting back a look of feverish anxiety.

"If that wasn't a stiff 'un," said the Duffer, "my peepers ain't of no good to me."

"Here's a pretty go; we've only got vun of the subjects, and the vun that's worth least money too," cried his companion; "but it's a lucky thing we haven't dug the other up and left it there to peach on us."

"I'm glad we're where we are," answered the Duffer.

The resurrection-men stopped at a surgeon's residence situated in the neighbourhood of Somer's-town, not half a-mile distant from Old St. Pancras burial ground.

Three taps on the door gained them admittance. The two ruffians were ushered into the surgery.

"We have only got one subject," said Tim Roper.

"How so? What do you mean?" demanded the surgeon, hastily.

"We were interrupted," replied Tim.

"Indeed! No one has traced you here I hope?"

"No one."

"Are you sure?"

"Quite."

"Which one is it?"

"The stale 'un."

"Devil! I'm sorry for that. You know I only agreed to give you three pounds for that one."

"That'll do."

The surgeon at once laid down the sum specified in the hands of Tim Roper.

"Is that a friend of yours? I suppose he's one of the right sort?" said the surgeon.

"He wouldn't be a pal of mine if he wasn't," answered Tim.

The two resurrection-men left the surgeon's house, when the door was immediately closed after them.

The surgeon returned to the room in which his purchase had been deposited. On opening the bag for the purpose of examining the subject, he perceived that the resurrection-men had not provided him with the one he had bargained for.

"This is an abominable fraud," cried the surgeon; "but yet it is just possible that the fellows may have been mistaken. This must have been thirty years at least below ground: it will, however, serve my purposes nearly as well, for the skeleton is all I require, and that is all I have here."

A white roll fell out of the bag which, on the

surgeon inspecting it more closely, proved to be a sheet of parchment.

There was writing on it.

"What can this be," he almost involuntarily exclaimed; "probably some will or other document relating to property."

The writing was in the French language, and ran similar to the following :—

"This being the only means I am possessed of for consoling you with regard to my present position, I gladly avail myself of the opportunity of sending you this letter by an old and faithful follower—one who I know will deliver it. My only dread is that you may not be where he expects to find you; in that case he has promised to keep it about him till he shall meet with you. Painful as the topic is to myself, I am confident that it must be equally so to you. I am going to acquaint you with a few of the leading incidents connected with my unfortunate capture and subsequent imprisonment. On Thursday, March 15th, my house at Ettenheim was surrounded by a detachment of dragoons and picquets of gend'armes, in all about two hundred men ; they were commanded by two generals, the colonel of dragoons, and Colonel Charlot, of the gend'armerie of Strasburg. This occurred at about five o'clock. At half-past five the doors were forced, my papers were seized and sealed up, and I was conveyed in a waggon, between two files of fusileers, to the Rhine. As for my papers being seized, for that I care but little as they were the other day examined in my presence, but all they found were some letters from my relations, one or two from the king, and a few copies of my own, now these you know could in no way compromise me.

I was afterwards taken to Colonel Charlot's house at Strasburg, but have, since that, been transferred in a hackney coach to the citadel. The first night I lodged in the commandants parlour, and slept upon a mattress on the floor, with gend'armes in the next room, and two sentinels in the one in which I slept ; I am permitted to walk in a little garden, in a court behind my pavilion ; but a guard of twelve men and an officer is continually at my door. Although the precaution is extreme on all sides to prevent me from communicating with any one whatever, I have managed to forward you this letter, how, I will tell you on a more befitting occasion,

I sincerely hope that I may shortly obtain my liberty, as I am really innocent of being implicated in any conspiracy against the life of the First Consul."

"This, then, relates to Napoleon," said the surgeon, as he hastily turned over the parchment in his hand.

He then continued reading :—

"May God grant that I do so, let us not, however, flatter ourselves yet. I intended sending you this letter before, but contingent circumstances prevented my putting my purpose into execution, I therefore subjoin the very latest particulars concerning my imprisonment,—particulars, which if my mortal career is unjustly cut short, will never probably become known to the world, but through the medium of your exertions. I am credibly informed that a letter was sent to General Murat, governor of Paris, and another to Harel, commandant of Vincennes, respecting myself ; in fact I have enclosed what I believe to be a veritable copy of each."

"Secret Police,
29th Ventose, Year XII., 4 p.m.,
"To the General-in-chief, Murat, Governor of Paris.

"General,

"Agreeably to the orders of the First Consul, the Duke d'Enghien is to be conducted to the castle of Vincennes, where arrangements are made to receive him. He will probably arrive to-night at this destination. I beg you will make the arrangements necessary for his safety as well at Vincennes as on the road of Meaux, by which he will arrive. The First Consul has ordered that his name and everything relative to him should be kept strictly secret, consequently the officer in charge of him must not make him known to any one. He travels under the name of Plessis. I desire you to give the necessary instructions that the intentions of the First Consul may be fulfilled."

"Secret Police,
29th Ventose, Year XII., half-past 4, p.m.
"To Citizen Harel, Commandant of the Castle of Vincennes.

"An individual whose name is not to be known, citizen commander, is to be conducted to the castle, the command of which is entrusted to you. You will lodge him in the place that is vacant, taking precautions for his safe custody. The intention of Government is that all which relates to him should be kept strictly secret—that no question should be asked him, either in regard to what he is or in regard to the cause of his detention. You yourself are not to know who he is ; you alone are to communicate with him, and you will not permit him to be seen by any one till further orders from me. It is probable he will arrive to night.

"The First Consul relies, citizen commander, on your discretion, and on your scrupulous fulfilment of these various orders."

"You may perhaps wonder how, I have obtained a copy of both or either of these letters, as I stated before, a more befitting occasion may present itself for my explaining all this more satisfactorily to you. Although the people around me are extremely obliging, I pine for freedom, and my grief increases the more I reflect on my cruel position. I have written to the First Consul protesting my innocence of the crime alleged against me, but alas, I have received no answer. In that letter I mentioned to him that if this plot existed, I had been left in total ignorance of it, and had even been deceived on the subject—that I, more than any one, was attached to France, and admired the genius of the First Consul, that I had often regretted my being unable to fight under his command and with Frenchmen ; and that perhaps, far removed as I am from the throne, and with no hope of obtaining it, I might have thought of doing so if the duties annexed to my birth had not imposed upon me the necessity of acting otherwise ; that, in short, I could not believe that the First Consul would consider it a crime in me to have maintained by arms the right of my family and of my own rank. But I fear that I am wearying you, yet believe me that even the limits of a large letter will not permit my saying all I have to communicate to you. Pray give my affectionate regards to your father. We must hope and wait. Do not forget to use any influence you may possess in my favour.

" Adieu, Princess. You have long known my sincere and tender attachment to you; free or a prisoner it will ever be the same.

L. A. H. De Bourbon."

For some moments the surgeon stood engaged in profound meditation.

" This skeleton must have belonged to one of the French emigrants, who came over hither in the ime of the famous revolution," exclaimed he musingly. " I am well aware of the fact that a great number of them were buried in that very churchyard. The parchment is addressed outside to the Princess Charlotte de Rohan Rochfort. But stay, here is some more writing, penned in another hand.

He then commenced reading again.

" It having been out of my power to deliver this to the Princess Charlotte de Rohan Rochfort, although commissioned to do so by the unfortunate Prince d'Enghien, of beloved memory, I have taken the liberty of prefixing an account of his royal highness's examination, which I am sure will add to its value in her eyes, should this precious document ever fall into the hands of the Princess, if it does not it shall be buried with me.

" The examination commenced at eleven o'clock, p.m.

" The prisoner was asked his surname, christian name, and place of birth.

" Answer. Louis Henri Antoine de Bourbon, Duke d'Enghien, born August 2nd, 1772, at Chantilly.

" Question. At what periods have you quitted France ?

" A. I cannot tell precisely, but I think it was the 16th of July, 1789. I went with the Prince of Condé, my grandfather, his father, the Count d'Artois, and the children of the Count d'Artois.

" Q. Where have you resided since leaving France ?

" A. On leaving France, I passed with my relations, whom I have always followed, by Mons and Brussels; thence we proceeded to Turin, to the King of Sardinia, where we remained nearly sixteen months; thence, always with my family, I went to Worms, and the banks of the Rhine. The corps of Condé was then formed, and I joined them. I had, before that, made the campaign of 1792, in Brabant, with the corps of Bourbon, under Duke Albert.

" Q. Whither did you go upon the ratification of peace between the French republic and the Emperor ?

" A. We finished the last campaign near Gratz ; it was there, that the corps of Condé, which had been in the pay of England, was disbanded, that is to say,——"

The rest of the manuscript was illegible.

" Would that I could keep th s," cried the surgeon, " but if I did, the manner in which I obtained it would be sure to transpire."

In another moment it was reduced to a heap of blackened charcoal.

Thus perished the last memorial of a man, whose death is deservedly regarded as the greatest moral blot on the character of Napoleon.

CHAPTER XL.

MR. STAMER.

It is now time to go a little into the history of Mr. Stamer's family, for without this explanation, some traits in his conduct may appear in the eyes of my gentle reader, not much to his advantage.

We have seen that he acknowledged to the baronet, that the name of Stamer was merely assumed, and that his mother was the daughter of a stockbroker. At the early age of seventeen, that lady had eloped from the house of her father with the Honourable Arthur Stamer Coningham, whose affairs were in such an embarrassed state, that immediately after his marriage, he was obliged to take up his residence in Italy.

Dora soon had reason to repent the imprudent step she had taken, for her father exasperated beyond measure, married again; and her aristocratic husband, ashamed of the connexion he had formed, entirely neglected her.

The bride but of a few months—she was left to mourn in silence through the day, and to watch in lonely solitude throughout the long long night.

At the end of twelve months, Dora, who had by the death of her father-in-law become Lady Stamer Coningham, gave birth to a son.

Gentle and affectionate, she hoped to find in the smiles of her infant a solace for her sorrows.

Her pale cheek resumed the blushing colour of the rose, the bright flashing of her fine dark eyes, which had been replaced by an expression of melancholy, again illumined her countenance. But the hope she indulged in was visionary; by command of her husband the little Arthur was committed to the care of a foreign nurse, and the weeping mother was compelled to deprive herself of the only tie which bound her to life.

This arrangement was made at the request of the Comtessa di Villa Nova, the lady of a foreign Ambassador, with whom Lord Coningham was at that time deeply enamoured, and who imagined that by pretending an extraordinary affection for the wife of her lover she would be enabled more effectually to lull the suspicion of her husband ; but the precaution proved vain. Lord Coningham in one of his nightly perambulations, was assassinated in the neighbourhood of the castle inhabited by his mistress.

Dora, who notwithstanding her husband's neglect, was entirely devoted to him, was for some months in a state of the deepest affliction. But time softened her calamity, and by the advice of her father, she dropped her title, assumed the second name of her husband, and retired into the West of England, where in a small country town she brought up her son.

At the death of his grandfather, the little Arthur came in for the greater part of his property, but it was thought advisable that the money should accumulate till he was of age, as he would then be enabled to take up his title without embarrassments.

At sixteen years of age the boy was sent to college, and the anxious mother purchased a small house in the neighbourhood of Oxford, where they resided for three years ; at the end of that time, Arthur left home for London preparatory to a tour on the continent, and it was then for the first time that he was informed of his noble birth and family connexions, and strictly enjoined to secrecy.

Let us now return to Mr. Stamer at the moment he concluded his interview with the baronet, and continue our narrative.

When Mr. Stamer left Grosvenor-square he returned home to his lodgings at the Blenheim, and determined immediately to communicate with his mother, and obtain her permission to inform the baronet of his true rank and condition. He wrote, and received an immediate reply, but it contained a death-blow to his hopes, for he learned for the first time that his grandfather, from prudential motives, had left him his fortune only on the condition that he should conceal his name and title, till such time as he could take possession of his inheritance free from all embarrassment. His mother concluded her letter by advising him to begin his travels without further delay.

" My travels," hastily repeated Stamer, throwing down the letter upon the table. But he took it up again, and, affectionately pressing it to his lips, " How little, dearest mother," thought he, " are you acquainted with the influence of love, or you would know that, notwithstanding the earnest desire I feel to fulfil your wishes, it is impossible for me to withdraw myself from the presence of my Amelia."

Stamer had little or no fear that, as soon as he was of age, and at liberty to disclose his circumstances, the baronet would give his consent. But he was now only twenty. One year must necessarily elapse before he could explain himself, and what if Amelia should cede to the solicitations of her brother, and accept the man he had chosen for her. The thought was maddening, and Stamer, who had thrown himself upon a couch, intending to pass the night, rose, and walked petulantly up and down his apartment.

" Please, sir," said an aged female, putting her head in at the room door, " the old gentleman down stairs sends his compliments, and begs you won't make such a noise, sir, for he hasn't had a wink of sleep all night ; and please, sir, he'd be much obliged if you'd just let him take a nap, sir."

" Give my compliments to your master, and tell him to go to the devil." said Stamer, angry that his meditations had been so unceremoniously disturbed.

" Well, I'll never believe that there is any goodness to be found in young gentlemen again," mumbled the old woman, as she re-entered her master's bed-room, and closed the door. " I did think that Mr. Stamer the most innocentest, harmlessest creature alive ; but I find he's like the rest of 'em—all well enough so long as they've got everything their own way, but the moment anything crosses 'em, then we find out what they really are."

" What age is Mr. Stamer do you call him ?" said the old gentleman, mildly.

" Please your lordship, about the age of your own master Freddy, and very like him, too, my lord—just his look when he came from Oxford, before he set out on his travels."

The old gentleman groaned audibly, and for some time remained silent, but, resuming the conversation,—

" Present my compliments to Mr. Stamer, and tell him I shall be most happy if he will favour me with his company to breakfast to-morrow."

Mr. Stamer received the message and in the morning sent a note expressing his regret that an early engagement prevented his accepting the polite invitation, but promised to pay his respects to him in the evening.

Stamer intended that day to obtain if possible an interview with Amelia, but he recollected that she would inquire for the little beggar girl and her family.

His mind had been so engrossed by his own concerns, that he had neglected to visit the poor creatures since they had taken possession of their new abode ; he therefore took a hasty breakfast and proceeded to Peter-street.

Arrived at the house he mounted the stairs to the second floor. The door of the room was partly open, but he knocked and the voice of a man invited him to enter.

Mr. Stamer obeyed the summons, but stood some moments on the threshold, uncertain whether or not to advance, for the room was darkened, and a solemn silence reigned throughout.

Leaning on the table, with his face buried in his two hands, sat the man, apparently absorbed in grief. At the sight of Mr. Stamer he lifted his eyes, but immediately resuming his former posture, he groaned mournfully. The same child which was on a former visit sitting helpless on his knee, was now standing by his side, but, on perceiving Mr. Stamer the little fellow advanced confidently, and taking his hand led him towards a small bed on which the inanimate remains of the woman and infant were laid out. The young girl wearied with watching and crying, had fallen asleep with her hand unconsciously grasped within that of her deceased parent. "Mammy's asleep" whispered the little boy, at the same time pressing his finger upon his lips, as if to enjoin silence.

Deeply affected, and conscious that in his selfish regard to his own affairs he had neglected to pay that personal attention to the sufferers which the urgency of their case demanded; he turned towards the man expressing a hope that every necessary care had been taken to supply the wants of the deceased.

"Everything, everything that could be done was done, and may God bless you, sir, for the ample means you have afforded us. But it was too late. For the last three months, sir, the poor dear sufferer never quitted her bed; lying sometimes three whole days without taking any nourishment but a little cold water; and I unable to leave the room. My right side, sir, is disabled," added the man, passing his hand over his shoulder and down his side. "I caught the rheumatics while I was in prison."

"In prison!" exclaimed Mr. Stamer, internally shrinking from holding converse with a being apparently so degraded.

"Yes sir," repeated the man, "I was in the Fleet for upwards of two years, and since that time have never been the man I was before. It's a sad story, sir, and though I don't say I havn't deserved all that I met with, yet that dear blessed angel that lies there, sir, did nothing wrong. She was the most affectionate, managing, clever creature you ever set eyes upon; and respectably born too, sir, for her father kept a large boarding-school near Fulham; but he got into trouble and destroyed himself, but that didn't make her any the worse"

"By what means did you earn your living before you were so unfortunately disabled? inquired Mr. Stamer, endeavouring to divert the man from the contemplation of his misery.

"I was originally in the navy, sir, but a school-fellow of mine, named Prigmore, having turned lawyer, persuaded me to quit the service and take a situation in his office. My father, who was a half-pay officer, was too poor to lay down money for me to enter the legal profession as a gentleman, I therefore engaged myself as copying clerk till my services should become more valuable and entitle me to better remuneration. Five years passed merrily, Prigmore earned plenty of money, and in consideration of my having on several occasions rendered him important services he paid me tolerably well. At the end of that time my master was employed to arrange the affairs of old Spellwell my wife's father. Susan Spellwell was a pretty girl; we had many opportunities of seeing one another, and at last we got so over head and ears in love that we began to talk about buying the ring; but Susan was a prudent girl, and she thought we'd better wait till I'd saved money enough to furnish a lodging. We agreed that it should be so, but some-

how or other Prigmore found out that we were engaged to one another, and one morning while I was sitting in the outer office he called me into his private room. 'Inkhorn,' said he, 'so I understand you are going to get married but want the means; your reasons for dissembling with me are best known to yourself, but I cannot forget that you have rendered me some essential services, and I should desire nothing better than an opportunity of expressing my sense of the obligation I am under to you.' I was going to make him an appropriate reply, but he stopped my mouth, begging that I would be silent and hear him to the end. 'It is my intention,' said he, 'to request your acceptance, I won't say of a gift, because gifts are burdens of gratitude, sometimes very uneasily borne, but a loan of one hundred pounds you can have no objection to receive.' With tears in my eyes I assured him that fifty would be more than sufficient, but he persisted in giving the hundred, and, astonished at his generosity, I bitterly accused myself for all the evil surmises I had on several occasions formed concerning him. I took the money and flew to my beloved Susan, and the following week we were married."

Overpowered by his feelings, the man was for some time unable to continue, but he recovered himself, and, regardless of Mr. Stamer's entreaty to finish it another day, he resumed it.

"For five or six weeks after our marriage Mr. Prigmore was our continual visiter; he was very familiar, and at last his attentions to my wife became so pointed that I could endure it no longer: I sent her privately away, and for some time visited her by stealth. But with all my precaution the villain discovered her retreat, and insultingly declared his intentions; I resented the injury, and the following morning I was arrested for the money he had advanced me. Two years I remained incarcerated, and at the end of that time was suddenly released; a relation of my wife's having died and left us a little money. Among the inmates of the prison, I had made acquaintance with several rather equivocal characters, and by their advice I set up a gambling tavern, to which there was a great resort of noblemen and others. We went on swimmingly for fourteen or fifteen months, when I'd suddenly a run of dice against me, and lost to the amount of fifteen hundred pounds. Not having sufficient money to discharge the full sum, I commenced a system of plunder and robbery, and at last became so notorious that I was compelled to leave the country. I however returned in a few months, but all my substance had been seized by my creditors, and I found myself with a wife and two children with only a few shillings in my pocket, compelled to seek shelter in the wretched habitation you found us in. I however did what I could for my wife, who was shortly afterwards confined. But the loss of my limbs, which took place a week after the birth of my infant, entirely disabled me. God only knows how we have managed to live through all the misery we have endured."

The man finished his narrative, and Mr. Stamer slipping a purse into his hand, recommended the nurse, who had returned from an errand, to see that every thing was properly attended to.

He then took his leave, and set out in the direction of Grosvenor-square.

CHAPTER XLI.

THE SUICIDE.

ALTHOUGH the Mudlark was possessed of the five sovereigns he had obtained from Abednego Levi on the occasion of his selling the ring to the Jew in the shop of the marine-store dealer, and which, although unconscious of it, he had deposited in the Barker's cellar, yet he wished to hit upon some means of obtaining an honest livelihood, and thus keep that small sum in his possession as a support, on which he might rest, provided any emergency should arise, without sinking into a state of destitution or returning to his former miserable occupation.

With this laudable intention he sallied out in far better spirits than he had previously experienced for a long period.

It was nearly eleven o'clock in the morning. Whilst walking along he arrived at a baker's shop, which he immediately entered, but found it unoccupied.

Shortly, however, the master made his appearance.

" What can I serve you to?" asked he, eyeing the Mudlark suspiciously.

" I wanted to know whether you were in want of a porter, or a boy to run of errands?"

" So you call yourself a boy, do you? Come here again and I give you in charge. I'm up to gentry of your description."

The mudlark left the shop.

He came next to a brewery.

" Holloa, you vagabond! what are you at?" cried a man, as the Mudlark entered the yard.

" I've come to see whether you've got any work to do?"

" None of that gammon. Be off, or I'll let my dog loose at you."

Again the Mudlark desisted.

" I must seek some filthier occupation—something more wretched—but let it be vot it may I'll live honest if I can," soliloquised the Mudlark, after the failure of this second attempt.

At this moment a piece of paper, hanging in a chandler's shop window, with " Wanted a shoeblack" inscribed upon it, caught his eye.

" I'm surely fit for that." And he entered.

" Please, mum, I've come about the sitivation."

" Oh, indeed! And have you got a character from your last place?"

" It's my first time of going into sarvice, mum."

" Then you won't suit me."

" Although I never tried it, I knows I could black boots well, mum."

" Will you go? or shall I be put to the necessity of calling a policeman?"

" Thank ye, mum, no necessity votever," replied the Mudlark, leaving the shop as he did so.

" It's the laws of society made me vot I am, and they seem determined to make me worse too, for I must either work or steal, or starve, and without a character I can't do the first, human nater's agen me doing the last, so I'm driven to do the second. However, I'll make one effort more, and if that don't answer I must fall back on the five pounds I've got."

The Mudlark directed his steps to the London docks.

He accosted a seaman and inquired of him whether there was any thing to be done.

" I can't say, mate, may be there is, there's some bricklayers working over there, and p'r'aps they might want some one to carry the mortar back'ards and for'ards for 'em."

The Mudlark thanked him and acted upon the information he had afforded him

" Are yer in want of hands, sir?" said he addressing the foreman.

The foreman eyed him from head to foot.

" Yes, we are in want of one or two; do you understand the business?"

" No sir, I thought you wanted somebody to run back'ards and for'ards with the mortar,"

" We only give boy's pay for that—eight shillings a week."

" That'll do, sir."

" And you must find your own hod."

" I could manage that, sir."

The Mudlark hastened home intending to tear up the boards at the bottom of the stairs, and thus obtain the five sovereigns.

While he was away, endeavouring to find employment, the Barker was anxiously awaiting the arival of Bill Waters.

At length he came.

" Oh, bill!" cried she, as he was walking up the stairs, " I've been in luck's way to day."

" Have yer found any thing then?"

" Yes, that I have."

" What is it?"

" Guess."

" I can't."

" Five sovereigns then, as sure as I'm alive it's true."

" Are you sure they're good uns?"

" That I am, but how they come where I found 'em, I can't tell. I should have thought my old man put 'em there, only where was he to get such

a sum? and besides, if he had have got it, he's a deal too knowing to put it in my way; but to be sure he isn't aware as how I should be sure to find it."

"What do yer mean to do with it?" asked Bill.

"Git drunk to be sure."

"Vot a good thing it would be if your husband vos out of the way! how cozy we might be together!"

"For my part, I shouldn't much mind putting him out of the way," said the Barker.

"We might make quite a little fortin' with them young 'uns."

"How?"

"By bringing 'em up to the perfession of cant-ng; they'd soon become fly at their tender hages."

"As I said jist now, for my part I shouldn't stick at putting him out of the way," reiterated the Barker.

'That's a awk'ard thing to do, d'ye see? It's almost sure to be found out some time or another, and he's a little 'un that 'ud make some slight op-position, too, I guess."

"Well, well, it was only a suggestion," observed the Barker; "but I shouldn't try it that way; I'd poison him."

"Then there's the poison inside of him to prove it agen yer."

"That wouldn't be so not if I strangulated him, though," said the Barker.

"P'r'aps not; howsoever, we'll talk about that 'ere anither day. I shan't want the babbies this time, cos I'm a-goin' to spit blood and have fits," ejaculated Bill Waters.

"You might have told me that afore, mightn't yer? cos then I could have let 'em to somebody else, p'r'aps; but have yer got yer traps all ready?"

"Not quite; I'll get 'em ready now. I thought

as how I'd better come to tell yer I didn't want 'em to-day," exclaimed Bill.

Bill Waters produced a small bag, from which he abstracted a piece of soap and an empty bladder. He then produced a glass phial, containing a crimson-coloured liquid, with which liquid he filled the bladder.

The liquid was sheeps'-blood. He placed the bladder into his mouth, and then pressed it between his teeth, when the sheeps'-blood gushed forth as though it had been the veritable stream of Bill Water's life.

"That hoperates vell," cried the Barker. "Now try the convulsion fit."

The impostor then put a slice of soap into his mouth.

Having worked it up into a state of fermentation, he commenced a series of convulsionary movements, well calculated to deceive the most acute observer. The soap oozed out from between his teeth like foam; his fists were clenched firmly together, and his whole appearance was that of a person suffering under the influence of a dreadful fit of convulsions.

"Oh, Bill!" said the Barker, "votever you do, don't stay making them faces any longer; but that 'ere 's just like you; I'm sure, with your talents for chousing, yer might have been a attorney, or a forger, or even a prime minister, though he sartinly is the biggest rogue of the lot."

"No, my dear," replied Bill Waters, "I arn't quite gumption enough for the last sitivation; but yet I do think myself skilful in my own business."

"You'd better go now, hadn't yer?" exclaimed the Barker; "but mind yer come back agen soon, and then we'll talk about my old man. I m quite in earnest, I can tell you; I arn't a-goin' to let him stand in the way of my happiness."

"You're right there; he 's a reg'lar bad 'un."

"A brute! a monster! a beast!" cried the Barker.

Bill Waters hastened out into the street.

Shortly afterwards the Barker followed his example, not forgetting to take the two unfortunate children with her.

She had quitted the house about ten minutes when the Mudlark entered it.

"I hope that all my misery is now at an end. Oh! how often—how fervently have I prayed for an opportunity of earning an honest livelihood by the sweat of my brow! but—thank God!—my prayer is at last granted."

He provided himself with an old bent poker, which he inserted into the slit in the boards at the bottom of the stairs, intending to tear up the planks, and thus obtain the five sovereigns, and, with a portion of that amount, to purchase a hod.

To his astonishment the poker met with no opposition, but the boarding opened up with facility, when his olfactory nerves were assailed with the vilest of stenches.

And then, with a cold shudder, he looked into the vile vault beneath.

"Is it possible? What new horror awaits me? But yet my money may be safe. Oh, God! may it prove so; if it does not, there is—yes, there is the last resource of despair." And emotion choked his further utterance.

Having obtained a light, the Mudlark descended into the cellar, eager to explore the place, as well as anxious to discover whether or no his money was safe.

What an awful spectacle met his gaze!

Oh, this is too horrible! horrible! horrible! My wife is yet a viler monster than I took her to be. Compared with this 'ere, the deed of the murderer is innocence itself. For the sake of a little money, how many a one may she have slowly poisoned! P'r'aps my children too." And the Mudlark covered his face with his hands.

Till now he had forgotten to look after his money.

"Unless that wretch has been here, it must be all right; but vy has she gone out and taken the babbies with her? P'r'aps she don't intend coming home agen."

He groped about in a state of feverish anxiety.

"I see it nowhere."

Ever and anon he would slip upon some foul piece of offal, or his distracted gaze would rest upon some more convincing proof of his wife's disgusting practices.

"I mustn't lose my hope," cried the Mudlark, half aloud, and as if communing with his own spirit, "for, at all events, the last extremity is always open to me."

But search as he would—and it was eagerly that he did search—the discovery of the object of his anxiety did not reward his perseverance; and how could it when it was in the Barker's pocket?

"Is there any hope left?" the Mudlark mentally ejaculated.

However desirable a quest hope may be considered in the breasts of most people, it too frequently eventually proves an *ignis fatuus*,. and, after leading its worshippers through many a quagmire, vanishes from their sight, and leaves them much deeper in the mire than they were previous to their holding any intercourse with the ever-shuffling daughter of to-morrow.

Repugnant as his feelings were to the ungracious answer, common sense suggested "No."

Would that this most useful yet most outraged of all our mental qualities and attributes, real or fictitious,—for he who acts according to the dictates of common-sense seldom errs—had retained its dominion over the mind of the frantic man!

But a heart rendered desperate and callous by social injury, and a mind warped by despair, are alike incapable of entertaining any reasonable ideas. When once an overwhelming avalanche of misery appears, it bears all before its impetuous tide—sweeping, like a defertilising stream, over a spot already too barren, it carries away, in its remorseless speed,—virtue, honour, common-sense, and probity: all are engulfed in one giddy vortex.

The mudlark ascended from the vault, the inspection of which had caused him so much mental anguish, and, having closed the trap-door, and extinguished the light, he mounted the staircase.

On arriving at the first landing he perceived a piece of rope lying at his feet.

As if afraid to trust his thoughts to their own custody, he availed himself of the opportunity chance had thrown in his way, and in another moment he was suspended from the banister above. A few throes of convulsive agony agitated his frame. Then all was still.

Presently the silence was broken by the shouts of a drunken party in the next house, and then an organ-boy played a merry tune in the streets without—a tune which strangely contrasted with the listlessness which pervaded that empty house of death; but both were mute to the ears of him who had committed suicide; his spirit had fled—whether to higher or lower regions, whether to realms of eternal bliss or infinite misery, who can determine?

Thus were the Barker's wishes fulfilled, without her being put to the necessity of executing them herself.

CHAPTER XLI.

THE DENTIST.

WE will now return to Mrs. Dobbins, who, as soon as breakfast was finished, set out with Miss Talbot to the residence of the dentist. They arrived at the house, and, upon inquiring for him, were immediately admitted. The dentist had no recollection whatever of having seen Mrs. Dobbins before, but when she recalled to his mind the particulars of her upset and his attentions, he immediately remembered her.

" I told my husband, sir," said she, " about the five-pound note, but he wouldn't give no more than three, so you must take 'em, sir, and do what you can for the value of 'em." Mrs. Dobbins put the money into the dentist's hand.

" Why, my dear madam, really three guineas is such a small sum that I am afraid we shall be able to do very little for it, but, if you can manage to pay the remaining two pounds within three months, I'll see what I can do for you."

" Well well, sir," returned Mrs. Dobbins; " we'll not quarrel about that."

The operating chair was wheeled out into the middle of the floor, and Mrs. Dobbins had no sooner seated herself than the dentist displayed before her some of the whitest and best-formed substitutes he could select.

" What are these made of?" said Mrs. Dobbins, picking out three of the largest; " because I can't afford to be buying new teeth every day, so be sure and give me the sort that'll last."

" Those, madam, are ivory; but they do not retain their colour. Those made of the teeth of the hippopotamus are more durable."

" Well, then, sir, I'll have of the sort you mention, sir—the hippopottypottimus—for I should think bulls'-teeth would last for ever; shouldn't you, Miss Talbot?"

Agnes blushed. The dentist smiled, and, assuming a rather familiar air, inquired upon what condition the young lady would consent to part with some of her pearly teeth.

Agnes made no reply, but the calm gravity of her countenance expressed her displeasure.

" What a funny man you are!" said Mrs. Dobbins. " When I was that lady's age, sir, I can tell you my teeth were the admiration of every living creature: they were as white as snow, and, oh, so reg'lar!"

" I've no doubt of it, madam," answered the dentist, examining her mouth attentively. " Those which remain are beautiful specimens of what the others must have been."

Mrs. Dobbins, who was aware that the interior of her mouth, in its present state, presented a sad spectacle of ruinous decay, looked doubtingly at the dentist. But he continued his inspection.

" If I am not very much deceived, madam," said he, " at the early age of eighteen months you were so ill with a fever that your life was in imminent danger. About five years of age you must have suffered very severely from the effects of small-pox; at seven——"

Mrs. Dobbins, who was not prepared for these revelations, stared with astonishment.

" Lor bless me, sir! why, you can be nothing short of a conjuror! However did you find out what happened to me when I was a babby? I've heard my poor dear mother say that I lay for six hours and she didn't know whether I was dead or alive, till father come with the doctor who had been physicking me for nearly two months. ' It's no use, Mrs. Lockyer, your sending for me,' said he; ' the child's had the brain fever, and now she's dead, and now I can do nothing for her.' But mother knew better, and, unbeknown to father, she'd sent for another doctor, who came in just in time to save my life. The moment father's doctor saw him off he scampered fit to break his neck. Mother's doctor looked after him and shook his head at him, then he turned towards me, who was lying stretched out as stiff as a corpse, and shook his head again and again and looked very melancholy, and, when mother asked him what he thought was the matter with me, he shook his head again, but said nothing. But presently, all of a sudden, a new thought seemed to strike him. ' Mrs. Lockyer,' said he, ' send for this powder.' The powder was got, and he somehow or other poked it down my throat. I opened my blessed little eyes, and presently began to choke. ' The hooping cough, if I don't mistake,' said the doctor, turning to mother. ' The brain-fever and the hooping-cough?' asked father, frightened out of his wits. 'Not the brain-fever, my good sir,' said the doctor. ' but the hooping-cough, and, with care, I've no doubt that the little patient will get round again.' Mother cried with joy, and father skipped about the room as frisky as a young kitten, declaring all the time that the other doctor should never enter his house again. But the doctor didn't forget to send in his bill, though ; and a pretty one it was, too."

The dentist, who had made several efforts to break the thread of this uninteresting reminiscence, smiled pleasantly when it came to a conclusion, and immediately resumed his examination.

"I must beg leave to contradict your assertion concerning the hooping cough, Madam," said he, " for I can assure you that certain marks upon your teeth give incontestable evidence that you were afflicted with that complaint about the age of seven."

" Oh dear no, Sir," returned Mrs. Dobbins, "I can assure you that you're quite out there at any rate, for mother told me over and over again how I used to turn black in the face with coughing, baby as I was, and how she used to pat my back."

" Very likely, madam," replied the doctor with some asperity, " many children are afflicted with convulsions during their teething. You may have had convulsions, and may have had a cough, but I positively assert that you didn't have the hooping cough till you were seven years of age. And I think that after having spent some twenty or thirty years of my life in studying the effects produced by sickness upon the teeth and gums, I have some right to expect that my decision will be considered conclusive."

" Well, don't let us quarrel about it sir, never mind whether I had the hooping cough at eighteen months or seven years old, though I know I had it at eighteen months, but I say never mind, I came here to get my teeth done, and perhaps you'll be good enough to do what you're going to do, and a done with it."

" No, madam," said the dentist gravely, at the same time turning down the cuffs of his coat, " No no, madam, when a lady thinks fit to deny the truth of my revelations, founded as they are upon experience and profound study, and to deny the truth of them only out of pure malice, I must beg to decline her custom. My charge for time and the examination of your teeth is one guinea, the other two I return."

" Why, lor', sir," said Mrs. Dobbins, " you surely aint going to keep back one of my guineas ; why its a regular swindle."

The dentist walked stiffly into another apartment, and Mrs. Dobbins, after putting on her bonnet, took Miss Talbot by the arm and quitted the house,

declaring that she never met with such a scandalous impostor in her life before.

"Had you not better go to some gentleman of established reputation, Ma'am," said Miss Talbot, " the person we have just left is, I fear, nothing but an ignorant quack. I have seen him several times in the country. On one occasion when I was on a visit at Brighton a friend of mine purchased a set of teeth of him, which he charged thirty guineas for, but though she made several attempts, she never could make any use of them. At Worthing he was so very unsuccesful in extracting teeth and performing other operations that he was compelled to leave the place."

" The good-for-nothing villain !" exclaimed Mrs. Dobbins. " And, now I think of it, he certainly does look very like a rogue ; he 's got such a palarvering sort of way with him. But what am I to do about my guinea? I'm sure Dobbins won't give me another ; and it 's no use my buying two teeth when nothing less than three will do. But no matter, I suppose I must wait a week or two and see if I can't squeeze it out of the living. Depend upon it, Miss Talbot, that the teeth that fellow kept taking in and out of his mouth all the while I was telling about my sickness wasn't his own making. If I thought they were, I wouldn't mind, after all, going back to him."

Mrs. Dobbins stood for some moments irresolute, but finally concluded that perhaps, after all, he would be cheaper than any body else.

Miss Talbot was of a different opinion, as she considered that teeth, badly made and ill set, would be of little or no use : consequently, however trifling their original cost, the money spent upon them could only be considered as thrown away.

But Mrs. Dobbins had made up her mind, and she turned about to retrace her steps, to the great annoyance of Agnes, who at that moment perceived Lord Oxburn in the act of presenting his arm to a lady who had just descended from her carriage.

Why did a blush of the deepest crimson spread itself over the pale cheek of Agnes? Why did her breast beat with a quicker, with a stronger pulse? Why did she tremble?

Reader, be not too inquisitive ; in due time the cause of Miss Talbot's blushes shall be unveiled to you ; let us not, therefore, ungenerously endeavour to pry into the hidden secret of her heart, but be content to know that, when Lord Oxburn entered into the house, and she saw the door close after him, she felt a sad, desolate sense of her own humble condition. Her spirits painfully depressed, she walked in silence by the side of her companion.

" What a pity, Miss Talbot, you didn't walk a little quicker ; I wanted to have caught a sight of that lady's gown before she went into the house. But it don't matter, for, as the carriage hasn't gone away, I suppose she 's coming out again presently, so we'll wait a bit. You see, I've got a new silk gown to make, and my gals will always make my things their own way; but, if I can catch a sight of that lady's gown, I shall see if I'll have one made like it, and then I can tell 'em how I'll have it done."

Mrs. Dobbins continued pacing up and down before the house regardless of the entreaties of Agnes, who now endeavoured to persuade her to return to the dentist.

"It will be so late, ma'am, that he'll not be able to see; hadn't we better go?"

"Why, as to that," said Mrs. Dobbins, resolutely maintaining her post, "we can go there another day: but, as I'm a-going to have my gown cut out to-morrow, I should like to make up my mind about it now, and I think the pattern of that lady's gown would exactly suit my shape."

Agnes was too well bred to contradict the assertion of Mrs. Dobbins, but she possessed too much sincerity to flatter her. She therefore contented herself with observing that the lady in question had a very slim figure, whereas that of Mrs. Dobbins was rather stout.

"Stout, miss!" exclaimed Mrs. Dobbins, while her face reddened with displeasure: "I can tell you that, if I chose to tighten and squeeze myself in as some people do, my waist wouldn't be more than a quarter of a yard round; but I couldn't bear it. I'd rather look as big as a barrel of beer than suffer so much misery."

Mrs. Dobbins, who, to do her justice, always contrived, by tight lacing and bracing, to make the least of herself, puffed and blowed as if quite indignant at the idea of being thought to have a larger waist than the delicate little creature who had stepped out of the carriage.

But presently the door of the house re-opened, and the same lady, accompanied by an older lady, Lord Oxburn, and an invalid elderly gentleman, advanced towards the step of the door.

As the younger lady passed she glanced admiringly towards Agnes, and whispered a few words in the ear of the old gentleman, who gazed first at Agnes and then at her companion with an expression of thoughtful inquiry, which touched Agnes to the very soul.

Since the death of her father the presence of an old person had always impressed her with a feeling of respectful tenderness, but, on the present occasion, the sight of the venerable stranger had occasioned an emotion so powerful that she could scarcely suppress her tears.

The carriage drove away, but as long as it was visible she was conscious that the eyes of the old gentleman were fixed intently upon her.

Mrs. Dobbins, who had observed nothing but the pattern of the ladies' dresses, was quietly trudging along by the side of Miss Talbot, debating, in the profundity of her own mind, how the body of her dress should be cut out, and whether the skirt should

be made plain or trimmed with flounces, till, wearied by the many *pros* and *cons* which started up in continual opposition to her half-formed intentions, she condescended to lay before Agnes the subject of her meditation; not that she had the remotest idea of following that young lady's advice, but because that, in all the important events of her life—and the making of a new silk dress was, in her opinion, a very important matter—she made it a rule to act in opposition to somebody.

"For my own wear," said Agnes, "I prefer skirts full and plain for walking out of doors, and trimmed for dinner and evening dresses."

"Your taste, then," said Mrs. Dobbins, "is very different to mine; for I can't a-bear to go tumbling up and down stairs, tearing my flounces all to pieces. Now, without you mean to sit stuck up all day long a-doing nothing, whatever can be the use of going to the trouble of making flounces to sit in a little back parlour, where nobody can see what you've got on? No, no, Miss Talbot; you governesses know nothing about management; you make wretched wives. If I had a hundred sons not one of 'em should marry a governess. If I have a well-made, handsome dress, I like my neighbours to see it, or I don't care a fig about having it at all. Whenever I go by Mrs. Thingamee's shop-window, lor! how she does peep through the glass at me, fit to bust, if I've got anything new on!"

The two ladies now found themselves in face of the dentist's house, and were about to knock at the door when the gentleman himself opened it.

"Well, madam," said he, bowing the ladies into the parlour, "I suppose you've come back again to have your teeth arranged, and I can tell you that, for your sake, I am very glad you've done so, for there's a scoundrel in this neighbourhood, who, taking advantage of my celebrity, entices people into his place, breaks their teeth and dislocates their jaws, and I can assure you that several deaths have been the result of his unskilful operations. After your departure, I reproached myself severely for having permitted my jealous concern for my own reputation to get the better of my duty, for I consider it, madam, the duty of a professional man to make any sacrifice rather than allow the unsuspecting public to be maimed and wounded by an impostor."

"I'm sure, sir, its very good of you," said Mrs. Dobbins, "here are the other two guineas, and if you'll please to be as quick as you can, for my husband 'll be wanting his dinner, sir, so I must hurry back again."

"But I must beg leave to observe, madam," said the dentist, "that we must consider what is past as done with, for I cannot consent to count the guinea I received as part of payment for our future transactions. I have no objection, if you will give me your address, to defer the payment of the remainder of the money for a month or six weeks."

"Well, sir, that'll do," returned Mrs. Dobbins, "what are we going to do first?"

The dentist, who now appeared in perfect good humour, entered a small closet and began certain mysterious preparations.

Fiz went a lucifer match; then crack, crack, crack was followed by a strong smell of fire.

Next gurgle, gurgle, proved that water was being poured out of a bottle.

Then came forth sounds as if something was being violently squeezed between two hands,

Mrs. Dobbins, whose curiosity at last became unbearable, rose from her chair, and approaching the closet, inquired "if he was making teeth."

"Keep in your place, madam," said the dentist, "I am only getting ready a preparation which you will presently be kind enough to put into your mouth, but my fire having gone out I have some difficulty in getting the substance into form."

"Oh pray do let me see it," said Mrs. Dobbins, I hope you don't put the same stuff into everybody's mouth; do you, sir?"

"Really madam, your remarks are quite insulting," said the dentist, working harder than ever in his endeavours to efface from the composition the teeth marks which had at least a dozen times been imprinted upon it. "If I hadn't already lost so much time, I positively declare that I would even now decline proceeding any further. Now ma'am I'm ready, and you will oblige me by taking your seat again and opening your mouth as wide as you can."

Mrs. Dobbins did as she was told, and the dentist stepped towards her with a small pan containing a preparation resembling wax which he requested she would put into her mouth and bite into the composition as hard as she could. After several attempts Mrs. Dobbins succeeded in giving a bite to the dentist's entire satisfaction, and they parted upon the whole pretty good friends, the dentist promising that before the end of the week the teeth should be ready.

"Well, I don't think I shall have any reason to complain after all," said Mrs. Dobbins as soon as they got into the street.

"I hope not," returned Agnes, who had certain misgivings as to the professional ability of the gentleman.

"What a mercy it is that I didn't fall into the hands of that villain who dislocates people's jaws, for most likely by this time he'd have done my business for me. Depend on it, Miss Talbot, I should never have spoken another word again if I'd by any chance a gone to him instead of the other."

Mrs. Dobbins then began to talk upon indifferent subjects, but Agnes was fatigued and replying only in monosyllables, the conversation soon dropt, and they pursued their walk for some time in silence.

But Mrs. Dobbins was not a woman to remain long without talking. Her thoughts had wandered from the contemplation of splendid shops and gaudy equipages, to the delight she should experience when she should again be able to laugh and talk without danger of exposing the ugly vacancies occasioned by the loss of her teeth. But as she did not feel quite assured that she could wear false teeth without detection, she inquired of Agnes, who was unable to give a satisfactory answer.

"Then, if you don't mind coming with me," said Mrs. Dobbins, "I think an acquaintance of mine who keeps a baker's shop in our neighbourhood, will be able to settle our doubts upon that matter, for I've heard from very good authority that she's got a false tooth in the bottom row, and while I'm talking to her I wish you'd examine and see which tooth it is, and tell me afterwards if you'd a found it out if I hadn't a told you. Here's the shop," and Mrs. Dobbins led the way into the back parlour.

"I'm coming directly," exclaimed a very smartly dressed little woman, thrusting her head from behind the counter half way into the back parlour; "I'm coming directly, Mrs. Dobbins."

But the lady was mistaken, for at that moment a tall thin gentleman with light bushy eyebrows and rather a savage physiognomy stalked majestically into the shop. A scanty cloak, lined and trimmed with scarlet shag, covered his bony person, while his hat, an uncommon shabby one, was pulled very much over his eyes, which were fixed indignantly on the bustling little woman.

"This morning," said the gentleman, deliberately taking a two-penny loaf out of his pocket, "this morning, Mrs. Twist, I sent my servant," he stepped towards the door and beckoned to a very small beggarly looking girl, who immediately advanced and stood by the side of him, "I sent my servant, this young person, to purchase a two-penny loaf for my breakfast. A two-penny loaf, we all know, is a small thing, but small or great I choose to have good weight."

The gentleman laughed sarcastically, and added, "Pray, Mrs. Twist, what do you pretend is the just weight of a two-penny loaf?"

"Why, really, sir," returned Mrs. Twist, "it's impossible for me to say. We divide the dough as equal as we can, but still there always will be a little difference."

"You can't deceive me, madam, by that sort of foolish talk. In the first place, do you acknowledge having sold the bread to this young person? In the second, tell me exactly what the weight of this loaf ought to be? Lastly, I insist upon your weighing the same before my face."

"Lor' bless me, sir, you don't suppose I'm going to be such a fool as to take all that trouble about a two-penny loaf?"

"Then by jingo I'll make you," said Mr. Tift, springing over the counter, and drawing from under his cloak a rusty sword, "then by jingo I'll make you."

Mrs. Dobbins, who had recognised her lodger, screamed with amazement, while the woman, trembling with affright, prepared to execute to the very letter the commands of Mr. Tift, who, satisfied that the loaf was weight, expressed his approbation, and smilingly informed her that, for the future, she might always count upon having his custom.

As soon as Mr. Tift had quitted the shop, the journeyman, who, at the sight of the sword had run into the bakehouse, came blustering through the trap door, declaring " he would be the death of the scoundrel."

" Oh Billy Dough you've come too late, the bird's flown," said Mrs. Dobbins, grinning provokingly; " but do look at your missus, she's fallen into a fit." Everybody set to work to restore Mrs. Twist, but it was not till a bottle of lavender and two of rose water had been poured over her that she began to revive.

" Well I never saw such impudence in all my life," said she, endeavouring to mop up with her handkerchief some of the sweet scented water with which her person had been deluged, " I never saw such impudence. This comes, Mrs. Dobbins, of being a poor lone widow. If poor Twist had been alive no man breathing would have dared to serve me so."

" Neither should they now," muttered the journeyman, " if I'd a been here."

" Why I was never more astonished in all my life," said Mrs. Dobbins, " why the gentleman's our lodger, Mrs. Twist. " I wonder what Dobbins'll say to it. I know he's a little eccentric, but that you know is nothing to us, if, he pays his rent that's all I care about."

" That ain't my way any how, Mrs. Dobbins," replied Mrs. Twist, " people must do something more than pay their rent to please me, and you, a mother of two grown up daughters, I think ought to be ashamed of yourself to own such sentiments."

" I don't exactly know, Mrs. Twist, what you mean to insinuate. My lodger is a gentleman, and I dare say you've sent him short weight before this or he'd never have served you as he did to-day. However, it'll be a long while before we shall have any more bread out of your shop again, I can tell you that, so you needn't trouble yourself to send it."

Mrs. Dobbins quitted the shop, and in a few moments after was seated by the side of a good fire in her own parlour, informing Miss Talbot how Mr. Twist died through the neglect of his wife, and how Mrs. Twist had since been courted by no less than seven lovers.

" So I call her a disgrace to her sex, Miss Talbot, no honest woman ought to countenance such a crittur."

CHAPTER XLII.

THE MUDLARK'S END.

IT was eight o'clock at night when Bill Waters arrived at the Barker's house. Finding that the Barker had not yet returned, he seated himself on the door-step, and there awaited her arrival.

Presently she appeared in company with the two children.

" Well, Mr. Waters," said the Barker, " I hope I ain't kept yer waiting long ?"

" Vy, you sartinly have ; but I vanted to see yer about your old man."

" Hush ! P'r'aps he's come home. You go over the way, then I'll kick at the door, and, if he comes and opens it, you needn't come in to-night; if he doesn't, you can."

Bill Waters crossed the road, and the Barker kicked repeatedly at the door.

" He isn't there. Come in, Bill, and we'll have some lush and a pipe together."· And the two impostors entered the house with the Barker's latch-key.

Bill Waters started back on the landing.

" Lor ! what's the matter ?" cried the Barker.

" Your old man——"

" Vot of him ?"

And then her eyes fell upon the remains of her husband.

Bill advanced towards the banister, probably with the intention of cutting him down.

" Leave him alone, yer fool, can't yer ? How do yer know he's dead yet ? He's just done for himself what I was a-goin' to do for him. I ain't over partickler how my ends are gained. Look yer there ; his leg's a-resting on the banister."

The Barker disentangled the limb, and clapped her hands firmly on the mouth of the Mudlark, intending to suffocate him, provided he had not yet perished from strangulation.

" That ere's the best hact he ever did in his life," said the Barker. " Quiet them ere squalling brats, will yer ?"

" Hold yer jaws, both on yer," cried Bill. " It giv' me a bit of a turn, though."

" Come and have a drop of some'ut, then, for he's stiff enough ; he must have been swinging some hours; and then we'll talk matters over a bit."

" I think I will wash my mouth out," replied Bill Waters, as he walked up the stairs.

" Sit down, Bill."

The Barker produced the liquor, and, having taken a pull at the flask, handed it over to Bill Waters.

" Now, yer see, I've got four pun' ten left, and nothing stands in the way of our union."

" Marriage do yer mean ?" cried Bill, eyeing her interrogatively.

" I don't."

" Sartinly not ; man and wife never live comfortable together long," said Bill.

" I couldn't a-bear to be saddled with marriage," observed the Barker ; " but what I vants is this—to make all the tin we can, and drink all the lush we can swallow."

" I admire your notion exceedingly, ma'am," quoth Bill, filling his glass as he spoke ; " and here 's to the success of it."

Bill Waters swallowed the liquor at a draught, and then ignited his pipe.

The Barker resumed.—

" Now, it seems to me as how we might sell my old man : do yer take it ?"

" Can't say I do," answered the beggar.

" Vy, I means he'd do for the dissecting room."

" To be sure he would."

" But how are we to do it ? I don't know of any resurrectionist."

" Leave that to me. I'll settle it to-night. I heard some fellers talking about body stealing at the ' Nimblefingers', so I'll step over there presently, and nail a bargain with 'em if I can."

" That 's doing business," observed the Barker.

" And about the young 'uns, vot can we do with them ?"

" The big 'un 's beginning to do well, and the little 'un will, I think, almost keep us drunk three times a-week without working."

" Oh, no ! she ain't so fly as all that."

" You're out agen."

" Vy, what 's yer plan ?"

" Blind children git lots."

" Well," impatiently ejaculated Bill, " but she can see, can't she ?"

" That 's no reason why she always should."

A pause ensued.

" I knows how to do it," resumed the Barker.

" How ?"

" Vy, tie a couple of walnut-shells, with black-beetles in 'em, on her eyes."

Bill Waters looked inquisitively at her.

" Vot do they do then ?"

" Eat 'em out, to be sure."

Bill Waters had lied, had deceived, was not by any means scrupulous of the means by which a purse was to be filled—aye, had even murdered ; yet there is always some good feeling or another in the breast of every man which, however depraved he may be, cannot be altogether eradicated : it may be apparently smothered, but underneath, the fire still burns, and, even in the most callous hearts, a little smoke will occasionally testify its existence. Of all abhorrent spectacles, none is more striking than that of an inhuman mother, and it was now that this feeling of the beggar's heart started from its lurking place.

" Are yer in earnest ?" said he, regarding the Barker with a fixed stare.

" To be sure I am ; vy shouldn't I be ?"

" Then I'm positive I needn't mind about it."

" I'll send the big 'un out alone to-morrow, and put 'em on the little 'un. Yer see, vot I looks at is this—she won't be of no use to us in another point of view for a tidy lot of years yet to come. We couldn't send her on the town till she 's twelve or thereabouts, and now, when she 's blind, she'll always have her bread in her hand.

" In her eyes yer mean, don't yer ?"

" Now don't be a fool, Bill ; but go arter my old 'un—will yer ?"

" Ay to be sure I will, gal ; shall I call yer by yer maiden name ?"

" Yes, Gal Briggs, if yer please."

" Then good night, Gal Briggs."

And Bill Waters repaired to the " Nimblefingers."

*   *   *   *   *   *   *   *

" What a while Sam Soame's been a-going at it ; what a buck he is ; what a devil of a run he's had," said a man in the parlour of the " boozing ken," addressing himself to Tim Roper.

" He's taking up my trade now," replied the resurrectionist.

" You calls him the Duffer, don't yer ?"

" That's my name," said the Duffer, who had just entered.

" And how did you come by it ?" asked the first speaker, who was a notorious coiner.

" I followed that line once, and I gloried in my calling, but my history 'd take a long time to tell," exclaimed the Duffer.

" Let's hear it."

" Can't now, but you shall another day, for there's a mine of instruction in it, and you know I'm always as good as my word."

" Time slips away in good company," said the man, who followed the profession of making counterfeit money : " we'll have yer tell the story to-morrow night."

" That's the ticket," replied the Duffer.

The coiner left the " Nimblefingers."

" I say, Sam, we must git another subject ; I'm hard pushed," observed Tim Roper.

" So am I," growled the Duffer.

" That old vagabond, Levi, hasn't put much in our way of late," added the resurrectionist ; " if he don't soon I'll be at him ; I believe we might git sum'ut if we frisked a bit in his house."

" No, no ; we won't try that yet."

" Perhaps not."

" But about the subject—we must go agin to the churchyard."

" I'd go to—to the treadmill first," replied the Duffer, doggedly.

At this moment Bill Waters entered.

" So you're in want of a subject, are yer gen'le-

men," cried he, having overheard the last part of their conversation.

"You ain't agoin' to sell yerself, are yer?" inquired Sam Soames, better known as the Duffer.

"We don't buy live'uns, we ar'nt such noodles," gravely observed Tim.

"Stuff! you can kill him whenever yer want him," suggested the Duffer, with a coarse laugh.

"It ain't myself I've come to sell, but a stiff'un," interposed Bill; " a feller of forty or thereabouts, who did for hisself vot the Jack Ketch should have done for him."

"If it's vun as suits us we don't want nothing better than a subject just now," observed the Duffer.

"Yer may have it to-night then for the matter of that," responded Bill.

"What do yer want for it?" inquired Tim Roper.

"Five pounds, and not a tanner less," answered the beggar.

"We'll come along with yer now if yer like it,

and if the subject suits us ' we'll drop the glanthem'* in no time," cried the resurrectionist.

" Come along then."

The Duffer, Tim Roper, and the beggar proceeded to the house in West-street.

The door was ajar. They reached the landing.

" Did he do that 'ere bit of kindness for himself?" asked the Duffer.

" To be sure he did, and his old 'ooman's short of tin, so she wants to get rid of him," was the answer.

"I arn't got no money now," said Tim, " but I'll be with yer agen in no time."

" Mind yer are."

The Duffer and Tim Roper left the house.

" How are yer goin' to get the glanthem?" demanded the Duffer.

"There's a flasher, a friend of mine at the ' Nimblefingers,' so he and I'll do it together, only yer know we must snack the bit."

* Pay the money.

" That can't be helped," said the Duffer.

" Besides, we've got the three pound I'd from the surgeon yer know," resumed Tim.

" There's only two to make up then."

" He must take four pound for it, 'cos it really arn't worth more, you know we mayn't get more than five for it ourselves."

The two ruffians entered the " Boozing Ken." Tim Roper whispered a few words into the ear of the landlord, and then beckoning to the Duffer, the whole party retired to a back room.

" Well Tim," cried the landlord, " there isn't a flash feller about the house."

" Nor a flimsy kid neither ?" asked the resurrectionist.

" No."

" Hold hard," exclaimed the Duffer, " can't I doff a few flash togs ?"

" To be sure yer can," answered Tim.

" So say I," observed the landlord, " yer see he's got a deal the tidiest figure."

" Let's have 'em then," quoth the Duffer.

" I charges two bob an hour for the loan of 'em, vich must be paid when yer brings 'em back, and twenty bob must be left on 'em."

This was immediately complied with, and the Duffer was soon equipped from head to foot when he assumed a swaggering strut, for the purpose of concealing his naturally vulgar gait.

The two men returned again into the street.

Presently they perceived a gentleman carrying a gold headed cane.

Tim Roper walked immediately up to him and deliberately spat in his face, and then ran slowly away.

" Ah the insolent filthy scoundrel," cried the Duffer, advancing quickly to the spot, "lend me your cane a minit, and I'll lay it across his shoulders in good style."

" Do,' exclaimed the stranger gratefully.

" I will."

" Don't spare him."

" I wont."

And the Duffer started off cane in hand.

Tim Roper increased his speed, but the Duffer strove to catch him manfully, till they were both out of the sight and hearing of the owner of the gold-headed cane.

Then they returned to the " Boozing Ken."

" Twenty bob for this," said the landlord, after having examined the cane minutely.

" And a glass of lush a-piece" added the Duffer.

" Then yer shall have it," chimed in Tim.

The landlord assented.

The resurrection man and the Duffer were now on their way to West-street.

Bill Waters had been anxiously waiting their return, and readily agreed to take four sovereigns for the subject.

The purchasers disposed of the Mudlark at a dissecting room, and the two men separated.

Let us accompany Tim Roper.

The neighbourhood at the back of Smithfield is inhabited by a lawless and depraved set of people. The men are thieves, and the women prostitutes.

Thither were directed the steps of the resurrectionist.

There is an alley still in existence, at the corner of which stands a tobacconist's shop, which alley is denominated "Sharper's Alley," and up it Tim Roper went.

At the farther end he entered a house and walked up to the first floor where was seated a young woman who might have been tolerably good looking in her time, but dissipation had already begun its deadly work, and its presence was denoted by her dim eyes, and hollow cheeks.

" Lor, Tim, how I've been a-waiting for yer; there's been a feller fallen down dead in an apoplectic fit nigh here, and the inquest came off to-day."

" Go on," impatiently ejaculated the resurrectionist.

" His body's in the work'us, and the officers have had bills about, giving an haccurate account of his dress and person, so as how it might be claimed by his friends ; now I thought I might git it."

" But it's late, yer know."

" Never mind that, it 'll have the better appearance ; besides, nothing dare, nothing have."

" Try it," said Tim Roper, after a pause.

The girl hastened to attire herself as respectably as she could, and then went to the workhouse

On arriving there she appeared to be in a state of the most anxious agitation—indeed, her manner was alarmingly wild.

" May I have a look at the body of the deceased ? I'm sure it's my poor dear uncle, who's been missing from his home ever since the other day—true as gospel, I am."

Of course her request was immediately granted.

The body lay in the dead-house, and on beholding the countenance, she gave a piercing shriek,

" My uncle, my uncle ; oh, my own, dear uncle.'

Then she threw herself upon the body, caressed it repeatedly, and really appeared almost heartbroken with grief.

" Oh, do let the body be taken home directly, as the family are in the bitterest affliction at the melancholy accident."

" Where do you live ?" asked a parish-officer.

" Number eleven, Little Thames-street."

" And what's your name ?" demanded another.

" Mary Martin.'

These answers were inserted in a book.

" Does anybody of the name of Martin reside there, I wonder ?" observed the first speaker.

" To be sure he does," ejaculated the second.

" What trade was he, ay ?"

" A cobbler."

" That's right. You may take him now.'

" I've got my cousin and a friend of his outside to carry him home; will yer call them in, please ?"

Tim Roper and the Duffer, who were in readiness outside, in case of the stratagem succeeding, with many efforts to pacify the unfortunate young woman, who howled so loudly that the parish-officers were well pleased to get rid of her, came in when called, and carried away the body.

It is needless to add, that it was consigned *instanter* to the dissecting rooms of a celebrated anatomist.

CHAPTER XLIII.

HE MARRIAGE.

" Must raise money somehow or other, Wilson," said Sir Richard Vyvian.

The honest butler looked doubtful as to whether there yet remained any untried method of " raising the wind."

" This infernal old house has been disposed of so often that I believe it is no longer in our power to get money upon it."

The baronet paused.

" The family plate," added the butler, blushing deeper than his crimson smalls,—" the family plate is also in safe custody."

" The estates in Yorkshire," resumed the baronet, " are mortgaged, ditto in Norfolk, ditto in Devon; consequently, nothing now remains but Miss Vyvian's jewels, and I cannot make up my mind to send them away. The poor thing put them into my hands the morning after the robbery in case of another attack, but now she is becoming more confident, it is not unlikely that she may ask me for them again; at present they're all safe, but how long they may remain so is another question."

At this moment the door opened, and Amelia entered, but, observing that the baronet was engaged, she was about to withdraw."

" Don't run away, Milly," exclaimed the baronet " I have matters of some importance to communicate to you."

The butler placed a chair and quitted the library, but the door was scarcely closed when Amelia, throwing herself into her chair, burst into tears.

" You're not well, dearest," said the baronet. " We will defer our conversation till to-morrow."

" Oh, no, no!" exclaimed Amelia. " I am ready now to hear anything you have to say, Richard."

" Are you very sure ?" said the baronet, smiling faintly. " I warn you beforehand that you will have occasion for all your courage."

Amelia blushed, and the baronet, guessing the cause of her excitement, proceeded to inform her of the conversation which had passed between Stamer and himself a few days ago.

" The other evening, Amelia, I rejected his proposals, but upon reflection I think I acted too hastily, for perhaps, after all, he may make a kinder and more considerate husband than Lord Oxburn. He loves you, my own sweet sister, with all the romance of a first love, and, if his fortune and family connexions are as unexceptionable as his character, I think there is every reason to hope that your union will be one of uninterrupted happiness. I have despatched a letter requesting him to call upon me this evening, and it now remains for you to inform me whether or no you are inclined to accept his proposal. I am aware that a little flirtation has passed between you, but have you seriously reflected upon the nature and importance of a wife? I speak gravely, my dear girl, because at this moment I am deeply impressed by the necessity of doing so. Your brother Francis is lying upon a bed of sickness, while his heartless, unfeeling wife has fled to the continent with Captain Dashington. But his affairs are in such disorder that he will be compelled ere long to visit England. I shall watch his return, and——"

" What then ?" exclaimed Amelia, recoiling with horror. " Surely, Richard, you will not counsel Francis to challenge a wretch who has re-paid the hospitality he received at his house by seducing his wife. Oh! rather let him live an object of scorn and contempt; let his name——"

She could say no more; the words expired on her discoloured lips, and she would have fallen senseless upon the floor had not the baronet hastened to her assistance. As soon as she was sufficiently recovered he carried her into her own apartment, and delivered her to the charge of her maid, under whose care we will for the present leave her while we return to Mr. Stamer.

He left Peter-street in the intention of proceeding straight to Grosvenor-square, but finding that it was later than he expected he retraced his steps and returned to his lodgings at the Blenheim. When he entered his apartment the first object that met his view was a letter from the baronet. He hastily broke the seal, and, after perusing the contents, set out immediately for the residence of his beloved.

The letter was worded in such a conciliatory tone that Stamer at once anticipated that all impediments to his happiness would be removed, he therefore pursued his drive in high spirits, and arrived in Grosvenor-square just as the baronet had given up all hopes of his responding to the invitation.

The two gentlemen met upon the most friendly terms. All remembrance of their late difference seemed entirely forgotten.

The baronet, with one of his blandest smiles, expressed the happiness he felt at the prospect of this alliance and proposed that the marriage should be celebrated as soon as the necessary preparations could be made.

" You will perhaps be surprised that I, who the other day was averse to your union with my sister, am now so anxious for the completion of it ; but circumstances have occurred which render it imperative that Amelia should marry, and as I am convinced that you alone are in possession of her affections, I feel that I should be acting injuriously towards her if I persisted in preferring the pretensions of another in opposition to your own. And need I add how deeply I have since regretted the inconsiderate expressions, the offspring of pride and prejudice, which escaped my lips in the course of my conversation the other evening, but I candidly confess, that, upon consideration, your good qualities have prevailed, and the first wish of my heart will be gratified when I entrust to your care and keeping the hand and person of my beloved sister." Tears started into the eyes of the baronet. " You've no doubt,' said he, " heard of my brother's illness and misfortune, but thank God he is now out of danger, poor Milly was ignorant of the whole affair till this morning, and the intelligence has so entirely overpowered her that I think it will be prudent to defer seeing her till this evening, when we shall expect you to dinner."

Stamer could scarcely find patience to submit to the delay, but he acquiesced in the propriety of doing so, and took his leave of the baronet, entirely fascinated by the graceful suavity of his manners, and alternately accusing himself and others for the apparently unjust suspicions which they had so freely indulged.   According to his appointment Stamer dined and spent the evening at Grosvenor-square. The clock struck three as he retraced his way back to the Blenheim. He walked thoughtfully for he had that evening lost three thousand pounds. He resolved never to touch another card. but attributed his evil fortune entirely to chance.

The sum lost was sufficient for the present purpose of the baronet, who, on his sister's account, seriously admonished Stamer to refrain from play.

Affected almost to tears by the parental demeanour of the baronet, Stamer pledged himself faithfully to observe his advice, and, in a letter which he subsequently addressed to his mother, after giving a glowing description of the beauty and perfection of his intended bride, he concluded with an exalted panegyric upon the manly virtues and elegant deportment of her brother.

Three weeks after the conversation recorded in the fore part of this chapter, Amelia Vyvian and Arthur Stamer Coningham, attended by bridesmaids and relatives, stood before the altar in St. George's, Hanover-square. The beautiful bride was dressed in white satin. A wedding bouquet ornamented her fair bosom ; bright jewels sparked amid the graceful ringlets of her dark brown hair, while the exquisite delicacy of her form contrasted admirably with the manly appearance of the bridegroom, whose fine eyes were now and then turned with an expression of tender anxiety upon her blushing countenance.

At the conclusion of the ceremony the party returned to an elegant déjéune in Grosvenor-square. The bride changed her apparel, and, after receiving the congratulations of her friends, departed with the bridegroom in a travelling carriage and four.

" Where is Richard ?" anxiously inquired Amelia as the carriage drove rapidly from the door of her brother's house, " It does seem so very strange that of my three brothers he only was present at our wedding, and then for him to disappear so suddenly. What can be the meaning of it ? Oh Arthur how can you keep me in such suspense ? I am sure by your dejection something terrible has occurred."

" Your brother Francis, dearest, is not yet able to leave his house ; the marks of the small pox are still red upon his face, and he would by no means have been an ornamental addition to our party," returned Stamer endeavouring to smile cheerfully.

" And Richard ?" inquired Amelia.

" Richard has gone before us to Brussels, where, please God, we shall speedily rejoin him."

" I don't much care about the loss of Frederick's company,"said Amelia, laughing, ''but still he is my brother, and I should have felt more happy if he had been with us this morning."

Stamer was silent, anxiety for the fate of the baronet, who was at that moment in danger, subdued the transport of happiness he felt in the possession of his beloved Amelia. She was now his own and for ever.

He pressed her to his bosom, he raised her beautiful hand to his lips and covered it with rapturous kisses. The carriage passed through London at a rattling pace, and we will leave the travellers to continue their journey

---

CHAPTER XLIV.

THE FUGITIVE.

IT was a stormy night, and though the air was still cold, flashes of lightning broke at intervals through the dark clouds, and threw a vivid light upon the figure of a female closely enveloped in a large mantle. She had just descended from an omnibus, and was resting against the garden gate of one of a row of houses situated in the Bayswater-road. Though exhausted by fatigue and agitation she remained some time before she could summon courage to ring at the bell and give notice of her desire to obtain admission. At last she did so, and almost immediately the summons was obeyed, and the lady was admitted into the presence of Dr. Dunwiddy, who we have already mentioned in one of the early chapters of our narrative.

Surprised at the unexpected appearance of a lady drenched with rain and scarcely able to support herself, the doctor advanced to meet her. On his approach the lady threw back her veil and sunk inanimate into a chair.

" Mrs. Veevian !" exclaimed the doctor, " What can hae brought the puir budy here all dranched wi' rain, and on fute. There must be something uncummun haypened to hur."

" Uncummun, indeed !" said a stiff-starched lady; " and uncummun deseegreeable it is to hawve all our neece cawpet soiled by hur wat fute, and our chair cuvers deertied. Really, Dunald, you'd batter cawry hur into the pawsage an lat Paggy breeng up aw wat flawnel an weepe awa' the mawrks bafure thay gat dree."

" Seelence, wuman ! Dinna luk at her deert, bat du what ye cawn to reveeve hur."

" Bat she wunt paw us far spoiling our gudes, Dunald. Reach or puir I wadn' shut my dure agin her, but I dinna ken the use of her satting all wat upon aur bast chairs.—See, nuw sha opens hur eyes. Gie her a glaws of water, and lade hur gantly into the hawl, the air 'll du hur gude, she'll ba batter than hare."

The doctor gave an impressive tug at the lady's dress, and she comprehending that he had reasons for what he did, suddenly became very amiable.

" Mayhawps tha water 'll ba tu culd for hur puir stumawk. Tree just a wee drap of brawndy, it cawn du na hurm, Dunald."

Dunwiddy took the hint, and a tumbler of warm brandy and water speedily restored Mrs. Vyvian to animation, and without asking any questions, she was released from her dripping apparel and put into a comfortable warm bed.

" An pray, Dunald, wha may this ludy ba?" said Mrs. Dunwiddy, stealing softly into the parlour, and speaking, as if fearful of being heard.

" Breeng yure chawr nearer the tawble, I'll tall ye aw I ken abute hur fawmily, but ye maunna spak lude. You've heard me spak of old Seer Pawtrick O'Sullivan, an Irish baronet, ane o' the brawest mun that ever stapt in shoe leather; my ain fayther always excapted, for he, guid mun, was seex or saven feet, I dinna ken which, and three inches, whereas Seer Pawtrick wa' only seex, but na mawter. This Seer Pawtrick mawried early in life a reech lassie, the dochter o' a country-gantlemun, and he sattled in England, whare Miss Alexandrine was barn; but Seer Pawtrick had sat hees meend upon having a son, sa he was awfu' sarry at the beerth of his daughter.

Bat the mither lo'ed her enteerely, and spoiled, and patted her till not a single budy cauld live in the huse wi her; and sa it's been ever sin' she was a breede. Her husband was at feerst vary fund of her, bat nuw he seems pretty weel cured of hees lave, for I hear he's scarcely ever at hame, and they 're saldum, if ever, at the same pawty. I

suppose she's mat wi' same opposeetion, but he'll tak' care that we shall loase nathing by keeping her here, sa ye need na fume abaut that."

" Wall, wall, if you 're vary sure o' that, let her stay as lang as she fancies; there's nai fear, she 'll soon gang hame again when she fends what puir suber budies ye an' I are, Dunald."

The following morning Mrs. Vyvian rose, apparently refreshed in mind and body; she had descended the staircase, and was about to enter the breakfast parlour, when the gruff voice of a man suddenly burst upon her affrighted ear; she opened the door, but remained upon the threshold, listening in an agony of suspense to the following dialogue :—

" I tell you I want to see that woman I saw at the window just now," roared the man. " I don't mean to stand any gammon, so you needn't try it; I've come up to London, all the way from Dover on purpose. She and another woman and a man, who called himself a captain, came and lodged at our hotel. At first, they passed the other woman off as a servant; however, servant, or no servant, she's marched off with the honest captain, and left the fine lady you've got in your house to pay the bill. But she's a reg'lar out and outer. All the day long she sat crying, with her head leaning on the table as if her heart was going to break, never said he couldn't pay the bill though, but as soon as we're all snug in bed, what did she do, but steals down stairs and creeps out at a back door, and off she sets to London. But I soon got scent, and followed close upon her heels, and, as good luck would have it, got into the very same omnibus she stopped at your door in last night. I got down as the driver directed, and sure enough there was my lady stuck up at the window, so you know it's no use your telling me she isn't here, because I seed her with my own eyes."

" Really, mee guid maun," said Doctor Dunwiddy, " you're enteerely meestaken ; the lady I've got in mee huse cartainly came last neeght, but she's the lawfu' mawrid weefe of Mr. Francis Veevian ; and if it's ony sawtesfaction to yau, I daw say my weefe 'll ha'e na objaction to lat ye stap into the pawlour just to luke at the leady, fur it's not a playsant thing of ye to cume and deesturb quiet suber people leeke us, maun. You're either nai batter thun ye shauld be yaursel', or you're a deceived maun."

" Well, all I ask is, to see the woman herself, and I'll soon let ye know whether I am deceived or not."

The man advanced towards the room into which Mrs. Vyvian had hastily retreated, and, the doctor leading the way, threw open the door. A faint scream escaped the lips of Mrs. Vyvian, and, throwing herself on her knees at the feet of the doctor, she earnestly besought him to pay the amount due to the man, and shield her from further insult.

Dunwiddy, dumb with astonishment, threw himself into a chair, and, turning his head in an opposite direction, gently requested Mrs. Vyvian to rise.

"Indeed! indeed! you must assist me," exclaimed Mrs. Vyvian; "for I've not a friend on earth to whom I can apply but yourself, and never will I rise from my knees till that insolent wretch is paid."

"The beel shall immediately be settled, madam," said the doctor, endeavouring to overcome his emotion. "But wha shall restore breeght honour to the name you have tawnished? wha shield you, a puir, halpless women, fra the loud reproach and burning scorn of your fallow-creatures? Bat dinna be too much caust down; perhaps matters may be settled; ye may live in peace with your husband yet."

"Oh, never, never!" exclaimed Mrs. Vyvian. "You have said that you will pay my bill; do so, and let him go. I never can return to Francis. I hate, I detest him, and would rather die than live under the same roof with him again."

Mrs. Vyvian rose from her knees, and the doctor, beckoning the man into his study, paid the money due to him.

"You'll send the lady's luggage safe and sound, maun," said the doctor; "and I hope that you'll not go and expose the welful weckedness of that wratched wuman, but jast keep it yoursel', an' pray for her puir soul, maun; for it's nae long sin' she was a pratty, innocent creature; and we all hae our mithers an' our sisters, or our weeves and daughters, so we mauna bear too hard upon their weakness."

The innkeeper expressed his sincere regret directly, and offered to apologise to the lady for his roughness.

"Na, maun; gang your way, and show more consideration anither time."

The doctor conducted the man to the door, and then returned to the breakfast-parlour.

Mrs. Vyvian, delivered from her creditor, had regained her usual spirits, and began, with the most unfeeling levity, to relate the circumstances of her elopement.

"I am quite delighted," said she, "now that nasty man is paid, that you are acquainted with all that has passed. I should never have had the courage to give you the explicit explanation you received from him; but now you do know how I am situated, what would you, doctor, as a man of the world, advise me to do?"

Doctor Dunwiddy was prepared for tears, for sighs, for repentance, and regret; but not for the heartless indifference the unfeeling woman exhibited.

"Return to your husband, wuman, and, on your bended knees, implore that he will receive and protect you from further injury and ruin, for, sooner or later, destruction will come upon you. Like a puir rose-bud, nipped by the early frost, your leaves shall decay, and the flower of your youth pass away."

Tears stood in the old man's eyes as he gazed pitifully upon the youthful countenance of the misled woman.

"The fact is, doctor," said Mrs. Vyvian, "that you have got a set of queer, old-fashioned notions in your head which, though they serve to frighten you, take no effect whatever upon me. Captain Dashington told me of at least fifty ladies of quality who had lovers unknown to their husbands."

"For shame, wuman, to be the reporter of such awful lees! Dinna you ken that bad men and women always try to make it seem that others are as bad as themselves. But you're nae come to that yet, though you're a puir silly fool to credit what is said to ye by the like of him."

A crimson flush covered the face and neck of Mrs. Vyvian.

"I cannot, I will not bear such insolence," said she, dashing her cup in the doctor's face. "Take that; and the next time you presume to insult a lady recollect the warm cup of tea I have given you. I suppose the conversation of the innkeeper has been reported to Mrs. Dunwiddy as she has not made her appearance at breakfast this morning: however, no matter; I have made up my mind, now that I have delivered myself of one tyrant, not to submit to another. My own resources are amply sufficient to enable me to enjoy the sweets of life without tasting any of its bitters."

"An' may God grant, puir, thoughtless budy, that the cup you are mixing for yourself may not be all bitters and na sweets," returned the doctor.

Mrs. Vyvian, colouring deeply, rose from the table and quitted the room, and in a few moments afterwards a violent bang of the street-door induced Dunwiddy to put on his hat and go in pursuit of her. But she walked so quick that, old and feeble as he was, he was unable to overtake her; still he pursued her in the distance. An omnibus passed; she entered it, and drove away in an opposite direction. For some moments the old man stood leaning on his stick sobbing like a child.

"If I was only sure that she'd money in her pocket," said he, "I should na feel sa sad about her."

CHAPTER XLV.

THE RENT.

It may well be supposed that, as Mr. Tift was resident in the house of Mr. Dobbins, no great period could possibly intervene before the hosier became aware of the fact that the son of the Queen Mother was his lodger.

One evening he met that eccentric gentleman in the passage, and immediately recognized him, but purposely forbore appearing to do so, as he knew it would prove impossible to eject him at all events without a week's warning, and, moreover, he was for the moment rather taken aback at the unexpected and not very welcome occurrence.

He had not escaped the observation of Mr. Tift.

On reaching his own room Mr. Tift began to ponder on the safest course he could pursue; he knew that unless the money was forthcoming, now that a fortnight was due, and after the unpleasant discovery the hosier had made, the consequences would infallibly prove unpleasant to himself.

Mr. Dobbins communicated the circumstance to his wife, who immediately dispatched Molly up stairs with a bill, and an order to request the immediate settlement of it.

" He says, Mum, it won't suit him to pay it just now," said the servant, returning from her errand.

" Then tell him," said Mr. Dobbins, " he must go."

" But pay first," interposed his wife.

Again the servant quitted the room for the purpose of fulfilling the mission intrusted to her.

" Lor' how unfortunate we are," said Mrs. Dobbins, " we might have all had our throats cut by that monster."

" Never take a man with that countenance again," replied her husband, with the air of a profound moralist.

The dialogue was interrupted by the return of Molly.

" He says he's very sorry at your insolent behaviour, sir, he says he'll quit the house immediately, and never enter it again as long as he lives."

" Tell him I'll stop his portmanteau if he dares do it," ejaculated the hosier.

Mr. Tift returned an answer pregnant with menaces and full of defiance.

" Leave that door open," said Mr. Dobbins, " and then if I hear him coming down I'll stop him."

" And mind if there's any piece of work you fetch a policeman immediately," added Mrs. Dobbins.

Presently the footsteps of Mr. Tift were heard on the stairs.

Mr. Dobbins immediately posted himself at the door.

Mrs. Dobbins ran up the stairs, and with one hand seized hold of Mr. Tift's portmanteau, while with the other she clung to the banisters.

" You mustn't do that," cried Molly, from the bottom of the stairs, " that hisn't legal."

" Leave him alone," exclaimed Mr. Dobbins, speaking as loud as he could, and never for an instant quitting his post, " let him come here if he

dare. I'm a strong man—a very strong man when my blood's up, it's a hissing now, I feel it beginning to boil."

The apprentice, who had slipped out unobserved, now returned with a constable.

Having told that functionary an exaggerated tale as they came along he evidently expected that nothing short of a burglary, or perhaps a murder had been committed, but when he perceived the true state of the case he assumed a careless indif-ference.

" What does the law let me do with this lodger ?" asked the hosier of the constable. " He hasn't paid my rent, and now he wants to go away without doing it."

" You can't stop him, but you can his goods.' was the reply.

" Then I'll do it."

" You're a nice set : this is what Christianity teaches you, isn't it ?" cried Mr. Tift.

" Does it teach you to run in debt with people without intending to pay ?" inquired the hosier's wife.

" Sunday after Sunday passes and you never go over the door to church. You must be all infidels, or fire-worshippers, or Mahometans," observed Mr. Tift.

" You disgraceful wretch! I wonder how you dare to mention such a solemn subject on such an occasion as this," indignantly ejaculated Mrs. Dobbins, who was really much piqued at the circumstance being revealed to the constable.

" Policeman," cried Mr. Tift, " am I entitled to take my portmanteau out of this house ? I think I am."

" I should say not, sir."

" Then of course I'll abide by your opinion."

And Mr. Tift retraced his steps to his own bed-room.

Mrs. Dobbins asked the constable into the back room, and gave him a glass of something to drink, which certainly smelt like anything but water.

This step was doubtless taken by the hosier's wife for the purpose of preventing the officer leaving the house with the idea in his mind that they were a family unaccustomed to pay due regard to the Sabbath, and therefore, without forgetting to abuse Mr. Tift, she took especial care to disabuse the constable.

As soon as the policeman had left the house Mr. Dobbins sat with the door open, fearful of his lodger even now effecting his exit with the only piece of property which he apparently possessed, the portmanteau.

Mr. Tift had listened attentively to passing events, and was determined to hazard a bold stroke; he felt that to pass through the passage would be impossible, how then was he to elude the hosier ?

He heard the daughters return from their business, and then there was a great bustle, perhaps they were being informed of the occurrences to which the evening had given birth, but speedily it all subsided.

"Now is my time," said Mr. Tift.

Having taken off his shoes, put on his hat, and provided himself with his portmanteau, he crept stealthily down stairs.

On arriving at the drawing room door he opened it cautiously and entered the room, which was situated over the shop, so that there was little chance of his movements being noticed.

He opened the window, and then looked into the street beneath, to see if any person was passing.

"I must wait a little longer."

The clock struck the hour of eleven.

Then Mr. Tift, as cautiously as before, retraced his steps to the drawing room.

The hosier did not intend retiring to rest that night, and was still sitting up in the back parlour, with the door ajar.

Again Mr. Tift opened the window and looked out.

There was discernible but here and there a straggler.

He dropped his portmanteau from the window into the street below.

For a time he waited to observe whether the noise thus occasioned had attracted any notice, but all was quiet.

He mounted the window sill, and lowered himself as far as he could, till his feet came into contact with the shop window, then he relinquished his hold and alighted without much noise on the pavement.

But this had not escaped the notice of Mr. Dobbins.

Mr. Tift perceived a light shining in the passage, and in an instant the truth suggested itself to his mind; without a moment's pause, he snatched up the portmanteau, and was speedily far beyond the precincts of the hosier's residence.

On arriving in the New Road, he was stopped by a policeman.

"Is that portmanteau yours?" he was asked.

Mr. Tift took the key from his pocket, unlocked it, and locked it again.

"That is all it's your duty to see; if I possess the key, that's sufficient."

Mr. Tift soon arrived at the Queen Mother's abode.

After a great deal of hammering and knocking he obtained admittance, and made up his bed for the night on the sofa.

There for the present we must leave him.

CHAPTER XLVI.

THE OFFER.

"This must, surely, be the house," soliloquised Agnes, as she approached the door of a tolerable sized house, in Eaton-square. A timid knock was the result of her conviction, and the knocker had scarcely escaped from her hand, when a man, out of livery, appeared at the door, and she was immediately ushered into the back drawing-room. She had not been seated many minutes, when a gentleman, apparently about fifty years of age, entered the apartment. He bowed, and colouring slightly, inquired, if the young lady had come from Mrs. Dobbins?

"I came here, sir," said Agnes, "in consequence of a letter which I received this morning, informing me that a governess was required to instruct two young ladies. I believe I am correct in the number of the house," and Agnes took the letter out of her pocket, and looked at the number.

"Perfectly correct," returned the gentleman, and the lady will be here shortly. In the meantime, Miss, you will perhaps give me some particulars concerning your birth and parentage, for we are very particular who we receive into our house, and I think that you will have time before the return of the lady to respond to some of my questions. Your father, Miss, is he still alive?"

"He has been dead some years, sir," exclaimed Agnes, sadly."

"Your mother, then?"

"I lost when I was very young; but the affectionate attentions of my father, prevented my feeling my loss so acutely as I should otherwise have done; but when it pleased God to deprive me of him also, then, and not till then, the full consciousness of my unprotected situation came upon me." The recollection of her parents brought tears into her eyes, and she wept long and bitterly, during which time the gentleman amused himself by looking out of window; but as soon as Agnes recovered herself, he resumed his seat by the side of her.

"Then it is as I thought," said he, fixing his small twinkling luminaries admiringly upon Agnes, "it is as I thought, and you will no doubt be surprised and delighted, when I inform you, Miss, that it is my intention to make you an offer of my hand and person. I am in earnest, Miss; for I consider that your beauty and accomplishments make amends for your want of fortune, and, rest assured, Miss, that of your conduct yourself with prudence and economy, it will be the pride and glory of my life to merit your esteem and tenderness."

The little man bent his crooked knees, and

placing his hand upon his heart, implored a favourable reply.

For some moments Agnes was so completely astonished, that she lost the power of utterance, but as soon as she regained the use of her tongue, she gave a decided negative.

"Then, Madam," said the gentleman, stretching his diminutive person to the fullest extent, " I am sorry to inform you that henceforth you must take up your abode in the country, some hundred miles from London; in fact, I am myself in possession of a solitary habitation suitable in every respect for a person of your melancholy turn of mind."

" I am at a loss to comprehend, sir, by what authority you take upon yourself to address me in the manner you have done. But beware; for sooner or later, rest assured, your insolence shall meet with the chastisement it deserves."

As Miss Talbot finished speaking a loud knock-

ing at the street-door proclaimed the arrival of a visitor, and, before the gentleman had time to make a reply, the room-door was thrown open, and Lord Oxburn entered the apartment.

Without uttering a syllable the gallant master of the house passed him and rushed down stairs.

" Prigmore, Prigmore! I can't stay a moment. I desire to speak to you upon particular business," exclaimed his lordship.

But the lawyer had decamped. Agnes had also risen to depart, but, being unable to support herself, she had sunk down upon her chair entirely overcome.

Lord Oxburn, mute with amazement, eagerly inquired how Agnes had come there? what she did there? and many other questions—to which he at last obtained satisfactory replies.

" But is it possible that that little scoundrel—Prigmore—enticed you here under the pretence of engaging you for a governess, and a single man, too? But your mother — how is it that she did not accompany you?"

"My mother," returned Agnes, "died many years ago."

"Thank God!" ejaculated Lord Oxburn; "for the figure of the person I saw you with the other day has never since been absent from my imagination. I am indeed sincerely delighted that she has not the honour of claiming you for her daughter."

A flush of crimson coloured the fair cheek of Agnes.

"I am conscious, Miss Talbot, that I have no right to make any remarks concerning your friends or relative. I would that circumstances had enabled me to become a candidate for your favour and given me an authority to do so. But I am too poor to marry at present, and in your defenceless position it would be ungenerous of me to make any proposition that might influence you in the rejection of a more fortunate suitor."

When Lord Oxburn ceased speaking he gracefully presented his arm to Agnes, and requested that she would inform him where he should conduct her to,

"I am at present residing with the person I was in company with when your lordship observed us the other day. But——"

Agnes blushed deeply.

"You feel, Miss Talbot, that it will not be in unison with your notions of decorum to allow me to escort you home," said his lordship, with some embarrassment; "and perhaps you are right. But at all events I can put you into a cab which will convey you in safety to your place of residence."

Agnes gratefully accepted his proposal, and Lord Oxburn, after pulling the bell, desired the servant to fetch a carriage.

For a man accustomed as Lord Oxburn was to every possible indulgence, it was a noble effort of self-control to assume the cool, indifferent air of an acquaintance rather than expose the fair girl he loved to the grief of seeing him perhaps at some future time become the husband of another. "If indeed I could really feel assured that she loved me," said Lord Oxburn, as he gazed musingly after the carriage, "I believe I could make any sacrifice to call her my own. We might even defer our marriage till, by the strictest economy, I had reduced my affairs to order."

Lord Oxburn continued his walk, while the cab, in which Agnes was seated, rattled carelessly over gravel and stone till, arriving at the corner of Hyde-park, it ran violently against a carriage and was immediately upset.

The coachmen mutually accused each other as the cause of the accident.

"What sort of a driver do you call yourself?" said the cabman, "to run bolt up again a poor man's vehicle in that sort of a manner. Do you know your master there'll have to pay a pretty

sight of money for the damage you've done my cab?"

The gentleman's coachman contented himself with muttering two or three unintelligible oaths, while the servants and cabman, assisted by some of the bystanders, endeavoured to disentangle the wheels.

An old gentleman, who was in the carriage, put his head out of the window and inquired if anybody was hurt.

"Can't say, your honour," said the cabman. "I've got a fare inside here, but can't say whether she's hurt or only frightened, for I fancy she's in a fit. I'll get her out in a minute, and see what we can do with her." Then, turning to the coachman, "I say, coachee, hadn't your governor better get out in case any more mischief happens.

The old gentleman, overhearing the remark, looked nervously at his valet, and intimated his intention of alighting from the carriage. The servant assisted him to do so, and, respectfully presenting his arm, led him to the spot where Agnes, who had with some difficulty been extricated from her perilous situation, lay extended.

She was just beginning to show signs of returning animation, and her first act was to pass her hand searchingly over her neck and round her throat. The old gentleman, with ready politeness, stooped forward, intending to place a small miniature, which he concluded was the object she was searching for, into her hand; when suddenly he dropped the miniature, and, without any apparent reason, staggered into his carriage.

"A sudden spasm," said the cabman; "and if you take my advice, gen'men, you'll give your master a good glass of warm brandy-and-water. 'Smever, a-course you'll do as you please.' The driver smacked his whip and conducted Agnes into another coach, which conveyed her to Oxford-street.

Mrs. Dobbins, who had for some time been anxiously expecting the return of her visitor, had posted herself in the shop near the door.

When the coach drew up a momentary feeling of alarm suspended an exclamation which was ready to escape from her lips. But at the sight of Agnes her fears subsided, and extending her hand, she welcomed her with genuine hospitality.

"We've been waiting dinner for you these two hours, Miss Talbot; what in the name of fortune has detained you all this time? I felt sure some accident must have happened to you, so I sent Mr. Dobbins off to Eaton-square, and he'll be glad enough when he comes back again and finds you here all safe and sound. However, come in and tell us where you've been to, and we'll eat our dinner, for I dare say you're hungry enough."

Agnes followed Mrs. Dobbins into the back parlour, and after dinner related the occurrences of the day.

" Well I do declare you've had a very lucky escape," said Mrs. Dobbins ; " Did you never read in the newspapers about a set of scoundrels who advertize for governesses, and when the poor innocent creatures go, expecting to obtain situations, they get them into trouble, and won't let them upon no account get out of their clutches again till they're ruined, or else good for nothing, and if they can't make anything bad of them why then they don't scruple about putting them out of the way, and they're never heard of again, take my word for that. But what the man could mean by offering to marry you, Miss Talbot, I don't understand, unless indeed it was a trick of some kind or other, for it is impossible to fathom those cunning wretches however much awake one may be. But Mr. Dobbins is the man for these kind of tales, Lor' bless you, my dear, if he knows one story he knows a hundred of young girls being decoyed from their homes, and that's why I always says to my gals, never upon no account go after sitivations alone. It isn't by no means a prudent thing for young females to do."

" Well Miss Talbot," said Mr. Dobbins, who had just entered, " I am happy to see you are all safe. I've had a pretty dance after you I can tell you ; that gentleman down in that square there must be a regular little villain. Before I went to the house I inquired in the neighbourhood what family lived there. ' No family at all sir,' said the woman, 'the house belongs to a single gentleman, a lawyer, I believe, he's got two or three servants, and keeps several clerks I understand, but that isn't his office, he only comes there sometimes;' so up I walked to the door, 'pray sir, said I,' can I speak to th young lady who came here this morning after a situation ; ' Don't know what you're talking about,' said an impudent puppy almost slamming the door in my face. However, I wasn't going to be got rid of so easily ; tap, tap, tap, went the knocker, again and again, for some time nobody came, but at last another man made his appearance. ' I tell you what,' said he, ' if you don't take yourself off the step of my street door, and go about your business, I shall be under the necessity of calling a policeman.' ' Call who you like said I, but quit this house, till you tell me what has become of the young lady, I won't.' Seeing I was determined, he requested that I would walk in, as he now recollected that a person had called that morning, but upon what errand he was ignorant. I made no scruple of telling him that I had made inquiry, and found that he was a single man, and considered that he must be a very great blackguard to send the letter he had done, addressed to my house, written as it was, in the handwriting of a female, and signed Charlotte Something, but none of us could make out what. After muttering a great many curses, and stamping about the room like a maniac, he suddenly became more reasonable ; and, seating himself by the side of me, ' Perhaps the best thing

I can do is to confess the truth at once,' said he smiling grimly, ' the fact is, Mr. Dobbins, that I had very important business to communicate to Miss Talbot, and I desired to speak with her entirely alone ; I thought it no harm to employ a little stratagem ; but, just as I was about to make certain disclosures concerning her mother's family, who should burst into the room but a certain Lord Oxburn, and I understood from my servant that after I left the house, the young lady, of her own accord, stept into a cab and drove off in company with his lordship ; where they went, I can't pretend to say, but if the lady should return to Oxford-street, and you really wish to do her a service, advise her to trust to my honour, and she will find that I am by no means the scoundrel, sir, you have had the impudence to call me. However, as circumstances are very much against me, I will forget what has passed, and when you have seen Miss Talbot, she will herself inform you of the nature of my communication.' I took my leave promising only to tell you what had passed, but I decidedly advise your having nothing more to do with the fellow."

Mr. Dobbins had scarcely finished speaking, when a man respectably attired entered the shop, and requested to speak with the master of it. " I have brought a letter," said he, " which I must deliver into his own hands in private, and that immediately."

William informed his master that he was wanted, and remained in the parlour while Mr. Dobbins hurried into the shop.

" Anything in my line ?" said the hosier, lowering his spectacles, and glancing inquiringly over them.

The man answered in a low tone of voice, and after a few minutes conference, Mr. Dobbins placed his arm in that of the stranger, and walked into the street.

" Well I never did see anything so strange," said Mrs. Dobbins, who had, through the window which separated the parlour from the shop, been anxiously watching the movements of her husband. " Where can Dobbins be gone to ? but I suppose its something about the Pearsons—their pride 's had a pretty fall, Miss Talbot—where Pearson 's gone to nobody knows, and as for his wife, I don't suppose at this present time that she 's got a stick or a rag belonging to her, except the things she 's got upon her back. Far better have stayed where they were in St. Martin's-lane, than to have played the fool in Guildford-street, pretending to be so grand."

" I wonder whether Miss Lucretia's going to marry the lord now," chimed in Miss Sophy.

" No, ha, ha," laughed Mrs. Dobbins, " no fear of it, Soph, the exposure in St. James's-street was enough to scare away a dozen lords, my dear."

" I hope the poor children will be taken charge of by somebody," said Agnes.

" Depend upon it, Miss Talbot, nobody will be very anxious to burden themselves with Mr. Pearson's children. Dobbins thought of taking the boy, but I wouldn't hear of such a thing. A nasty, mischievous little monkey. I suppose they'll all be obliged to go to the workhouse, for not a crittur belonging to 'em can give 'em anything. But Lor' bless me if here isn't poor Mrs. Winter."

At this moment an elderly woman leaning upon a stick entered the parlour.

Agnes rose to leave the room.

" Pray don't run away, Miss Talbot. This is a very old friend of ours. She's been obliged to go into the workhouse, poor crittur, and I haven't seen her since she's been there," whispered Mrs. Dobbins. Then with a loud shrill voice she turned to her visitor, " And how do you do, Mrs. Winter?"

" A very fine day, ma'am, indeed," replied the old woman.

"; Why you're deafer than ever," bawled Mrs. Dobbins.

" No, my dear, I havn't dined yet, I left the workhouse directly after breakfast, and have been walking ever since. Called at the old place, Mrs. Dobbins, found it quite empty, all gone away."

Tears trickled down the old woman's face.

" Well never mind, Mrs. Winter, we'll get something to eat, and then you shall tell us how you're getting on. Where's your daughter?" inquired Mrs. Dobbins, putting her mouth close to the old woman's ear, and raising her voice louder than ever.

". She'll be here presently," returned the old woman, seemingly delighted at having at last comprehended something that was said to her.

" And here I am," said a pretty young woman, leaning over the back of her mother's chair, and looking smilingly in her face.

The old woman pressed her hand, and after mutual inquiries concerning health and family matters, the visitors seated themselves at the table and dined heartily off some cold roast beef, and the remains of a pudding.

During the repast Mrs. Dobbins, in an under tone informed Miss Talbot that her guests were the wife and daughter of a respectable shopkeeper who formerly resided in the neighbourhood. Upon the death of Mr. Winter his effects were sold, and the produce given to the creditors, and poor Mrs. Winter with her daughter, was compelled to go into the workhouse.

" Well I havn't had such a good dinner for a long time," said Mrs. Winter, drawing back her chair from the table.

" Glad of it," said Mrs. Dobbins, " and now you shall have a good glass of brandy and water. Suppose you fare but poorly at St. Pancras?"

" Well I don't know, the meat's pretty tolerable. They allow us six ounces a day three times a week and a pint of small beer."

" And what sort of bread do you get, Miss Winter?"

" Bad enough, Mrs. Dobbins, I can tell you, and I think it a very great shame that better is not provided; the very smell of it makes me sick."

Miss Winter did not speak loud enough for her mother to hear, but the old woman watched the motion of her lips, and as long as she spoke appeared anxious.

" What's the matter with your mother?" inquired Mrs. Dobbins, " she seems all of a fidget."

" Why the fact is," replied Miss Winter, laughing, " that mother's been told that if she speaks against the house, if ever she goes back again they'll put her into the ' Black Hole.' "

" The ' Black Hole,' " said Mrs. Dobbins, " and pray where's that?"

" Why it's a stone-built room, very cold, and very damp, situated under the workhouse. They lock up refractory paupers in it, and keep them without food or fire."

" But surely they wouldn't serve your mother so, who was once a respectable housekeeper."

" Why I don't know; it's a sad thing to be shut up from the world in the power of anybody. They pretend to punish only the vicious and unruly, but some of the overseers are very hard hearted and tyrannical; they forget that when people are suffering from poverty they may be driven to commit many faults, and sometimes even crimes, which they would never dream of at another time. Others again, who show more kindness and forbearance, are generally respected, and have it in their power to effect more good, even among the worst of the paupers, and there are some of them certainly very bad. But there is another place of punishment called the ' Oakum Shed,' in which persons of the most infamous character are shut up and employed in picking oakum. These are not allowed to mix with the other inmates, but it not unfrequently happens that the respectable poor are thrust into the shed and compelled to remain there simply for having made some remark displeasing to the authorities, for if they suspect that you are at all inclined to complain about anything, they, one and all, turn against you. However, there's a great deal to be said on both sides; we can't expect to be as well off there as we were at home, and though, for people who have seen better days, it is a very sad place, still it's better than wandering about the streets. The worst of it is sleeping two or three and sometimes even four in a bed. We are now, thank God, out of the nasty place, and I trust we shall keep so. A relation of my mother's has left us a little property which will keep us comfortably enough in the country. And now, Mrs. Dobbins, before we take our leave I must tell you that you're the only friend that hasn't turned your back upon us during our trials, relations and all included, the moment they found we really wanted, there wasn't a name they could speak bad enough for us."

Miss Winter rose from her seat, and her mother followed her example.

" But surely you're not going to leave us before tea?" said Mrs. Dobbins, taking Miss Winter by the hand.

" We have taken our places in the stage-coach," said the old woman; "and shall lose our money if we're too late."

" Then God bless you both." said Mrs. Dobbins.

" I'll write and send you our address as soon as we're settled," said Mrs. Winter,

" A charming girl that," said Mrs. Dobbins, as she closed the parlour-door. " I only wish I had a son alive and old enough, and you may depend upon it that she should be Mrs. Dobbins number two before the year was out."

CHAPTER XLVII.

THE DUEL.

ON the same morning that Amelia Vyvian became Lady Coningham, and about one hour after the ceremony had concluded, a gig might be seen driving rapidly towards one of the most secluded spots in a remote part of the environs of the metropolis.

Presently it stopped in a narrow lane, where it was almost entirely screened from observation by numerous thick and lofty trees, whose spreading branches formed a natural arbour.

Two gentlemen descended, and repaired to a retired spot situated in a field close by, and with them they carried a moderate-sized box.

One of them was Sir Richard Vyvian.

" They must soon be here," said the baronet, addressing his companion. " Were this not such a sequestered spot, we might fear interruption at such an advanced hour of the morning, but the circumstance of my sister's marriage prevented my appointing any other time."

" However great a craven Captain Dashington may be, he is too much of a ' star in the west' to avoid a meeting of this nature. He would not forfeit his name at the clubs for being the ' best fellow going' for a whole universe," answered the other, who was a captain in the Rifle Corps, and about to act as second to the baronet.

" They are coming," exclaimed Sir Richard, as two figures appeared advancing towards them.

The officer in the Rifle Corps and Captain Dashington's second exchanged civilities.

Then the two seconds stepped apart, and for a moment conversed together for the purpose of making arrangements.

" Why," cried Captain Dashington's second, on examining the pistols, " some person has removed the pistols I placed in this case, and substituted worthless ones."

A pause ensued.

" Y-y-you must have mistaken," stammered Captain Dashington.

" Pray don't mind that, gentlemen," somewhat sarcastically remarked the officer of the Rifle Corps; " I am not unprepared for this emergency."

He produced a box, which, on being opened, sure enough presented a pair of rather large duelling pistols, with the necessary appurtenances.

" I am glad of that," cried the captain's second, firmly.

" So am I," echoed Captain Dashington, in a somewhat fainter voice.

" Time flies," ejaculated the baronet, impatiently, " measure the ground."

The ground was measured—twelve short paces.

The principals took their pistols and their places.

" Fire."

Sir Richard Vyvian, still trembling with rage, enveloped his right arm in a handkerchief, for the limb was desperately wounded.

Captain Dashington looked unconcerned—he even attempted to yawn.

The baronet took his neckerchief from round his throat, and walking up to Captain Dashington, presented him with one end.

" I neither came here to murder, nor to be murdered," exclaimed the captain turning pale.

" Load them again, will you?" said the baronet, addressing his friend.

" Do you think to frighten me in this way?" cried Captain Dashington. And then, turning to his second, he added, " Load again."

The pistols were again charged, and both presented with one—each took a corner of the neckerchief, then they fired.

In another moment Sir Richard Vyvian lay rolling in his blood, his eyes fast glazing, and after one wild bound of intense agony, he was silent for ever.

* * * * * * *

Captain Dashington had also fallen.

On his second opening his waistcoat, there appeared a fine sheet of mail, perfectly impenetrable to a pistol bullet.

" I hope you do not consider me an accessory to this," said he.

Captain Dashington soon recovered, for he had only fallen from an excessive fit of passion, which he had but ill contrived to suppress.

" Our passports are for France," said his second, " but I shall decline your company."

" Then you will not, I hope, refuse to give me the satisfaction of a gentleman?"

" I shall refuse most certainly what cannot belong to you."

The Captain left the field overwhelmed with confusion.

There was a wound in Sir Richard Vyvian's temple, though small, nevertheless, deep and deadly.

His mouth was frightfully contorted, his eyes stared wide open in their blue ghastly stare, and in one hand he had frantically clutched a heap of grass.

CHAPTER XLVIII.

THE DUFFER'S HISTORY

"Now Sam for yer history," said the coiner mentioned in a preceding chapter, to the Duffer, both of whom had met according to appointment at the "Nimblefingers."

Ben Bendy and the resurrectionist were also present.

"Are yer all ready?"

"Yes."

"Then here goes."

"If there's one trade worse than another it's that of a coal-whipper, and coal-whipping was the trade my father followed. My mother was from the coal mines in Cornwall, and as soon as I could run alone she returned there agen, because she and my father, it appears, never lived happily together. I heard afterwards that she was dashed to pieces by the falling in of a part of the mine."

"Them haccidents often happen in the mining districts," observed the coiner.

"Well, when my mother went away I was left to run the streets, and there I remained sometimes with a dinner and sometimes without one, till I was ten years old. Then I determined to do something for myself. I soon found out my mistake as to getting work, so what could I do but turn prig? My father was always drunk for he received part of his wages in liquor, and if he couldn't drink it he might throw it away if he liked, but still he got no more money. One day when he was intoxicated he fell overboard into the river, and his companions held him below water till he should hold up his hand as a sign he would stand three gallons of beer which they always get for saving a feller. He was too drunk to do it, so they held him under water till he died. Then I was hard pushed. I was too young to turn coal-whipper, so I became a regular prig. After a run of two or three months I was sent to Parkhurst, where I remained for half-a-year, at the end of that time I came out agen without a shelter or a bit of bread. But one day I met a friend of my father's, he seemed to feel for me, and said he'd make a man and a river pirate of me; I accepted his offer, and till he died lived on barges and about the water-side; then I was again alone, but chance threw me in the way of an old Ikey of the name of Levi, and he finished what Parkhurst and the streets had begun for me."

"What sort of fellers are the river pirates?" inquired the resurrectionist.

"There's a great many kinds of 'em," answered the Duffer, "the *light horsemen* confine their hoperations principally to the West India ships, and board any vessel in the night they think unguarded. The *heavy horsemen* pretend to go aboard to sell things, or else to assist in moving goods, but they have rum dresses, with pockets all round 'em, and pouches in 'em, which they fill with anything they can stow away in 'em." "Then there's *game watermen*, who are the Thames receivers, er Ikeys as ve calls 'em, and without them the trade would'nt pay, but besides them, there's lots of marine store dealers on both sides of the river who never asks no questions."

"Well one month arter I became acquainted with him, I was become as hardened as a bit of granite. I followed "buzzing" till I could set up on my own account, and he took all the swag, then I turned "duffer," which got more profit and a deal less risk."

"And yer succeeded?" inquired Roper.

"I made so much that Levi didn't like to lose me, but I was'nt agoing to mar my future prospects for him, so one day I perlitely took my leave. I was blessed with a fertile invention, and by continnally shifting my ground, was capable of inventing a 'knowing go' pretty well for every day in the year. Things went on well, and I'd a two-year's run, before ever I saw the inside of a jug. The jug I was lumbered in, was Norfolk goal. I got there for prigging grunters from the farmers, for although a throughbred towney, I did sometimes condescind to do that, or turn 'lully prig.' I got out by the assistance of a feller who's stiff long ago. He was transported for pig stealing; but he was in the last stage of consumption when he sailed, and he sartingly was one of the staunchest prigs ever seen. When he landed, while he was supporting himself round the hospital man's neck, he managed to pick his pocket of a pocket-comb and a penknife: next morning he was a corpse."

"Never mind him, tell us the adventure," cried Ben.

"He, poor fellow, was out of jug, so one morning the turnkey looks in, and says he, 'yer mother's come, and wants to see yer.' "Show her in, says I, for I guessed it was a pal."

"And it proved to be him?" said Ben.

"To be sure it did. He came in, panting and blowing at every blessed word he spoke, but, when the turnkey went away, 'Sam,' says he, here's a fine hair-saw, here's a jemmy, and here's a centre-bit. I'll be outside to night at eight, and when I hear you whistle, I'll throw the rope ladder over for yer.' I thanked him heartily, and that night fortune was perpitious, so I got out of the first jug I ever was in. The rest of my history yer pretty well all on yer know."

The Duffer leant towards the resurrectionist.

'I'm hard up, we *must* go to Levi's, we'll frisk there, and frighten him into giving us a clue to where he keeps his swag,"

"Agreed," answered Tim Roper, "and if he makes any opposition, we'll be prepared to quiet him."

"And that's easily done, what say you to ten to-morrow night?"

"Could'nt have a better time," responded the ruffian.

Although this conversation had been carried on in a low tone, Ben had overheard the greater part of it.

"And I'll be there too," said he, as the two companions left the boozing ken."

"What are yer muttering about," asked the coiner.

"Oh, nothing, I'm given to that habit they say. Would yer like a glass now?"

"If you'll stand one."

"Come to the bar, then."

CHAPTER XLIX.

AN EXPLOSION.

THREE weeks had elapsed since the incarceration of Frederick Vyvian in the Bench prison.

At the termination of that period he was liberated by the interference of Mr. Stamer.

The night was bitterly cold; the wind howled mournfully around, making the windows and doors crack and strain, and moan like tortured things; but the raging elements without were as tranquil as a calm, when in comparison with the contending emotions which agitated—even tore the breast of Frederick Vyvian.

The news of the death of the baronet had reached him, and he now perceived the folly of the compact he had entered into with Abednego Levi. His only hope was that of calling on the Jew, and threatening to reveal the secret of his birth—although he was himself ignorant who his father really was—unless the miser should consent to lay down an ample sum of money.

The duel had only occurred that morning, but he was already looked upon as Sir Frederick Vyvian. Presently he arrived at the Jew's den:

"Ah, my dear!" said Abednego; "what a time it is since I had the pleasure of seeing you last. What have you been doing with yourself?"

Frederick took the Jew's arm hastily in his grasp.

"I wrote asking you for money—money to liberate me from prison; that money you refused; now hear me."

"I'm all attention," responded Abednego.

"As my entreaties failed in having the desired effect, I had recourse to threats—threats that I would expose my birth, and thus prevent your establishing a claim to the Vyvian property, which property I sold you."

"You did," said the Jew, trembling violently, for this was touching the chord which was strongest within him.

"I am not in the habit of breaking my word—at least, in those matters. I am now come to make you a proposition; if you accept it, well and good; if you do not, you will be a material loser."

"I am ready to hear anything, my dear."

"You are doubtless aware ere now of the death of Sir Richard Vyvian. I am not his brother, and I was conscious of that circumstance when I sold my chance to you. No living soul save myself is cognizant of this, and, if you advance me a good round sum of money, I pledge myself to be silent."

"You lie," cried Abednego. "I believe you are his brother, and that this is but a plan laid to entrap me; at all events, you are not the only person aware of all this."

"What do you mean? Who else can know anything about it?" exclaimed Frederick.

The Jew took a long breath, and then said, in slow and measured accents, "Mr. Prigmore."

"Do you know him?" asked Frederick.

"I do."

"But there is no fear of him, as I myself quieted him long ago."

"There is not now, p'r'aps, but there was. called on me to-day, and threatened to expose the whole affair unless I paid down thirty pounds: that I've done, but will lay down no more money; therefore you needn't expect it."

"Very well, very well; we shall see how this unpleasant matter will end."

"I shall act as I have spoken, and leave the result to providence," exclaimed the Jew, with a hypocritical leer.

"But I say you must advance me some money; I mistake, you *shall* do it."

"Both my boys—such clever boys as they were, too—are transported, and I really fear I shall be left penniless in my old age."

"You'll lose more by refusing than you will by granting my request."

"You wouldn't expect me to rob myself for you. You're a liar, and you've had my answer. You'd have got my money out of me when you knew Prigmore was in the secret."

"I'm desperate," shouted Frederick Vyvian, "in desperate circumstances, and in a desperate humour."

"You wouldn't hurt a poor, defenceless old man," said the Jew.

"But I'd crush a viper."

"You think to intimidate me," exclaimed Abednego, trembling with fear and rage; "but I defy you: rather than lose a penny—one penny, mark you, think of the coin well—I'd send both you and myself— But you see my meaning."

" I'll search this room through and through," ejaculated Frederick, in a state of fearful frenzy; "and, if you interrupt me, may your blood be on your own head."

Frederick Vyvian rose to execute his threat.

The Jew threw himself savagely upon him.

In another moment the young man felt his throat grasped in nerves of iron.

He hastily seized a large knife that lay on the table, and, with a desperate lunge, plunged it into the breast of the Jew.

Then Abednego Levi lay upon the ground, while the gates of death were being unbarred, seeing frightful visions of a future state.

When Frederick looked up, the first object that met his gaze were a pair of fiendish eyes peering at him through a small time-bestained window. Suddenly they vanished from his sight.

Frederick Vyvian rushed impetuously from the house, where for the first time he had stained his hands with blood.

The impression left by the two eyes felt in his maddened brain like molten bullets.

He had scarcely left the house when two figures approached the doorway.

One of them was the Duffer, the other was the resurrectionist.

" There's som'ut wrong here, Tim," said the Duffer.

The two villains walked cautiously up the stairs.

The Jew had lost the power of speech, but he still breathed.

" There's no time to be lost, Sam," cried Tim Roper. "Search the room quick. I'll set fire to the house, so as how the affair shan't be diskivered. He thoroughly desarves it—he does, the avaricious old warmint."

The Jew understood the meaning of these words, and appeared in an agony of despair when the Duffer commenced searching the room.

On the Duffer touching the china mantel-piece, it fell to the ground, and revealed a store of sovereigns to the delighted eyes of Sam Somes, and Tim Roper.

This sight appeared to inflame the old Jew to madness.

He crawled along in the direction of the treasure, as if to perish on that which he loved best on earth; at least so thought the Duffer and his companion.

Then the resurrectionist began setting fire to the room, while the Duffer filled his hat with the money.

An awful explosion tore asunder the Jew's den.

Ten thousand dismembered fragments for a moment glittered in the air,—the atmosphere was convulsed with a terrific shock.

The den of Abednego Levi had ceased to exist.

The Jew had always kept several barrels of gunpowder concealed beneath the flooring, for the pur-

pose of evading the law, should the officers come in search of him. He had now ignited them, that he might have the gratification of perishing with his treasure.

The following morning were found the blackened remains of Abednego Levi, the Duffer, Tim Roper, and another body.

The other body was the corpse of Ben Bendy.

CHAPTER L.

THE TRIAL.

The morning after the awful explosion related in the past chapter, a man apparently bent nearly double with age, leaning upon an oaken stick of considerable dimensions, toiled up Holborn-hill. A large straw hat, torn and dirty, entirely covered his head and throat, as well as the upper part of his face. A dirty coloured handkerchief was tied over his mouth.

Having passed the wall of St. Andrew's church, he made several ineffectual efforts to cross the road.

Suddenly a policeman, who had for some time been watching his movements, stepped forward, and arrested him in the name of the Queen, for the wilful murder of Abednego Levi.

This was Frederick Vyvian.

* * * * * * * *

An eager concourse of people were assembled the Old Bailey.

Before the entrance of the Judges, a commotion among those present, announced the presence of the accused.

An ashy paleness spread itself over the features of Frederick Vyvian.

After the Judge had taken his seat, the indictment was read, and the interrogation of the accused commenced.

Frederick contradicted, with audacity, the whole of the charge.

The counsel for the prosecution enlarged much upon the strange circumstances attending the discovery of the murder. He said that like the sun piercing through clouds, Providence had by one unforeseen event, brought the crime within the reach of justice. What that event was, he was going to tell them. A Mr. Prigmore, by profession an attorney, had been with Mr. Levi on the night of the murder, nay—had received money from him to the amount of thirty pounds, nay—he would go still further, had seen the act committed by the prisoner at the bar.

These words had the effect intended upon the wretched young man. He fell back swooning.

" You see the effect of my statement," cried the

representative of the law, raising his voice in proportion to the success which attended his oratorical powers, " you see that *he* too remembers this circumstance." He then wound up his harangue by observing that the mark of the knife was still discernible on the calcined body of the Jew, and that the jury would of a verity shake the pillars of society to the foundation, if they thought of acquitting the prisoner at the bar.

The counsel for the defence having been heard, the jury retired for a short time, and on their return, convicted the prisoner of wilful murder.

The Recorder, after a pause, addressed the prisoner as follows :—" The crime of which you are found guilty, is one of an aggravated nature. I have in vain looked for mitigating circumstances, but have found none. When I consider the rank in which you have moved, although you did so without the right of birth, and when I see you in the position in which you are now presented to me, I feel pained in the extreme. This case affords to bystanders, to society, and to the public at large, an exhibition of the great truth inculcated by every act of our courts of justice, that education and position, whether real or imaginary, are not considered as palliatives, but rather aggravators of an offence. If you feel as you ought to do, I don't wish to add poignancy to your feelings by dwelling longer upon so painful a topic."

Mr. Prigmore rose, and stated aloud, that he had a further communication to make. Having received permission, he exclaimed " the man he murdered was his father." Astonishment was depicted on every countenance.

Frederick Levi, better known as Frederick Vyvian, again swooned away.

Sentence was deferred.

CHAPTER LI.

SIX SCENES.

SCENE I.—SUFFOCATION.

It was nearly midnight. A pale, sickly light was emitted from a solitary charcoal fire, which burnt in the chamber of the Barker's house in West-street.

"We can never face our doom," exclaimed the Barker, addressing Bill Waters, "now we have murdered that child; the officers are sure to be arter us."

"You yer mean: how came yer to do it?" demanded the beggar.

"I kept the walnut-shells on too long, so, arter they'd eaten the eyes, they eat the brain too."

"The traps are arter me too; but how did they find out about the babby?"

"I sold it to the resurrection-men, and they sold it at a dissecting-room, when, arter it was done with, it was pitched among a lot of muck. Well, it was carted into the country, and there it was found, and an inquest was held upon it; the rest yer know."

"If we finish ourselves, shall we do it for that ere babby over there?"

"Sartinly; otherwise, if we puts her out of doors, she'll raise an alarm."

"Then yer'd better begin a-filling up the crevices, 'cos I'd sooner die like that than swing from the gibbet."

These were soon filled up with clay, with which the Barker had provided herself. Then she commenced blowing at the grate, and a blueish flame rose up, and tinged her now pale countenance with an almost unearthly glare. The preparations were completed; then a faint and sickly odour filled the room.

"How giddy I gits," said the Barker.

By degrees the deleterious gas of the charcoal filled the apartment, till it had expelled all the vital air previously contained therein. Then the atmosphere appeared full of blue figures.

     *   *   *   *

There is night upon London—dense midnight. From many a steeple sounds forth the hour, and, deep and sonorous above them all, the great bell of St. Paul's proclaims the solemn time. Four men are seen hurrying rapidly along, carrying on their shoulders two coffins. At length they stopped in a place of gravestones.

There are no mementos of by-gone mightiness, no comfortable cherubs looking archly from among stony clouds; but it is a bleak and barren spot, the last long home of the poor—the workhouse burial-ground.

A hole is already dug, and into it are carelessly flung the two coffins. Then the heavy mould was quickly shovelled, and that unhallowed grave was closed in which lay the murdered child and the suicides.

SCENE 2.—THE DEATH.

It was evening. An elderly gentleman was reclining at his length upon a sofa.

A ghastly paleness—the paleness of long disease was upon his cheek. His dim eyes were turned with an expression of melancholy tenderness towards a young girl who was attentively counting the drops as they fell from a small phial, which she held in her hand, into a glass of water. An old woman stood at a respectful distance.

When the mixture was ready she advanced to receive it, but the young lady bending gracefully on her knees by the side of the sofa, presented the medicine to her grandfather.

"Are you sure, child, that you have counted the drops correctly," inquired the invalid in rather a petulant tone of voice, "Parker has always been used to attend to the directions of the doctor—in my feeble state, the most trivial mistake would, I have no doubt, prove fatal to me."

"Indeed, grandpapa, I have been very careful," said the young lady, "and if you only knew the happiness I feel in attending to your wants, I am sure that you would not deny me the gratification of doing so. But if it is your wish that Parker should resume her duties"—

The old gentleman pressed her hand affectionately, and taking the glass swallowed the mixture. For a few seconds he remained entirely overpowered by the exertion, but presently he half rose, and desired his grand-daughter to seat herself beside him.

"I desire to relate to you some particulars respecting your mother," said the invalid, "but God knows whether I shall have strength to perform my intention. But listen, and I will endeavour, as briefly as possible, to enlighten you—

"My father was the Earl of Torrington, the second son and was bred to the army. Upon the death of my father and eldest brother, I succeeded to the title and fortune. I had previously married a rich heiress, she died four years after our marriage, and left me with two children. Your mother was the eldest. She was a gentle creature, but my mind was too much engrossed by parliamentary and other duties to cultivate domestic affections. I was proud of her beauty, and my sight loved to dwell upon the noble bearing of my handsome son. But the former disgraced herself and her family. Yes child—she formed an attachment to one of the officers of my own regiment—the son of my bitterest enemy. She eloped with and married him. And at that moment I swore never to acknowledge her, or hers. But touched by the withering hand of time my mind has become enfeebled, consequently my resolutions have crumbled and given way. My son died abroad. I have long since felt the want of a comforter. In you, child, I have found one, and in return, I have not been unmindful of your welfare; I have, by my will, secured to you a handsome fortune, and in the person of my heir, I trust you will find a husband worthy of your affections. I have written to inform him of mv intentions. I have entreated him, as he values my blessing, to make a kind and considerate husband to you—but he comes not—and, I feel—I feel that before to-morrow, perhaps even this verv night, stern death may seize upon my poor withered form, and number me among the children of the grave. A convulsive shudder shook the enfeebled form of the dying man —he grasped the hand of his granddaughter— "Pray for me child—oh, pray for me—for I have been severe and unforgiving—selfish—uncharitable murmured the sick man in a thick husky tone of voice,—" I cannot pray."

The young girl kneeled by the side of her grandfather—she buried her face in her hands, and unable any longer to restrain the violence of her sorrow, burst into an agony of tears.

The invalid, overpowered by emotion, sunk back upon the couch, when suddenly the door of the apartment opened, and a gentleman, accompanied with two ladies, entered the room and stole softly to the side of the sofa. The sick man opened his eyes, still moist with tears, and a gleam of satisfaction, almost of joy, illumined his countenance. He strove to articulate, but the sounds died upon his lips—he grasped the hand of his nephew, and placing it within that of his granddaughter—he expired.

"Agnes"—murmured Lord Oxburn."

*   *   *   *   *   *   *   *

It is now time to acquaint our readers with the circumstances which led to the introduction of Miss Talbot into the house of her grandfather.

Mr. Prigmore had many times been requested by the Earl of Torrington to use every possible endeavour to discover his granddaughter. The worthy solicitor, aware that his lordship had bequeathed her a very handsome fortune, never ceased his inquiries till he did discover her. But he kept the secret to himself.

He found Miss Talbot dependant upon the bounty of Mr. Francis Vyvian, and immediately determined, that, as soon as the feeble health of the Earl should give way, and threaten dissolution, he would propose to the granddaughter, and make her his wife, just in time to come in for the legacy. We have seen how, by a forged letter, he enticed Agnes to his residence in Euston-square, we have also seen how her courageous rejection of his suit, and the unexpected appearance of Lord Oxburn, thwarted his intentions.

Agnes, after leaving his house, returned to Mrs. Dobbins. She congratulated herself that the portrait of her mother, which she always wore about her neck, had received no injury from the accident, but she was not aware that it had attracted attention, or that the coachman who drove her, had given her address. She was therefore overpowered by amazement, when, on the return of Mr. Dobbins, he requested that she would prepare immediately to accompany him to the house of her grandfather.

As soon as she was sufficiently collected, she took an affectionate leave of the Dobbins', and slipped into the carriage, which was waiting at the door.

The Earl of Torrington received her with more pride than affection, but the dutiful tenderness of the granddaughter prevailed, and during the short time she resided with him, she gained entire possession of his affections.

———

SCENE III.—THE EXECUTION.

OUR story conducts us back to Frederick Levi.

In the condemned cell of Newgate—that cell which has seen tears shed of bitter remorse, where the guilty and the innocent have alike pined previous to expiating their crimes upon the scaffold— chained hand and foot, lay the murderer.

*   *   *   *

In the front of the prison-doors was the scaffold, which somewhat resembled a box upon wheels, painted black, with a cross-beam over it.

Close to the barriers were the most depraved of the assembled crowds, men and women, whose voices were hoarse with disease and intoxication.

A spirit of reckless hilarity and coarse mirth pervaded the crowd, and the bursts of animal laughter were incessant. Echoed as that laughter was by the surrounding buildings, with what fearful distinctness must it have reached the ears of the parricide.

This melancholy occasion constituted a festival —an orgy and merry-making.

" He'll be finished off soon," said one.

" Here 's a good seat for two shillings." cried a man.

" Where the beam comes right in the way, and all the best of it 's hid," bawled another. " Here's a seat for eighteenpence."

Immediately around the instrument of death was a large body of policemen, all carrying their staves.

Perhaps one-third of the whole mass consisted of women, by whom the most foul blasphemies were uttered.

The toll of the prison-bell was the first announcement that the dreary procession was on the move. In two or three minutes a small door under the pent-house of the scaffold opened, and the executioner, the culprit, the chaplain, and one or two functionaries came out.

Then all the men took off their hats in the same manner as they would in a playhouse, and a death-like stillness reigned around.

The face of Frederick Levi was completely blanched.

The executioner drew a cap over his head, then, at a given signal, pressed down a handle attached to the scaffold, when the whole platform fell away from beneath the feet of the criminal.

The body of the murderer was several times drawn up as if in convulsions. He was in the agonies of death.

Thousands had assembled in the same spirit that would have led them to a dog-fight or a bull-bait, and now those thousands went away more hardened than they came. None were awed by the ghastly sight they had just witnessed; on the contrary, they admired the "pluck" of the criminal for "dying game."

At nine the executioner again appeared, and, having cut down the body, it was carried into the prison by some assistants.

———

SCENE IV.—ST. LUKE'S

IT was the latter end of February, 1843.

In a large room, tenanted by many persons, all of them of the male sex, was Peter Prigmore, the attorney.

The loss of the Vyvian property, and the non-success of his schemes with regard to Miss Talbot, had weakened his brain. After this, by some strange fatality, he forgot to insert his own name in a will, which unlooked-for circumstance completely bereft him of his reason. But why is he so eloquent? He is evidently defending an imaginary cause.

He imagines himself to be at the oar of Minos, but when there how very different will he find the practice of that court, to any he has hitherto been accustomed to.

By the side of him is a venerable looking mad-man, who also appears to be engaged in addressing shadows. He fancies himself in earnest conversation with the sages of antiquity, Plato, Aristotle, Demosthenes, Cato, and many others of a kindred disposition. Perhaps his, is on the whole, a happy delusion.

But who is that running backwards and forwards, crying piteously, and shaking his head?

A sentimental youth, who would fain have acted Hamlet, but the managers underrated his tragic abilities, and by so doing, have caused him to become an inmate of St. Luke's.

There is a sportsman who bore the death of five wives with the patience of a stoic, but lost his reason on hearing of the demise of a favourite pointer,

Here is a young fellow who is in a constant agony of uneasiness, lest his father should come to life again and claim his property.

There is a strange variety among the unfortunate inmates of a mad-house.

———

SCENE 5.—BEHIND THE CURTAIN.

It was a dingy room.

The walls were hung with black drapery, and behind a table, in a dark corner, was seated a conjuror.

He appeared to be in great request, for as soon as one of his applicants retired, another invariably entered.

Each person paid half-a-crown for a peep into the secrets of futurity.

His professional avocations over, the conjuror laid aside all the mummery of the "dark art," and hastened into an adjoining apartment.

Then Mr. Tift, for he it was, supped with the Queen Mother.

———

SCENE 6.—THE GIN PALACE.

About two years had elapsed since we first introduced Mrs. Francis Vyvian.

Reclining on a butt of beer, in a gin-palace, and in the last stage of a consumption, was the remnant of one who had once been so lovely.

There were yet about her features, remains of her former beauty.

From the gin-palace she went to a temple of Venus, situated in the neighbourhood, which alternately with the streets, had been her home for many long months—months of intoxication and abandonment, and of intense suffering.

*   *   *   *   *

Another month has passed away.

In a half-lighted attic, in a brothel, expiring on a worn out mattress, lay the unfortunate woman.

—

CHAPTER LII.

CONCLUSION.

A few words, more and our tale is completed Time has given birth to the year 1846.

Captain Dashington may be seen any day at the Reform Club House, or in a box at her Majesty's Theatre, or driving in an elegant curricle round Hyde-park. He has grown considerably stouter than he was, and is perhaps a little bloated. He plays much, drinks deeper than he did formerly, and it is rumoured in some circles, that he recently discovered himself to be affected with that old enemy of *bon vivants*—the gout. He is much courted in society, particularly by the women, is ever ready to shoot anybody that looks at him; has many acquaintances, but no friends, and carries with him the character of an egotist, a coxcomb, and a man of the world.

Lord Oxburn and his wife are generally considered the happiest couple in the fashionable world. It is not certain whether his lordship will ever become an M.P., but he is thought not disposed to discountenance the idea.

Lord Coningham has proved himself equally successful in drawing a ticket for the marriage lottery. He resides somewhere by Richmond,

EPILOGUE.

Our labour is terminated; our narrative is completed.

Where we have seen roguery we have unmasked it; where we have observed tyranny, we have deprecated it; where we have noted injustice, we have exposed it: what then remains for us to do that we promised in our prologue?

We have entered the palace of the peer, we have supped with him on delicious viands, we have reclined in his luxurious apartments, and for a while we have sported in the gay realms of fashion; then we have adjourned to the humble hovel of the artizan, there we have partaken of a scanty meal o. the coarsest food, there we have seen dire-faced poverty, but we have not yet become acquainted with crime, next, we have been introduced to the "boozing ken," the "smoking crib," the retreat for "cadgers," and other sinks of infamy and haunts of iniquity.

Where we have discovered vice we have lashed in, and if, in the preceding pages, we have altered the names of persons and of places, our characters are not the less real, nor are those places the more fictitious.

May every one who peruses "Life in London" have some good and useful sentiment thereby awakened in his breast.

THE END.

CONTENTS.